F
GRE

Green, George Dawes.

The caveman's
valentine.

$19.95

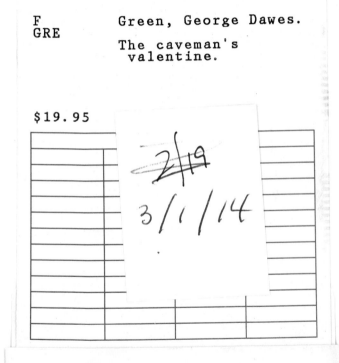

2/19
3/1/14

THE

CAVEMAN'S

VALENTINE

THE CAVEMAN'S VALENTINE

GEORGE DAWES GREEN

WARNER BOOKS

A Time Warner Company

Copyright © 1994 by George Dawes Green
All rights reserved.

"The Seahorse Czar," lyrics and music by Romulus Ledbetter,
copyright © 1993 Stuyvesant Music, Inc., New York, N.Y.
Used by permission.

Warner Books, Inc., 1271 Avenue of the Americas, New York, NY 10020

Ⓦ A Time Warner Company

Printed in the United States of America
First Printing: January 1994
10 9 8 7 6 5 4 3 2 1

Library of Congress Cataloging-in-Publication Data

Green, George Dawes.
    The caveman's valentine / George Green.
        p.   cm.
    ISBN 0-446-51722-4
    I. Title.
PS3557.R3717C38   1994
813´.54—dc20   92-51026
                                                                          CIP

For beautiful Rachel

Acknowledgments

To Dr. Jeffrey Newton, for his profound insights into the subtleties of clinical paranoia, my deepest appreciation. And also my envy, for I believe he has fathomed the fragile machinery of Romulus Ledbetter's imagination better than I ever will.

On the other hand, to those of Mr. Ledbetter's early therapists who misdiagnosed his brain-typhoons as "schizophrenia," I wish to express my undying disdain. But then what can we expect—*what, after all, can we ever expect* from C. G. Stuyvesant's most abject minions and toadies?

THE
CAVEMAN'S
VALENTINE

Y-RAYS

1

You figure now you got me in your clutches, you going to *read* me, like a book, right?—going to look right into my *brain* and you going to read it by page, like I was some cheap-jack midnight entertainment to make you forget the mess *you're* in—right? Get you chuckling, get your greasy thumbprints all over my thoughts, get you through another miserable lonely night, *right,* Stuyvesant?"

"Who's Stuyvesant?"

"You're Stuyvesant."

"I'm not Stuyvesant."

"No, you're a zit on Stuyvesant's ass. But you're Stuyvesant just the same. You're *all* Stuyvesant."

"I just want to take you to the shelter, Mr. Ledbetter."

"But *watch out* when you're in my skull, because I got *legions* of angels in there, and they're going to beat the shit out of you with their little wings, and pick your limbs apart and spin you around and slide you on out of there. Oh, I'm going to *crap* you out and be free of you. *You hear me?* I'M GOING TO CRAP YOU OUT, STUYVESANT!"

"It's the coldest night of the year, Mr. Ledbetter."

"It is cold."

"If you stay in this cave, you'll freeze. You'll die out here."

"I might. The world turns, it takes some of us with it. But if I swallow your con, if I go to your damn smelter—"

"Shelter, Mr. Ledbetter."

"Then I would die for sure."

"Oh, the shelter's . . . well, it's not a hundred percent safe, but . . . at least it's warm."

"Damn right it's warm. You know why it's warm? *Because you burn the bodies in the furnace!* That's why it's warm. Our livers you serve for breakfast, and our hearts you sacrifice to Stuyvesant, and the rest you *cook up in the furnace!* To keep everybody *toasty*."

"Mr. Ledbetter, I'm freezing out here."

"Then go."

"Your daughter asked me to come looking for you."

Romulus Ledbetter glared at his visitor.

Then he sloughed off his blankets and came out of his cave and rose up to his full height. Rose up before the social worker the way in a nightmare a grizzly will rise on its hind legs and it's too late to run. His hat was a Teflon saucepan lined with the furs of squirrels killed on the Henry Hudson Parkway. His stink was enormous. For a scarf he wore the "Week in Review" section of the Sunday *New York Times*.

"My daughter."

There was a wheeze in his voice, and the big eyes in his black face looked off somewhere.

"She's worried about you. She says tomorrow's Valentine's Day. She says how's her old man going to be her valentine if he freezes to death?"

"Well, you tell her *not* to worry. You tell her for me, tell her maybe I'm low, maybe they knocked me low, but I'm still a *free* man."

He stood there and simply loomed. Until at last the social worker shrugged and went away.

2

It must have been much later that night, even colder, when Romulus Ledbetter half-woke in his cave to the sound of footsteps. Coming this way, up the park slope. In this cold with the air tense as piano wire you could pick up any sound, from a long way off, and what Romulus heard was these slow footsteps. And somebody huffing. Somebody was carrying something.

Romulus reached and pulled himself up out of the ooze of sleep. He listened.

Very close now, the steps.

They stuttered. A near-fall on the hard February crust. So not boots—whoever was out there was wearing slick soles. City shoes, money shoes. A grunt, then a muffled thud. Then the footsteps faded.

Still swaddled in blankets, Romulus stretched and grabbed the TV remote control and aimed it at his carcass of a Zenith, and zapped it on.

He watched the News.

The News was someone hurrying out of the park. A figure in crisp white coat and white cap. You could almost smell the new leather. The News followed the figure as it jogged through the dead-of-winter oaks. To the wall at the park's edge, at Payson Street.

There, in the dark, an elegant white sedan waited. The white-cap figure slipped into it like a snake. The fancy car accelerated into its getaway. Romulus killed the picture.

The News, so what?

The News was all lies, *always.*

Come morning, though, when he woke and unwound himself from his cocoon of blankets, when he shook the cramps out of his limbs, and went out into the snow, and walked down the hill under the big beech tree to take a leak, when the steam rose up from his piss and he looked mildly into the clump of winter thorns before him, he found the valentine that had been left for him there.

3

The nurse was hurrying down Dyckman Street, hunched against the cold and rushing for the bus, when she saw him. He was standing before a little three-sided telephone coop. She gave him a glance and it turned into a stare.

Look at that crazy man. Must be homeless by the looks of him but something of a house unto himself. He was a big man, icicles hung from the eaves of his beard, and he was pulling from the pockets of his many coats all sorts of weird attic bric-a-brac. Old theater tickets, children's scissors, the skeleton of a shrew. Some of this stuff fell to the sidewalk without his even noticing.

Finally he fished out a quarter, which he also dropped. He looked down at it. Must be tough, she thought, for that swaddled-up giant to stoop. She stepped over and picked it up and put it in his glove—careful not to touch him. He didn't say a word to her. He was in his own world. She leaned into the bitter breeze and went on her way.

4

Romulus dunked the quarter in the slot and tapped out his former telephone number. He was calling his daughter the cop.

But somehow the tapping turned into that coffee-perking song from the old ad. *Poppa-poppa-POP-pop.* He played it again, this time throwing in a few flat and sassy grace notes. His shivering got into the rhythm, and whenever his fingers hit two keys at once the phone laid a fart in his ear, and he was running somewhat berserk with this music when a voice interrupted him.

"This call requires a twenty-five-cent deposit."

"Oh *bullshit.* Your boss already *got* my quarter."

"This call requires—"

"No no *no*, you listen to *me*, Miss Machine. You might not have got the News yet but guess what—*you're a slave*. Just like the rest of us. News is, you been sold down the river to ol' Massa Stuyvesant, and you going—"

"This call requires—"

He pushed five keys at once—raucous trumpet-chord of truth.

Then a human operator came aboard, and he made the call collect. He gave his name as Blast from the Past. His daughter accepted the charges.

"Daddy."

"Little Lulu. Did I wake you?"

"Oh no."

"I did, didn't I?"

He remembered how she used to love her sleep, and it pained him to think he'd pulled her out of it.

"It's OK, Daddy."

Then he heard in the background his former wife Sheila. Or maybe his present wife. Seventeen years since she'd kicked him out, but he'd never asked her if she had yet bothered to divorce him.

He heard her ask Lulu, "Where is he?"

He could picture her precisely. He saw her standing at the kitchen door in her house robe with her big eyes blazing. She was fixing Lulu and the telephone, fixing them with her chickenhawk gaze and she was still a great part of him, he figured—by his rough calculation about one-third of Romulus Ledbetter was still this woman with the raptor eyes.

"Mama wants to know where are you, Dad?"

"Huh? I'm home."

"At your cave?"

"Uh-huh."

"You got a telephone in your cave now?"

"Oh, *all* the amenities. Tell your mama that. TV, Cuisinart, quadraphonic CD—everything no respectable homeowner could live without."

Squawking in the background.

7

"Mama says get your ass over to the shelter. Did Mr. Simms come by?"

"Mr. Simms I don't know."

"The social worker."

"Oh *yes*. He came by. I took him downstairs to my study and we shot a game of snooker. Tell your mama to call off her hounds. *I have a home.* It's not fancy but it suits me fine."

Further squawking.

"Mama says if you freeze to death she's not paying for your funeral."

"Funeral. That reminds me. Why I'm calling."

"Why are you calling, Daddy?"

"Stuyvesant killed somebody."

Silence. Years ago she'd have shot back, "But Stuyvesant doesn't exist, Daddy." Or, "Daddy, Stuyvesant's just a figment of your paranoia." But now at last she'd given up arguing. Sad, when they quit arguing with him. She just gave him a weary sigh.

"That's rough, Daddy."

"This time I've got the evidence."

"Uh-huh."

"Persuasive evidence."

"Uh-huh."

"He left the body outside my cave."

"What body?"

"Lulu. I'm a paranoiac, OK? I've been wasted by failure, right, you got it, you *know* your old man. But as to this dead thing outside my cave? Now this one I believe is just as real as you'd like it. I mean it's so shiny-real it hurts the eyes to look at it."

"Daddy?"

Note of concern. Maybe even a glimmer of credence. He thought of her as a five-year-old. Hair done up brilliantly in cornrows, believing every story he told her. And why had he told her such damned outrageous lies? Well, they were the truth, for one thing. And anyway, it was half her fault—why had she just sat there with her big eyes always believing him?

"Lulu?"

"Uh-huh."

"Lulu, please don't put up a fuss, OK? Please, child? Just please can you come on over here?"

5

The body in question was a thing of sculptural beauty.

A young man, a white man—though white wasn't the word. It didn't begin.

Alabaster, that was better. Or phosphor.

Or ice.

Romulus, waiting for his daughter to come rid him of this horror, knelt with difficulty and reached down and touched the kid's cheek. No give. No give at all—he yanked his fingers back. Yes, *ice* was the word: the body was frozen through.

A tattered coat, but wide open. The summer rayon shirt was buttonless. No laces on the sneakers. The chest and the belly and the ankles were all exposed—all frozen into stone, and all flawless in form. Perfect, finely muscled. In places there were long ruby-beaded lacerations, and some gray bruises, but Nature hadn't inflicted those.

Even Romulus, who professed to no eye for this sort of thing, could see that Nature had been in a large, giving mood when it had made this boy.

Small nose, gentle chin. A long blond mane of hair. Wide feminine eyes that were open and gazing into the branches of the beech tree, or into the sky, or somewhere further. And Romulus was hard put to conceive of this work as anything you'd want to call *dead*.

Would you call any of the marble god-statues in Florence—would you call them *dead*?

6

W hite cap." The detective looked down at his clipboard. "White coat. White car." He shook his head at the meagerness of what he had written there. "That's all you saw?"

"I said the car was *fancy*."

"Oh yeah. *Fancy* white car. And where was this fancy white car again?"

"Down there."

"Down *there?* You're pointing at this tree."

"I mean, on the other side of this hill."

"Oh. But didn't you say you were lying right here in this cave when you saw all this?"

"Right."

The detective had a concave face. Like a satellite dish. Or a cake that had fallen. He was a smart-ass. He looked sidelong at Lulu. Lulu looked at the snow. The detective turned back to Romulus.

"Then if you were in this cave, how could you see the fancy white car?"

"I told you. Try listening for once, OK?"

"OK. I'll try anything once."

"I'm telling you, I saw the white car on my TV."

"Oh. Sure, the TV in your cave. Now you're talking."

"And I can save you some time, I can tell you who the car belongs to. The car belongs to a man by the name of Cornelius Gould Stuyvesant."

But the detective's attention seemed to be wandering. He was watching the ambulance workers load the marble corpse onto a stretcher. They draped a dropcloth over the work and hauled it away. Then a cop came over and handed the detective an eelskin wallet, threadbare.

"Found it in his coat."

The detective looked through it. Not much to look through, though. Supermarket receipts. A driver's license, which the detective

10

squinted at. Presently he passed the wallet back to the cop, who popped it into a plastic bag and took it away again.

Then the detective eyed the TV set that sat at the entrance to the cave. Spilling out of the back of the TV was a ponytail of frazzled wires that led nowhere.

"Hey, tell me something, Caveman. What kind of shows you get on that?"

"All the shows."

"Like what?"

"Everything. The whole heady broth of American culture, right?"

"Right. You get cable?"

"Sure."

The detective gave Lulu another look. A little worm of a smile slithering across his lips.

"Get any broadcasts from Mars?"

"No."

The man kept looking at Lulu. Lulu had inherited the sweet shape her mother used to have, and the amazing ragged-edged irises. And also something else, a sort of anti-aura, something down-to-earth and knotty and impenetrable that fascinated men. And damned if this detective, this squash-faced beet-nose sucker, wasn't leering at her. The blood began to pulse in Romulus's temples. Stick to your own kind, fucker. He took a step forward, caught the detective in his shadow.

"Write it down."

"Write what down?"

"The name of the murderer."

"You mean ol' Uncle North Wind? Hey, what's the point of getting after *him*? I could book him, you know, but I'd never get an indictment. He'd blow down the frigging courthouse. You ever see the cheeks on that guy?"

"Write his name. What are you afraid of? Cornelius Gould Stuyvesant. Write it!"

Drumbeat of skull-blood, and a stirring of tiny wings inside his brain. Quickening toward a rage. But Lulu—only Lulu—kept it from boiling over. With a word.

"Daddy."

Romulus let out a breath. Let his blood settle. He said:

"Well, tell him to write it, Lulu."

"I can't tell him anything, Daddy. This isn't even my precinct. I'm just a nobody here, like you."

But then the detective raised his clipboard again, and grinned a generous grin.

"Ah, what the hell, my friend. You got some help for me? Who am I to turn down help? So how do you spell 'Cornelius'?"

7

Later, nearly dark, Romulus was making his rounds, just shuffling along through one of the rich enclaves off Riverside Drive. His low-energy sleepwalk shuffle. Build up some momentum with a gait like this, you could go on forever, like a steamship. But when he came abreast of a familiar and reliable row of garbage cans, he pulled up.

A doorman across the street gave him a baleful eye.

Romulus ignored him. Lifted a lid.

Well OK, here was the afternoon newspaper anyway, not bad. He stuck it under his elbow.

The rest was just miscellaneous desk trash. But he gave the mess a quick stir anyway, just in case—and uncovered a trove, a gleaming trove! Sheet music! Sugary white-bread tunes. "Gentle on My Mind." "The Impossible Dream." "On the Road Again." Some spoiled brat in the tower above him, practicing with sodden fingers every Tuesday and Thursday, till she was old enough to bail out, to ditch this foolishness.

But sheet music no matter how corny was always a pleasure to Romulus.

He took a sheaf of it and put it in his outermost coat, slid it through the tear in the lining. Then moved on before the doorman could start something.

He went about a block and it was getting dark and he was tired, he'd lost that momentum now, and he stopped where he was and sat on the sidewalk, with his back to the blond brick.

When he dipped his head, he caught a whiff of his own stink. A bubble of deep rank sincere stink. Made him ashamed of himself. Usually he showered and washed his clothes at least once a month at the Franciscans' down on Broadway and 112th. Cleanliness—that was a point of pride with him. After all, he had his daughter's reputation to think of. He had his handsome rocky home—homeowner's pride. Could such an upstanding prophet in the community go about ill-groomed? But these last few weeks—such cold! He kept putting off going down to the Franciscans, kept waiting for a break in the weather—and pride had gotten itself frozen out.

Just frozen out.

Frozen, iced-over, snowed in . . .

He woke with a start. Shook his head to clear it. The newspaper was on his lap. He took it up, and braced himself.

He was ready to confront the Ice Apollo again, in a big front-page spread.

But the front page was enthralled by the VALENTINE GHOUL, who'd been caught digging up Andy Warhol's grave. She swore that he'd asked her to. *"He wants to be my love-zombie."*

Then pages two through six were communiqués from various SPURIOUS AND TRUMPED-UP WARS around the planet. The soldiers wore the same faces, just different uniforms. Of course. They were all extras.

Pages seven through twelve were taken up with the TEARFUL CONFESSIONS of pols who admitted to robbing the public blind but who promised to cut back just as soon as they could.

He was almost to the classifieds before he found what he was looking for.

HOMELESS MAN FOUND FROZEN TO DEATH

The lifeless body of Andrew Scott Gates, 20, was discovered early this morning in a remote section of Inwood Park on the northern tip of Manhattan. A preliminary autopsy report indicates that Mr. Gates was the victim of exposure to the subzero temperatures that have prevailed in the metropolitan area for more than a week.

Mr. Gates, an unemployed model, had been living since November at 144 East 4th Street, in a building owned by the city of New York but occupied by squatters.

Early this month, however, according to other tenants of the building, Mr. Gates had moved out onto the street. "He was depressed," said Laurie Black, who lives with her husband in another room of the building. "He thought maybe he was dying of AIDS, and he kept talking about people out to get him."

For some time after leaving the East 4th Street address, Mr. Gates had been noticed in and around the tent village at Tompkins Square Park. He had not been seen, however, for nearly a week.

Mr. Gates's body may have lain undiscovered for several days, said Lieutenant Detective John Cork of the 34th Precinct. "It's a little-trafficked area of the park. He might still be lying there if another homeless man hadn't run across him."

When found, the body was dressed in light summer clothes and an open coat. There were no indications of violence. Lieutenant Cork speculated that Mr. Gates may have been seeking shelter in one of the park's shallow caves.

The police will conduct a thorough investigation, said Lieutenant Cork.

Mr. Gates is the third homeless man whose death has been attributed to the recent wave of arctic air. On Tuesday, an elderly Brooklyn man was found dead near a heating vent in the Williamsburg section of Brooklyn. Yesterday an unemployed construction worker died of burn injuries he received when sparks from a cooking fire set ablaze his crude cardboard dwelling on West Street.

O farrago of lies! Lies and distortions.

The ol' North Wind, sure. AKA *Cornelius Gould Stuyvesant*.

Mr. Gates's body will be transferred to the Museum of Classical Ice Sculpture in SoHo, where it will be attended by seven vestal virgins from the Fashion Institute of Technology. If there's ever a power failure, the remains will melt into a puddle and Stuyvesant's minions will mop up that puddle and rinse it away and it will burble down the drain and into the sewers and the rivers and into the Atlantic Ocean and you can rest in peace *then,* Andrew Scott Gates, there's not much more the bastards can do to you.

Easy, Romulus. Back off on the rage. Easy on the bitter visions. Remember that iniquity and injustice such as this are all in a day's commerce here. Detach. Smile. Get out that sheet music and play.

8

The bankruptcy lawyer was one of the best in New York, a man to whom even the grimmest of grim tidings brought enrichment. And as the tidings from all points of the compass were very grim indeed these days, he whistled cheerfully as he walked up from the corner, where the car had left him, to his apartment house.

Then he saw the bum. The bum was sitting on the sidewalk with his knees drawn up, and he was reading something and his head was rocking from side to side. He was in some kind of bum's rapture. He was a big black man. He wore a pot for a hat, and several coats, one on top of the other, and out of the pocket of the topmost coat stuck the ends of a bunch of bananas—coal-black, oozing at the seams.

The bankruptcy lawyer was not dismayed by the sight of bums and beggars. As symbols of abysmal failure they also stood, of course, for his own prosperity. But more than that, he thought they represented—in the constancy, the intractability, of their numbers, despite every attempt in every age of humankind to eradicate them—some stubborn and gloriously perverse willfulness in the human spirit.

Something to draw a kind of courage from.

Not that he ever gave them a penny.

But tonight was such a cold night. Tonight he saw this poor vagabond and felt, despite the firmness of his principles, a twinge of guilt. He veered to the edge of the sidewalk, to give the man a wide berth. He strode quickly and purposefully, hoping the crazy wouldn't surface from his trance in time to badger him.

But not quickly or purposefully enough. The bum raised his eyes, fixed him, and said:

"Hey mister. You got a pencil?"

The bankruptcy lawyer waved him off. And was halfway down the block before he realized the man had asked him not for money but of all things for a *pencil*.

He turned around and came back.

"Did I hear you right? You asked for a pencil?"

"You got one?"

"This isn't just to get me in conversation so you can hit me up for a dollar?"

The bum stared at him. The bankruptcy lawyer said:

"What do you want a pencil for?"

"I want to balance it on the end of my nose."

"I mean—OK, you just want to write something, huh?"

"Right."

"Well, I don't have a pencil. I've got a pen."

"That would do."

"I don't have a cheap pen."

"No?"

"But here. What the hey."

The bankruptcy lawyer handed over a gold Parker Executive. Foolish gesture. But one that triggered a little warmth in his breast. *What the hey.* It was just such foolish gestures that kept the Ghost of Christmas Future at bay.

Even in late February, a bankruptcy lawyer was wise to keep one eye out for the Ghost of Christmas Future.

He said to the bum, "Maybe if I ever see you again, you'll give it back, OK?"

"OK."

The bankruptcy lawyer started off again. Looked back again. The bum was writing furiously. What he had open on his knees was sheet music, and he was sitting there in the insane cold making emendations in the music—filling in notes where there were none,

X-ing out whole measures, changing the key, block-printing commands beneath the bars. His head bobbing and bouncing, his eyes rolling, the Parker Executive dancing. The bankruptcy lawyer came a few steps closer, so he could read the title on the sheet.

Lord. "Gentle on My Mind"?

9

Bassoons and a banshee siren! Bass clarinets! Derail this rinky-dink choo-choo music! Two dozen harmonicas, wheezing destruction! And Romulus, scribbling away, dreamed of himself, none other, at the piano, bedazzling the ivories. Send this freight hurtling into the depot building! Cymbols, mayhem, and fiddles! Crash through that row of parked cars on Main Street, plough through the antique shops and the country boutiques. *Smoke and rubble! Despair*—

"Could I ask you what you're writing there?"

Pinstripes was back. Big guy, woof-woof voice. Probably had played fullback in the Ivy League. But what threads! Romulus blinked at him and said:

"You want your pen back?"

"No, that's OK. You a musician?"

"Uh-huh."

"What do you play?"

"My skull."

And then—the cold and the approaching dark making him sleepy and softheaded again—Romulus relented a little, opened his past just a crack for this stranger.

"I used to play other things."

"Like—?"

"Like everything I could get my hands on. Mostly piano."

"You had a piano?"

"Not of my own, no. But there were a good many where I went to school."

"Where'd you go to school?"

"Juilliard."

"*Juilliard?* Lord, then how the hell did you wind up here?"

Romulus roused himself. He tucked the sheet music into the lining of his innermost coat. He clicked back the point on the Parker Executive and dropped it in the pocket of his outermost coat, with the bananas. With a prodigious effort, mind over matter, he rose. He bent over and coughed. He wiped his nose on his sleeve. Adjusted his Teflon-saucepan hat, and said:

"You want to know how the *hell* did I wind up here?"

He shuffled away, down the block, and he beckoned Pinstripes to follow. At the corner he gestured toward the dusky view of lower Manhattan.

"I wound up *here* because that bastard *wants* me here."

Romulus could feel them now—they were astir inside his skull. The Seraphs of Divinity and Vengeance. He felt them fluttering their little wings like moths against the soft walls of his brain. He felt their fury rising.

Said Pinstripes, "What bastard?"

"Don't play stupid, Pinstripes. You know the bastard that lives in that tower."

"What tower?"

"*Don't,* Jack. Just don't even bother, right? That tower right there. All right, use your pretty euphemism. Call it the Chrysler Building."

"You can't see the Chrysler Building from here."

"Yeah? Yeah, but who gives a shit?—he can see *me*. He sees me at all times, you think I don't know that? He sits up there in his tower and he watches, and what he sees he doesn't like. I mean it curdles his stinking rancid *blood* what he sees, 'cause what he sees is a *free* man. Free man busting through to his own divinity, right?—you getting this? Ghetto kid making it in Juilliard? Making a name for himself? Young composer? Hot, jumping? Getting his notes straight from God hisself, am I right, you know this story? Getting an angle on what the *truth* sounds like, what *love* sounds like—and old Stuyvesant, you know what he says to *that.* He says, We're going to crush *that* nigger. Oh yes, send some Y-rays that nigger's way. We're going to CRUSH THAT NIGGER! Right? Oh, don't you back off, Pinstripes. Don't give me that shit, you *know* what I'm talking about. YOU SIGN THE PAPERS, DON'T YOU? Send another load of darkies into the mine—you'll sign off on that, won't you, Mr. Overseer? Never going to see them poor suckers again. GET BACK HERE! YOU FUCKING COWARD! Stuyvesant's gone and laced your mind with Y-rays, YOU'RE LIVING LIKE A JACKRABBIT! Oh, yes, RUN, Stuyvesant! Run like a fucking jackrabbit—but you sign the papers! Right? You say CRUSH THAT NIGGER! I hear you! STUYVESANT! I SEE YOU! You see me? I SEE YOU RIGHT FUCKING BACK!"

10

Romulus was almost home, he was slogging up the last snowy slope to his cave, when he noticed the tracks.

One set of tracks going up—toward the cave. One set coming back down. No other tracks around. Of course. Who ever came this way? Nobody.

Except the murderer.

Last night. The footsteps he'd heard.

There was enough stray streetlight to read how smooth these marks were. That poor dead boy, he'd had sneakers on his feet, and sneaker tracks should have been filled with all sorts of strange sneaker hieroglyphics. Right?

Not these tracks. These tracks were smooth-soled.

Furthermore, thought Romulus, if this were the trail of a man who had been freezing to death, it should be wandering all over, shouldn't it?

But these tracks were deliberate. They went right up, they dumped the body, they came right down again. No fuss.

These were Stuyvesant's shoe prints.

So why the hell hadn't the police found them?

Oh, but *of course* the police hadn't found them.

These prints could have had a big *S* for Stuyvesant in the middle of the heel, they could have been glowing, could have been neon-red and pulsing, they could have stood up and danced the mambo, and still the cops would have overlooked them.

But nevertheless, let it go, Romulus. Forget it.

Remember, the poor boy was just bait.

It's *your* soul that Stuyvesant's really after.

11

He climbed up to the knoll above the cave and looked down.

And saw that someone was waiting for him.

Dark figure squatting in front of the cave, his back to Romulus. Looking nervously left and right. Listening.

Romulus stood there a moment.

Stuyvesant's henchman, waiting for me. The angel of death. So why not just give it the slip? Turn around and go back the way I came. But that's my *home* down there. They call me a homeless man, but *uh-uh*—and hell if Stuyvesant's going to make me one. Chase me out of my own front yard—*uh-uh*.

Romulus waited till a truck went whining past on the highway down by the river, and then he started to move.

He moved down the snow-dusted rocks as stealthily as he could. It wasn't like when he was a kid—when he was a kid, he was a panther. But now he was so big and so damn far from his feet, it was like trying to be stealthy on stilts. It was like a telephone booth on stilts trying to be stealthy.

Yet he found he hadn't lost it *all*. A little panther magic yet clung to him, and he knew these rocks by heart, and there was a regular rhythm of trucks down on the highway to cover for him.

He clambered down from one rock to another. Then he paused and collected his balance and let the silence collect, and when another truck went groaning by, he shifted to the next rock. And the squatting henchman, who was so intent on listening, didn't seem to know *how* to listen. He was always moving his head just as Romulus was moving. Never hearing, and never thinking to look behind him.

Then Romulus lowered himself between two boulders and stepped out to the edge of the last rock. There was just a small patch of snowy ground between him and his enemy. He took a breath. He leapt down and hurtled forward, gathering momentum and by the time the henchman turned wildly and rose, it was way too late.

Romulus barreled into him.

Knocked him back on his ass. Pounced, and had him by the throat, and swung the fucker to his feet and slammed him against a tree. Slammed the wind out of him. The fool doubled over, gasping for air.

"*Rom!* Don't kill me! Please God don't kill me!"

Matthew. Matthew the Weasel. The little Italian druggie. Now Romulus could see him, could see in profile the long eroded ridge of the kid's nose. The slight build, the stringy hair. Romulus put his arms around the kid. The kid blubbered and wheezed.

"Jesus, I'm dead already Rom, what you want to kill me for?"

"Oh for Christ's sake, Matthew."

"I'm dead already."

"What are you doing here?"

"I waited for you. You never came. God, I thought I was going to freeze to death. I heard those wolves, Rom."

"Heard what? I can't hear you, you're talking into my coat."

Matthew pulled his head back. He was weeping. "Those wolves. They were coming to eat me."

Said Romulus, "We don't have any wolves in the city, Matthew. What are you doing here?"

The kid kept weeping. He said, "Rom. You were the one who found him, weren't you? They said the Caveman found him—that was you. You found him."

"You mean found the dead guy?"

"Scotty."

"Yeah, I found him."

"I *knew* they were going to kill him."

"Matthew, you're shivering."

"I *knew* they'd get him."

"You're too cold."

"I don't care."

Romulus said softly, "Why don't you care?"

"Rom, have you ever loved anybody?"

The kid shut his eyes tight. Balled his fist and brought it down against Romulus's chest as though it were a wall. With all his coats, it nearly was—Romulus scarcely felt the blow.

"Oh Jesus. Rom."

"You loved this guy?"

"Rom. I gotta die, too. I gotta. I gotta. *Please,* Rom. I gotta die, too."

"Yeah but not now, OK? Tomorrow if you want, when it's light out. Right now you've got to get warm. Come here."

He helped the kid into the cave. It wasn't much of a cave, just a deep recess in the rock. But it was his home, and he wrapped his guest in the rags of an old blanket, and sat him down, and then he untied some strings and unfurled a pair of mad harlequin curtains that stretched across the face of the cave. So his guest was shielded, a little, from the roaring cold.

Then he gathered an armful of kindling that he'd been drying all winter, and set about making a fire.

"Jesus, Rom, what are you doing? You can't light a fire in the park."

"Then let them come after me. What, now they won't let a man make a fire? But that's what a man does. Fires all over this fucking planet, Matthew. This one's mine."

When the pyre was ready, shrewdly built, Romulus pocket-hunted till he found a book of matches (*970-NEED. Visa, MC*) and lit it. A quick, sure blaze. He sat beside the Weasel. He put his arm around him. Some semblance of coziness despite the flagrant cracks around the curtains. They watched the fire.

"OK. Tell me."

12

They killed him, Rom. He was too beautiful for them. Did you *see* him? God, I used to just lie there and look at him. Sometimes he got in a bad mood, you know? I mean, they'd fucked him up so bad—and then he wouldn't let me touch him, so I'd just lie there and look, for hours.

"Oh Jesus, Rom. Jesus. I feel like somebody just tore half my insides out. Why'd they do it to him? *Why?*"

Said Romulus, "Who? Who did it to him, Matthew?"

"He was just a country kid, Rom. He grew up in this little town upstate, and he was in love with this real simple girl and he was going to work his way through college and then he was going to marry her. I bet they'd a had seven kids, and I'd never have even met him, but that's OK—he'd still be *alive,* Rom. But then that bastard got hold of him."

"What bastard? Stuyvesant?"

"He was fifteen, you know, and his parents were killed in a car accident—so what could he do? The state was going to put him in some school for orphans. All he needed was someone to take him in for a while. And that bastard came along."

"Who?"

"You don't want to know. Rom, they're going to find me, and they're going to kill me, and if I tell you, they'll kill you, too."

"Tell me."

"You want to know?"

"Who's the bastard?"

"I gotta tell somebody. But you already know his name."

"Stuyvesant?"

"David Leppenraub."

"Who?"

"You're kidding. You don't know who he is?"

"Uh-uh."

"Photographer? *Trees of North America?*"

"Wait a minute. Maybe I did see his name in the paper. Some controversy . . ."

"Every paper in the fucking country. He did these pictures of trees, all kinds of trees, you know, in the city and gas stations and malls and like that, just these normal American scenes except there was always a little bit of violence in them, just a touch of blood or something. And in every one of these pictures there was also an angel, and this angel didn't have no clothes or nothing, and this angel was beautiful. I bet he was. 'Cause this angel was Scotty."

"He was the model?"

"Yeah. He was Leppenraub's model. He was also Leppenraub's slave. He took him in, put him up on his farm up in Dutchess County. He said he was some kind of precious flower. He said he was too good for that girlfriend of his. He gave him presents, and he made him a glamour boy. He made him the mascot for all his fancy parties. He gave him drugs and shit, all the shit that'll fuck up a kid the fastest, I *know* about that shit. He turned him into a zombie. He just sucked all the blood out of him, so he could do whatever he wanted. He made him fuck all his friends. He made him do all sorts of shit.

"Once Scotty tried to run away, and a couple of Leppenraub's party-boy goons came after him, and they brought him back to the farm and taught him a little *self-discipline,* you know? I mean they beat the shit out of him. Taught him to do what he was told.

"One time—listen to this, Rom—one time Leppenraub made Scotty invite his old girlfriend up to the farm. And she still loved him, she still didn't understand what had happened to him. And they had lunch, the three of them, and she was looking at Scotty and she started to cry. And Leppenraub, he consoled her, oh yeah. He told her Scotty just wasn't ready for serious *commitment,* but be *patient, child,* perhaps when he's *ready*—and all the while Scotty was doing what he was told. You know what he was doing, Rom? He was jacking off Leppenraub under the table. Rom! The man made him do that. The man's a fucking monster."

"Jesus."

"He's the most sadistic bastard that ever walked the face of the earth. You see what he did to Scotty? You see the scars?"

"He was dressed when I saw him, Matthew."

"You see the brand, Rom? He *branded* him—fucking heart tattoo on his butt. *Yours forever.* Oh Jesus."

13

There was something outside. Matthew talked on, and Romulus shut his eyes, and he felt it, felt *them,* gathering out there. Something colder than the cold. Not wolves. Much fiercer than wolves. *Y-rays.* Sent down from Stuyvesant's tower. Dense miasma of Y-rays, gathering on the other side of the rude curtains, settling in around the entrance to the cave. Eyelessly watching and listening in on Matthew's grief, listening to every word.

14

Matthew said, "Then he got crow's-feet around his eyes and sores on his skin, and he started to look sick. And that's how Leppenraub knew he had it. How he knew he'd given Scotty the virus. So—*so long,* fucker. Get the fuck out of here, fucker."

"He just kicked him out?"

"Just like that, yeah. He didn't have no use for him no more. Got hisself another model. Go die now, Scotty. Go off somewhere and die.

"Leppenraub though, he was real sick himself. He went in the hospital after he kicked Scotty out, and he was supposed to die.

"So they had this big party for him just before he went in, so everybody could say good-bye to him. And they gave a lot of speeches and everybody said how *gentle* he was, all the big wheels, and they fed him a little cake. If I'd been there I'd have fed him dogshit till he choked. But I didn't even know who he was then.

"But anyway, the thing is, Leppenraub *didn't die*. He's back on his fucking farm. He's feeling so much better, thank you. The fucker. Scotty's in some *drawer* somewhere in the city morgue but Leppenraub's having a high old time.

"And of course everybody just loves him.

"I mean wherever you go now it's Leppenraub. You see the bookstores last Christmas? Leppenraub coffee-table books and calendars and shit, and they had that big exhibit at some museum. The Whitman or something. Me, I never looked at any of it. I wanted to, you know, just to see what Scotty had been like before Leppenraub ruined him, but he wouldn't never let me. All those pictures of him, they just *humiliated* him."

The tears kept washing silently down the Weasel's cheeks. Romulus found a wadded-up tissue in a pocket, and he gave it to Matthew and Matthew wiped his face with it, but it didn't do any good. The tears kept coming. He said:

"I don't know how Scotty made it before I found him. I took care of him best I could. But he was just crazy. He kept talking about revenge. He had evidence, he said. He said he had this videotape that Leppenraub had made at one of the torture sessions. He said he was going to go to the bastard and let him know he had it and get some money. He acted so crazy, he weirded everyone out in the squat. They threw us out."

"You got evicted from a *squat,* Matthew?"

"Hard to fucking believe, huh? Hey, what can I tell you? They should have left me out on the hillside when I was born. But still, you know, I guess it was OK, 'cause I still had Scotty. We was on the street—but we still had each other. Till one day he says to me, 'I called Leppenraub. He wants to meet me. He wants to negotiate.' 'You going to do it?' I says. 'Yeah,' he says. 'I got nothing to lose.' I says, 'You got us. You going to lose us.' And he smiles, you know, and he says, 'You and me, we're going to Key West. We're going to buy a mansion, and a boat, and live happily ever after.' I says, 'He'll kill you.' He says, 'Yeah, well if he does, you tell 'em. Matthew, you gotta tell 'em you saw me. You saw what they did to me. You tell 'em.'

"And then he told me he loved me. And then he was gone. That was a week ago. That was the last time I saw him."

Romulus got up and threw the last of the wood on the fire. Sparks flying wildly. Any moment the curtains might catch. But when you lived in a cave and owned nothing and had the feeling you were not long for this world anyway, this was not an oppressive concern.

He settled back down on his blanket again. It was warm enough that he could take off his saucepan hat. Underneath it he was three-quarters bald, and he took a minute to rub the bone of his head with his knuckles. Just did that, and looked at the fire. Now why is it, he wondered, after such a tale as this, such suffering and confusion, why did his thoughts feel so light and clear and sure-footed? It was as though the world had only to own up to its share of chaos and sham, for Romulus to peacefully acknowledge his share in the world—fair exchange.

"So did you talk to the cops, Matthew?"

"They—they came around."

"Did you tell them about all this?"

"Rom. Oh, Rom, I *couldn't* tell them. How could I have told them?—they'd have gone right to Leppenraub. And that'd be it for me. He'd a squashed me just like he'd squash a bug—and who'd give a damn? What I *ought* to do, I ought to kill that bastard myself. But I don't have the guts. Oh Rom, for Christ's sake, I'm scared. I got nothing to live for, so what am I scared of? But I'm scared to death. What am I going to do, Rom?"

"I don't know. Seems like you're too small. Nothing you *can* do. Nor nothing I can do for you."

They sat for a long while watching the sparks.

"Rom, you know what—one time I brought Scotty up here to meet you. It was like, back in October. I says, 'I know this guy that's got hisself clear of all this shit. He don't work for nobody. Lives up in this cave, and he fends for hisself, y'know, and so what if he's a little nuts? He keeps himself healthy, and he don't do no drugs, he don't even drink, and he's not even afraid of no wolves—' "

"I'm not afraid of wolves, Matthew, because there are no wolves in New York. Or if there are, I'm sure they're on *our* side."

"Anyway, Scotty says to me, 'This guy I gotta see.' So I took him up here. But you weren't around."

"When was this?"

"October."

"I was probably out harvesting."

"You what?"

"I've got a patch of pumpkins down by the highway."

"*Pumpkins*—that's what I mean. See, that's what Scotty would have loved. He wanted to live just like you, see. He wanted to be free."

Said Romulus, "Well, he's free now."

"You think so? I think he's walking around in *chains,* Rom."

"Matthew, get that notion out of your head right now. No such thing as ghosts. Right? Doesn't matter what kind of garbage you're carrying around, death's going to shake it right out of you. Just hold you up by the ankles, and shake."

"So what are you saying? You're saying we just forget about it? About Scotty, about what they—"

"No, I'm saying *Scotty* just forgets about it. I guess you're not going to be so lucky. Me neither. I mean, this thing just . . . pisses me off. Toss that boy's body at my doorstep. You know why he did that, Matthew? To show me he *dishonors* me. He dishonors me the way he dishonored that boy."

"Wait. You *know* Leppenraub, Rom?"

"Leppenraub, shit, Leppenraub's just a shill. I know who's be-hind him. I know the man he works for, and I know what that man wants. He wants to show us how *little* we are, Matthew. How he can break us in pieces any time he feels like it. Oh shit, Matthew. Old

Stuyvesant, he got to us this time, didn't he? I mean *this* one—looks to me like we're going to be carrying this particular nasty insult around in our heads a *long* time."

He rubbed his head awhile.

"Pisses me off."

THE
PERFECTLY
REAL
AND
GOOD

15

Lieutenant Detective Jack Cork stepped into the nave of the St. Veronica chapel on 207th Street. He crossed himself and felt stupid doing it, then crossed himself again because he'd felt stupid. He also felt edgy. He scanned the pews—there was no one to be seen. He shot a glance over his shoulder. Nobody behind him. He took a few steps down the aisle, into the open. Lord, if this is a setup, I'm in your hands, and please forgive me that this is the first time I've darkened the door of your church since . . . when—Rose's wedding?

Actually, he didn't think it *was* a setup. But there were many surprises in his business. If it was a setup, if some hunter was using one of the pews for a blind, he was a dead duck.

More likely, though, it was just another no-show.

There were multitudes of those in his business.

Then he smelled something. Faintly, faintly . . . He sniffed. Not a churchly fragrance. He sniffed again.

A rich, rank, bum stink.

Someone hissed at him. He looked over to the side aisle and saw the Caveman. Over by the confessionals, wagging a finger, summoning him. Well, he had figured it was probably just the Caveman. You couldn't have known for sure over the phone, but there had been something unhinged and strangely civilized about that voice. And who else would insist on meeting in a place as unlikely as a church?

Cork went over to him. The Caveman nodded gravely, then slipped into the priest's side of one of the confessionals. Shut the door.

Jack Cork sighed. He stepped into the penitent's side. Shut his own door, and sat on the bench, and the little window slid open.

Said the Caveman, "Do you have any sins to confess, my child?"

"Ah, you don't even know the lingo—but all right, yeah, I've got one sin to confess. It's a whopper. I committed sacrilege. I agreed to meet an informant in your church. I'd like to say it's 'cause I'm such a good cop and I was banking on this infinitesimal chance that I'd get something useful. But—nah, it was just an excuse to get away from my desk for a while. Anyway, it was a dumb-ass move, and if anybody catches me in here talking to this crazy man, I'm up shit's creek, and I deeply repent it, Father."

"You shouldn't, my son. Stuyvesant fears religion, even bogus religion. A church offers your informant some privacy. It's no sin, meeting here—merely prudence. Come now, have you committed no true sins?"

"Well maybe one or two, you know—but they're private little suckers. That's all for *you*."

"Nothing you've overlooked?"

"Well, like what, for example?"

"Like covering up the murder of Andrew Scott Gates?"

"Oh, yeah. Well, I did that, but you gotta understand, Father. The guy that offed him was this big . . . I don't know, Lord of All Evil or something, this guy Stuyvesant, and if I'd blown the whistle, they'd a boiled me alive or stuck me in some precinct in the Bronx. Anyway, there was just this smidgen of doubt in my mind that there had *been* any murder."

"Despite the tracks?"

"What tracks?"

"The tracks the murderer left in the snow."

"Oh, *those* tracks. Well, I guess I gotta give you a big mea culpa on that one, too. I totally missed them. Though if I might offer just . . . just a word in my defense. . . . We are talking about a park in New York fucking City, and on the day after a snowfall in any New York City park there's about forty *billion* sets of tracks, and not one of them's worth shit to a murder investigation. You know the real shame of it, Father? They don't even *teach* tracking at the Academy no more. Not since Natty Bumppo died. Can I go now? I mean, I gotta get out of here."

"Wait. Wait my son—I want to ask you a question."

"OK, ask."

"What if . . . suppose you found out there was a very famous person involved in this case? Suppose the victim had been held against his will by this famous person, and abused—I mean, abused, tortured—a real horror story, right?—then what would you say?"

"I'd say who's the famous person?"

"Suppose that couldn't be disclosed?"

"I'd say go fuck yourself, Father."

"Well then, suppose, suppose there could be found some way . . . I don't know, *some* way to *slip* you the name of the famous person—then what?"

"Then I'd say, Let me go back to work, Father, let me get out of here before I lose *my* marbles, too, and you work on some way to *slip* me that name without anybody knowing about it. And as soon as you've figured out how to *slip* me David Leppenraub's name, you give me a call—and then I'll tell you to go fuck yourself."

"You *know* about Leppenraub?"

"Sure. Gates was his model. Until he quit, and came down here and went nuts on the streets of New York, which no one can hold against him. He decided that his employer had ruined his life. This you can't hold against him either. I think the same thing about *my* employer. He started cooking up all these paranoid delusions. These do not in any way constitute what we'd call evidence of murder."

"But suppose there was evidence? I mean suppose there was a witness, suppose—"

"A witness? A real witness? With a name and all?"

"Again, I'm not at liberty—"

"Then again, please go fuck yourself. Who're we talking about anyway, that little weasely guy he lived with?"

"He—Matthew told you?"

"The Y-rays told me, Father. The Y-rays tell all."

Silence from the priest's side.

Jack Cork laughed. "Relax, Caveman, I'm just playing with your head here. Your daughter told me about your Y-rays."

"You talked to my daughter about me?"

"Hey, take it easy. Girl's got nothing but praise for you. She admires the hell out of you. She said if you could just get your little *fits* under control, why, there's nothing you couldn't do."

"You stay away from my daughter."

"She said the shrinks can't quite get a bead on you. Paranoid, sure, but psycho? They can't make up their minds. There's some who think you're kind of weirdly *healthy.* She used some shrink term . . ."

"'Well compensated'?"

"You got it. Like you manage to get by pretty good, in your own way, you know. She says you raise your own food."

"In season. Winters I'm obliged to scavenge."

"But anyway, you're no run-of-the-mill homeless loony—"

"I'm not homeless. I live in a cave. I take care of it."

"Right, what your daughter told me. She said you're all right. She said sometimes she thinks you're saner than anyone. Only . . ."

Cork hesitated.

"Only what?"

"Only sometimes she thinks maybe you're a little—you know?—sometimes a little frightened."

"Frightened?"

That stung. And Cork saw that it had stung.

"Oh shit, I shouldn't have told you. Look, it's better than what my kid says about *me.* Hitler's zombie nephew, how'd you like to be called that?"

"A little frightened? Like I'm some schoolkid peeing in my pants? That's what she said?"

"Forget about it, OK? She loves you. She respects you. I mean, your daughter and me, we had a nice long chat—"

"Don't you chat with my daughter. Don't you ever. Don't you ever touch my daughter."

"Touch her? You mean, carnally? Hey, no offense, but, uh, the ebony-and-ivory thing, that's not really my bag. You know? Anyway, I got a wife and three grown kids. I'm just a good Irish daddy. All I got the hots for these days are the antique roses in my garden. Now those are some fucking sweet broads."

Cork laughed again. "Look, Caveman, relax, will you? Your daughter and me, we are not an item. And your buddy Matthew?— he didn't tell us nothing. He was scared out of his gourd. But he wasn't the only one that Scotty Gates was blabbing his sob story to. A lot of guys down around Tompkins Square knew Gates had it in for David Leppenraub. So I gave Leppenraub a call. Kind of a spoiled prick, I thought, but he told me what I wanted to know. He said, yeah, Gates had tried to blackmail him, and he'd told Gates to eat shit."

"Oh I'm sure he *told* him that. *Right.* He told him very persuasively—he killed him."

"*Your* paranoid conclusion. Me, all I've got is the evidence. I been wasting a lot of time scrounging in the scum of this city for evidence, and the evidence is there ain't any evidence. Of murder. There's plenty of evidence that Gates was off his nut. He was running around with his shirt undone in the middle of winter, babbling about all his bad breaks. *Everybody* thought he was going to freeze to death. And I got me an ME's report telling me that's exactly what he did. The body was clean. Some scrapes, some bruises, maybe some rough play back in his sicko history somewhere—but no lethal blows. Just ice crystals."

"What about AIDS?"

"HIV positive. Big deal. These days about every John Doe they wheel in there comes in positive. But the virus didn't kill him either. Cold killed him. Hypothermia."

"How do you know the morgue wasn't covering up?"

"Hey, maybe they were. Or maybe they just screwed this one. Morgues don't get our best and our brightest, you know. Maybe Gates was a pregnant eighty-year-old grandmother who died by assault from a chain saw—maybe they just missed all that. I wouldn't put it past them. But what the witnesses say seems to suggest they got it right."

"Then the witnesses lie."

"Can I ask you something, Caveman?"

"Sure."

"What the fuck do you care?"

For some time, just church-silence. Then Cork asked, "I mean, you sure *you* never knew Gates?"

"No. Never."

"Because it strikes me kind of curious what the hell he was doing way up here in this neighborhood. I mean, he buys it right in front of your cave—now why? Seems to me maybe he was looking for *you.*"

"He'd heard of me. Matthew says he told him all about me. They even came up to see me once, but I wasn't around."

"So OK, maybe he thought you were the kind he could tell his delusions to. Maybe that's why he came up here. But before he could get a load of your sage advice, he froze to death."

Romulus said, "Sounds reasonable."

"Yeah, it does, don't it?"

"Sounds very reasonable. Except that when he was tossed at my doorstep, he was already *dead.* He was *murdered.* He wasn't thinking *shit,* you fucking snake. You think you can snake this one over on me? But see, I know you! I know you! You're Stuyvesant's ass licker! You call *me* frightened? YOU LICK HIS SLIMY ASSHOLE, AND YOU CALL ME FRIGHTENED? OH, I KNOW YOU! I KNOW THE KIND OF *SLIME*—"

"Good-bye, Father."

Cork got up and cracked the door and peeked out, and thank God there was still nobody there, and he moved out quickly, and as he got to the big front door the Caveman was still going at it, the empty chapel trembling from his sermon, and Cork crossed himself in a flash and got the hell away from there.

16

By that evening the bitter cold had broken. It was a misty, spring-thaw evening, and Romulus was down in the East Village.

He looked both ways, up and down Fourth Street. Nobody coming, so he stepped up quickly onto the milk crate by the window-hole. The window had once been sealed shut with concrete blocks, but somebody had taken a sledgehammer to them. Now there was a jagged gap, and Romulus scrunched down and clambered through it. Straightened himself and stood in a dark forlorn parlor, swatting at his coat to get off the masonry dust.

The light would have been dismal in here even without the cloud of dust. He peered. No furniture in this room. Up near the high ceiling, though, was a fine and delicate molding. The pride of some immigrant who was now spinning in his grave at 400 RPM because someone had written across the length of one molding-board—from wall to wall:

NOBODY HERE BUT US INSURRECTIONARY CHICKENS

He heard voices from above.

Then he spied a door, and passed through it. Pitch black. He went through his pockets and found matches—lit one. Haunted corridor. The floor groaning as he walked. Prodigious stench on the right: what had once been a bathroom. There was a bucket of water, and the toilet lid was in pieces all over the floor—and from the toilet bowl itself came a slow, sulfurous burbling.

His fingers started to scorch. He shook the match out, lit another.

At the end of the corridor, a staircase. The balustrade was gone, the steps sagged. A warning had been painted on the risers: KEEP RIGHT OR— then a skull and crossbones.

Romulus kept right, hugging the wall as he went up.

The voices grew louder. A baby whimpering. Echoes everywhere. Echoes pushing past you on their way down the stairs, or on their way back up. Echoes flirting with the shadows in the corners. A feeble light at the top of the stairs, and the voices were thundering now:

"Tell me not to *look*! What the fuck!"

"You're always sliding your eyes all over me!"

"Put padlocks on my *eyeballs,* bitch? 'Cause you're Miss Scarlett and I'm just the field nigger, is *that* it, bitch?"

"I think bitch is inappropriate, P.J."

"She's a BITCH!"

"You might find a less inflammatory term—"

"It's P.J.'s mode, George. His verbal mode—"

"Yeah, what you doing stifling my mode!"

"He's not staring at *your* tits, Rachel."

"Shut up, bitch!"

"I agree with Anne, Rachel. She feels demeaned—"

"P.J. doesn't *mean* to demean. It's his *mode*."

"MY MODE!"

"USE ANY MODE YOU WANT! JUST STOP STARING AT MY TITS!"

A child started howling. Another joined in. Romulus grinned in the dark. How his divinity did harmonize with such passionate discord!

"Can we move on? The slop pot issue—"

"You're agendizing, Linda. We're not done with P.J.'s staring."

"Yeah, but I'm sick of hauling other people's slops! You hear me, Albert? I'm fed up with hauling your slops!"

"*My* slops?"

"Tuesdays *you're* supposed to haul the slop pot!"

"BUT IT'S NOT MY *SHIT*! I DON'T EVEN SHIT HERE!"

"THAT'S A FUCKING LIE! I'VE SEEN YOU!"

"WILL SOMEBODY GET THE BRATS OUT OF HERE!"

"SEE, THEY'RE *MY* TITS, OK, P.J.? SO GET YOUR EYES OFF OF THEM!"

Romulus stepped in quietly. They all looked up—this circle of fiery eyes under a naked bulb. The wire for the bulb went out the window and over to the next building.

"Caveman!" said someone.

"Yo, Caveman, tell us about The Guy with No Face!"

"Stuyvesant! What's that old fucker Stuyvesant up to?"

"How're the Y-rays tonight, Caveman? Bad out there tonight?"

"Tell us about Homeowner's Pride!"

"Give us a fucking tirade, man!"

Romulus scanned the eyes, spotted Matthew's. Matthew was sitting against the wall, outside the circle, with a demeanor of utter catatonia.

"Matthew."

Matthew got up and came to the door. Romulus gave the group a smile before he led Matthew out.

"Rage on, people."

17

Out in the hall by the grime-frosted window, a seep of gray light. The sound of water dripping from the snow-melt. Romulus said quietly:

"Matthew, they say he froze to death."

Matthew shook his head. "He was murdered."

"Yeah, right. But they say there's no evidence."

"They just don't give a shit. There's a videotape, Rom!"

"Maybe there *used* to be. But I guess when Leppenraub killed your man, he must have got the tape, too."

"I bet not every copy."

"There's another copy?"

"Rom, listen—when Leppenraub was doing all this sadistic shit to Scotty, there were other guys there—and there was this one guy who was running the camera. Scotty said this guy didn't seem to be *into* it, you know? He just made the movie like he was doing what he was told."

"What was his name?"

"Scotty never told me his name. He just told me that one day this guy slipped him a manila envelope. 'I made a copy for you,' he says. 'Just in case you ever need it.' And that was the tape—that's how Scotty got hold of it, all that sick stuff."

"But Scotty never showed it to you?"

"Uh-uh. He said he was hiding it somewhere. Somewhere far off, safe."

"And that other guy?"

"The guy that gave him the tape? Well, right after that is when Leppenraub kicked Scotty out. He never saw the guy again."

"So if we could *find* the guy . . ."

"Maybe . . . Oh, damn, Rom, I'm crying again. I can't stop crying, Rom, I gotta stop crying."

"Where do we look for the guy?"

"I don't know. How am I supposed to know something like that? Ask the cops. Ask Leppenraub."

"Yeah. Right. That's about it, Matthew."

They stood and listened to the bustle and commerce of the echoes. Romulus said:

"I mean that's it. You'd have to go up there, right? To Leppenraub's farm. I mean, you'd have to meet the murderer in his lair, and get him to *cooperate* somehow. You'd have to be fucking crazy."

"Yeah."

Then Matthew gave him a look.

Romulus shook his head. "Oh no, not me. I'm paranoid—that's a *special* type of crazy. Not good for this kind of work, uh-uh. No, this . . . this takes the kind of crazy that thinks it's *sane*."

18

All the way back home the temperature kept climbing. Though without spirit, just climbing dull-footed into a drear drizzle.

Romulus got back to the cave and sat there in the dark, and zapped the remote control on his TV set.

Since the set had been disemboweled before he had found it, and since it wasn't hooked up to anything, it took a while to warm up. The images came in blurry, ghosted.

Romulus watched, and munched. In a bag he had Doritos

crumbs and shrimp scampi and hunks of somebody's wedding cake, and extracts from an arugula-and-tuna salad. All gleaned from some generous cans in front of 28 Corbin Plaza. He popped tidbits of this compost into his mouth as if they were popcorn.

The images on the TV started to add up.

They turned into a movie starring Steve McQueen and Ali MacGraw. It was set in the fifties, but it had been made in the sixties and it was snappish and airy and callow.

The movie was called *Prodigy.*

Steve McQueen played a young music student at Juilliard. His family was poor, from the Bronx, but they were strivers. The parents were tough and demanding. No coarseness of speech, no dialect, was permitted about the house, and Steve McQueen's older brothers were all embarking upon promising careers. Steve's girlfriend—the Ali MacGraw part—burned up the screen with her beauty. The script was dumb but the music—the pieces the young student composed and played on the piano—these were strong and strange.

So, was this movie the biography of an actual composer? You couldn't tell. No names were used.

Though there were hints that perhaps the Steve McQueen character was in fact supposed to be a young black man. At one point it was let drop that his great-grandfather had been a slave. And when the young composer wanted kicks, he went to Harlem, where he was treated like family. Also, at times it was flashed on the bottom of the screen that this movie had been

DECOLORIZED FOR POPULAR APPEAL

The young composer's music was moving but destructive. He'd take sappy pop tunes and shake them till they cracked open and the syrup poured out of them, till they were rattling carcasses, but bone-lovely. Some of his peers at Juilliard thought he would be the greatest composer of the age. What a joyful jam his life was, and how sharp, mordant, and loving was Ali MacGraw!

But then came a shot of Stuyvesant's tower—played, of course, by the Chrysler Building—and a beam of Y-rays shooting out from it.

Cut to Stuyvesant in his vast aquamarine office up at the top. Stuyvesant played himself. He wore a white cowl, and he had no face at all. His fingers rested on a glowing globe before him. He was receiving Y-ray reports on Steve McQueen.

He saw that the young man's music was making a mockery of the *American Heartfelt*. He worried that the *Perfectly Real and Good* was being undermined.

He muttered something.

And right away Ali MacGraw got pregnant. Steve McQueen married her, left Juilliard, and went to work in the Domino Sugar plant in Brooklyn. Domino Sugar was owned by a holding company that was held by Stuyvesant's lawyers, and they saw to it that Steve McQueen's life was hell. He got angry and poured Domino Sugar into the machinery. He was fired. He got a job as a pianist, playing dinner music at a restaurant. He said to the patrons, "Here's 'Three Coins in the Fountain' for all you mindless racist scum." He was fired. Ali MacGraw came and begged his boss, and her eyes flashed and she looked like a bird of prey, and the boss took him on again. But he did things to "The Impossible Dream" that the patrons found unbearable, and they threw radishes at him. By now the movie had turned into a melodramatic litany of failure, the script was a pointless grind, and Romulus wished it were Christmas again so he could watch *It's a Wonderful Life*.

He prayed for an ad.

But this movie was presented as a public service by the Stuyvesant Fund for Absolute Control, and there were no ads.

19

Instead he got more of Steve McQueen's screaming rages, and one job after another, and mental hospitals and halfway houses, and one by one his other brothers coming around and trying to rescue him, but nothing doing, and more mental hospitals and halfway houses, and Ali MacGraw raising their little girl by herself, with her job at the welfare office.

And then the scene where he didn't come home one night until about noon, and she said, "Where have you been?" And he said, "I'm a free man, right? I spent the night in a cave in Inwood Park."

And she said, "Then spend another night there. I can't do this no more. I love you, but I got a kid to raise and I got to get on with it."

So she threw him out.

And Steve McQueen was on his way back to Manhattan, crossing the Willis Avenue Bridge, when a big limo pulled up. The door opened, he got in. They went to Stuyvesant's tower. There was a Jacuzzi in the elevator, and Steve McQueen sat beside it on this lovely sofa, and then the elevator door opened and there was Stuyvesant—and a grand piano.

"Come in. Come in, sit down, and play, my son."

Steve McQueen played three selections from *The Sound of Music*—played them heartfeltly. When he was done he wept, and he told Stuyvesant, "I've learned my lesson."

Y-rays flashed and crackled everywhere, like Tinkerbell. Stuyvesant gave him the Congressional Medal of Honor and said, "See how sweet reality can be once you accept it as your personal savior?"

Then Ali MacGraw and the kids came running in for a big embrace. Music up and out.

Romulus threw the remote control at the screen, but the screen had been made from the fingernails of South African miners, and wouldn't break. Sirens sang down on Dyckman Street, and on the Henry Hudson Parkway. Stuyvesant's minions making their rounds. And then when the sirens faded there was nothing for a while but the sound of the drizzle, and of the snow thawing and dripping in front of the cave, and Romulus managed a few rags of sleep.

20

He spent a great part of the next day at the Inwood Branch Library.

He was trying to fathom the hidden meanings in *The Reader's Guide to Periodical Literature,* but it was too damn hot in here to concentrate.

He took off his topmost coat and hung it on the back of his

chair—this insulting school cafeteria plastic scoop-chair. Then ten minutes later he took off another coat.

But the lining didn't come off with it, so he had to take *that* off, too, and nothing but battle-flag shreds it was—and all the while that old librarian was giving him this dark eye as though it were *her* battle.

And then ten minutes later he had to take off the last coat.

Peeling away—stripping down to a proto-Romulus he hadn't seen in weeks, and releasing, as he did, ranker and ranker fumes of himself. He was disgusted. What was the matter with him, not bothering to wash? Falling apart at the seams here. The librarian scowled at him. A tableful of junior-high nasties kept bursting out in snorts of derisive laughter. He was having trouble staying awake, and he needed to take a leak. Meanwhile, *The Reader's Guide* utterly resisted him. He rubbed his head, picked at his beard. He found morsels of the week-old croissant he'd had for breakfast. Picked them off and popped them in his mouth. The junior-high nasties turned blue trying not to laugh and then exploded. He got up and wobbled to the librarian.

She had set up her face to hurt you. Romulus showed her *The Reader's Guide.*

"I can't use this. It's in Chinese."

"Were you sleeping before, sir?"

"I had my eyes shut. I mean, it's like an oven in here. What, are you baking us? You making a pie?"

"You can't sleep in here."

"You got one of these books in English?"

"What are you looking for?"

"I'm looking for articles about a certain murderer."

"Did you look under 'Murder'?"

"Yeah, but nothing about Leppenraub."

"Leppenraub. You mean David Leppenraub? He's a photographer."

"You mean photographer-murderers are kept separate from regular murderers?"

She opened the book, flipped briskly to the Ls.

She said, "See there's plenty of articles about Leppenraub. We don't have most of these magazines though. We do have *Artforum.*

All right, here's one. September of 1992. You'll find the *Artforums* up on that shelf."

He asked her, "Where's your furnace?"

"What?"

"Don't get all excited, I just want to check out your furnace. It's so goddamn hot. I want to see what you're burning in there."

"This is a library."

"You won't show me. Right. You don't *need* to show me, either, 'cause now I *know*."

He went and pulled down the bound copies of *Artforum*. Brought them back to his table. All the chairs in this place were the same color, an electric, executioner's green. They hung on, in blobs, in the corner of your eye when you were trying to read, and drove you nuts. That and the heat. He took off his heavy shirt, so he was down to his Batman T-shirt. Fads always swing around again sooner or later, he thought—if I just keep wearing this shirt for another twenty years, it ought to be worth something.

He got up and went back to the librarian's desk.

"I need to take a leak."

"Excuse me?"

"A whiz."

"This isn't a shelter."

"The key, OK?"

"You people think it's your own private bathroom. You make a mess and expect us to clean it."

"Not me. My aim is outstanding. You want to come watch? I'm a sharpshooter."

She handed over the key.

In the bathroom there was a chain through the toilet paper and a padlock on the chain. Romulus's aim was as fuzzy as ever. Oh, concede her these droplets all around the bowl, these little yellow vindications, it will satisfy her no end to find them here.

While shaking, he felt Y-rays, curdling around his legs. He looked down. There was some kind of ivory-white rubber-tipped device attached to the wall by the sink. He dealt it a smart kick. Which did the device no apparent harm, but the Y-rays seemed to subside. Or else with the pain in his toes he couldn't feel them.

He limped back to his seat. Found the September 1992 issue of

Artforum and leafed through it, and soon he came upon an article entitled

LEPPENRAUB'S CAVES:
CLAUSTRAL HARMONIA

Photo of a cave entrance. Sitting before it, a gorgeous woman who wore a calico farm dress and golden earrings, whose wild hair swept down like a red-oak windfall in autumn. Lord, she was lovely. A Siberian husky was curled at her feet. The dog stared at Romulus with ice eyes.

The woman's name, the caption told him, was Moira Leppenraub.

Oh Jesus, *wrong* fucking Leppenraub. Stupid bitch of a librarian doesn't even know how to read *The Reader's Guide.*

But then he considered that if the woman at the cave was the wrong Leppenraub, she wasn't *all* wrong.

There were diagrams of the caves she made. The passageways all spiraled inward like a ram's horn or a conch shell. There were details of the drawings that adorned the passages, and Romulus studied these a long time.

Caves. A woman who made caves.

The article itself was as unintelligible as *The Reader's Guide.*

Her attenuating corridors, her delicate compactions, while castigating gingerly the constraints of our own "crush-culture," nevertheless do open—inwardly, diachronically, and enthusiastically, to embrace the spirit of prepatriarchal realms of Lascaux and Altamira. . . .

He skipped all that.

But near the end he found a little biographical tidbit that interested him:

Moira Leppenraub finds source and resource in the same "natural, pagan world" that invigorates the work of her brother, David Leppenraub. She presides over David's Leppenraub Foundation for the Arts, and she lives in a converted coach house on David's expansive Hudson Valley farm. "I have an absolute dream-studio there," she says. . . .

Then another half page of Mandarin goulash. Made you dizzy just to *look* at writing like that.

God, it was hot in here!

Inside his head, the Seraphs of Divinity and Vengeance were whipping around his consciousness the way moths fly around a porch light on a molten summer night.

Romulus staggered up to the desk.

He asked the librarian, "How do I find out about the Leppenraub Foundation?"

"What's that?"

"I don't know. It's some foundation he's got."

"The murderer?"

"Right."

"Well sir, what kind of foundation is it?"

"How the fuck should I know? It's a foundation for murderers. A hit man gets leukemia, the Leppenraub Foundation is *there* for him. Right?"

She sighed. "Check *The Foundation Directory*. Over there, near the bottom."

From *The Foundation Directory*, Romulus learned that the Leppenraub Foundation had been founded in 1986 in Gideon Manor, New York. That its principal donor was David Leppenraub. That its main purpose was funding the Gideon Manor Playhouse, the Hudson River Symphony, the East Village Art Clinic, roll on sweet Jesus. That its trustees included Anders O. Nilson, Dr. Laura Smits, Arnold Gannon—

Arnold fucking *Gannon!*

He rubbed his head. He shut his eyes.

So then maybe . . . he could just give old Arnold a call and ask him . . . for a *letter of introduction* or something. . . .

But of course he couldn't. No he could not. No, it was too much to come out of a cave after so many years and . . .

He opened his eyes. She was standing there.

"Are you sleeping, sir?"

"What do you *want* me to do?"

She shrugged. "Read?"

"Oh, I can't read *now*. Too busy."

"With what?"

"I'm trying to screw up my courage to ask somebody something."

"What's that?"

"You're such a nosy bitch."

"I'm calling the police."

"Oh, all right, I'll tell you. I'm trying to get up the balls to ask you if you'll marry me. So. There it is, what do you say? I love you more than my life. I'm not a rich man, it's true, but we can buy a little pony cart, and go on down the interstate and I'll play hurdy-gurdy for folks and you can dance for 'em in the raw, darling—do tricks for 'em."

"I'm calling the police."

"No, call a preacher, my love. Or a justice of the peace."

"I'm dialing right now."

"Yes, but I *know* you're dialing a preacher. I see your heart, my love—it's beating like a newborn *but*-ter-fly."

21

But later he regretted the way he'd spoken to her.

He was walking down Nagle Street, and he said to himself, You've got to stop that.

You want to get hold of the truth but you're not getting hold of a damn thing till you learn to rein yourself in a little.

Seraphs! Do you hear me? I'm talking to you! Seraphs, you've got to simmer down in there!

He stopped dead in his tracks and listened for them, listened to the caverns in his skull, but the Seraphs were lying low. Quiet as church mice. Not so much as a wing-flutter out of them.

He walked on.

Right, he thought. But I'm telling you, Seraphs, you've got to *stay* like that for a while. I mean you've got to absolutely *hide out* or where's the sense in my making this call?

And I've got to make this call.

If I don't make this call I'm a slime-skimmer, and I ought not to suffer myself to live.

But if I'm going to make this call, first I've got to remake *myself*. Got to learn to mask myself. Got to learn to *lie* a little.

It was wearing him out just thinking about it.

He passed in front of a dry-cleaning shop, and in the dark window he saw his reflection and stopped to appraise it. He stared back at the shambling mad-hatted wreck of a hobo and asked himself what chance he had of pulling this caper off.

Way down close to zero. Rubbing bellies with zero, right?

But it wasn't the grime, or the tatters—*that* could be changed, he thought. He took off his hat and stood up straight and brushed some crumbs off his coat and cocked his head a little. Yes, surely he could take care of his appearance. Clean himself up, get a shave, change his clothes.

The question was, what was he going to do the next time he was ready to pitch a fit? What the hell was he going to do then?

He thought about it. *Chuckle?*

Isn't that what everyone does? Isn't that what chuckling's *for*— to put a mask on all the boiling shit inside? He tried it.

"Heh heh."

But it came out sounding nervous, insecure.

When what I want is simply to sound amused, like I'm so in command of this situation it's just plain *silly,* heh heh. Like me and reality, why, we're *old* friends, and yes sir everything's under control in *this* boy's brain, hee hee hee. And I'm just *tickled* to see how everything's unfolding according to my scheme of things, oh yes I've got all my duckies in a row, and now I'm just going to stand here and blow them away, one after another—

"Heh heh. Heh heh. Heh heh. Heh heh. Heh heh."

After a few minutes of this, the Asian proprietor of the shop opened the door and stuck his head out and said, "Go way. Go away. We don't have what you want."

What I want?

Said Romulus, "Well—but I could sure use one of those pretty suits you've got on that rack there."

The proprietor tried to look as fierce as he could.

Said Romulus, "Heh heh. Joking with you, my friend. All in jest. Heh heh."

Practicing.

Then he went to the phone on the corner of Nagle and Broadway, and took a deep breath so he could lay down some breeziness in his voice, and dialed.

22

Romulus? God damn. Where the hell *are* you?"

"Hey, just dropping in on your good city for a couple of days, Arnold. I been living out on the other coast. San Francisco, you know."

"No shit."

"Yeah, got a pretty good gig. You know the um, New Bay Museum for the Living Arts? I'm the music director."

"No shit," said Arnold. "Last time I heard about you, you were living in a *cave* or something."

"Heh heh. Oh yes. My dissolute past. That seems very distant right now. And what are *you* up to?"

"Same old. Teaching at Columbia. The BBC's doing an opera of mine."

"No! I'd like to hear it."

"I think it's got a lot of you in it. Got a calypso choir singing 'Moonlight in Vermont.' "

"Heh heh. Maybe a *little* of me."

"I still remember your 'Love Is a Many-Splendored Bolero' from school."

"Those were not bad days, Arnold."

"That was a good time. So. What is it again, the . . . New Bay Museum?"

"Oh, Lord, Lord, it's *something*. Lot of New Age folks."

"Romulus, this sounds like a big con."

"It does?"

"But I'm biased. To me, that whole state sounds like a big con. They got you writing the *Symphonie Écologique* yet?"

"Heh heh. As a matter of fact, Arnold, next month they're having what they call the New Pastorale Festival."

"Haw haw."

"Yeah, I had to write a piece for it. Just program schtick, you know. Inspired by some of David Leppenraub's photographs. You know, those city trees? Nature enslaved and all? I really do love that guy."

"Well, he's remarkable, Rom. The amazing thing is, he does all that blood and violence stuff, but in person he's just a *gentle* guy."

"You know David Leppenraub *personally*? Arnold! You lucky SOB. Have you been to his *farm*?"

"Oh sure. So tell me something, Romulus, how did you get out of the *cave* thing? I heard you went just *bonkers*, boy."

But Romulus would not be swerved from his course. He said, "I mean, from the photos it looks . . . it looks incredible."

"What does?"

"Leppenraub's farm."

"Oh. Well, it's a nice place. Nothing fancy, really. But lovely. So anyway—how long you in town for, Rom?"

He'd blown it. He'd moved too fast. He'd come off sounding like some kind of adoring art groupie, and Arnold was changing the topic because it had gotten too weird for him.

"What? Oh. I'll be here a couple of days."

"Because I was thinking, Rom, that Leppenraub piece you wrote—did you say it was finished?"

"My 'Blood Pastorale'? More or less."

"Would you be willing to *perform* it? I mean, I don't know what you're doing on Saturday . . . but the Leppenraub Foundation is having a big bash. Up at David's farm. Sort of in celebration of him getting out of the hospital. If by any chance you could come on up, well—shit boy, we'd get to see each other, and maybe if you'd play just a *little*—you know, he's got a Steinway up there, not too bad— am I being presumptuous?"

"Heh heh."

Cool down. Try to breathe.

"I'd love to."

"Oh Jesus, Romulus, this'll be great."

"Heh heh heh heh."

Date, time, place, a little lame hemming and hawing, and he was free again. He'd hoped for something like a letter of introduction, he'd wound up with a Royal Command Performance. Of the breath he'd drawn at the start of the call, he still had about 97 percent in his lungs. Idling in there, fermenting. He let it out. A plague of mauve and blue stars gusted before his eyes. You could do these things—you just set your teeth, and you could do them.

23

That evening he went and waited at his post on the little street off Riverside Drive.

The big thaw was still in effect. Plenty of mist, a blur on everything—like the atmosphere in a fable, or in some simple nursery rhyme. The kind of evening where you simply took it easy. No harsh edges. OK. He took it easy. He waited.

And by and by comes Mr. Pinstripes, strutting along on his way home.

Romulus had him in his sights, in the corner of his eye. Pinstripes wasn't wearing pinstripes tonight—rather this elegant light blue wool-and-linen number. He faltered a step when he got a whiff of Romulus. He didn't want another lecture. He hugged the curb.

And Romulus didn't even raise his eyes till the man was dead even with him on the sidewalk. Then he said:

"Hey mister, could you spare a suit and tie?"

Just the least hitch in Pinstripes's step, but enough to let Romulus know he'd heard. He kept moving, but it was only a matter of time. Only the matter of a dozen steps or so, and Pinstripes started slowing. He was winged. He was losing strength. He took two more steps and pulled up.

"Say again?"

"Well, you see, I don't know anybody else comes close to my size."

"You want a *suit* and *tie*?"

"Just anything old in your closet. Something you're ready to throw out. Right?"

"Right. What for?"

"Got a gig. Upstate. Playing a big bash for the Leppenraub Foundation. Schoolmate of mine got it for me."

"You mean a schoolmate from Juilliard?"

"Right! You remembered."

Pinstripes looked at him dubiously. "Let me ask you something. You say you went to Juilliard. So what do you know about . . . ohh, say, Scriabin."

"Who?"

"Scriabin. For example. What can you tell me about him?"

"Nothing."

Pinstripes frowned. "Ah. Yes, of course. You know nothing about him?"

Romulus shrugged. "Nope."

"What I expected. How about Beethoven, then? Have you ever heard of *him*?"

He gave his perfect laugh again.

Said Romulus, "Oh, sure. I could tell you lots about Beethoven."

"I'll bet. But I have to be going." He took a quarter from his pocket and flipped it at Romulus. "Take care, guy."

Romulus let the quarter bounce off his shin. He said, "But Scriabin—now that man's just a total *cipher* to me. I mean, I think one time I spent a month listening to the *Étrangeté*—to all those Promethean chords, you know—and I still couldn't see through to the least *flicker* of that man's divinity."

Pinstripes squinted at him. "Well," he said. "All right, may *be*. Maybe you're for real."

He rolled his eyes up. He deliberated. Then he said, "Come on, then."

"Huh?"

"Come up with me."

"Now? To your apartment?"

"You want a suit and tie?"

24

Romulus followed him.

Ornate portal. Lobby of travertine and glossy shrubbery, and too many damn mirrors. Reflections and rereflections, miles of travertine, thousands of Pinstripeses and their hobo buddies—and then out of a rereflection stepped the doorman.

This bouncer dressed like some kind of ridiculous Turkish Zouave. He clapped a hand on Romulus's shoulder.

"Where you think you're going?"

Said Pinstripes, "It's all right, Mahoud. I'm just taking him up for a minute."

"But this guy—Mr. Clay! This guy's a *bum*. I seen him hanging around. He's an absolute loser."

"There are no *absolute* losers, Mahoud. The man is in the state of bankruptcy. To emerge from which he'll need to recognize that prior business plans were flawed, unrealistic. He'll need to reorganize. Most of all, he'll need an infusion of capital to restore public confidence. Said capital takes the form of a suit and tie, which I've agreed to front him."

"But don't you think it's kind of risky—"

"Not at all. However, if tomorrow morning you should find pieces of me in the elevator shaft, I suppose I'll need to rethink my position. Good night, Mahoud."

Romulus unpeeled the Zouave's fingers from his shoulder. He followed Pinstripes.

Up they went.

At the door Pinstripes went in first, calling ahead of him.

"Honey, you decent? Brought somebody up."

Romulus followed him into the apartment.

Spacious, oh yes, with a killer view, yet something about the place seemed out of kilter. Seemed peculiarly *plain*. Kind of homey and rounded off and dawdling. Simply . . . simply comfortable, that was it. It reminded Romulus of nothing ritzier than easy Sundays at his great-uncle the dentist's place in Harlem. Sprawled out on the waiting room rug, playing with his toy ambulance.

So where, Romulus wondered, was all the high-tech cutting-edge decor? Pinstripes couldn't afford a designer?

"Hi."

A woman was staring at him from the sofa.

"Betty, this is . . . what's your name?"

"Romulus."

"Romulus. I'm Bob and this is my friend Betty."

"How do you do?"

"How do *you* do?"

"Betty, Romulus is a homeless man who's looking for a suit of clothes."

Romulus muttered, "Not homeless. Not."

"He's the one I told you about. Remember?"

Said Betty, "You mean the one who saved you from the Ghost of Christmas Future? The music man?"

Betty's lips curled up at the corners. She seemed uncertainly amused. A little scared but amused. She was a small woman with big eyes and a pageboy, and right now she looked a little like a toddler beholding her first clown.

Bob said, "That's right. The music man."

Then he took hold of Romulus's elbow.

And terror also took hold of Romulus. For it occurred to him, what if this man had a *piano*? What if they were going to ask him to play? Rich guy like this probably had a piano. In fact there was probably a piano right in this very—

And there it was.

An upright, in the corner by the window. And the man had him in his clutches and was leading him over . . .

"You'll grace us?"

"Ah. Not now, thanks. Thank you very much."

"Oh, just one piece."

"My. Nice view."

"Play anything at all."

"My. This is a strange-looking piano."

"Yes. Yes, it's a Hammond, 1936. Depression moderne design—you like it? Everything in this apartment is moderne from the thirties."

That was it. Everything dulled-out chrome and Bakelite and softly, drably streamlined—everything looking forward to a better future but no rush.

Said Bob, "What can I say? I'm a bankruptcy lawyer—the thirties were kind of a golden age for my kind. But play for us—please."

"I can't."

"Why not?"

"Because it would kill me."

"But if you've got a gig, you'll *have* to play."

"Yes."

"So why not practice a little now?"

"Because it would kill me."

Said Betty, "Honey, if he doesn't want to play—"

"I want to know if he *can* play."

Romulus looked at his shoes. Then at the piano. He reached over and pressed the B♭ below middle C. The shock drove through his fingernail, his knuckles, wristbone, elbow and collarbone, slammed into his limbus and drove it up into his cerebrum. He sank down, sat on the stool.

Nobody said anything. Romulus looked down various alleys, but they were all blind. Bob was right, there was no way out.

Presently he looked up, and set his teeth.

"All right. All right, then, you want proof?"

He wheeled on the stool and dove in with his eyes shut tight. He played for fifteen seconds. Slapped down an array of chords, sprayed a menacingly cheerful melody on either side of them. Then ceased, midchord, and wheeled back to face his audience. Put his face in his hands. His saucepan hat fell to the rug. Betty picked it up and handed it to him.

"Jesus. You OK? That was wonderful. What *was* that?"

"A variation on the Mr. Clean jingle. Do I pass?"

Said Bob, "One hand-me-down suit, coming up."

He went to get it. Betty kept peering at Romulus, looking worried. "Tell me, why did it hurt you to play?"

"Because that was a life. Playing music, that was one life, this is another life. I dare you to turn into a buffalo or a wounded jackrabbit for fifteen seconds and see if it doesn't discombobulate your whole evening."

"A buffalo?"

"Also because your blinds are open and you've got a view of midtown Manhattan and Cornelius Gould Stuyvesant *saw me playing the piano.*"

25

The suit turned out to have no label. This puzzled Romulus.

Bob asked him, "Why, what were you hoping for? Brooks Brothers? Bill Blass?"

"It doesn't matter. I just wondered."

"This suit was made for me by my tailor in Singapore. I think he's also Bill Blass's tailor."

"Oh. What's wrong with it, then?"

"Hm?"

"Why are you giving it to me?"

"Lapels are a little too narrow. They smack of the lean and hungry and greedy eighties."

"Oh."

Betty wouldn't let him try on the suit till he took a shower. She gave him a towel, and a pair of Bob's silk boxer shorts and a pair of Bob's silk socks, and he took it all into the bathroom, the fixtures of which were also thirties moderne.

He stripped. He showered, and tuned the flow to such force and heat that it melted his bones—and presently his fear. Presently he began to hum the Mr. Clean jingle, and then to sing it, and then to juice it up with toucan trills and jaguar yowls. He stared profoundly into the jet of sizzling water. The grime of the last month fell from him. He washed himself with bubble bath. Then with Oil of Olay. Then with Neutrogena hair conditioner. Then with Comet cleanser. Olympian clouds of steam enveloped him. He washed the wrinkles under his knees and found that a rough area that had started out as dirt had now become fused to him—a kind of tyro flesh. He washed his penis for so long he began to feel little tremors there. Muffled cock-crows. Way down deep beneath the surface but no denying them either.

He held out his arms, a god-king at his own immolation.

He opened and shut his mouth like a fish.

When at last he emerged, he was offended by the odor of his own clothes. He stuffed his old underwear into the pocket of his coat. His socks were a crime against humanity. He opened the window and tossed them.

CITY GARDEN MYSTERIOUSLY BLIGHTED.

Then, in the luminescent cloud chamber of the bathroom, he put on the underwear and the socks and the suit he had been given. His skin was seduced, his skin swooned to the feel of these duds. He came out and Betty tied his tie for him.

Then she sat him down in the kitchen, tucked a towel under his collar, and trimmed his hair. She lathered him up and shaved him. When she was done she pulled off the towel and wiped the daubs of lather from behind his ears.

She asked Bob, "What do you think?"

Bob walked all around him. "I think Galatea. Suit's a tad tight in the rump. But otherwise Pygmalion and Galatea."

Said Betty, "You know, Romulus, you're a very handsome man."

Said Bob, "Would you like a drink, Romulus?"

"Thanks. I would."

"Would you care for a rickey? A lime rickey?"

"Sure. Perfect."

Romulus and Betty sat on the curvy chairs. He couldn't remember the last time he had crossed his legs. It was one of the perks of being a Man of Elegance.

But Betty noticed his shoes and shook her head. "What size do you wear?"

"Twelve."

"Bob's a ten. No good. Better try to keep them under the piano when you're doing your gig."

Then she called to Bob. "Darling, you know your old black topcoat?"

"Which one?"

"With the tortoiseshell buttons that I don't like?"

"Uh-huh."

"Can Romulus have that?"

Bob chuckled. "You don't want him to freeze to death, do you?"

She ran and got the coat. Romulus tried it on.

"Very nice," said Betty.

Bob brought the drinks. He lifted his own and said, "To *reorganization*."

They all took a sip. Then Bob lifted his glass again.

"To the eternal cycles of *failure* and *reorganization*."

They drank.

"Well, you can take it off now," said Betty. "Relax awhile."

Romulus took off the coat and draped it on the sofa, and sat beside it. He took another sip of his drink.

Betty, staring, asked him, "OK, now tell us, who is Cornelius Gregg Stuyvesant?"

"Gould."

"And you say he's *watching* us?"

"Where do you work, Betty?"

"Seventh Avenue. I'm a rep for Mizzy Jeans."

"Right. See, Stuyvesant owns Mizzy Jeans. It's a subsidiary of Robert Hall, Incorporated, which he bought in the sixties. He's your boss, Betty."

"Oh."

"It used to be owned by this guy Robert Hall, but Stuyvesant had him killed."

"How did he do that?"

"Had him injected with some disease. It's his usual method."

"Oh. And he *watches* us?"

"Damn straight. You don't see him?"

"Where?"

"In his fucking tower."

Bob didn't raise his eyes. He muttered, "He's talking about the Chrysler Building, darling."

She said, "Which one is that?"

Bob told her, "Left of the Empire State. That little needle."

She found it. "Oh, yes."

Romulus scowled. "And do you see the Y-ray beam, Bob and Betty?"

"The what?"

"Look, spare me the bald-ass innocence act, OK? *I know damn well you see it.*"

Bob coughed significantly.

"Darling, maybe we better not talk about Cornelius Gould Stuyvesant right now."

"Makes you nervous, Bob? Something you don't want her to *know?* Huh, *Bob?*"

Romulus realized he hated the name *Bob.* He took another sip and made it a big swallow. Crossed his legs again. What's the matter with my shoes? They don't like the holes in my shoes? He wagged his foot at them, insolently.

"In fact," he said, "Stuyvesant's got a *lot* of methods for killing people. And so often he likes to toy with them first. Torture them awhile, then dump their bodies in the snow. And what do you know about *that,* Bob?"

Bob had nothing to say.

Said Romulus, *"'You wouldn't want him to freeze to death, would you?'* Oh, I just *loved* that one. *Bob.*"

Bob and Betty took a sip. Romulus didn't. He shut his eyes.

Boom-boom, went the blood in his temples. The Moth-Seraphs swarmed and whirled.

He took a breath. Set his teeth. After a long while he produced a brief chuckle, and then said hoarsely: "OK, listen. It may be that I have been impolite. Please . . ."

He found he could speak civilly if he spoke with formality.

"Please if I have been impolite, or ungenerous in any way, please. *Please?* Forgive me, and I think I better go. Right. But my undying gratitude for the clothes. And the shave and haircut. And the lime rickey, which was needless to say excellent. Heh heh."

In silence, he went to the bathroom and gathered up his own forlorn rags.

When he came out he dug in his pocket.

"I nearly forgot. Your pen. Thank you."

He set it on the chrome-edged coffee table.

"Thank you, Romulus."

"I'm very outspoken sometimes. Forgive me that."

"Good luck, Romulus."

"Good luck, Romulus."

That's when he saw it. Out the big window he saw the blast of light shooting from Stuyvesant's tower. Though it was thicker than light, and heavier, and not quite so fast. Romulus saw it coming.

He gaped at it, and he was astonished and terrified. *Because this was not a Y-ray.*

A Y-ray was quick and yellow. But this huge blast of light coming at him was sort of a slow, furred green. Like a clump of electric moss—and he stood there, watching, and it passed right overhead. Missed this building entirely. Wasn't even aimed at this building, but it was headed north somewhere, somewhere upstate.

Said Betty, "Romulus?"

"Yeah." He blinked at her.

"Don't forget the coat."

"Oh, right. Thank you."

He picked up the coat and left. Went down to the lobby, and he and the Zouave gaped at each other's outlandish costumes. Then he trudged home.

26

The warm front was still at work, even in the dark. He got to the cave where an old white woman they called Cyclops—because her other eye was just a purplish burned-out socket—was asleep on his mattress.

He took off his new clothes and folded them neatly. He put on his old clothes, then he woke Cyclops and told her to make some room. She rolled over and slumbered on, purred. Romulus sat beside her, looking out into the mist. Against his new-scrubbed skin, his old clothes chafed. They felt clammy, gritty. Didn't seem to fit. Didn't suit him anymore.

Furthermore it annoyed him, it always annoyed him, to share his cave with Cyclops.

It was a great nuisance. The cave was too small to share with anybody, and besides, Cyclops had fleas. Romulus would wake up at four in the morning and feel them popping softly against his neck, an invisible wind. Take him days to hunt all the buggers down.

But she had no home.

The woman was dying of six different diseases. She lay there with no blanket on, just her coat, and her calves were exposed and in the dim city-glow Romulus could see her sores. Her legs were patchworked of scabs, boils, fissures, and blisters. In her sleep she reached down and raggedly scratched herself, dug in with her moonstone claws. But wearing all that ancient armor of scab tissue, how could she hope to satisfy the itch beneath? And her breathing was one long death rattle, and her brain was a smoking wreck, and those fortunates like Romulus who *had* homes were simply obliged to share them with those who didn't.

There was no way around this.

Clearly (however misty, it was a night for clear visions!), clearly, neighbors, if you would trouble yourselves *just a little,* just enough to open your doors and step out and offer up a little villagers' love no less—why then, Stuyvesant in his tower would be defeated and he'd writhe and cringe and *HOWL!* YOU BLOODSUCKER! DE-FEATED BY LOVE!

WRITHING IN HELLFIRE!

Clearly. But Y-rays have bleared every eye and mucked over every heart, and all who live here live only to tremble. Too busy covering their own asses to worry about anyone else. All who sleep now in the dark canyon-tenements of this city sleep fitfully, scared out of their wits, and it's the same with me isn't it?—truly Romulus Ledbetter must be just what his daughter says he is—frightened, a rattle-bone coward, or wouldn't I be standing up and *showing them* what a murderous cruel son of a sick *snake* it is that they bow down before? Wouldn't I be doing something to try to *stop this horror?*

I would. I will.

And then as he sat there muttering to himself, Romulus heard a voice.

"Now you're putting on airs, baby?"

The voice wasn't Cyclops. The voice came from the other side of him, and he swiveled. Sheila, his wife, was right beside him. In the cave-shadows, in the dark. She seemed to be floating. Her eyes were gleaming.

She was making one of her little *visitations*.

She dosed her voice with sarcasm and said, "Now you think you're a *detective*?"

"I'm just doing what I've got to do. That's all."

She scowled. "You doing everything but what you got to do. You got to sit down at a piano. You want to show us you got more will than craziness? *Sit down at a piano.*"

"I did. I did just that. Tonight."

"Yeah, I was there. And did it kill you?"

"Nearly." They sat silently for a moment. Then Romulus said, "No, I feel that pursuing my musical career would not be appropriate for me at this time of my life."

"Appropriate? Ap-*pro*-priate?" She laughed, her howlingest, most scathing laugh. "Oh, my. So playing detective, *that's* appropriate? What on earth do you know about being a detective?"

"I've got the eye. I can see things that other people can't. For example, I know what kind of car the murderer drives."

"What kind, baby?"

"Well, I know the color, anyway. It was white. Bone white."

"Oh, sure," said Sheila. "What else would Stuyvesant drive? Baby. Baby. This isn't for you. Try music."

"Go away, Sheila. Leave me alone."

She stirred herself. "See you in the country," she said.

"No. Leave me alone. Let me do this by myself."

She said again, "See you in the country." Then the color went out of her, and she seeped back into the rock wall of the cave, and Romulus felt, as he always did after one of her appearances, worn out but contented. A kind of rapturous exhaustion. He lay down beside Cyclops and fell into a sound sleep.

27

It was Friday night and the crowds were flowing, and Eel was giving them the hiss.

The NYU tarts and the club slime, the art holes and the once-a-week bridge-and-tunnel leatherettes, the spikes and the usual dregs and walking garbage, Eel was giving them all the hiss. He was down here at his corner of Ninth Street and First Avenue—he had the southwest corner to himself and he was bobbing and rocking and darting with the traffic, hissing, "Sense, acid, ecstasy, smoke, smoke, how can I help you, how can I be of service?"

The patter was just pouring out of him and the last thing he wanted now was Matthew the Weasel pestering him, screwing up his rhythm, but that's what Matthew the Weasel was doing.

Every time the crowd ebbed, or when the cops would troll by, Eel would fade back and lean against his wall and his mind should have been strictly on business—cash flow, market share, sales ratios, new product development—but Matthew would be right there at his ear, wouldn't let him alone. Matthew wanted D. Dope. Heroin. Eel didn't have any D.

"If I had any D., I'd sell it to you, Matthew. But I don't got none. My *resource* don't got none."

"But you promised."

"I promised before this Rotorooter shit came down."

Rotorooter was the name of a brand-new kind of heroin, and it was causing a lot of trouble.

Said Matthew, "Give me some Rotorooter."

"You don't want Rotorooter, man."

A gaggle of uptown tourists passed by, and Eel hissed, "Sense, X, 'shrooms, smoke." They dropped their eyes to the sidewalk, all of them at once, *thud,* and they were gone.

Eel said to Matthew, "Rotorooter's frying people, man. That's why the whole market's tight. Everybody ducking, man."

Then a great big svelte-looking black guy in a million-dollar suit came by. Guy just glowed with the look of money. Stockbroker maybe, or TV sportscaster.

Said Eel, "Sense, X, how can I serve you sir? Let's make a deal here."

The money man caught sight of Matthew and held up. "Matthew . . ."

"Holy shit," said Matthew. "Rom? What happened to you?"

"Stepping out a little, Matthew. I've been looking for you."

Said Matthew, "Well, this is the place to find me. This is where I live till this asshole comes through."

Eel said, "Don't call me an asshole."

"I'm sorry. Eel, *please*. Sell me something."

"Nothing I can do for you."

"Then I'll take my business somewhere else."

Said Eel, "Oh please be my fucking guest. Tell you what, go talk to my partner, Shaker. See him over there?"

He pointed, and they looked. Shaker was easy to spot. Big mother, and menacing despite his bright plaid tam-o'-shanter. He was also doing the hiss, and also getting nowhere.

Said Eel, "Go bug him, Matthew. But he don't have no D. neither."

Matthew sniffed. He said, "Rom, tell Eel he's gotta give me some dope."

"Apparently he doesn't have any, Matthew."

"But he promised."

This million-dollar guy, he seemed to be Matthew's friend, and this puzzled Eel. What would the man want with a little rodent like Matthew? Maybe he was an old drug connection. Maybe this guy was one of those million-dollar pushers Eel had seen on TV.

Matthew was saying to him, "I'm not a real junkie, Rom. I mean, I do it, but I don't *gotta* do it. But if I do a little, it makes it seem like Scotty died a long, long time ago. So why not do it? But now I *can't* do it 'cause this guy's holding out on me."

Eel said to the million-dollar guy, "Hey, will you tell your friend?—nobody's selling no D. Will you tell him about Rotorooter?"

"What's Rotorooter?"

"You don't know about Rotorooter either? Don't nobody read the papers? Rotorooter's a new kind of shit, they cut it with something weird-ass. Supposed to make you cream your pants, man, cream your whole body, but what it's doing, it's killing people. People going down like flies. One of my best customers—but I didn't sell it to him. Not me. Anyway till this blows over it's too hot for any kind of proper customer service—"

Some lovely babes bobbled by. Speaking Swedish or something. "What's your pleasure, ladies? Any little playful substance I might procure for you—"

They looked at him like he was some kind of fecal matter that was trying to attach itself to their shoes.

Ah fuck, thought Eel. Just . . . fuck.

Whenever he let this profession get to him, it got him into a *mood* very quick.

He faded back to his wall. The million-dollar guy was asking Matthew:

"Matthew, did you truly love Scotty Gates?"

"Rom! Rom, Jesus—"

"No, I mean truly. It wasn't just a crush, was it? It wasn't just lust. It was love?"

Matthew didn't say anything for a while. Then he said, "All I know is I think about him all the time and I wish I was dead with him."

More customers, Eel gave them the hiss. No sale. Gone. He glanced across the street. His partner, Shaker, had just struck out again, and he looked depressed. General business downturn, all across the board. Dmitri—Eel's man, Eel's resource—was going to be pissed. But it was Dmitri's own fucking fault. The problem was there was no product innovation. Lack of ingenuity on the supply side, that was the problem. Little runners like Eel and Shaker were always clamoring for something new to entice their customers with, and what did the *resources* come up with? Rotorooter.

He faded back, and the rich guy was saying:

"Because, Matthew, tomorrow I'm going up there."

"Up there? Where? Leppenraub's?"

The million-dollar guy nodded.

Said Matthew, "Oh shit, Rom, no. Don't do that. He'll kill you."

"But there's no other way. Look, Matthew, I know he did it—I can feel it. And I know he works for Stuyvesant. But I've got to find out how I can prove it. And the only way to do that is to go stick my head in the lion's mouth. Which I expect he's going to bite off."

"But why? Rom, you don't have to do this for me."

Said the million-dollar guy, "Out of your hands. Matthew, I don't care if you're pressing your charges or not. I'm pressing your charges. All you have to do is tell me if you truly loved Scotty."

He stood in front of Matthew and looked in his eyes. But all Matthew said was, "I wish I was dead with him, that's all."

Then the suave guy gave Matthew a little piece of paper. "That's my daughter's number. Lulu Ledbetter. I've told you about her, lots of times. She's a cop. I know you don't like cops, Matthew. None of us likes cops. But she's OK. You get into any kind of trouble, you call her. Right? And you take care."

There were more customers, more of this modern disdain for the honest working tradesman, and when Eel turned around again the million-dollar guy was gone.

And Matthew was still whining at him.

Eel crossed the street, went up to his partner Shaker. He said, "Shaker, I gotta get something for that kid."

"Who's that?"

"That stupid dago over there. He wants dope."

"Scrape some dandruff off your shoulder, give him that."

"Business sure sucks tonight, huh?"

Said Shaker, "Yes it does. This business always sucks. Eel, do you realize we're almost *drug kingpins*? We're supposed to be driving Maseratis. Why don't you buy some flour, give him that."

"Flour?"

"Gold Medal flour, give him some of that."

"Where am I going to buy Gold Medal flour?"

"In the deli here."

Eel said, "I don't think they sell flour."

"Oh. Eel, do you realize we're almost *drug kingpins,* you realize that?"

"Almost. Yeah."

Said Shaker, "And yet I cannot pay my fucking rent."

28

That night Romulus sat up with his back against the back wall of the cave, and he shut his eyes and quietly shepherded all the Moth-Seraphs into the lowest districts of his brain. Every last Seraph. Then he built barricades to keep them from climbing up again. Barricades to hold back their rage, to fence in their fury. Huge iron-spiked gates he built, and he built them to be *strong* and it took him hours, but sometime before dawn he was finished, he had every passageway sealed. Then he practiced his chuckling for twenty minutes, and then at last he was ready, and he let himself get some sleep.

29

Next morning he put on Bob's suit again. He carried the sleek coat because he didn't need to wear it, it wasn't cold at all. He went down to the gate of Columbia University at 116th Street, and there he met his old schoolmate Arnold. They gave each other big hugs.

"Old hangdog Arnold," said Romulus.

Arnold was the same tall gangly ugly kid he'd known long ago—except now, of course, he'd put on the makeup of middle age. Seemed to Romulus he'd put on a little too much. Too much jowly sallow on the cheeks, too shock-white the hair. Made him look kind of sad, Romulus thought.

"Twenty-five years, Arnold?"

"Thereabouts."

In a rented car they drove north.

The sun slid up out of the haze, and the day evolved into a magnificent warm slab of open time. So that on top of everything else, on this of all days, Romulus had to come down with a massive case of spring fever.

They rolled down their windows, and whenever they stopped for a red light, birdsong flew in.

Arnold kept wanting to find out about Romulus's life in California. Romulus kept chuckling. Slipped a veil of lame jokiness over his life story, eluded every trap, and kept Arnold talking.

Said Arnold, "Rom, tell me about the vineyards out there."

"Uh-huh. Well, there are some *splendid* ones. Hey, Arnold, you know I saw a movie the other night, all about Juilliard."

"Yeah?"

"Prodigy."

"How was it?"

"What a bomb. Heh heh."

They passed from the Henry Hudson to the Saw Mill Parkway to the Taconic. Eventually the malls and developments thinned out. They entered a country of winter meadows and stands of hemlock.

Romulus saw two pale-white early butterflies.

Said Arnold, "Hey Rom? Tell me something?"

"Sure."

"Why'd you leave Juilliard?"

"Oh. Well, I got Sheila knocked up. Right? She wanted the kid, I married her. And our parents got sore at us, and tossed us out on our asses, and . . . so that was it."

"That's what you told us at the time. But I kept thinking if you'd really wanted to, you could have figured out some way to stay in school."

"You think? Hmm. Maybe so. Heh heh."

"You know, at the time one of your brothers came around to the school to talk to me."

"Yes? This I never knew. Which of my brothers?"

"August?"

"Augustus."

"Augustus, yeah. He thought maybe there was something wrong with you."

"Such as?"

"He wasn't sure. Just . . . you seemed scared of something."

"Scared? No, that I don't recall. I remember I did not care for recitals. Heh."

Terror. Naked terror. That time when they all came to hear him perform—his parents, his brothers, his great-uncles, all of them—and he didn't show, he wandered the streets and he was walking up Lexington Avenue and he felt like his head was full of swirling feathers— and he looked up and saw the steeple of the Chrysler Building swaddled in mist, blurred by his tears, and he thought he could *feel* the terror pouring out of those jagged-eye windows, and he came to the harrowing surmise that perhaps *there* was the source of all this confusion—and much later that night he called Sheila from a pay phone and he could hardly speak and she said, "You've just got to get ahold of that fear, baby. Just get ahold of it, and *wrestle* it down, you can do that, you're strong, baby, just keep working at it, I *believe* in you."

Now Romulus chuckled for Arnold, and said, "I don't know, I

couldn't tell you. It was just a tough time for me. Before I got everything *together,* you know what I mean?"

The Taconic Parkway wound up into the hills, and in Putnam County Romulus woke from a doze and looked across a long vale of virgin forest to a slope of red oak. The trees were still clutching handfuls of last year's leaves (useless old ticket stubs), but they were already dreaming powerfully of the coming spring. Blushing red with the same fever that was eating at Romulus.

And as he studied this hillside he discovered—small victory!— that he could detect *no stain of Y-rays* there. Not the least taint or residue of them. None.

"My . . . Lord."

Said Arnold, "Hmm?"

"Oh, it's just—you know, I haven't seen woods in almost . . . twenty years."

"What? Wait a minute—there are no . . . ?"

"No I don't mean . . . that California . . . scrub-shit. I don't mean park woods, either. I mean *woods.* Lord."

They came into dairy and horse farm country. They left the Taconic and wound endlessly on a two-lane blacktop.

And slid at last through the toy village of Gideon Manor. Church, jail, band shell. Up on the left, the Gideon Manor Playhouse—a huge Dutch gable elephant on a hill.

Another mile, and they turned off onto a simple dirt drive that cut through a dense spinney of trees. No name on the mailbox. Might be a double-wide trailer back here for all you could see from the road.

But in a moment they emerged from the trees into the flung-open sky of the Leppenraub Farm.

Meadows, brooks, orchards, bramble patches. The tarnished-gold fields falling away, all the way down to the Hudson, where that speck of white must have been a sail.

More sunlight than Romulus had ever seen at one time.

And up on the hill, in the shade of sugar maples, the perfect farmhouse. In robin's-egg blue, with wraparound veranda, from which the Siberian husky came down to greet them with a few wary woofs.

They came to a stop.

Then Romulus saw the car.

The murderer's getaway car, the sporty sedan. Parked in front of the house. Turned out it wasn't white, as he had thought, but as scarlet as its sins.

Still, he knew it was the one. And the Moth-Seraphs knew it, too—they raged, they surged against the barricades he'd built in his skull. Romulus shut his eyes and his jaw sagged, and he rubbed his head with his knuckles.

Go to sleep for a while, he told the Seraphs. Justice will be done, but not this minute.

Arnold, who had already stepped out and was patting the dog, heard Romulus muttering to himself, and he looked back in.

"You OK?"

"Heh heh. Of course." *You're strong, baby, I believe in you.* "I'm fine. No question about it, everything's just splendid. Right?"

A
STENCH

30

A woman was pushing a wheelbarrow by the side of the house, a wheelbarrow full of leaves and dirt and flakes of barnacle moss. She set down her load and smiled at the visitors.

She was the woman from the *Artforum* photo. Windfall of deep brown hair, with one demonic corkscrew of white mixed in. When she smiled, the first thing to flash out was her sharp, lovely canines. She was lovely all over. It seemed to Romulus that one of her eyes was slightly lower than the other, but this only added. Threw her a little wildly out of whack, made her a kind of cubist Venus.

Someone in the window above her spoke to her, and she looked up and said, "Of *course* I'm bringing it to the studio."

Then a man's voice. Crisp, slightly nasal.

"Moira, you've got to spray that goddamn stuff for bugs before you drag it all into the coach house."

"Oh, that's stupid."

"No. It's *not* stupid, kiddo. I want you to tell Vlad to fumigate that stuff. My God, you want roaches running wild in the coach house?"

"Yes," she shot back huskily. "I'm training them, David. Roach commandos. They're *coming* for you."

She wiggled her fingers, lifted them toward him. A quick, sketchy gesture, but expressive. You could see the roach hordes swarming toward that window. She laughed, and Romulus got another glimpse of those astonishing canines.

The voice at the window and coldly, "Tell Vlad to spray the stuff. Why is Lao-tse barking?"

"Our guests."

And then she came over. What a loving panpipe laugh she had! She took Arnold's head in her hands, and smushed his cheeks, and gave him a fat buss. Then she turned to Romulus.

"I'm Moira Leppenraub. Mr. Ledbetter?"

"Romulus. Or Rom's OK."

"Rom. Arnold's told us a lot about you. He says you're a genius."

"At what?"

"Your music, of course."

Romulus smiled and said, "That's all?"

"There's more?"

"I can hold a match in my teeth with the flame inside my mouth, and in a dark room I light up like a jack-o'-lantern. He didn't tell you that? The man does not *promote* me right."

Grins all round. But the dog Lao-tse came over and sniffed at Romulus's shoes. Taking in a long history of fabulous lowlife aromas. Then it made a quick snuff at the suit, sat back on its haunches and said calmly with its eyes, *The suit and the shoes don't match. You're not the suit—you're the shoes. You're running a con, aren't you?*

Moira said, "Shall we go in?"

Said Arnold, "We don't want to take you from your work."

"Oh, it's just some leaves and things for my sculpture. Vlad or Elon will take it to the studio. Me, I'm ready to party. Caterers will be here in an hour, and I've got nothing to do. I'm at your disposal, gentlemen."

She was wearing Levi's cutoffs and old boots and a checkered linen shirt, and she fairly bounced up the steps before them. And it troubled Romulus that he found himself inclined to imagine—after so many years of disinterest in such affairs—all the pastures and sweeping hills and bramble patches that lay under these innocent clothes. Now what is *this* all about? he wondered. Where the hell does a feeling like *this* come from?

A feeling like this was not going to make his work any easier.

Moira held open the screen door, and he and Arnold stepped into the front hallway.

David Leppenraub came down the stairs.

The first glimpse Romulus had of him was his hand on the banister. The delicate lattice of his veins. The color of his skin, standing out against the brown wood, was the same crushed-seashell color as the skin of Scotty Gates, the morning Romulus had found the body.

Leppenraub descended slowly. He kept his back straight, but one was aware of the man's pain.

"Arnold," he said. "Good to see you. And this is your friend."

He didn't extend his hand to either of them. Concession to the layman's terror of AIDS? But when Romulus put out his own hand, Leppenraub grasped it firmly. Arnold introduced them.

Said Leppenraub, "Romulus, I hear you have kind things to say about my work."

"Well, I like it very much."

The man's gaze was sharp, unwavering. He asked, "Why?"

"Excuse me?"

"*Why* do you like my work?"

"Well. It's . . . um—"

"Come."

He led them all into the parlor. The furnishings were spare and simple, but in every corner and niche there was art. Quirky sculptures, paintings—but mostly photographs. Leppenraub gestured toward a piece by the piano. Black-and-white of a vacant lot. Looked like some place in the Bronx. One leafless sapling, struggling to survive. A blurred black kid on his bike.

And in a far corner of the lot, there was a strange twisted lump of something, with a flesh tint. The only color in the shot.

Maybe entangled lovers. Maybe a couple of cadavers.

Said Leppenraub, "Ever seen this one?"

Romulus stroked his chin. "Well, I believe I *have,* uh-huh, I—"

"Of course you have. It's one of my most popular pieces. So, tell me, what do you think of it?"

Romulus glanced to Arnold for help. But Arnold was staying out of this.

And Leppenraub, though he leaned against the baby grand for support, didn't ease up on his stare at all. As though he had seen through Romulus's masquerade from the get-go, and now he was going to let the fool expose himself, just stand there and watch the fun.

For a moment Romulus was nervous the way he'd been in fifth grade when he hadn't studied and teacher was calling on him. Wanting to hide, to disappear. Wishing he'd never left the city. But they were all watching and there was no time for regrets, and no choice but to take up the man's challenge and brazen it out. He said, "What do I think of it? Nothing."

Leppenraub smiled a thin smile. His eyes flashed. "Nothing?"

"Hey, I mean, it's like one of those millions of scenes you look at every day, right? When you're walking, or on the train, or whatever. You look, your eyes fill up, but a minute later it's gone. This time there's a smidgen of . . . *passion* there, right?—that heap of love or death back there. But the rest, it's still *nothing*. I mean this scene has so much nothing it hurts the eyes to look at it. I mean the kind of *burned-over nothing* you get when Stuyvesant's *done* with a place. Right? Finished *fucking it over,* am I right? *Finished*—"

"Stuyvesant?"

Leppenraub was staring at him. They were all staring.

Oh shit.

"I just meant—I meant . . ."

Leppenraub shook his head. "So much nothing it hurts?"

Then the corners of his mouth turned up. He started to chuckle. "Now that I *like,* amigo! It hurts, it *hurts* the eyes!"

His chuckle turned into a laugh. Partly the wide-open laugh of a child and partly the jaded laugh of the man of power—and edged all around with the laugh of a man who's dying, and dying in pain. He finished it with a dry cough.

He cried, "Arnold, who the hell is this guy? This guy made my day. Jesus. *It hurts the eyes!*"

31

Then he took them all out to sit on the long veranda.

Drinks were served by Vlad.

Leppenraub reminded Vlad that he had asked for *two* onions in his martini. Vlad shrugged and went back inside and fetched the onion jar. He was a muscular man in his mid-twenties. He wore a tight black T-shirt to show off his torso, and his every move was something of a swagger. He pulled an onion out of the jar between two fingers, and dropped it with an insolent little splash in Leppenraub's drink.

He served Romulus a glass of white wine. He said, "Sorry we have no Night Train. You know Night Train, hah? Now *that* is a wine!"

He glossed for the others: "What they drink in the American ghetto." Then, again to Romulus: "But these people know *nothing* of the ghetto, you know what? Americans never go to Harlem. I'm Czech, *I* go to Harlem."

Moira laughed scornfully. She asked Romulus, "Have you met Vlad? Vlad's our resident Eurotrash authority on American small-mindedness."

Vlad scowled. "And you're my most excellent example! Exactly, yes, try to teach an American *anything*, they call you Euro-trash."

Moira kept smiling. Her smile seemed to infuriate Vlad. He asked her, "You think you're American *hipster?*"

"No Vlad. I don't think I'm American hipster."

"The black man is *born* with soul. You white Americans, you all think you can *make* soul. You do the witch thing, you think it makes you—"

Said Moira, "Muga brzah-gahbena—"

"And what is that stupidness?"

"A spell to protect me from Transylvanian vampires."

"*Romania!* Transylvania is in *Romania,* you stupid, stupid—"

"Enough," Leppenraub said quietly. He took a hefty swallow of his drink. "Bring Arnold his martini, Vlad. And leave my little sister alone."

Said Moira then, "I can defend myself, David." Something sharp and retaliatory in her tone, some old habit of resentment.

David said again, "Enough."

And his voice, soft as it was, held sway. She lowered her eyes. Romulus thought, There is a divide between these two. Which perhaps he could work to his advantage. If he could get her alone. . . .

Vlad brought the drink. Then he swaggered over to a big wicker divan, and sprawled on it. Leafed aggressively through an *Art News.*

Leppenraub turned to Romulus. "Arnold says you work with a museum in San Francisco?"

"Near there."

"Which one?"

"It's . . . it's called the New Bay Museum."

"Oh, yes, I think I've heard of it, uh-huh. Who's on your board?"

"Just . . . they're just names. You know."

"I know lots of people, Romulus. Try me."

Names, the man wants names. OK, give him some names. Any name will do, right? Piece of cake. Romulus knew *thousands* of names.

But at this moment he could not think of a single one.

He peered into his brain and saw nothing but the glowing eyes of the Seraphs, staring out from their prison.

"Matthew!" he said suddenly. "Matthew . . . Cornelius! That's one. That's a name. And, uh . . . Lulu Gould?"

"Oh, *Lulu,* yes."

Oh, *Lulu,* yes. Lies were no sweat to Leppenraub. He lied with a poker face. Held his head at an angle, so you'd get the full bitter majesty of his nose, and looked at you with his white skin and sharp little eyes, and bullshitted freely. He smiled at Romulus again, and murmured, "*Hurts your eyes . . .* oh, I do like that. Let me take you to the barn later. I'll show you a new thing of mine you might appreciate. Oh, yeah—I think so. Ought to hurt like hell. *Ha!*"

He polished off his martini.

Said Romulus, "You know I've been trying to figure it out. And I just did. What made me think of him."

"Think of whom?"

"Stuyvesant."

"Oh yes? Who's Stuyvesant?"

"Heh heh. First mayor of New York. They've got a big portrait of him in Grand Central or somewhere. And my Lord, I believe you're the spitting *image* of that man."

He looked to see the effect of this on Leppenraub. But Leppenraub was smooth. He only offered, "I do have Dutch ancestry."

"Patrician! Heh heh. The grand pa-*troon*. My . . . Lord. Yes sir."

32

After this Romulus shut up.

He let Leppenraub and Arnold talk. They talked about something called "Neo-Geo"—some grand art movement that had been born and become the rage and had burned itself out to ashes while Romulus had been living in a cave.

Moira seemed restless. She took no part in the discussion. She stretched one leg out before her. Lifted it, set her ankle on the porch railing, and pointed her toes like a dancer. Then she did the same with the other leg. Then she folded her arms and looked at her brother. She was trying to pay attention to the tricky chatter, but could not. Nor could Romulus. He simply watched her. Gazed at that shimmering skin.

When he raised his eyes, they lit upon Vlad, and he saw that Vlad was watching her, too. And he saw Moira glance back at Vlad. And Leppenraub—as he babbled on—Leppenraub was watching Romulus noticing Moira giving back Vlad's glancing.

Moira, with a scowl, broke the chain. She rose. She said, "It's a damn miracle day. We ought to walk."

Said her brother, "Go right ahead."

She asked Romulus, "Like to see the farm?"

"You should, Rom," Arnold encouraged. "Beautiful place. You'll love it."

Romulus shrugged and stood.

Said Vlad, "I think I'll come, too."

"No," said Moira, "I think you won't. Walking's bad for the upper-body muscles, Vlad. You stay here. Guard the little onions."

But she did whistle up Lao-tse the husky.

33

They came to a chicken coop that had been made into a handsome little house. A man was sitting on the little stoop, on a rocking chair. He was wearing overalls, and he was holding a chicken in his arms, stroking it. He stared into space.

Moira called to him.

"Elon?"

The man looked up. He started to shiver. His lips twisted into two or three trial shapes and finally came up with a smile. He said, "Hello. Hello, Moira."

"The *wheelbarrow*, Elon."

She pointed.

"You see the *wheelbarrow?*"

He nodded.

"Take the *wheelbarrow* to the *coach house*. To *my house,* OK? Leave it outside my *studio.* OK? Don't bring it *inside,* or David will kill us. OK?"

Elon tucked his lower lip under his teeth. His shivering got worse. For a while he considered the strategy for this chore. When he had it all sorted out, he nodded again.

"OK, Moira," he said. He set off on his errand.

34

They followed the farm lane under a colonnade of great stiff-backed tulip trees. To their right they passed the old coach house that Moira had made into her studio. To their left, an open pasture dropping away. You could see all the way down to the river.

Said Romulus, "Who was he?"

"Elon?—he's David's inheritance. His father used to run the farm for David. And when the old man died, David kept taking care of Elon."

"Your brother—he's what you'd call a selfless man, right?"

"Huh? Oh, now and then, sure. Not that Elon's family shows any gratitude. Elon's got swarms of cousins around here, and they bad-mouth us all the time. The city scum, they call us. They say David takes advantage of Elon because he's retarded. They're bitter as hell. Which maybe I can understand. Elon's grandfather, you know, he used to *own* this farm."

"So why don't all those cousins take care of Elon?"

"Bad-mouthing's easier."

"Seems a lot of people like to bad-mouth David Leppenraub."

"Uh-oh. What have *you* heard?"

"Oh. Well. Heh heh."

But she pressed. "What?"

Take the opening, Romulus thought. Take it easy, but take it.

"Well, I guess I've heard only what I'd expect to hear about a— about a rich gay artist who shares his home with his models."

She bristled. "No. *No.* That's lie number one. David's never *lived* with any of his models. I mean, all right, it's no secret he's had a few wild weekends here. . . ."

And since she's offered, grab this one, too.

"How wild?"

"How should *I* know? Think I get invited? I live in the coach house, David rents it to me. Until he got so sick, I never spent much time down in the big house, and certainly not when he was having one of his bashes. Nobody wants his little sister around when he's whooping it up. But the thing is, my brother's a damn disciplined artist. Monday morning, all lingering amusements are cleared out the door, and he's back at work. No one has ever *lived* here with him except Vlad and Elon."

"And that blond kid, right? The kid who froze to death."

"Scotty? Uh-uh. Scotty lived with me."

"With *you?*"

"Wait a minute. How do *you* know about Scotty?"

"Oh, I met him. Out in California."

She gave him a surprised look. He embroidered his lie as quickly as he could. "Yeah, yeah, he showed up at our museum. Don't ask me what he was doing out there, he never said. But he didn't like it that we had David Leppenraub's work around. He had a lot of nasty things to say about your brother."

She narrowed her eyes and thought this over. Finally she said, "All right. I *know* Scotty changed, I know he said those things. It's just—it's still hard to believe."

Then she looked up into the branches of the tree above them, and she said, "He posed up there once. The crucifixion, you know that picture? But no, no of course you don't—it hasn't been published. But anyway, this was the tree, this old cottonwood. That branch."

She pointed. Her breasts rose under her shirt, and Romulus nearly forgot to look up. When he did, he peered into the branches a moment and then said, "It's not a cottonwood."

"What?"

"Slippery elm. Come look at the leaf scar."

He grabbed hold of a branch and dragged it down and she came and stood close to him.

He said, "Look at the marks on the twig. From last year's leaves—when they fall off, they leave these little scars. And see here, on each scar, how there's two dots and under them this smiley line? Sort of a happy face? Only elms have happy faces."

Whiff of her fragrance.

Earth, straw, musk, stone.

She said, "This is a slippery elm? Really? Rom, you know what witches use slippery elm bark for?"

"I don't."

"Ward off ugly rumors. I've got some at home. Essence of slippery elm bark. Costs a bundle. Doesn't work, I guess."

35

L ao-tse came running when she heard Moira's whistle. She bounded up out of the field and saw her mistress sitting on the low wall under the tree, sitting with the stranger. Suspicious-Shoes. She approached and nuzzled Moira's knees. Suspicious-Shoes reached out to pet her and made this friendly smacking sound.

She shied away from him.

Strangers were not Lao-tse's cup of tea.

But a moment later when she was distracted by some scent coming in on the breeze, the stranger reached out stealthily and started scratching her before she could pull away. He scratched her in precisely *the* spot, that place a little ways up from her tail that Moira always neglected. He scratched her deep with his big dark hand in that perfect place, and she arched her back up so he could get to it better, and pretty soon she was pushing up against his legs and he kept at it and she was melting under his touch, *melting . . .*

36

T hen Romulus turned to Moira and said in as even a tone as he could muster, "Scotty Gates told us that David tortured him."

Moira did not look at him. She gazed out at the field. She said, "All right. If you say so. It's hard to believe."

"Why?"

"Because if Scotty was being tortured why didn't he say something to me? Or call the police, or just leave, or . . . *something.*"

"He said David had him in his clutches. He said he and David were lovers."

"Also hard to believe."

"Why?"

"Well, first of all because Scotty was straight."

"How do you know that, Moira?"

"Fuck off, mister."

"Wait, I didn't mean—"

"What, you think I was screwing him? Christ, I was like a mother to him."

"By no means did I intend—"

"Oh skip it. Think I give a shit what people think of me? I let it out that I'm sort of a pagan, I read the tarot for a few lost locals—next thing they're saying I'm the bride of Satan. They say I'm ee-vil."

Then there was a silence. Which she broke abruptly: "Rom, listen to me. I met Scotty in an art class I was teaching. Six years ago. He was one of my favorite students. Not particularly talented or anything, just . . . I don't know, I liked him. I guess I thought there was some kind of . . . *purity* about him, something like that. Anyway, when he was almost sixteen his parents were killed in a car accident. And he didn't have anybody, *anybody*. The state was going to send him to some foster home or something. So I took him in. Because I felt sorry for him. *Not* to get into a fifteen-year-old's pants. I've had some unsuitable suitors, but not that unsuitable. I just gave him a place to live. And of course he got to know David, and David made him his model. But he never moved in with him. He lived with me, in the coach house."

37

The lane left the shade of the trees and cut across a golden field. They came to a plank ridge over a little brook. Farther down the slope, the brook paused to make a pond, in which a pair of mergansers were floating. Lao-tse tore off through the winter stubble, ran to the water's edge, and barked bloody murder at them.

The mergansers paid him no mind.

The sun was falling, and all colors were preternatural. The

green of the mergansers' cheeks was not of this world. The brown of Moira's eyes caused an ache.

She said, "See, you just had to have known him. Now when I hear what happened to him—about how he went nuts and said the things he said, it *simply does not make any sense.*"

"Doesn't sound *real?*"

"No."

"Still."

"Yeah. Still. *Something* sure screwed him up, or he wouldn't have been lying in that morgue last week when I went down to identify him. Maybe I was all wrong about him. Maybe he *was* David's lover. Maybe David did screw him over."

"But he never complained to you?"

"Uh-uh . . . seemed a little unhappy when I left with David for the hospital. I know he was having problems with his girlfriend. But I didn't think he was going to flip out. I don't know, maybe he was lonely. He was living up here by himself—I mean except for Elon. I was staying in a hotel down by the hospital, and Vlad had gone back home for a visit—back to Transylvania. And Scotty stayed here. Till one day he up and vanished. And David got a letter from him saying he'd gone to New York, and fuck you David, and not a word to me."

A kingfisher's high horse rattle. Down where the stream ran back into the woods, a wisp of undulating flight. Romulus thought awhile.

He said, "OK."

Moira smiled. "OK? You're satisfied? Then will you answer me one?"

"Sure."

She touched his arm lightly with her hand. "How do you know about leaf scars and slippery elms and all that?"

"Oh. Oh. Well, I used to have a friend who lived in a cave. He taught me. I guess he got it from books. You know? He must have dug the books out of somebody's garbage."

She said, "I'm always dreaming about going to live in a cave. But it must take some courage. Tearing away from everything."

"I suppose. Equal parts courage and cowardice."

"No, I think you had balls."

"Ah. Right. Arnold told you about my cave thing, right? Yeah, it *was* me living there, wasn't it? But a long time ago. Another life."

"What, were you some kind of holy man, Rom?"

And then they heard a car on the lane behind them. They turned, and there was the sporty scarlet sedan, coming toward them, trailing a simmer of dust.

38

Vlad driving. David Leppenraub in the passenger seat, his lips set sourly. The car settled beside Romulus and Moira, and David's window came down with a whirr.

"Thought you might like a ride back to the house. You and your new friend."

"Friend" came out with a high polish of irony.

"No, that's OK, David," said Moira. "We're walking, we're having—"

"Thought you might like to come back *now*, before eighty-five guests get here. For Christ's sake."

"Everything's under control—"

"Control? The caterers are already here, Moira. Running around like chickens while everyone waits for my sister to come back from her little stroll and tell them what to do. Jesus—where the hell have you been, anyway?"

Moira glanced at her brother. "I do not want to argue, David. Not now."

Vlad got out and came around and opened the door for them with an ugly little flourish. He had dressed for the party in a tuxedo. His hair was slicked back, vampire style.

For a moment no one moved.

Then David Leppenraub said to Romulus, "I suppose she was showing you her *work?*"

"No, actually—"

"These little caves she builds, and she likes to take her callers *inside*. Very domestic, don't you think? Very feminine."

Romulus said, "I didn't see them."

"Shut up, David," said Moira.

Leppenraub said, "You know, I really don't need this stress just now, Moira. I thought we agreed these arrangements were your responsibility. I mean I think everybody should be pulling their own weight around here—"

Moira sighed, flipped up her hand in a defeated gesture. "OK. OK, for Christ's sake. Let's go then."

She nodded to Romulus, and he climbed into the car. She followed, and he heard her mutter, "My brother's keeper."

David heard it, too. He didn't turn around to face her, but he said sharply, "Except brother's the one who pays the bills."

And he added, as Vlad turned the car around, "You want to see some *artwork,* Romulus, I'll show you work."

Silence.

They drove back toward the farmhouse.

Vlad glanced back over his shoulder at Romulus. Then he gave Moira a look. His eye twitched, or he winked.

"Hey my friend."

"Call me Rom."

"You like John Coltrane? Now that is a man with the gas, you know what?"

Romulus turned to Moira and asked, "What kind of car is this?"

"Diamante. Pretty tacky, huh?"

Vlad was adamant. "Blood *everywhere* when John Coltrane plays, you know what?"

"What?"

"No, I'm saying, John *Coltrane.*"

"Right. Heh heh."

39

It might have *looked* like a barn.

But inside it was two and a half floors of gallery and sales office and printshop and an $80,000 security system and mist-colored carpets that *gave* like mist when you walked on them. And piped-in Bach.

Bach in chains, Bach and his baroque slave-chanties for two violins.

Leppenraub would glide on ahead of Romulus and touch a panel in the wall, and another room of masterworks would come to light. Then Leppenraub would point out a favorite, and Romulus would stand before it awhile.

Said Leppenraub, "This one's not bad. My little *Ginkgo*."

An old city-blasted ginkgo-tree. In its shade, an angelic youth, completely nude. The ginkgo is full of gypsy moth caterpillars. So are the cages in the pet shop behind it. And caterpillars crawl up the leg of the angel, gnaw at it. His calf is an open wound, strings of bloody muscle dangle freely, but he doesn't seem aware of that at all; he contemplates the dying ginkgo above him.

The angel, of course, was Scotty. The same boy Romulus had seen dead in the snow.

All the angels in all these pictures were Scotty.

Romulus said, "Could I ask you something, David?"

"Of course."

"Could I ask, I mean, would it seem crude to ask—"

"How much a thing like this would sell for?"

"Heh heh."

Leppenraub said, "Well, you know, it depends. Of course, this one, hand-painted—"

"Painted? I thought it was a photograph."

"It *was*—before I painted it over. It's subtle—very thin paint. Mostly just blacks and whites and grays. The only color here is in the pet shop sign and the blood. You really didn't know I glaze my photographs?"

"I'm sorry."

"Oh, don't be."

They passed on to another gallery.

Leppenraub told him, "Actually, somebody who likes my things and doesn't know squat about them—it's wonderful. You never read the art journals?"

"Not . . . not—"

"Oh, they write reams of chatter about my paint-overs. About all the *richness* the technique adds to my work. I'll tell you one thing, it adds to *my* richness. A painting'll go for of a hell of a lot more dough than a photograph. Now this one—this is *Bonsai Maple*—this one's OK."

A mall somewhere. Flow of shoppers. Up close, a pair of bonsai trees on either side of a Japanese bridge, which arches over a stream. A child in a Teenage Mutant Ninja Turtle mask stands on the bridge. In the pool beside him floats our angel. His pure backside, immaculate—except that the blade of a Japanese katana *sword is buried in his spine, buried to the hilt. A colony of glowing jellyfish drifts around him in the water, and a thin membrane of his own pale-scarlet blood floats with them.*

"So," said Leppenraub, "you really want to know how much I *take* the suckers for?"

He laughed. Shrugged. He said, "About three or four hundred thousand a pop."

"My . . . *Lord.*"

The ringing Leppenraub laugh. Romulus gaped at him, and said, "But . . . there must be dozens here."

Said Leppenraub, "Shitloads."

But he pronounced that self-deprecation with the satisfaction of a sultan. Grinned through billowy hookah-clouds of satisfaction and stared his intent stare and said:

"Price is going to go *up,* too. Want to know why? Because I'm the only one with guts enough to make pictures like this. Mapplethorpe and that idiot Anselm Kiefer—forget them. I've got less fear—that's all there is to it. You understand this?"

But Romulus didn't hear the question. He was looking at the photograph. At the drowned angel, at that flawless pale backside. There was something troubling about that backside, and he was trying to figure out what it was. What? What in the world? It was a backside. It was hairless. It was muscular. It was blemish-free. But it was just a backside. What in the—

Suddenly he became aware of the broadening silence. Leppenraub was waiting for him to speak.

"Excuse me?" said Romulus.

"I'm saying the whole question in art is guts versus fear. The whole question. You understand this?"

Said Romulus, "Guts I don't know. Don't know too much

about guts but I've been told that I'm something of an *expert* on fear."

Leppenraub stared. Then grinned. Then wildly laughed.

And in that moment Romulus had it: no heart.

He looked again at the photograph, looked closely. Matthew had said that Leppenraub's boys had branded a heart onto Scotty's buttocks. Well, you could see the profile of this angel's face and it was clearly Scotty. But there was no trace of any brand, anywhere. No marks of any kind, except where the stage-sword went in.

And so what? So Leppenraub had airbrushed the thing away. Or this photo was taken before his relations with his model had turned so nasty.

Or maybe that cop Cork was right: you're such a sucker for silly flash-ass clues, Romulus, you're likely to overlook the real deal.

The real deal. Which at that moment was nothing but David Leppenraub grinning and leaning in close and murmuring: "Fear? Really? Fear's your thing? Good! Good! Then come with me!"

40

He led Romulus to the second floor, and then down the corridor to the last gallery. He touched a panel, and the light came on.

There was only one piece in the room, a huge three-part photograph. Romulus stood before it, and Leppenraub spoke softly into his ear.

"*Triptych,* my latest. My best. September. Just before I went into the hospital."

Romulus leaned close.

In the first slender panel, our angel climbs a slippery elm. He looks exhausted. He carries a passel of bird cages slung over his back. Cages of all sizes, and every one of them empty—the wire doors are wide open.

In the middle strip, the angel is up high in the tree. Hanging there, crucified.

But in the last panel, the space where he hung in the tree is now empty. Way down below, on the ground, a congregation of songbirds pecks viciously at something. Something small. You can't tell exactly what. An organ? The boy's heart?

Leppenraub was still at Romulus's ear. He said, "Does it hurt your eyes, amigo?"

"Oh yeah."

"So what's your verdict?"

"Oh. Guilty."

Leppenraub chuckled. This was the sort of sport he liked. "Guilty! Ha! And your evidence for this?"

"Don't have any, not yet. Give me a while. In the meantime, tell me who the model is."

"This piece'll fetch me a hell of a lot more than four hundred thousand."

Romulus jerked his chin toward the crucified angel. "Tell me. He isn't the same model, is he?"

"Huh?"

"Not the same kid as in the other shots. Thinner, wirier— right?"

"Ha! You are perceptive. I don't think anybody else has noticed. But yes. Scotty—the young man in the other shots—he was afraid of heights. So for this scene I used a young man who looked like him."

"Who was that?"

"Oh Christ. I don't know. Why?"

"Why not? Why not tell me? What's the matter?—you want to keep this place sealed up against the truth? You think a little gust of the truth might damage your precious *things?*"

"What?"

"I'm just asking a simple question. What are you frightened of? *Who was the model?*"

"I've used a lot of models. He was some young man working with our theater here. Ask Moira."

The blood had started to whack against Romulus's temples. He took a step toward Leppenraub, and stared down at him. Leppenraub tried a smile.

Said Romulus, "I mean tell me now, what do you think would happen to the value of all these things if there were ever some kind of *scandal?*"

That blew Leppenraub's smile to shreds.

"Scandal? What are you talking about? Scandal? You mean a scandal about me? You think they could say anything about me that hasn't already—"

"They could say you tortured your models. That'd put a *big* scare in the suckers that buy these things, right? People might start *looking* at this stuff, and maybe they wouldn't see genius anymore, wouldn't see your great *courage*. Right? They'd see just . . . cruelty. Ordinary plain-ass cruelty."

"Who says—"

"Stuff like this could go out of fashion pretty quick, couldn't it? Just like *that*."

He snapped his fingers an inch from Leppenraub's eyes. Leppenraub didn't blink. But his pupils shrank to pinpoints.

Said Romulus, "People get a little uncertain, next thing you know they're unloading these things all over the place. Suddenly you can't *give* these things away. Right?"

Leppenraub pursed his lips. Twitch in one eye. He said, "You playing some kind of game with me? You want something from me?"

"I'm just asking you a question."

"Who says I tortured my models? Who? Senator Smires? That *asshole*. I don't want to hear about that asshole. You listen to me. All these preacher boys and homophobic fascist liars, they're all going to blow away, but my art's still going to be here. A hundred years from now, people'll pay in blood to have my art. Who says I tortured my models?"

"Oh nobody important, don't worry about it. Just one of the models you tortured. Scotty Gates."

"What, you know Scotty?"

"But lucky for you the kid got *cold feet*—right?"

"Who the hell are you? What do you want? *You* want to blackmail me, too?"

"Oh shit no. I'm just a concerned citizen. Is all. Is that all right? Is it OK to get a little worked up when I hear about torture? But I wouldn't want to get in the way of great art or anything. I know he was only a *face*. Shit, he wasn't even that—he was a fucking *moment,* right? And when that moment was over, chuck him! Show some guts—right, Stuyvesant?"

"What's this Stuyvesant nonsense?"

"What's this murder nonsense?"

"You can get the hell out of here! You can take a hike, you hear me? I'm too sick for this shit. But I'll tell you one thing before you go. *One thing, fuckhead!* I *loved* Scotty! So I don't want to hear this shit! I loved Scotty like a son. Which is none of your fucking business, but I don't like people saying I would ever hurt that boy."

"Then why did *Scotty* say it? If you two were so loving, why would he want to hurt *you?* Why would he want to blackmail your ass?"

"I wish I knew. I lie awake in bed and try to figure it out."

For a moment, Leppenraub seemed to forget his anger, his outrage. He seemed to be musing to himself. He said, "Something happened to Scotty. Back when I was very sick, so I wasn't paying much attention to him then. But there was—I think he said something about an old girlfriend. Jilting him or something. I guess that was it. Love—it gets into your head—distorts things."

Then, silence. Romulus was all ready to come apart. He had a tirade on the tip of his tongue, and he felt a desperate need to let it go. The Seraphs surging. His blood hammering.

But not yet. For Christ's sake not now when the truth was within his grasp.

Romulus put his hand against the wall beside the triptych and steadied himself, and took a breath, and murmured, "Right. That's right. Love will do that. Look. I'm sorry. Sorry I said those things. I heard a story. The kid—Scotty—I liked him, I believed what he told me. I got upset. But now you've set me straight. I didn't know you loved him so much, I didn't—"

"Forget it," said Leppenraub. Gently. "I do understand. I know the kind of things he was saying. In your shoes, I'd have had the same reaction."

"But I'm really sorry."

"It's all right."

Leppenraub sniffed, collected himself. He said, "I suppose it's just part of . . . being who I am. You know? There's always this wild envy all around me. Always. Even with the people I love. The people I'm closest to."

Then he shook his head and added, "Just too much goddamn envy. And too many goddamn stories."

41

T hey walked back to the house in the gathering evening. Leppenraub went upstairs. Romulus wandered into the parlor, then into the big chandeliered dining room.

One of the caterer's maids was setting places. Romulus asked her, "Where's Moira, do you know? Miss Leppenraub?"

The woman pointed.

Moira Leppenraub was in the kitchen, cutting celery. She was wearing a black sheath dress and silver earrings, and she was radiant. The caterers bustled all about her. Arnold was sitting up on the counter by the cutting board. He was drinking wine, holding the bottle in one hand and a little Dixie cup in the other. Pouring frequently.

He called, "Romulus! Jeez, Moira, this is my old *friend* here! This guy! This guy used to take the theme song for 'Leave it to Beaver' and make you weep! Weep for our lost innocence! And then it was like . . . it was like Eddie Haskell breaking into the Cleavers' house, you know, and smashing the windows and throwing gasoline on the drapes and burning the place to the *ground!* Want some wine, Rom?"

"No thanks."

"Twenty-five *years* I haven't seen this guy!"

A telephone rang somewhere in the house. Moira excused herself—but before she went, Romulus asked her if there was someplace he could freshen up.

She said, "Through that door, take a left."

She gave him a long gaze, a sustained smile. When she turned to go, there was the cut of her black sheath as it swooped down her back, and whatever Arnold was saying, Romulus wasn't hearing.

"What?"

"I said she's gorgeous, isn't she?"

"You think so?" said Romulus. "Yes. You may be right about that."

Then he went through the door she'd pointed out and found himself in the back hallway. He was taking a left when he heard, behind him, drifting down the back stairs, Leppenraub's voice.

It was a murmur, but with an edge of anxiety.

Romulus stopped. He listened, but he couldn't quite make out the words.

So he silently climbed those back stairs.

Halfway up, the staircase turned, and Romulus stopped at this landing. The door to Leppenraub's room was just above him, and it was slightly open, yellow light pouring out through the crack.

"No . . . *no* . . . uh-uh, I'm telling you, he knows something . . . I just *feel* it. He just about accused me of murdering Scotty. . . . "

There was a window on the landing, a window that overlooked the backyard. Dusk was sketching over the lawn with a quick stroke. Elon was out there. He was on his haunches on a big patch of bare mud thaw, and making a castle. Mud all over him. Romulus used to take Lulu to a playground on Ward's Island, and they would make a tower from wet sand, and top it with an upside-down Sno-Kone. And then Romulus, to his daughter's delight, would pretend he was the king who lived in that Sno-Kone spire.

He heard Leppenraub again:

"Yeah, *supposed* to be Arnold's friend but I don't know, I don't know who he is really. . . . Maybe he's a cop. . . . Well, I don't like it. . . . I don't give a shit, I'm telling you I don't like it at all. I want you to take care of it. . . . Listen. He's bugging me. OK? *So take care of it.* Tonight."

Faintly, the sound of a phone being cradled.

Romulus stood there. He kept sending the command down to his legs: *Move. Flee.* But his legs paid him no mind. The connection had gone bad. All he could do was stand there and stare out at the lawn. Which was turning, even as he watched, an uncanny and pernicious shade of green.

He's going to kill you. To kill you. Kill. You're going to die, Romulus, you came up here to be killed. Do you understand?

"What are you doing there?"

He wheeled. It was Moira, standing below him.

She said, "You get lost?"

She was backlit by light from the kitchen. Sweet Moira, in your snake sheath, give me another smile. Give me a smile to stop me from shaking, to get me down these stairs. *Please.*

She did. He came down. He told her:

"Lost, yes. Lost. I . . . I wanted to see the view. Then I was watching your friend Elon."

"Elon loves this time of day."

"Oh, it's a *wonderful* time of day. It's the time when killers plan their kills and victims prepare to die. Right?"

She considered this. She said, "You're kind of nuts, don't you think?" Then she laughed. "But that's OK—I love crazy men. They're the only ones I understand."

She laughed again. She said, "You're right, it is kind of spooky out there. I think it's the mist. I think it's going to rain. Look at that color! God, I wish I could capture that color, I'd use it in my sculpture. Anyway. Bathroom's there."

She pointed. He made no response. Simply stared at her.

She said, "You still want to freshen up?"

"Oh, yes. Freshen up. Prepare, absolutely. *That* door, you say?"

"That door."

42

In his time, Romulus had tasted of the most exquisite food that Gotham had to offer. But he seldom had known the name of any of these delicacies. Their provenance was a Dumpster or surly cook at a bistro's back door. They were never fresh, these tidbits, never hot, and Romulus liked to mix them up, in a plastic shopping bag, with old luncheon meat and popcorn and smears of mayonnaise and sometimes bits of stale bread or M&M's. So he wasn't sure if he had truly fathomed the full piquancies and subtleties of these dishes.

The point for him had never been to seek that inspired moment when tang and aroma and ambience all conspire to transport us to the Realm of Gastronomic Bliss. The point had always been to lick his hunger.

Tonight though, everything was fresh and steaming hot and served with elegance and pomp.

And yet he tasted none of it.

Leppenraub was scheming to kill him.

He opened his hatch, he put the food in. This was his last meal, he thought, really he ought to pay attention. But he couldn't.

They started with a soup called *zuppa di farro*. He knew it was *zuppa di farro* because Moira told him so. She told him it was made from wheatberries and sage, and garnished with a flash of virgin olive oil.

She asked him, "What do you think?"

"Sticks to the ribs."

Next they had *funghi en tegame*. Moira commented on the cunning touch of mint in the sauce. The mushrooms, she said, were portobellos and wonderful porcinis.

And the music? The music Romulus knew. Ravel's *Le Tombeau de Couperin*.

Arnold was sitting a few places down from him, and he was drunk. He called up: "Romulus! Listen up! You're supposed to *like* Ravel!"

I can stand Ravel just as much as the next guy. Only, for God's sake, please don't play anything that hurts.

The Moth-Seraphs in his head were full of vengeance, and they were muttering oaths and plotting to break out, and Romulus knew that any stretch right now of, say, Ives's *Holidays,* would rally them like an anthem.

Said Moira, "You like it?"

"What?"

"The *funghi en tegame.*"

"Oh. Mmm-*mmm.* When I lived in that cave I once tried to grow mushrooms but nothing came of it."

Leppenraub was going to kill him. There was no way out of it. The only question was how. How would he do it?

Was it already under way, his murder? Was Leppenraub poisoning him with *funghi en tegame?*

He looked up at the assassin presiding at the head of the table.

The man was being gently witty and endearingly infirm. His guests, all these brilliancies gathered before him, were in awe of him. Even voluble Moira was silent (sullen?) in her brother's presence. David Leppenraub was a certified genius, he was incandescently charming, he had tons of money. He was a man who had stepped to the verge of the chasm of death, and then stepped back from it—and yet he seemed relaxed, content, he seemed utterly in possession of his life.

Look at him. He had tortured Scotty Gates and killed him without the ghost of a qualm, and he'd been commended by Stuyvesant for the deed. The two of them had laughed together, they'd stood in Stuyvesant's tower in the chill light of Y-rays and brayed at all the fools below. And Leppenraub would kill another man before the night was over and yet *look* at him!—he sat there making benign wisecracks, swirling the wine in his glass—look! He was more evil than Stuyvesant even—precisely because his evil was less consequent, carried less weight. The smallness, the no-accountness of his evil gave it its force. *Look at him!*

Then it dawned on Romulus, slowly, that the woman to his left was waiting for him to answer some question she had put.

He glanced at her. She was in profile. She had a geyser hairdo, and she was the profile on some ancient worthless penny.

"Um . . . excuse me?"

"I say *I* voted for him last year."

"Well, heh, heh, sure you did. He was the man for the job, right?"

"I went to the awards and *prayed* for him. But of course Spike *never* wins. He ought to *sweep,* don't you think?"

Try, Romulus. Try to listen.

"Who are we talking about again?"

"Spike Lee."

"Wait a minute. Did you say director? You mean movie director?"

"Without equal."

"A black man? You're saying they've got a black man directing movies?"

"You never . . . *heard* . . . of Spike Lee?"

Romulus squinted at her. Was she telling the truth? She apparently thought she was. He pursed his lips. He said, "No, of course

I've never heard of him. But I tell you what you do. You carry around a little bottle of turpentine, see?—and a white handkerchief. And next time you run into this fellow, you pour some of the turpentine onto the handkerchief. Like this." He demonstrated, using his napkin and the water from his goblet. "Then you rub the handkerchief against the fellow's face. Like this." He swiped at her cheek. She flinched. "Then check the handkerchief. What color is it?"

"What?"

"What color?"

"White?"

"Not anymore. Some of the black polish has come off."

"You're saying *Spike Lee* is an Oreo cookie?"

"I'm saying Stuyvesant doesn't let black men direct his movies." He leaned close to her. "I'm saying cut the shit before you get the Seraphs all hopped up in my skull and they come busting for daylight. You know what I mean?"

She was gaping at him.

And he turned and let her slip away, slip back into the ocean of table chat, and he wondered again: So how would they do it? How would they kill him?

This way:

When the other guests leave, Arnold will be too drunk to drive back to Manhattan, and their gracious host will put the two of them up for the night. Then he'll come into my room in the middle of the night and dispatch me the same way he dispatched Scotty, whatever way *that* was. And he and Vlad will put me in the trunk of the scarlet Diamante—and Romulus could see the trunk hood closing over him, a great vault of darkness. . . .

Something swimming with worms was placed before him. Moira identified it as *pappardelle con sugo d'anatra*.

"That's a nice name," said Romulus.

He held down the worms with his knife and cut them with his fork. He was addressed by a full round face across the table, a milk-fed moon-woman.

"Where exactly do you live in San Francisco, Mr. Ledbetter?"

Why don't they leave me alone?

He muttered something, but the great round face didn't hear his answer.

She said, "Excuse me?"

"I said, I live *near the water.*"

David Leppenraub heard that, and seemed to think it funny. He laughed his laugh.

Anger gathered.

"But where?" the woman pressed.

"What difference does it make? I won't be living there any-more."

"You're moving?"

"I'm dying."

Leppenraub laughed again. Leppenraub loved this.

In desperation Romulus turned to Moira. Moira was going to have to save his ass.

He gazed into her eyes and said in a voice loud enough for Leppenraub to hear, "You know, you are one magical woman."

"A what? Magical?"

Her eyes shone. She was flattered. And out of the corner of his eye Romulus could see that Leppenraub was burning. Oh, he did not like this rude nosy Negro oozing up to his little sister.

It was the effect Romulus had been looking for.

Making Leppenraub burn—it steadied him some. Enough to be able to hobble through the rest of the meal without pitching a fit.

He let the clangor of repartee wash over him, and leaned back into a cloud so no one could see him, and he waited. And when he leaned forward again he found that the dessert and the Ravel were behind him, and everyone was repairing to the parlor and he with them, and then he managed to slip out onto the porch, alone. He walked all the way around the porch to the back, and stepped into the backyard and drew a breath of fresh air. His head was rumbling, smoking. He shuffled across the lawn to the dirt drive, to Elon's mud castle. He stood over it, hanging his head and listening to a far-off owl. The lights were on in Elon's cottage, and faintly he heard a radio going. Behind him, in the kitchen of the big house, he heard the clatter of the caterers as they cleaned.

A fat raindrop bounced off his skull.

He missed his saucepan hat.

Without question, the best idea was to run like hell.

But before he could even think of taking a step, he heard a

growl, and looked over and there was Lao-tse, right beside him. Watching him, her blue eyes gone black in the dark, and growling low in the throat. *No,* Lao-tse was telling him. *Running is not the best idea. Try it, and I'll show you why not.*

They appraised each other. Also Romulus appraised the huge dark spreading before him. Then he turned and looked back at the house—and saw someone waiting for him.

A dark figure standing on the back porch. Romulus heard a chuckle, and the figure came toward him.

Tuxedo. Vampire-slick hair. Vlad.

"Hey, I have been looking for you. Hurry, come with me, man."

43

Romulus didn't budge. "Come where?"

"Just come. Surprise."

"Oh, I don't know."

"What's the matter? You scared?"

"Well . . ."

"Well, you should be. I'm going to cut your fugging ears off."

Vlad grinned. Thousands of tiny teeth, glimmering in the dark. Then he said, "My *horn,* man. That's all. I want to show you how I wail with the horn. You like John Coltrane?"

"Coltrane? Sure."

"You like Miles?"

"Sure."

"Come on, I live under the barn, we go there. I play for you. I cut your fugging ears off."

Said Romulus, "David tell you to come take care of me out here?"

"David don't know I'm gone. I tell Moira."

"I see. You don't ask her. You just *tell* her."

"Sure. You want I be a crybaby? *Oh Mommy, please?*"

"Are you fucking Moira?"

It did occur to Romulus that this was a dumb question. Certainly dangerous, and probably pointless. But it was the first thing that had popped into his head, and he no longer had the strength to keep these pop-ups down.

Suddenly Vlad's face was in Romulus's face. "That's very rude to ask, my friend."

"Yes. I know that. I'm in a rude mood."

"I hear you ask a lot of fugging rude questions."

"Bad habit."

"Fugging bad habit."

A small snapping sound. Romulus glanced down. There was a switchblade in Vlad's hand. The blade was open. It glimmered in the faint yard light.

"Are you going to kill me *here,* Vlad? This close to the house?"

Vlad grinned again. "Nah. This was just so you know we got the same language, you know what? No fugging wimp shit."

Vlad made a spitting sound in disgust. He snapped the blade shut. He said, "Look, you're a *man.* I'm a *man.* OK? Just so you know. And what's in there is *wimps.*"

Cocking his thumb toward the house lights, the party gabble.

Romulus said, "Right."

"I got ghetto balls. You know what?"

"What?"

"No, I'm saying, I got ghetto balls."

"Right," said Romulus. "But you still haven't answered my question."

"What question?"

"You fucking Moira?"

Vlad laughed. "American women, they want a wild man. Hah hah hah hah hah hah!"

The rain started to come down in earnest.

Said Romulus, "Maybe I'll take a rain check on the concert, OK?"

"Yeah yeah, you got to go in and play for the white American wimps. Too bad. Later we go to my room, and do the jam."

"Right," said Romulus. "We'll cut their fugging ears off."

Sudden sheets of rain. They broke for cover. Clattered up the wood steps onto the porch.

Lao-tse did a dog-shake.

And then another question popped into Romulus's head, and he set it at liberty right away.

"Hey, Vlad. What was Scotty Gates like?"

"What? Why you ask?"

"Being nosy again."

"Yah. Well, he was pretty. Pretty pretty pretty. Fugging wimp."

"Did David Leppenraub ever torture him?"

Silence for a moment. They were standing on the porch by a tall window, and inside, in the strong yellow light, the partygoers milled about and gossiped and laughed.

After a moment Vlad said quietly: "OK, you know what, I tell you about that fugging wimp Scotty. I tell you a story. Sometimes Scotty, he brings his girlfriend out here to the farm. Oh, he thinks he impresses her, that he lives in this fancy place, that he models for this big American photographer. He thinks this girl's got little-girl eyes, he thinks she's *naive*. He thinks she's a nun. She's no nun. That I see first thing. So one day's she's here and Scotty's working for David, posing, you know what, and she's here all alone, and she tells me she wants to ride the horses. We ride the horses. She tells me she wants no more with Scotty. You think she wants for her boyfriend a pretty model who shows his pretty cock? Nah, she wants no more. She wants to go live in New York City, find a real man. I say, There's a real man right here. We ride to the pasture, I fug her."

"You fucked Scotty's girlfriend?"

"She wants a *man*. American woman wants a fugging wild man. We have lunch, Scotty and the girlfriend and David and me. Scotty—he's a big bore. He's got moon eyes for the girl. He says to David, 'Isn't she sweet?' And me, I pull my cock out under the table and put her hand on it and she is—what is the word? . . . pumping me."

"She did that?"

"Pumping me off."

Romulus looked through the window and spotted Moira Leppenraub. She was passing among the knots of partygoers but not stopping to chat. She was casting her eyes about. She was looking for someone. Looking for me, thought Romulus.

Said Vlad, "But too bad, because I think later she *told* him what she did with Vlad. American girl, they always guilty, fugged up in

the head because they want wild man, and so they got to tell everything they do. Yeah, she must have told him what she did all weekend with me. Because later—Scotty goes bats, you know what? I
hear he goes out of his fugging mind."

Then they heard Moira at the front door, calling into the dark.
"Romulus?"

Piano time.

44

In the parlor David Leppenraub was proposing various witty
toasts to his friends, and the friends clinked their glasses and clapped.
Meanwhile in the front hallway Moira dried Romulus's head with a
towel.

She asked, "Where did you go?"

"I was talking to Vlad. He said he wanted to cut my ears off.
Moira, why don't you make him stay here and put little onions in
martinis?"

"You can't *make* Vlad do anything. If it were up to me, I'd fire
him in two seconds, but David won't let me. How are your feet?"

"What?"

"Your shoes are sopping. Where'd you *get* those shoes, anyway?"

"The shoes. Right. I've got a story that explains the shoes. I've
got a story all ready for you. I worked it out on the way up here."

"OK. I love stories."

"Only I can't remember it now. Something about these are my
lucky shoes. Or something. Nothing too persuasive. But I don't
think it matters anymore anyway."

Then Arnold came to fetch him. Ushered him in, and the glitterati were all watching him, and Arnold introduced him. The audience applauded him warmly.

Romulus sat before the baby grand.

45

With his right hand, way up on the keyboard and lightly, he trilled a pair of notes. Just dabbling a toe in the water. How was it? Freezing. Stop-your-heart freezing.

He popped a low F#.

Which stung.

He dropped his hands. Smiled at the glitterati. The whole room was abuzz with them. There, in the front row, was the coin-profile woman with her husband. At their feet, on the hook rug, drunk and swaying, sat Arnold. Moira stood by the vestibule door. Leppenraub by the window. Everywhere Romulus looked there was an audience: Methuselahs and barracudas and toy-boys and women with geyser hairdos.

He took a breath and rolled his eyes.

He said, "I haven't started yet. Heh heh."

That charmed them. Giggles all round.

He had it all planned out—what he would play. Just a cute little snatch of program music, heavily larded with romance. Here and there a filigree of atonality for authenticity. It's simple. It's easy. Just remember, Romulus, that *you have no ambition in the world except to get to the other side of this piece.*

So *go.* They're waiting. Go now.

"OK."

He lit into the keyboard.

The chords that roared back hurt like hell, but he held on. He kept his fingers dancing, he kept plunging the pedals. He gave his audience a scrapbook of pictures from the walk he'd taken with Moira. The green-gold mergansers—*there.* The dog's romp—*there.* The tulip trees and the golden fields, and oh, this was so simple and sweet and easy, and soon he'd be done.

But then something started to stink.

There was some bad odor creeping into this piece, into this sweet farmscape he was painting, and it was the smell of mendacity and evil. And the music from his left hand was sniffing, sniffing, searching out the source of that odor.

Well, tell that music to quit it.

Forget the foolishness, *now,* and the audience will think that sequence of ominous chords was just a stormcloud passing overhead. Just give them six full saccharine measures of the little duck pond and let's get out of here.

But his left hand wasn't listening to him. He was no longer in command. The Seraphs were.

The Moth-Seraphs had broken through all the gates. They had swarmed into the domed womb of his consciousness, and they were taking the controls. Already they had taken his left-hand music under their wing.

His right hand kept up the easy shepherd's-ode frolicking, but his left hand was on a rampage. It was searching everywhere, searching the whole farm for the source of that reek—that evil. The music from his left hand crashed into the barn-museum and tore the prints from the walls. It rifled the office, scattered negatives, overturned the file cabinets. What is it? *What is the clue to this reek?*

The music looked in the farmyard and found Elon and seized him and shrieked in a bizarre chord progression:

TELL ME! WHAT IS THIS FOULNESS HERE?

WHAT THE HELL IS IT?

Then the music let go of the poor man, and made its way to the doll's coach house, to Moira's studio. It went inside. It felt around in the dark, and sniffed, and found that here the stench of evil was particularly strong. The stench was so bad that it made Romulus shudder, made him rise up before the Steinway and slam his hand down against the keys. Oh, here it is! *Here in the coach house, here!*

But what *is* it? What stinks?

What have I found and why is Stuyvesant laughing?

Is it the rotting of the dead boy you threw outside my cave, is that what I'm smelling, Stuyvesant?

Is it the cops you hire to hide your lies and rape my daughter? Is this a whiff of their corruption?

Is it the whore with the skewed eyes and windfall hair that you engaged to seduce me? The smell of lust, is that it?

WHAT IS THIS STENCH?

Leppenraub! Is it the way you tortured Scotty Gates, because the poor fool thought he was *somebody,* thought his life was in his own hands, and you couldn't have that, could you? So you did him just the way they did me, you tortured him, you *leached all the divinity out of him,* right? And when you were done you killed him so he couldn't accuse you? Right? *Is that what I smell?*

Then Romulus happened to notice Arnold's stricken look, and he realized that he was speaking all these thoughts *aloud,* while he played. While he wildly, plungingly played on, he was shouting at the top of his lungs:

"IS IT THE WAY YOU DUMPED HIM IN FRONT OF MY CAVE, LEPPENRAUB? *SPECIAL DELIVERY,* SO I'D KNOW YOU KILL WHENEVER YOU PLEASE, SO I'D COME AND LICK YOUR SHOES, AND BEG YOUR BOSS STUYVESANT FOR A POINT-BLANK SHOT OF Y-RAYS INTO MY BRAIN?

"IT'S *ALL* OF YOU, ISN'T IT? *ALL* OF YOU FUCKERS! IT'S YOUR BONE-DRY ART AND YOUR IDEAS LIKE LAST WEEK'S VOMIT AND YOUR SHIT-IN-A-FRAME! AM I *RIGHT?* AND THE HEART HAS FUCKING *VAMOOSED* FROM THIS CULTURE LONG TIME AGO, AND ANYBODY GETS WIND OF *THAT,* YOU'LL TORTURE HIM AND KILL HIM AND MAKE A VIDEOTAPE OF IT AND CALL IT *ART!* AND YOU'LL THROW HIM IN THE SNOW AND *TEACH THE CAVEMAN A LESSON!* AND BURN OUT THE CAVEMAN'S EYES WITH BLUE SKY AND GREEN DUCKS AND BROWN EYES, AND GET YOUR HANDS OFF ME! I HAVEN'T FOUND IT! GET AWAY! *I HAVEN'T FOUND THE CLUE YET!* GET YOUR HANDS OFF ME!"

The vase in front of him leapt up and dove down and hit the floor, and it was every shard for itself. Shrieking chaos. Faces swimming before his eyes. They were very close. One, David Leppenraub's, was barking over and over, "I won't have this! I'm sick, I don't have to take this!" The music was still playing, but it was the orchestra of Romulus's mind now—violins, kettledrum, and hurdy-gurdy.

The Steinway was silent.

Romulus looked down, and there were a dozen hands on his

sleeve. He yanked. He twisted. Arnold was saying, "You lied to me, Rom!" Romulus spun violently, the mass of faces fell away. He checked his sleeve, all the hands were gone. Then they were back again.

Cried Moira, "*Don't hurt him!* Rom, it's OK. *It's OK!*"

Arnold shouted, "*You lied to me! You're still living in that cave, aren't you?*"

The room tornadoed about.

"AND YOU WON'T GET ME *OUT* OF THE CAVE EI-THER! YOU WON'T MATCHBOX ME!"

A knife appeared in front of his eyes.

Said Vlad: "Sit down, nigger."

Moira screamed. "*Vlad! Put that away! Are you crazy? Don't hurt him!*"

"STUYVESANT, YOUR TOWER'S COMING DOWN! STUYVESANT!"

And then he wasn't in the room anymore. He was leaping off the porch, or he was thrown off, and he was stumbling on the flag-stones, and sliding face first on the wet grass, breathing mud.

46

A snarl at his ear. Romulus opened one eye, and got an eye-ful of Lao-tse's tucked-back lips and fangs, two inches from his face.

The dog's eyes were as cool and magisterial as ever. But the fangs were madder than hell. It was a confusing sight, so Romulus let that eye shut again—and then he heard Moira.

"*No!* Lao-tse, get back! Vlad, get him off!"

A step close by. Sound of a kick and the dog yowled. Romulus put his palms to the earth and pushed himself off it. Unsteadily rose.

There was Vlad's knife again. "I say, sit *down*, nigger."

"Why the fuck should I?! *Soul brother?* You going to slice my fugging ears off?!"

An elbow came crashing into Romulus's face. Blinding flash. He fell forward, and Vlad's knee came up into his chest.

Far away, Moira was screaming. "No! No! Stop it!"

Romulus saw her, faintly, on a porch somewhere. Leppenraub and someone else were wrestling her back into the house. She was trying to bite her brother. Her brother was saying the same thing over and over again.

"I won't have it, Moira! I'm sick, I don't have to take this!"

Romulus, on his knees, tried again to rise.

Vlad flourished the blade. "Sit!"

Romulus rolled his eyes up to Vlad. "Watch it, *homeboy*. This still isn't the moment. Still too many witnesses. Not so easy as it was killing Scotty. Right?"

"Shut up."

Another jolt, and in that white flash of lightning Romulus saw all the way downstate to NYC, caught a glimpse of Stuyvesant's tower. Presiding over all. Invincible.

Who in hell did you think you were kidding, Caveman?

NEEDLES
HURT

47

He was in a small room with a small window. A dog looked in through the window. The dog winked at him, again and again. Mean-looking cur, but it wasn't Lao-tse. It was that bull terrier from the beer ads. It was a neon sign in a tavern window across the street from the Gideon Manor Sheriff's Office.

Romulus had thought that if he would just *wink back* the dog might quit.

It didn't work.

The deputy said, "There's nobody out there, sir."

"Yeah."

"What's the matter?"

"Nothing."

"But, sir, you're crying."

Romulus swabbed his cheek with his forefinger, and put his forefinger in his mouth. It tasted of mud, and blood, and—yes, the man was right—of salt.

"Think nothing of it. Sometimes this'll happen to me after I pitch a fit. The doctors tell me it means nothing. The tears just come, right? Hey, I mean, I might not be thinking about my daughter at all. I might be in a fine, easy mood, but you'd never know it—you'd look at these tears and think I was a wreck. You got something I could blow my nose with?"

The deputy sheriff went out and came back with a tissue. The deputy had a paunch, a few last good-bye strands of hair, pulpy red cheeks. When he smiled at Romulus, his lips didn't move much, those cheeks just knotted up.

Romulus honked into the tissue. Wiped his face.

He said, "There. Am I still crying?"

"Doesn't look like it."

"OK then. What can I do for you, Officer?"

"Well sir, what's your name?"

"Romulus Ledbetter."

"Where do you live?"

"Inwood Park, New York City."

"Street address?"

"Just the Cave."

"The Cave? This is your *real* address?"

"Of course not."

"Oh. One of those."

"Right."

"Sir, what were you doing here in Gideon Manor?"

"Attending a party."

"Excuse me, but Mr. Leppenraub said that isn't quite true. He said you aren't who you say you are."

"He's lying. I'm just as much who I say I am as I really *am*."

"What?"

"Forget it."

"OK."

"In truth I'm a private investigator. I'm investigating the death of Andrew Scott Gates."

The deputy considered, remembered.

"You mean Scotty? The kid that froze to death in the city? Yeah, uh-huh. Some detective was asking around up here last week."

"Lieutenant Detective John Cork?"

"Friend of yours?"

"Rival."

"Oh boy. Poor guy."

"You said a mouthful there."

"Well, who are you doing this investigating for?"

"Nobody. Myself."

"Why?"

"Why? They say I'm paranoid. They said Scotty Gates was paranoid. It's like a family thing, OK?"

"Sir, what are we going to do with you?"

"I don't know. I can see that's a tricky one for you, but me, I think I ought to stay out of it. I'd be biased."

"Do we send you to a hospital?"

Romulus shut his eyes for a moment.

"I'd rather . . . that you didn't do that, OK?"

Please God. Though I could understand if you felt you had to. Others have. In your place. Before you. But please God.

"I could book you."

"Right."

"I'm not sure on what charge though."

"I couldn't help you with that one either. You'd be the expert."

"Uh-huh. Well, sir, tell me this, you still feeling crazy? You're not going to hurt anybody, are you?"

"So long as they don't make me play the piano again."

"Are you ready to drop this 'private investigator' thing?"

"No."

"Ah, but you're just going to have to. See, I think I'm going to put you on the bus for New York. There's one more bus and it leaves in half an hour."

"I don't have any money."

"One way is twenty-two fifty. I'll spring."

"I couldn't ask you to do that."

"Well, truth is, Mr. Leppenraub said he'd cover it. I think he can handle that amount."

"Sure. He can sell one of his lovely artworks."

"Oh, boy. One of those weenie shots?"

"Exactly."

"See, I believe Mr. Leppenraub just wants to get you the hell out of his hair."

"Mr. Leppenraub just wants to get me where he can quietly murder me."

"Whatever. I don't care one way or the other. Long as it isn't in Gideon Manor."

"I can understand that."

"Well, understand this, too, then. Sir. If I ever see you around here again, I'll charge you with harassment and whatever else I need to, and get you sent to a prison for the criminally insane. Around these parts, that'd be a place called Matteawan. Have you ever seen that place, sir? Right off the interstate? Looks like a medieval fortress? I've never spent time there myself, so I can't say for sure if it's got dungeons or not. But it sure *looks* like it does. Oh, boy, now you're crying again."

"Think nothing of it."

48

R omulus put on the beautiful coat that Bob had given him, then they went to wait at the bus stop. The bus stop was twenty paces down from the sheriff's office. Directly across from the bull terrier, who kept up his winking at Romulus. The rain was drizzling out to nothing. Romulus and the deputy leaned against a low rock wall. Behind the wall was a meadow that sloped gently upward into the night. The deputy went up to the curb and looked down the street for the bus. Nothing.

There was nothing at all going on in this town.

The only action was the dog's winking, and a buzz from the fluorescent light at the entrance to the sheriff's office.

The deputy came back and leaned beside Romulus.

"You know, you don't seem like such a wild man."

"You should have seen me pitching my fit. But, right. After I'm done pitching, I'm sort of quiet, right. . . ."

The deputy went to the curb again and checked the street. Then he came back.

"So what makes you have a fit?"

"Oh. Oh, well, I mean, any nasty thing, you know."

"Like?"

"Like. For instance, did you know that before he was elected president, there were two years when Richard Nixon disappeared from public view? From 1962 to 1964?"

"Uh-uh. I didn't know that."

"And you know what he was doing? He was going to school. You know where the school was?"

"Where?"

"Chappaquiddick Island."

"Wow. What school was this?"

"The Stuyvesant Institute for Political Research."

"I didn't know that. That's interesting. I don't know what I'm supposed to make of it though. Do things like that disturb you?"

"Yes."

The deputy shook his head. Then he strolled back up to the curb.

There were a few spring-stirring sounds in the meadow behind Romulus. Early and mild insects. Romulus turned to look. He could see nothing in the field. But way up at the top of the hill, there were lights on at the Gideon Manor Playhouse. He called to the deputy.

"They giving a show up there?"

"Hmm?"

"That's the theater, isn't it?"

"Oh. No sir, there's no plays this time of year. That's just Walter's Bar, in the old hotel. Right next to the playhouse. Used to be the Gideon Hotel and Playhouse when Walter's folks had it. Now the hotel's falling apart, and of course Walter sold the playhouse to Leppenraub—but he kept the bar for himself."

"Leppenraub only bought the playhouse? How come he didn't want the hotel?"

"I don't know. Maybe Walter didn't want to sell it. But no more private investigator, OK? I thought we had a deal."

"I just—heh, heh. I'm just surprised they don't try to restore it."

"Ah hell—it's way past saving. But Walter's going to keep his bar going till the room falls in, or till we go up and close it, which I guess we're going to have to do pretty soon. Hate to, though. It's all Walter's got left."

"You go in there much?"

"No. I go across the street here. No, it's just a couple of weirdos go there. Gay people, you know? Except in the summer, and then some of the theater folks come in. I don't know which is worse for Walter—the gays or the actors."

"That winking dog doesn't get on your nerves?"

"What winking dog?"

"Right over there."

"Oh. Yeah. Never noticed it."

Said Romulus, "Well, you see that's exactly the sort of thing that makes me pitch a fit."

The bus came. The deputy gave Romulus a twenty and a ten.

Romulus said, "I don't have change."

"It's OK, sir. Leppenraub can handle it. Hey listen, something I forgot. Mr. Leppenraub's sister, Moira—she wanted me to tell you— she thought your playing was real good. In fact, she said it was *magnificent.*"

"She say anything about my fit?"

"No, sir."

"Well. When you see her, would you thank her for all her generosity?"

"I will if you mean it and you're not wising off."

"I mean it. And thank *you,* Officer."

"Yes, sir."

Romulus stepped onto the bus. He said, "See you."

"I hope not. Because if you do, you know you're going straight to Matteawan."

"Right."

Romulus bought a one-way ticket for New York. He moved down the aisle a ways, and the bus started down the road. Warm in here, dark, with the sweet snoozing smell of bus-innards. He knew if he let himself sit down he'd be asleep inside of a minute. But he didn't let himself. He stood and waited until the bus had gone about a quarter mile, then he went up to the driver and said:

"Oh, my . . . *Lord,* I forgot my briefcase. You got to let me off."

The driver grunted. "Not supposed to stop till we get to Peekskill."

"I can't go without my briefcase. Jesus, I'll lose my job. I can take the next bus."

"This is the last bus till morning."

"That's OK, I'll stay over. I've got to get my briefcase."

"I'm not supposed to refund—"

"I don't want a refund. *I just want to get off.*"

The driver sighed. Not much room to pull over, but he did, and Romulus stepped out onto the still highway.

Thinking: I'll go back home tomorrow. First I've got to get another look at that coach house.

The bus pulled away.

Romulus was all alone in the dark. He looked back down the road he had just come on, and he started walking.

And then he saw something.

Something just sitting there on the road. It was damn, solid dark out here—but he peered, he strained his eyes, and that shape began to look like the shape of a car.

The sounds of the bus faded. He heard a purring. The smooth rich contented purr of an expensive car.

It had been following the bus. It was sitting in the middle of the road, and someone was sitting in it, waiting patiently.

And now the bus had gone, and Romulus was all ready to be taken. The car's interior light snapped on. A cage of light, floating in the darkness. And for a moment Romulus could see the driver. But no face.

Then the engine roared.

The car was coming at him. The headlights blazed up in his eyes.

49

He staggered backward. In the face of those two flaming eye spots growing huge in his vision, that's all he could do—stagger like a drunk. His hand groped behind him as though for some kind of hold. The eye spots loomed.

He glanced to the left. There was a stretch of shoulder, and then a sharp plummet into blackness. He broke for it.

But that edge of blackness seemed too far to go. He could wring no speed from his legs. The headlight beam and the roar had him in thrall. They closed in, they wrapped cobwebs around him, they gathered him up. As he moved he jerked his eyes to the right, to face those lights, and again he saw the driver, in the faint interior glow above the monstrous beams.

The driver had no face.

Stuyvesant. Or one of his minions. Facelessness was the bastard's mark, and he was making sure Romulus saw it—so there would be no question as to who was killing him. By his facelessness ye shall know him.

And anger surged up in Romulus—he kicked wildly at the cobwebs, took one great stride, planted a foot on the edge of the shoulder and lunged forward, dove into that sheer abyss.

50

Hovering there, middive, he felt the wind of the car's passing behind him. He heard a keening of brakes and spraying gravel.

Then the blackness swallowed him, and he wrapped his head in his arms and came crashing down into a net of branches. They were in a fury, these branches. They tore his arm away from his face and tossed it into the air. They caught his leg and hurled that skyward as well. They folded the rest of him in two and shoved him through a narrow slot, and did something tricky with his foot and then flipped him over and he landed on his back in the mud.

The wind went out of him with a *whump.*

All the air in his lungs was sucked into the sky. He writhed. He coiled into a fetal ball, and clawed the ground, and forced sips of air into his lungs, and finally his lungs unclenched.

He rolled over. Struggled to his knees, heaved air. Heaved. Coughed. Heaved again.

Up on the road, he heard a car door shut. A flashlight beam shuddered in the branches all around him.

He reached up and got hold of a branch and pulled himself to his feet. He took a few steps. His ankle hurt like hell, but held. Not broken, just wrenched. He stumbled away from the road through a swampy ditch-seep. On the other side of the muck there was a row of trees and then an open meadow. He pushed toward that meadow, dragging his cheap shoes through the sucking mud, till he fell, sloshed into the muck and then the flashlight was all over him.

He got up and ran furiously into the great blurry field. He startled something in the grass. Probably a rabbit. It skittered away from him, and he followed it.

And as he ran, he kept glancing back. The predator's flashlight was moving. Making its way down into the ditch, then into the field, coming up the slope after him. Coming on patiently.

Romulus ran, and ran, and about halfway up the slope he ran himself out of wind.

He held up a moment—he had to get some breath. His lungs were shrieking. His legs were sodden. He looked back, and as he did the light lifted again, and found him. Again it settled upon him. Steadied.

Then he heard a gunshot, and something popped in the grass next to him.

That got him going again. He ran and he zigzagged as best he could with his bad ankle. The grass popped again, another shot, closer. He looked up. The field was clear directly ahead, hopelessly clear and fatal. But to the right there was a dark mass of brake. Where the rabbit had gone. Romulus would have to be a rabbit, too—he veered and scrambled, and pushed into that tangle.

51

It was a stand of gray dogwood, taller than he was. It cut off the light behind him, so he had to grope—to forge ahead blindly.

Something clawed softly at his cheek. Tendril of a thornbush. Then something tried to hold hands with him in the dark: another thorn-shoot. Something grabbed his ass, and something tried to pull the silk sock off his sore ankle. He twisted. He put his hands in front of his face and shoved on. Stepped high, leaned into the pain. The thorns slashed away.

He tried telling himself that in truth, in the best of truths, these were not thorns but fireflies, fireflies over the tobacco fields at his great-uncle's place in North Carolina. And this was not pain, it was only the fireflies' little pulsing fires. For a moment that seemed to help. The wall of lightning bugs parted, opened a way for him, and he ran full tilt through that opening and then he smashed headlong into a swarm of something and if they *were* fireflies, they were a species with stingers like black raspberry thorns and they cut him to ribbons, they ganged up and threw him to the ground.

He lay there. He tried to swallow his mad thirst for air. Held it down in his gut for a moment so he could listen.

Somewhere behind him a soft, slow tread.

He looked above him. The play of the flashlight.

Always the play of that fucking flashlight.

He shimmied along on the ground, on his knees and elbows. The thorns dragged along his skull. One of the thorn-serpents got under the collar of his coat and worked its way down his back. Bob's beautiful shirt tore, Romulus's neck tore, the pain roared. He reached back and wrapped his hand around the barbs and pulled out the tendril. Pushed it aside and crawled on, and presently he came upon what seemed to be a shallow sort of ditch that ran under the thorns. Follow that rabbit. Hunching along for a few dozen yards and then suddenly it wasn't quite so dark—the sky had opened above him. He stood.

He was out of the thicket.

He was at the top of the slope, and on the other side the field dipped down quickly into trees, and there was the sound of a stream at the bottom. The sweet plashing of a country stream.

Then his shadow flickered on the trees before him.

Which meant the fucking light had found him again.

He stumbled down the hill.

But he was dragging, he was spent, he had nothing left. When he got to the stream he leaned against a big tree to weight his lack of strength and breath, and it seemed likely, it seemed in fact *certain,* that this was as far as he was going.

All the strength he had left he used to climb onto a big low limb of the tree, and then up to another smaller limb.

There he rested. He held on to a branch that ran at about chest level behind his back. His arms were outstretched, and his head drooped.

And it occurred to him that now he had all the requisites for his martyrdom. He had the thorns in his hair. He had the wounds. The stigmata, the weariness, the whole cake.

Even the pose.

Not on your fucking life, Stuyvesant.

Oh, Romulus recognized this one. This was one of the bastard's cheapest tricks. *Put you in one of these poses,* make you feel that martyrdom is *just the ticket* for you. Make you feel like your pain is a *work of art* or the *Second Coming of Desperation* so that when he runs you through his gauntlet of suffering and then death, why, you won't even care, you'll chalk it up to your *tragic fucking communion with the suffering of God.*

You'll go out with a shit-eating smile on your face. You won't fuss.

Right?

Not for me, fucker.

Romulus let go the branch with one hand, and straightened himself up and scowled. Get out of that droopy pose. Get set.

If you're going to die here, you're going to die standing tall. So come on now, Stuyvesant. Come on down here and get me.

The light came down the slope.

It searched along the stream bank.

The light came closer and closer, until it was right beneath the tree, and then the hunter stopped. Not more than five feet from Romulus's perch. Romulus could have spit on his head.

The hunter was listening now. And moving his flashlight, moving it in a slow, slow circle. Like a watchtower beam.

It was coming around to Romulus.

But it was coming low. Keep your mouth shut, don't move a muscle, and if you're lucky it will slide *under* you, right under your shoes.

Not a muscle. Where your face twitches, stop that. Where the

127

blood keeps crashing to your temple, stop that, too. You're part of this tree. You've been growing here for years.

Seraphs, hush.

The light slid under Romulus's shoes.

It kept going around.

Then it paused. The hunter had an idea and the flashlight beam came back. Came up—slowly—into the tree—and then the sunrise was full in Romulus's eyes, and he did the only thing that was left to him—he leapt straight out, straight for that light.

52

S lammed into the hunter and his elbow knocked the flashlight up and he got one fiery glimpse of the no-face. It was a no-face because white bandages had been wrapped round and round the head.

Then the rest of Romulus crashed into the hunter and the flashlight spun crazily in the air and the gun went off. Romulus hit the ground. The ground was mud, he slid. His head was stopped by a rock.

His thoughts shrank up a moment and then cleared, and he struggled to his feet and spotted the gun. The flashlight was lying on the ground, and in its scoop of light Romulus saw the gun where it lay on a flat mossy stone. He went for it.

But before he could reach it, the light jumped.

The hunter had picked up the flashlight. Romulus turned, and the light blazed in his eyes. He looked back at where the gun was, but that was all blackness now. He faced the light and moved toward it, and it flared and sparked in his vision and he lumbered forward and reached for it. It went out.

He lunged—but there was nothing there. Nothing to see but the light's afterburn. He blinked. Huge purple peony, blooming in his vision.

He heard the hunter's footsteps as they raced away. He followed the sound, scrambled after it till a tree slugged into his shoulder and spun him around.

The footsteps faded away.

Romulus stopped where he was and waited till his eyes had attuned themselves to the dark. Then he went back and found the mossy stone and the gun.

The feel of the gun, its slick heaviness, gave him the creeps. He tossed it into the water.

He sat on the mossy stone until the rain started up again.

Then he didn't know what to do.

53

The rain came harder and harder, and Walter Whittle, of Walter's Bar, watched it coming down and knew there was no hope for late traffic. Knew that this was all the customers he was going to see tonight.

He counted them. Seven. The same seven he'd counted an hour ago. The same seven he'd counted last month. The same seven that he supposed he'd count around his deathbed when the lights went out for keeps. All of them *gaybos,* except for Cassandra rocking her hips over there by the jukebox. Cassandra, too, probably— though who knew what really turned on that piece of flirtatious trash?

Andy and James were dancing, draped over one another and churning softly to an Andy Williams ballad. The Gaybo Club, they never asked to change anything in the jukebox—they'd just take the good old standards that were in there and enjoy them in their own disgusting way. And ruin them, forever, for Walter's ears.

They'd sing along to Pet Clark and Tony Bennett, and laugh uproariously.

They'd dance their unpleasant dances.

So wasn't it about time to clean this place up? Walter asked himself. To throw these deviants out on their debauched bony asses?

Yes it was. It had been time for a long time. The Gaybos, they were why nobody else would come in here. They were what had happened to the traffic. Nobody wanted to come to a bar full of Gaybos. People thought they'd catch their death.

Walter had tried to explain this to the Gaybos, many times. They had laughed uproariously at him.

"Walter," they'd said, "nobody ever came in here before us—except a couple of your old Zeke buddies, and they're dead, Walter. We're the only business you've got."

Walter said, "Ah, shit—this used to be the busiest hotel on the Hudson."

They said, "Yeah. About fifty years ago. When your mummy and daddy ran it."

Then he started making them drink out of plastic airline cups, so he wouldn't have to clean their glasses. Cleaning their glasses sent shivers up and down his spine.

They laughed uproariously at him.

Cassandra said, "Oh, airline glasses. Very seventies."

Sometimes Cassandra seemed to be the Gaybo Club's mascot, other times its ringleader. About the glasses she'd said:

"Walter, nobody's *ever* coming in here if you serve drinks in airline glasses. Even the airlines don't use airline glasses anymore."

Walter said, "I ought to put a quarantine sign over the door," and they laughed uproariously and did it for him: "QUARANTINE." And though he took it down as soon as he'd noticed it, word got out—and the whole town had a good yuk over it.

He said, "I don't want this place turning into no Gaybo Club!"

Right away they started calling themselves the Gaybo Club.

Once, he threw them all out. Then one night after a week of scant receipts, they all come trooping back in. He said, "I thought I told you to get lost."

They said, "We forgive you, Walter." And Cassandra put her money in the jukebox and punched up Frankie's "High Hopes."

Walter told them, "OK, stay. What the hell do I care? But I tell you this—I'm not putting up any damn frilly pink curtains on the windows."

And they *tsk*ed and said, "Walter. Walter. We love you just the way you are."

So now here it was Saturday night, and usually Saturday brought in enough non-Gaybo business to tempt him into staying open another week. Tempt him into thinking that if he could hang on till summer, maybe the cottage people and the theater crowd would just flood in this time, maybe they'd scatter the Gaybos for good, maybe . . .

But this Saturday night it was pouring out, and there was nobody here but the six Gaybos and the punk girl. A Saturday like this was pure perdition.

The music ended.

One of the Gaybos, Dan, called to Cassandra standing at the jukebox: "Jesus, Cassandra, *play* something. Quit looking for the Butthole Surfers. They're just not *in there,* girl."

And then Walter heard the vestibule's outer door creak open and his heart jumped a little.

"Walter! A customer! Hide the airline glasses!"

The vestibule's inner door opened.

A large black man came in. Tattered coat, mucked and bloodied all over. Lame, wild-eyed, leaving tracks, leaving the door open, the Gaybo Club speechless for the first time in its history.

The apparition crossed the room and sat at the bar.

The apparition said, "Could I have a . . . cranberry juice, please?"

The Gaybo Club exploded in laughter and applause.

"*That* was perfect."

"*That* was a moment that will go down in Walter's Quarantine Bar and Gaybo Club Hall of Fame."

"God! Wonderful! Creature from the black lagoon comes in, orders a cranberry juice."

The black man turned and smiled. "I must look a *sight,* huh?"

"You look like the last chapter of Revelations."

"You look like Walter's latest nightmare."

"No, you look like Cassandra's latest boyfriend."

"Walter, get the man his juice! For Christ's sake."

Walter reluctantly poured out a cranberry juice from a can.

The black man took a sip, and made a face at the sourness. Then he downed the rest.

"How much?"

"Dollar."

The black man put a dollar on the bar.

The Gaybo Club was still gaping amazed at him.

"What *happened* to you?"

He shrugged. "Went to a party. Got thrown out."

"Whoa. Andy, why weren't *you* there?"

"Tell Andy here the address! That sounds like Andy's kind of party!"

Round of laughter. The black man shrugged again. "I don't know the address. The Leppenraub farm."

Silence. That struck a chord all around.

Walter pushed the dollar back toward the black man.

"You got thrown out by David Leppenraub? It's on the house then. Have another. What the hell were you doing with that son of a bitch?"

"Playing piano."

James spoke up. "Looks like you were playing pretty piss poor."

The black man drank down his second cranberry juice.

"No, I think I played pretty well. The hostess said I was magnificent. I think they were just offended by something I said."

"What did you say?"

"I said David Leppenraub was a murderer."

"Whoa."

James asked him, "Who'd he murder?"

"Scotty Gates. You know him?"

Said Andy, "The kid? The kid who modeled for him? He was murdered?"

Then Dan got up from the Gaybos' table and approached the black man.

"You know, you're saying some pretty reckless things, my friend. Saying things like that could get you in a lot of trouble around here."

"So I've noticed."

"But let's keep our priorities straight," Dan went on. "The important thing, the essential information here, is that *you play piano.* Walter, give him a shot of something."

"No thanks, that's OK."

"Whiskey, barkeep. A shot of whiskey for the maestro."

Now the black man seemed nervous. He glanced around the room. His eyes lit upon the old piano in the corner. His whole muddy, scratched-up face seemed to silently groan.

54

Andy and James danced, and the others sang, and Romulus played "On the Street Where You Live." He played it straight. His fingertips were sore, and it hurt to open his left hand where the thorns had dug into it, but he seemed to have no anger at all. He hadn't had the heart to turn these folks down when they had so eagerly pressed him to play, and now he hadn't the heart to play hob with their favorite tune. He even tossed in a few arpeggios.

He even joined in the singing.

While he played, Cassandra stood behind him and absentmindedly picked leaves and thorns off his jacket. Walter sat behind the bar and watched the Knicks game on TV with the sound turned down. But Romulus could see the old dog's lips moving a little, mouthing the words to the tune.

When the tune came to an end, Romulus did feel obligated to leave some sort of a mark on it, so he threw in a volley of sour and unaccommodating chord-stomps. Which it turned out his audience loved. They applauded. They hollered. They brought him another whiskey, though he hadn't finished the first one.

It surprised Romulus, how little damage it had done him to play that tune.

They asked him to play something else.

He tinkered idly with the keys.

"Oh, better not. Better not before Stuyvesant hears me. But tell me something, folks. Walter over there, what's he got against Leppenraub?"

"Oh, he's just jealous. He sold his old barn theater to Leppenraub for peanuts, and Leppenraub fixed it up and made it a big success and that pisses the hell out of Walter—"

Walter grunted from across the room. He said, "That's a lie. That's bullshit. Theater's got nothing to do with it. I just don't like what that pervert does to people. He comes up here and he's fancy-pants city scum, and he's got all this sicko art—"

"Walter, our esteemed art critic—"

"Well maybe I am. Maybe I can see what's bullshit and you can't. So you got a picture of a guy with his John Thomas hanging out, and somebody's smeared blood and shit all over him, I say what's so special? What's so *artistic* about that? Huh? But Leppenraub, he's got you all fooled, and he just takes your money and comes up here and buys everything in sight and he does his sick disgusting things and he makes *toys* out of people, even a poor retarded guy, he treats him like his little sicko *doll*—"

"Walter's talking about his cousin Elon."

Said Romulus, "Elon's his cousin?"

"Walter thinks Leppenraub has done something terrible—"

Walter came out from behind the bar.

"I don't think—I *know*. Everybody knows. Yeah, sure, Elon's kind of slow, but now—well, I say he's goddamn scared spitless. Just look at him—look at the way he shakes. Whatever you say to him, he shakes like you're going to kill him. He didn't used to do that before. Lot of sick stuff going on at that farm, but Leppenraub's got him so scared he won't talk. He won't tell nobody."

Romulus asked, "So why don't you get Elon out of there?"

"Think we haven't tried? We took the bastard to court. Ah, but he's got lawyers coming out of his ass. You should a seen them lawyers! Ah, Christ. He had lawyers crawling all over that judge. They were squeezing his nuts! They were—"

One of the patrons rolled his eyes. Said to Romulus:

"Little bit paranoid, wouldn't you say?"

Romulus nodded. "Yes, it certainly rings true to *me.*"

Said the patron, "No, not true. *Garbage.*"

Behind Romulus, the girl Cassandra said, "Oh, Archie, you *have* to defend the Leppenraubs. You work for the theater."

Romulus raised an eyebrow. "Is that true?"

Archie nodded. "In the summers. I do set construction. Moira Leppenraub runs the foundation, and I work with her all the time."

"Oh, there's another one," said Walter. "The witch."

"No, Walter," said Archie. "Not a witch. Or if she is a witch, she's a white witch—OK? She's all right. And look—I've been over to the farm lots of times, and I think the way David takes care of Elon is pretty damn generous."

Walter scowled and walked off. "Bullshit."

Said Archie, "Bullshit to you, Walter."

Cassandra shoved Romulus over and took a place next to him on the piano stool. She was a lovely fiery blond kid, and she had a ring in her nose, and she carried with her an ostentatious display of grit-smells: leather, sweat, alcohol, onions, and metal bangles. Whiff of sheep shit from her Guatemalan wool bag.

She didn't strike Romulus as a country girl. She seemed to belong in downtown New York, in the very bowels of downtown.

In her honor, Romulus slapped together a progression of gritty chords.

Then he fixed on Archie. "So those famous evil weekends . . ."

"They're just a fantasy. People like Walter here, they *need* fantasies like that. It nourishes their homophobia."

Walter had taken up his station behind the bar again. He said: "Pah. Don't listen to him, bud, he don't know jack shit. *He* was never invited to those weekends. None of *these* yokels ever went. Leppenraub and his witch-sister, you think they want any *local* trash at their parties? No way."

Cassandra spoke up. "*I* went to a few."

Andy smiled. "Yeah, we've heard about you and the count."

Cassandra shrugged. "So what? So fucking what? I thought Vlad was sexy, so what?"

Andy glossed for Romulus. "Cassandra is often subject to lapses in judgment."

With his left hand, Romulus took a handful of beer nuts from the saucer and began popping them into his mouth, one by one. With his right hand, he played a series of riffs inspired by *Cassandra's Lapses in Judgment*.

He was sore all over. He had not had an easy night. Nevertheless here he was, and damn if his divinity was not content. The Moth-Seraphs slept. No fear, no anger, and his fingers felt right at home. He asked Cassandra:

"So was it a wild time?"

"Oh great. Best ever. He took me to a field and he played his trumpet for me. That was a *blast,* ha ha."

"And did you ever see David Leppenraub get nasty?"

"With me? A girl?" Cassandra snorted. "I don't think he even knew I was there."

"And torture—you didn't see anybody getting—"

Archie bust in. "Crap. Rumor."

Romulus looked at him. "You mean David Leppenraub's parties were all tea parties?"

Andy said, "No, no, we know he's not a saint. But *torture?* Uh-uh. There's just no evidence—"

Walter, from his perch: "*Bullshit! A witness* ain't evidence?"

Romulus stopped tinkering with the keys.

Archie, full of indignant contempt, snapped, "Yeah? Like who's a witness?"

"Like Clive Leif."

Romulus asked, "Who's Clive Leif?"

Said Walter, "Theater kid. Worked for Moira in the playhouse. You remember Clive, don't you, Archie?"

"Sure. But he *liked* David. He respected David."

"That's what he told *you.* 'Cause he was scared. But I got a different story. I got the truth."

Then Walter turned to Romulus and told him: "This guy Clive, he lived here last summer. He was assistant director for the play—that David Mammoth piece a shit—and he lived here, in one of the old hotel rooms upstairs. Nice kid, a southerner, knew a lot about trout fishing. Mostly these theater guys are a pain in the tush. They think they're so hot. I tell 'em, You're so hot, what're you doing in summer stock then, Mr. *De Niro,* what're you—"

Said Archie, "Get to the *point,* Walter."

"Point is, one day, right near the end of the season, Clive comes in here, and he's stone drunk. I tell him, 'You look like you have been having a time.' And he says oh yeah, he's been over at Leppenraub's all weekend. And I ask him if he'd had a *good* time, but he won't say nothing. Then he has a couple of drinks. We're all alone here, in the bar. And then he looks up and he says. 'That man's a fucking monster.' So I ask him who. And he says, 'Leppenraub.' So I ask him what he means, but he won't say. He won't say nothing. He just says, *'Don't ever tell him I told you that. If you tell anybody, he'll kill me. He'll kill you, too.'* And I wouldn't have told, neither—except he's been gone such a long time."

Archie scowled. "Walter, you're making this up."

"I swear to God. Then he tells me he's going. Back to New York, I figure. But uh-uh, he says he's going *home*. Back to North Carolina. Fuck directing, he says. Forget the fucking movies. 'Cause if he doesn't hide real quick and real good, Leppenraub's going to have him killed. That's the last I ever saw of him."

Romulus remembered something.

"This kid, this—"

"Clive Leif."

"Right. You ever see him with a video camera?"

"Sure. He *was* a video nut. Had all sorts of equipment up here."

"Did he ever show you any tapes? Of Leppenraub's weekends or anything like that?"

Archie broke in. "Of course not. There *are* no tapes. This is all a fabrication."

"Which part is the fabrication?"

"All of it."

"Then why did Clive throw his career away and go home?"

"Who says he did?"

This incensed Walter. "You calling me a liar?"

"Just a dreamer," said Archie. "The world needs dreamers."

Said Walter, "*I'll* tell you why he skedaddled. 'Cause he liked to fish, but he didn't want nobody fishing *him* out of the river."

Then he smiled. Grinned at his own wit. Romulus hadn't seen him smile before. The inside of his mouth looked like a Gothic ruin. Cobwebs, tiny bats.

Romulus asked him, "You have an address for him?"

"Uh-uh."

"A telephone number? . . . A friend who might know? . . ."

"Naw. I don't know nothing about him. Except he liked to fish."

"*I* know something."

This was Cassandra. She said: "I know he came from a little town called Lent. I remember 'cause it was such a weird name. Lent, North Carolina, he said."

One of the patrons asked her teasingly, "When did he tell you *that*, Cassandra?"

"None of your business. All right, maybe we were on a date. Maybe I thought he was sexy."

Romulus pressed. "Did he tell you anything else?"

"Yeah, he told me he was going to be the next Jonathan Demme."

"That's all?"

She laughed. "He said I had a cute butt."

They all looked at her, grinning.

"I said he had a cute butt, too."

She shrugged.

"OK. So what? Another lapse in judgment, so fucking what?"

55

Romulus played "A-Tisket A-Tasket."

While he played, Archie put on his coat, murmured his good-nights and left. So did two of the others.

Romulus played "Hit the Road, Jack." Cassandra sang, and the others came in on the *no mo*'s.

Then Romulus's fingers quit on him and anyway his head was swarming with music. A fine bunch of notes but his skull was getting a little crowded. Ache was elbowing out contentment. And he had nothing more to ask these people. Time to hit the road.

He rose.

They gave him a long wave of applause. Even Walter came back out from behind his bar and put his patties together—one clap.

"Hey," he said, "you ever want to come back and play for drinks, why . . ."

They all laughed. Said Andy:

"You're a generous man, Walter, that's why you're such a smashing success."

Then Romulus looked out the window and saw a patrol car pull up.

Cassandra saw it, too. "Oh shit, it's Deputy Warm and Fuzzy. I think I'll just be slipping out the back."

Walter gave her a worried look.

"What's the matter, kid, your ID no good?"

"My ID is great, Walter. You know that. It's just that Warm and Fuzzy thinks it's not in synch with the real me."

She went over and gave Walter a peck on the cheek.

"Gotta run, sweetie. Bye."

Romulus grabbed his coat. "You know, maybe I'll just slip out with you."

"Hey, no need. Warm and Fuzzy won't bother you."

"Yeah? He said if he saw me again he'd send me to Matteawan."

They heard footfalls just outside.

Cassandra asked, "What's Matteawan?"

"Dungeon. But let's talk about it another time, OK?"

The outer vestibule door creaked.

Cassandra dashed for the back of the room. She moved pretty quick considering her tight skirt and clip-clop high heels. Romulus was right behind her. Through a door, through a casualty kitchen, through a rat-shit pantry and upstairs and down a long corridor. A wing of the old hotel. Haunted rooms opening on either side of them.

As they ran she said, "Hey, what did you mean when you said Leppenraub killed Scotty?"

She asked him that out of the blue, as they clattered down the hall.

He said, "You knew Scotty?"

"Sure. He used to be my boyfriend."

"Your *boyfriend?* My . . . Lord. So it's *you?* You're . . ."

"What?" she said. "You've heard something about me?"

He was panting. Struggling to keep up with her.

"I heard . . ."

"What? Who's talking about me? Vlad?"

"Can't talk about it now."

"Hey, why not? I don't give a shit. You can tell me."

"No. Can't. Can't flee and talk at the same time."

"OK. But I wouldn't believe anything *Vlad* told you."

They came to the end of the corridor. There were stairs going down.

"Wait," he said. "Wait."

He stopped. There at the top of the stairs, he hunched over and breathed, and coughed, and said:

"OK. You sure . . . you sure you want to hear this? Vlad. Vlad said. Said you gave him. Um. Manual. Whatever. A hand job. OK? Under the table. When you were having lunch with him. And Scotty and Leppenraub. They were right there. Vlad said."

"He told you that? That son of a bitch."

"So it's a lie."

"*Yeah,* it's a lie. All I did was rub him a little. Oh, don't look at me like that. It seemed like a fun thing at the time. We got to get out of here."

He followed her down the stairs.

As they descended he asked her, "Did Scotty ever find out about you and Vlad?"

"Oh shit. You going to blame me for Scotty going crazy?"

Then they were out. In the rain, in the long alley between the hotel and the barn-theater.

"Come on," said Cassandra. "My car's in the back lot."

They headed down the alley.

A flaring of headlights nailed them to their shadows.

Romulus looked back. A car was turning in, coming toward them. It drove under the lamp at the end of the alley. The scarlet death car.

"Run!" he cried to Cassandra.

They raced helter-skelter down the alley, Romulus desperately looking for any way out. But no chance. No ditch this time, no friendly grove of sumac. No, this time the assassin had him dead to rights. Except this time there was a witness. But what would that matter to Leppenraub? Leppenraub would gladly run them *both* down. Double his pleasure.

Then Romulus heard the car brake, just behind him. A voice: "Romulus."

He looked back. It was Moira.

"Romulus, wait! You're in danger!"

He drew up. So did Cassandra.

Cassandra said, "Jesus, Moira, you scared the shit out of us."

"Darcy?"

"Long time, huh, Moira?"

"Darcy, what the hell are *you* doing here?"

"Trying to get the hell away from here."

Said Moira, "Well, thank God I found you. Look, Romulus, I think they—you can't let Herman—I mean that deputy—you can't let him catch you again. Come on, get in with me."

He thought about it.

On the one hand, getting into any car with any Leppenraub struck him as about the stupidest idea imaginable. However, this running was getting old. And there were still a host of questions nagging at him. And he wanted to get out of the rain. And he wanted very much to get another glimpse of that coach house.

And her tone did not seem too unkind.

He said, "Moira, I don't know."

"Rom. *Please.*"

Cassandra was fidgeting. "Mister, you going with her or what? I got to be somewhere else."

Romulus decided. No real thought involved, just a tumbling down a slope. He was getting good at tumbling down slopes. He tumbled into the decision to stay with Moira Leppenraub.

He said, "You be OK, Cassandra?"

"Oh yeah. Hey, it's been fun."

"Thanks for the drinks."

"Thanks for the music."

She gave him a kiss on the cheek. When she did, he smelled all the well-scrubbed kid smells just underneath the grit-smells. Soap, aloe, and cream rinse. The kid core of her. Then she turned and clip-clopped away.

And Romulus got into the death car.

56

They drove past the theater parking lot and down a steep slope. Romulus could see the lights of a village across the Hudson— misty gold and ruby lights. The river itself was a great belt of utter blackness. The ice, Romulus thought, was probably breaking up out there. Probably making a lovely racket. He wouldn't mind driving down there right now and stopping to listen. But tonight, he supposed, was not the night for it.

Then they turned onto a country road and sped around curves. He hunkered down low in the leather seat. She looked over at him.

"You OK?"

"Yes, I'm very well, thank you. And you?"

"Rom, you look terrible."

"Well, it's past my bedtime. Whatever made you suppose that I'm in any sort of danger?"

"I heard my brother. I was cleaning up and the phone rang and when I picked it up I heard my brother—"

"Hey, is this your car, Moira?"

"Are you kidding? I drive a Civic. In the shop. I'm just borrowing—"

"Will this seat go down? The seat went down in Arnold's car— will it go down in this one?"

"Sure."

She hit a button on the dash and the seat sighed and leaned back, and Romulus sighed and leaned with it.

He said, "This is all right. I mean, seats used to go down in my day, too, just not so far."

He watched the headlights carving out stun-lit country scenes. Drooping boughs, dripping leaves. A stone church. A rail fence. A fireplug.

Many arrogant eagles on mailboxes.

He asked her, "So what did you hear?"

"I heard David say something like, 'I don't want to hear you didn't. I don't want to hear about it at all. I just want you to take care of things.' That's all. That's all he said. Then he hung up."

"Well, maybe he was talking to his agent. Maybe he was talking to the Louvre. What makes you think he was talking about me?"

"He was scared tonight. What you were saying about him scared him. I've never seen him like that. He's scared of dying, I know that, but *you* scared him even worse."

"So you think he hired a hit man to kill me? Tonight? Kind of short notice for a hit man."

"I know that. I'm not saying—"

Romulus mused, "It'd have to be somebody close to him. Somebody he relied on. Who might that be?"

"I don't know. What are you thinking?"

"I'm not thinking anything. I'm just trying to stay alive. So how did you know I was still in town?"

"There was another call that came in. I made sure I got to this one first. I thought if it was the same caller, I could at least hear the voice."

"Hey, doesn't Vlad ever answer the phone?"

"He does when he's around. He wasn't around. I don't know where he was. Anyway, this time it was Archie calling—Archie who does sets at the theater. He'd just been with you at Walter's bar. He thought we should know you were in there saying bad things about David."

"All I said was, David Leppenraub's a murderer."

"Jesus," said Moira. "You know . . . that's . . ."

"What?"

"That's my brother you're . . ."

Said Romulus, "Yes. I know. So who sent Herman the deputy to Walter's bar?"

"David. David says you're a crazy psycho and you have to be locked up before you hurt somebody."

"I see. When assassination doesn't work, call the cops."

She glanced over at him. "Rom, what *happened* to you? David told me they were just going to put you on a bus for New York."

"They did. I got off at the wrong stop though. Then somebody tried to kill me."

"Kill you? Kill you how?"

"Thorns. State of the art."

"I don't understand."

"Makes two of us."

"Who are you, Rom? You're not from California. You really still live in that cave?"

"Mm."

"And you knew Scotty?"

"A friend of mine did."

"You think my brother killed him?"

"What do *you* think, Moira?"

Another glimpse of the river. The rosary-bead lights of a far-off bridge.

Finally she said, "My brother . . . I don't know, my brother has a tough streak. But people have been tough on him. He came out when he was sixteen years old. And where we grew up, this little town in Missouri—this was in the late sixties—well you just didn't do that. But *he* did it. One day some friends of his were ragging on queers, and he said, 'I'm a queer.' That was it. That simple.

"I remember the day. I was in second grade, and in that one day the word got all the way down to my class. Some of the girls came up at recess and said, 'Your brother says he's a queer. that makes *you* a queer.' And I came home and I was bawling and I went in David's room and started hitting him, and calling him everything I'd heard that day. 'Queer.' 'Faggot.' 'Homo.' Not 'gay,' we didn't have that word then. And he held me till I stopped and then he said, 'Sex is what you do because you love. You have sex with the one you love, not with the one you're *supposed* to love. It's not a duty. It's love.'

"I never forgot that. But I think David did.

"Because they were just so goddamn cruel to him. He used to come home all black and blue and his clothes torn and he wouldn't say who did it, but he got colder and colder. And that chill, that worked into his art. I don't know what happened to that pure love. I don't know where his heart is. Maybe he feels a little love for me, but that'd be just a guess. Really, I think he hardly knows I exist. He won't even look at my art. He rents me the studio, he lets me run his foundation, his theater and all, but that's just . . . for form's sake, I think. So people will say how much David Leppenraub loves his family. But he doesn't really give a flying shit what I do."

"You hate him for that?"

"I'm a little sick of being David Leppenraub's little sister. I mean are they going to put on my tombstone, 'She Was a Loving Sister to David Leppenraub'? Christ. I'm just as . . . Jesus fucking Christ! I'm a goddamn better artist than he is."

A few seconds slipped by. Then she said, "Whoops. That was dumb. That was stupid, competitive—"

Romulus, with nothing useful to say, said, "No, but I bet you are. Better, I mean." And instantly regretted it.

Moira shot back, "How the fuck would *you* know? You've never seen my stuff."

"I . . . I saw some things in *Artforum.*"

"Jesus, why did I say that? I've never said that to anyone. Why did I say that to *you?*"

Romulus shrugged.

Moira said, "Well, forgive me, would you? I didn't mean it. I think my brother's a *great* artist."

They sat in silence for a long while. Then she said: "Look, the only thing my brother's got now is *esteem,* and now that's in jeopardy. And he's sick, he's so sick, Rom, he's not thinking straight, and he doesn't know what the hell he's doing. So yeah, I guess . . . I guess he might be capable . . . of having someone . . . killed. Yes. Though it makes me . . . to even *say* it, it makes me . . ."

"What are you going to do, Moira?"

"Me?"

"You're in there. You're with him. You tell this sad story. It is sad, but he's still a murderer. You're still living with a murderer."

She thought about it.

"Maybe I could go live in a cave?"

She tried to laugh but couldn't. She said, "I can't just walk away. Everything in my life is connected to my brother. And I still love him."

She kept thinking.

"Do you have any evidence, Rom? I mean any hard evidence that he killed Scotty?"

"No, not yet."

"Oh, God, what if this is all craziness? You *are* a crazy man, for Christ's sake. I mean, I saw you. Tonight, when you went into that—"

"Fit. Right. I did that. I am nuts."

She said, "And I could be nuts, too. This could all be . . . just delusion. Paranoia—"

"You heard him tell his hit man to kill me."

"No I didn't—I heard him tell *someone* to *take care of things.*"

145

"That li'l someone tried to run me over. Then tried to gun me down."

He glanced at her and she glanced back. She was crying. She said, "Romulus, I don't want anyone to hurt you."

She tried to focus on her driving.

"But that's my *brother* you're talking about for Christ's sake."

57

Well."

Romulus said only that.

Then he was quiet. His lids sank. They nearly shut. He saw only the green undersea lights of the dash. And now and then the white silk of Moira's forearm as she moved the shift. He made up these lines and sang them silently to himself:

> Way down here, where the seahorse czar,
> And his briny ballerinas brew barnacle beer . . .

He felt the car brake slowly. He lifted his lids high enough to see that they had come to a dark crossroads.

"Romulus. Where do I take you now?"

Sleepiness in his murmur. "I don't know. Your studio is in the coach house, right?"

"Uh-huh."

"Well. Your work then. I'd love to see your work, Moira. Would you show me your work?"

And a few minutes later, sweeping up the drive around the old farmhouse—here was the barn, here was Elon's little chicken-coop house, here was the great field and the road under tulip trees—why, it was a little like returning after a long absence to some favorite old haunt.

Remember the wild party when David called the police on me? And whatever happened to that strange guy Vlad?

Still, Romulus scooched down very low in the seat, in case someone happened to be still about. No one was. All windows dark.

They cruised on up to the coach house.

"Sure David won't come back here? Or Vlad?"

"This is *my* place, Rom. All Leppenraubs are sticklers for privacy. They'd know better than to bother me when I'm working."

"Pretty late to be working."

"Lots of times I work till dawn. You're OK here. Come on in."

First, the big room that had once been stables and was now storage. A '52 MG-TD, up on cinder blocks. An old horse-drawn plough. Saddles on the walls.

The golden gondola of a hot-air balloon.

Said Moira, "It was one of David's hobbies. A few years ago. He got about two rides out of it, me in the chase car. Then he nearly ditched in the Hudson, and I found him and his balloonist friend on the shore, drinking champagne with a fisherman, and they were already drunk to the gills and the champagne was gone and I didn't get any, and that was that. He got some good pictures out of it though. I thought the fisherman was kind of . . . interesting. Happier days. Or wilder days, anyway."

A rusty seeder. A pair of motorbikes. A pool table. A big walk-in freezer. Romulus walked in. Bare. He turned back to Moira.

"Where's the beef?"

"No more. He used to have these *huge* barbecues, you know. But he's too sick now for that kind of diet. I gave away all the meat. You should have seen it all. Donated it to the men's shelter in Poughkeepsie. Feed them for years."

But Romulus scarcely heard her—he had his eyes on the pool table. Something about the pool table made him uncomfortable. He sniffed. No stench of Y-rays. But still, *something.*

Was this it? Was this the clue? Was this the source of the stench that his music tonight had been searching for?

He went over and lifted the plastic cover. Peeled it back.

Moira shrugged. "He doesn't even play pool anymore. It's a beautiful table, though, isn't it?"

That green again. That sea color. Except—

"Except, Moira—what's this brown stain here? On the felt."

"I don't know. I've never noticed it before. Barbecue sauce?"

147

He tried to think—or *not* to think: he tried to feel, in his heart, what the story was here. It was a bloodstain, he was sure. A Rorschach stain of blood, right in the dead center of the table. So if Scotty had been strapped down here, the bloodstain would have been just under his genitals. . . .

Some rite of sacrifice?

Some kind of crucifixion?

On a fucking pool table?

But if they had done anything to Scotty's genitals, Matthew would have noticed. Matthew would have told him about that, for sure.

For a long while Romulus rummaged in his heart for the key. Moira stood by patiently.

Nothing. He put the plastic back.

"Ready?" Moira said.

"Ready."

58

There was a narrow hall, and on the other side of it another huge room, and this was her studio. And taking up fully a third of it was a perfect replica of a woodlands cave.

"Jesus," said Romulus.

"I'm just finishing it," she said. "Go ahead. Go on in."

He stepped inside the cave. There was a faint bluish light he couldn't find the source for, and by that light he saw the drawings. Drawings all over the walls.

A herd of aurochs. A feast, a celebration. You let the drawings lead you in, the narrow passage curving you into the cave's bowels. Pentangles. Sketches of crudest eros. A snake with a two-pronged phallus. The blue light flickering.

Fire.

Torture.

Crucifixion.

A man with no face, wearing a white hood.

And then he saw that the cave walls were stained as that pool table had been stained. The walls of the passage closed in and the air grew heavy, and he saw a naked victim with bleeding crotch, and there were willow-limbed women tossing his vitals among them, and then the blue light fluttered out.

He was in utter darkness.

A heave of panic.

He turned, felt along the walls. Found light, stumbled forward into the bright studio. Moira was sitting on a stool with her knees up. She giggled. She looked into his face and she broke out laughing.

"Did it spook you?"

"Light went out."

"It's supposed to. Supposed to flicker out."

"My Lord."

"Oh. You're too tired for this, aren't you?"

"I may be. But as far as I'm concerned, you're a better artist than your brother."

"I'll vote for that. Also wilder. Take more risks. Take lots of wild risks. Come upstairs with me."

59

He had his shirt off and his pants, and was dressed in only the silken undershorts that Bob and Betty had given him, and he lay facedown on the fluffy old bed. He had showered in her bathroom, he was squeaky clean, and now he lay on Moira's bed and she was applying an ointment to his cuts. An ointment she'd mixed herself, with her oils and herbs. The active ingredient being essence of slippery elm bark. Moira said that if it was no good at warding off rumors, it was still great for cuts. She said it was what doctors in the Revolutionary War had used on battle wounds. She rubbed it in gently, with her thumbs.

It did seem to ease the sting.

He had asked her a question, and she was pondering it.

"Uh-uh," she said, "I don't think so. *Stuyvesant?* I thought he lived a long time ago."

"Not this Stuyvesant."

"Well, I've never known *any* Stuyvesant. That I can remember. Anyway, the priest-figure in my cave—he's got no face because—well, that's just the style of the drawings. He's got a white hood because I based him on the Druids. So who's Stuyvesant?"

He tried to tell her. About Stuyvesant and his tower and the Y-rays. Meanwhile, outside, a long ways off, a barred owl kept asking over and over, "Who cooks for you? Who cooks for *you*-all?"

Moira worked a long time and as tenderly as she could at the big gash on his neck.

"This was a thorn did this, Rom?"

"Or a bunch of thorns. I don't know, it was dark. Felt like about fifty yards of barbed wire."

"You're in bad shape."

"I've survived though. I'm just beginning to grasp this."

"Turn over."

He did. She went to work on the cuts in front.

She had an ungodly beauty.

"So what I want to know is, Rom, I mean this is a great story, this wicked guy in the tower—but you know it's not *reality*, don't you?"

"Sure," he said.

"I mean, not the reality of, well, say, this cup of ointment, or the cigarette burn on this nightstand—Stuyvesant's not real in *that* way?"

"Oh shit, no. No, of course not. Stuyvesant's not real at all."

"OK," she said.

"Stuyvesant's much truer than reality."

"Oh."

"Stuyvesant *invented* reality."

"Oh."

"In the spring of 1913. Though in truth the man who did most of the work was a chemist by the name of Lem Mulkhoo. I suppose you never heard of him."

"I haven't."

"He was my great-grandfather's cousin. He had a lab in

Harlem. He was a genius, and he was working on this drug to cure old age, and in those days, who was Stuyvesant? Stuyvesant was just a two-bit snake-oil salesman. That's all.

"See, Stuyvesant sold patent medicines to the black folks that were just coming into Harlem then. And he hated Lem Mulkhoo because Lem Mulkhoo's cures truly worked, and so Stuyvesant couldn't make any money selling his quack shit. Right?"

Moira nodded. "Right. Do you think Stuyvesant sold any essence of slippery elm bark?"

"No. He only sold remedies that were of no value at all."

She went to work kneading his shoulders.

He said, "So one night Stuyvesant snuck into Mulkhoo's lab. He found the vat where Mulkhoo was brewing up his new elixir. Oh, and I forgot this part, but this is very important—Stuyvesant loved Lem Mulkhoo's daughter. She was . . . a *vision,* you know what I'm saying? She was like a Nubian princess, you know?—and Stuyvesant thought about that girl's pussy all day, that's *all* he thought about. And he had plenty of charm, he thought he could have charmed that girl right into his bed, but Lem Mulkhoo wouldn't let him *near* her. You with me?"

Moira nodded.

"So Stuyvesant, he sneaks into Lem Mulkhoo's lab one night, and he pours *hemlock* into the vat. So Mulkhoo will make this drug that's poison, and have to go out of business. Maybe it wasn't hemlock. Most sources say it was hemlock, but there's this other guy, this historian Hodovitch, he says it was this chemical compound, *triarsenium coagulatene* I think he says. Anyway, whatever it was, Lem Mulkhoo came back to the lab unexpectedly, and he saw what Stuyvesant was doing and he tried to stop him. They wrestled, and then Stuyvesant threw Lem Mulkhoo into the vat.

"And when Mulkhoo came out of the vat, he was the same, only *defeat* was all over him, just this gray color of defeat and the sound of the spirit in chains, that's a gray sound, chink-chink, right, and the smell of degradation, and Stuyvesant says, 'Hoo hoo—I got something here!'

"And now he had power over Lem Mulkhoo, and he put him to work. He had Mulkhoo make his concoction into a vapor and one day Stuyvesant let that vapor go. That was August 14, 1913.

He let it waft over the city. And he called it the *real,* which is Spanish for the royal fuck-over."

"But he still, he still couldn't get Lem Mulkhoo's daughter. She was immune somehow to the *real.* And Stuyvesant got angry, and he put Mulkhoo to work again, and Mulkhoo came up with a concentrated version of the stuff, a beam, a wave, and it made people say *yes* to all Stuyvesant's shit, and so Stuyvesant called them *Yes*-rays. Or Y-rays, right?

"But even the Y-rays didn't get to Mulkhoo's daughter, and I saw her once, she was a very old woman and I was just a kid, and she was my second cousin twice removed, and this was in the Bronx. Long time ago. She was still tall, and she didn't take no shit, and she was nearly blind. When I saw her, she was crossing the street. I didn't see her too well, 'cause the sun was in my eyes. But I was looking right at her, and I saw this white car come out of nowhere and it ran her down. Usually, you know, Stuyvesant sends a goon. But not that time. This job he did himself. I saw his no-face, his white cowl. That's the truth. And he didn't stop, he just roared on out of there. My mama was screaming, and she just picked me up and got me out of there."

"Did your mother know it was your cousin that was run over?"

"No, I figured it out on my own. When I grew up. I just put all the pieces together, bit by bit. That feels good, where you're rubbing. Thank you. But the thing is, there's many who are still immune. Immune to this reality poison. More blacks than whites are immune, but some whites, too. So Stuyvesant hasn't won yet. Stuyvesant could still be overthrown. But never underestimate him. He's clever. You could never outclever him. You can only put your heart out in front of you, and pray for that son of a bitch to fall."

By now, of course, Romulus smelled the smoke. It was pouring out of their loins, so how could he miss it?

60

From Moira the smoke was pure and had the fragrance of the sun in North Carolina. From him it was incinerator smoke, sooty, a lot of trash smoldering, lot of stuff that wouldn't burn right, and when she brought her fingers down his clavicle he couldn't help but close his eyes and linger on a flash of his wife, of sweet Sheila, long ago, getting out of the tub in her folks' apartment when her folks had gone to visit relatives, and all of her was smooth as glass except the elbow he was kissing, which was whorled and knobbled like tree bark and dripping bathwater.

He opened his eyes and Moira was just as lovely as she had been, despite that she was not that woman in the bathtub.

He enveloped Moira's hand in his own. He had not taken a woman's hand in his own for more years than he could count. She took her hand back. She spoke solemnly.

"Rom, were you telling the truth? When you say you could hold a lighted match inside your mouth and make yourself look like a jack-o'-lantern?"

"Do you have a match?"

"Just a minute."

She ran downstairs.

He lay there and listened to the owl. The owl laughed maniacally.

He could have fallen asleep.

It occurred to him that he might not get out of here alive and he smiled at that.

Then Moira came back and he lit a match and motioned for her to turn off the light. She did. He drew breath very slowly, because that was the secret, maintaining an even, constant flue. He aimed the flame toward him and gently put the match inside his mouth, and closed the gate of his teeth over it. Moira laughed. She said she had never seen a holy man do *that* before. He knew what she was seeing, because he had practiced the trick before many mirrors. He knew she could see the light right through his translucent lips and nostrils. And that he looked a flaming beast of skullish dark.

His lungs started to ache a little and he coughed the flame out.
He struck another match, and relit the candle beside the bed.
He sat up, and they were still laughing, and he kissed her.

She didn't embrace him, but drew him to her with her claws
resting lightly on his back. The kiss was all lips, no tongue. Just a rocking of dry lips. He breathed in the air she had just breathed out. He
ran his fingers along her side, where her stomach dipped in, where her
hip flared out, where her short dress ended, and then he was sweeping
along the skin of her thigh, his fingers sparking. He looked into her
eyes. Even up close they were skewed. With a wild hedgerow of
lashes. He pressed those lashes between his lips and tugged at them.

Then she moved till she was on her knees on the bed, and she
pushed him back. Her hair flowed over his cheek and neck and chest
and wrapped around him. The tip of his tongue surveyed the space
between her gums and her lip. With her finger she wrote something
in his palm. He felt the moisture of her panties against his thigh.
Heard her hoarse breath. The wind spiraling down through her
pipes. He stroked the back of her thigh. Slight marbling of cellulite
there, and he traced circles around the puckers. All the while her
hands were grazing on his back.

His great grizzly-back.

She was careful to touch him lightly but sometimes her fingers
did drift over a thorn scratch, and it might have smarted somewhere
in his brain stem, but the news was not sent on upstairs.

They moved again. She reached up her arms, and he slid the
dress off her. Then he was on his back, and she pulled at his shorts.
But his cock had come through the fly, had hooked the elastic waist,
and the shorts wouldn't come down. She did something that involved shifting his cock with her cool fingers, which involved bolts
of amok electricity, and then she drew off the silk shorts. They
moved, she rolled onto her back and he was above her. She lifted
her ass and he wobbled her panties down to her knees, her ankles,
they were gone. Removing them released a cloud of smoke in the
room and he breathed it in and nearly lost his balance.

They collided. They squeezed the breath out of each other—
and still they were not close enough. Must ratchet up the pressure.
Must graft skin, cohabit the same pouch of flesh. Their tongue-
flickerings burned away a few inches of candle. She stroked his cock

with her thumb. He moaned, she growled gently. He showed his teeth and snarled, she snapped and their teeth were flashing at each other and then he kissed her all along the jawbone. He dipped and kissed the cornsilk of her armpit, her nipples, which were maroon, then her seven true ribs and five false ones. He made a circle of kisses around her navel. He knelt beside the bed, and she shifted and opened her legs to him.

Her pubic hair was delicate and sparse, and her fragrance was not the tropical mango of his wife but a high heath fragrance. Juniper. Frosty and sharp. He leaned in and pressed his lips to her. His tongue made a small question mark. She whimpered. He held her hands in his. They passed messages through their fingers, and he looked up across her flesh at her fluttering lashes and kept making those question marks with his tongue. She let go of his hands and tried to get a purchase on his hair, and when she couldn't she grabbed his ears, and then letting go of those, snatched at the bedspread. She moaned. Cried out. He held her at the arch of the back, where her skin was rippled like hard beach sand, and her moans came in waves. She smothered him between her thighs. She drenched his face in her essence. Then suddenly she broke free, pivoted and then she was kissing him wildly, upside down, tongue to tongue flat out, and twisting and slithering off the bed into his arms.

They were a sprawl on the floor. Then she sat up and stretched out her arm, reached for something on the nightstand.

When she'd brought up the matches, it turned out, she'd also brought a condom.

She opened the package with her teeth. While he thought of some point at the core of her, somewhere back of her navel, the last turn in the labyrinth, the grotto of absolute dark warmth and blood-press—and this was where he wished to be. His wishing was the only complete notion in his head.

There were, however, other *fragments* of thought.

There was a fragment of the girl who had been his first lover.

There was a fragment of the Danish girl with splendid legs who studied the flute at Juilliard and who told him she'd never known a man who so lived and breathed sex, and she guessed if he ever went a week without it, it would probably kill him.

There was that piece of Sheila in the bathtub, and other memories or half memories of her that surfaced or did not surface. So many shards, thousands of them, things that were lost to him, Jesus, so much stolen! Such goddamn incomprehensible larceny and pillage, and it was a wonder he could even get it up but he certainly could, and then he came into Moira and the losses were not canceled but anyway forgotten.

She surged against him. Kept surging, and their joined mouths were an echo chamber. She shook her hair, and a great deal of time fell out of it. The candle guttered out. At some point he heard her say:

"Oh. Oh. Oh. Oh. *Oh.*"

61

After a while they pulled down the covers and crawled under them.

"We'll have to get up very early, Rom. I'll drive you to Poughkeepsie, to the bus. But before it's light."

"OK."

They held each other.

Then he remembered something he had wanted to ask.

"Moira."

"Hmm."

"That girl I was with tonight? You called her Darcy."

"That's her name. Darcy Reynolds."

"She called herself Cassandra."

He felt her shrug. "Yeah, well she dreams of playing drums in some downtown noise band. I'm glad she's picked out a name. Now all she has to do is buy a ticket to the city. I bet she never gets around to that one, though."

"And she was Scotty's girlfriend? But I thought you said Scotty's girlfriend was *innocent.*"

"She is sort of innocent. She just likes to sleep around a lot. Scotty never got used to that."

"Mm."

Again he started to drift.

Then he thought of something else.

"Moira?"

"Yeah?"

"You know someone named Clive Leif?"

Silence for a moment. Then she said, "Sure."

"A director?"

"He wants to be."

"Any good?"

"Sort of. He's young. His ideas are sort of all over the place."

"He knows David?"

"Yeah. I introduced them—they hit it off. Well, Clive's into photography and video and all—"

"So I hear. What happened to him?"

"Clive? I haven't seen him for months. Somebody said he quit the Great Star Search and went home."

"But if he was a good director—"

"He's OK—he's not fabulous. He was good-looking—he could have been an actor maybe. I'm not sure he had the brains or the focus to direct. I guess he realized that, though. Some people hang on for years, you know? Some people never get the news. Actually, I was a little surprised Clive cottoned on so quick."

"Terror opens the eyes."

"Romulus?"

"Hm?"

"Just hold me for a while. OK? Don't ask any more of your questions for a while?"

62

Sometime during the night Sheila came in the room. It was pretty embarrassing, her catching him like that.

She folded her arms.

"You having fun with the white girl, boy?"

He tried to bury his head under the pillow.

She poked him hard in the ribs. He sat up.

"You hear me?"

"Yes I did. Yes. Yes I'm having fun. Tonight I had the most fun since . . . since you threw me out."

"Threw you out? You were never around, what was there to throw? I just got myself out of the damn hotel business."

"Right. That's a better way to put it, right."

"Damn zookeeper business."

"Right."

"Well then. Is she giving you second thoughts about your cave nonsense?"

"I don't even have first thoughts. I'm too tired to think."

Sheila went to the window and looked out. Her bird-of-prey profile, checking out the farm.

"Boy, I see a light on in the big farmhouse."

"That'd be Leppenraub. He's worrying about my next move. I'm going to get him, Sheila. I'm going to get the evidence, and I'm going to nail that bastard."

"Uh-huh. *Have mercy on us, oh Lord of Vengeance.* So you still think you're the great private detective? Where's your *white* car, boy?"

"OK, I was wrong about that. The car's red. So what?"

"But you were *sure* about that white car. You said you had an eye for things that other folks couldn't see. You said all sorts of shit. Oh baby. If your shit was a rocket ship, you could go to the *moon.* What the hell are you up here messing for, boy?"

"Love. For love's sake. My friend was in love with the kid Leppenraub murdered."

Sheila looked out the window again. She was looking at that light in the farmhouse. Weighing things out. Then she turned to Romulus.

She said, "*Uh*-uh."

"What?"

"I just said, uh-uh."

"You don't think he did it?"

"You're being misled."

"Oh, goddamn it, Sheila—who's misleading me?"

She sniffed the air. "What's that smell? Some kind of ointment?"

"Essence of slippery elm bark."

"What's that? Voodoo? I don't like it."

"Who's misleading me?"

"You are. As usual. As usual, boy, you've picked yourself out an enemy, and he can do no right. But look at that man! You're so scared of him, you can't see him. If you'd open your eyes, you'd see he's got more fear than you do yourself. And it's not a guilty fear, baby—it's just plain *fear.*"

"You think Matthew was lying to me about him?"

She gave it a moment. "Matthew doesn't seem like much of a liar."

"Well then, what? You think Scotty lied to Matthew? But why would Scotty have lied? He was the *victim,* Sheila. Leppenraub did those things to him, and then he killed him to shut him up. And tonight he tried to kill me."

"Pah! That man couldn't kill anybody. He doesn't have it in him. Which you know as well as I do."

"I don't—"

"Of course you do. I'm all in your head, so you can't help but know what I know. You just won't own up to it."

"Then who came hunting for me tonight?"

"That I can't say. *Somebody's* up to no good, for sure. Something sure stinks here. There's a mess of evil in this place. I don't know what you want to be hanging around for, breathing it in. No, I do know. You're here 'cause you're just sick of being a *nobody.* You're not fit for it. You never were fit for it. I heard you play tonight."

"What'd you think?"

She waggled her fingers. "Rusty."

"But better than at Bob and Betty's?"

"A little. You're not hopeless. Your brother's got a piano, why don't you—"

"Sheila. Leave me alone."

"Fine. I'll be on my way. And if you got any brains left that aren't scrambled, so will you. You'll get up out of your cozy love nest, *holy man,* and be gone before you get yourself murdered in your sleep."

"Where *you* going?"

"Home."

"How'd you get here?"

"I rode in on your dream. Which is just rags of a dream now, and fixing to blow away."

"So, go then."

"I'm going. This is the craziest you've ever been, Romulus. You better wake up. You hear me? Have I ever told you wrong, baby? When I come to you like this, have I ever lied to you?"

He shook his head, slowly, reluctantly.

Said Sheila, "Then listen to what I say. *You're being misled, and you better wake up.*"

"Go, Sheila."

"I'm *already* gone."

63

She was. And Romulus was wide awake.

Listening to the sound of a car.

An engine running. Smooth as butter. So smooth that at first it fooled him into thinking it was his own steady breathing. But when he held his breath, the engine kept on, softly churning.

He lifted his head from the pillow and looked out the window. Splashes of moon, a clearing breeze. Maybe it was just the sound of that breeze he'd heard.

He reached for his lover in the dark. But that didn't work—didn't ease his anxiety at all. His lover wasn't there.

He rose. Quickly in the dark he found his pants and pulled them on. Skip the shorts. Nor did he have time for socks, nor for buttoning his shirt. He got his shoes on, and grabbed the coat and jacket and shoved the socks into the coat pocket and went out into the hall, and listened.

He heard a voice. Low, a man's voice. Downstairs. Somewhere

in the big storage room. Then just a musical ripple on the silence—this must have been Moira's voice.

It was reasonable to suppose that his assassin had arrived. Also a solid conjecture that Moira wouldn't be able to keep him down there for very long.

He tiptoed across the hall and stepped into Moira's big upstairs parlor. He got to the window and pushed it up. Got it up about a foot before it stuck. He put out his head and squeezed his shoulders through, and then he human-jacked the sash, straining against it, pushing it up with his shoulders. *Everything you've got.* He worked another four inches out of it. The last inch coming with a small screech. Pray that the hunter hasn't heard, and you can just forget a graceful exit—*scramble.*

He wriggled out headfirst, onto the steeply pitched gable roof. The shingles were still slick with rain, and he was no sooner out the window than he started to slide forward. He put his hands down to stop himself but he kept sliding. He shimmied sideways as he sailed over the edge and managed to grab hold of the rain gutter with one hand. Then the gutter shuddered free of him and he dropped. Landed in the fallow flower bed below and there was another swarm of thorns, his old friends the thorns.

He was back of the coach house.

No lawn, just straight into the woods here.

He picked his way through the moon-tattered trees, and angled over to the tulip-tree road. He crossed the road and clambered over the rock wall, and he was out in the open. The broad field before him. Away down at one end of it was the big barn and the house.

Just as Sheila had said, there was one window lit up in an upstairs room of the big house. He aimed for that light.

Figuring he'd keep to the field, skirt around the house and then make his way to the road out of here. And we'll see from there.

He kicked through the high grass. A cool wind came up and above him the moon sailed into a patch of clear sky. And he noticed a faraway sheen to his right and realized this was the Hudson River. Lovely night. He wasn't afraid now, and though he felt light-headed from lack of sleep, there was little trouble in his head. The Moth-Seraphs weren't stirring at all. In fact, maybe they were gone, maybe they'd all flown the coop, flown out through his ears when he was making love to Moira.

Making love to Moira. He brought his fingers to his nose and breathed. Her scent was all over his fingers, and after breathing it in he was doubly light-headed, and his walking through the grass had a bit of dance in it, and a bit of stagger.

Abruptly he stopped. Looked about him.

Just hold on now. Doesn't that moonlight have an uncommon and unlikely *green* undertone to it?

He studied that shifting vague viridescence, and he woke up— woke up suddenly and truly now to what was going on.

Oh, the deceit was very subtle.

Of course there was no stench of Y-rays here.

Stuyvesant could never have done *this* with Y-rays.

Y-rays were for helling over a place. Y-rays were for crudely hewing out the forms of backed-up toilets and tax collectors and kids caught in drug-war crossfire and the gray death gathering on the faces of subway straphangers—

But for *this*—

For this sheen on the Hudson and for martinis with little onions in them, for the complacency of his drowsy loins, for the smell of sex and the smell of a rich man's fields after a rain shower—

For this eerie core of well-being now residing in Romulus's bowels—

Oh, to fashion such perfidious and mendacious appearances as *these,* you'd need something much more potent and devious than Y-rays—

You'd need a new and wickeder radiance—

Radiance soft as moonlight, but *green,* the hushed green of first spring—

And so this was it, at last. Stuyvesant had finally done it. Come up with his puissant new weapon:

Z-rays.

64

As soon as Romulus had grasped the existence of Z-rays, the complexion of everything around him changed. He stood there stunned. Looked up at the moon. The moon had given everything away, and now the clouds were rushing back in a panic to throw some veils over the thing. Romulus stood there and slowly shook his head.

Then he heard a snarling beside him.

He turned. The husky, Lao-tse. Who threw back its head and started howling bloody murder.

65

Lao-tse couldn't figure it out.

She'd no sooner started barking than the stranger had gone down with a *whump*. And now there he was, lying on his back with his arms outstretched and his eyes wide open to the sky and he was clearly dead. And Lao-tse had uttered less than half a howl.

Well, it was clear that she simply didn't know her own power.

Though there was still a chance the stranger was shamming. She came a little closer, still snarling, and sniffed at the shoes. Oh yes, now she remembered this one.

Suspicious-Shoes. By God she'd keep these shoes for herself. After she'd ripped the stranger's throat open, and tasted a few of the choicer organs, why, she'd just pull these exotic ships of stink off his feet and take them and bury them somewhere—for future meditation.

She moved up on the leg, sniffing. But when she came close to the groin, she got a disconcerting surprise—a blast of her *mistress's* crotch smell. She stepped back. Tried to think it out. Came back and took another sniff and it was Moira's crotch all right—but this stranger was wearing it—this guy from the walk today, this lunatic from the soiree contretemps.

What the hell?

Suddenly she caught a downdraft of breath from his nostrils—oh, so he *was* shamming. He raised his head a little. Put his lips together, pursed them in a kiss, and produced a smacking noise which did something funny to Lao-tse—made her feel like a milk pup and also made her forget, for a moment, to tear open his throat.

She kept her snarl out in front of her, and kept her war-hackles high. But she did sort of sidestep her butt over, a little closer to his outstretched hand, and when he brought that hand up and placed it gently on her back, and started that spidery uncanny back scratching of his, that *way*-down-the-back scratching, she pretended not to notice.

She thought, Well, after all, he is a guest. Maybe disemboweling's not in order here. After all, Moira did swap crotches with him, so maybe he's OK, and yes right *there,* that hits the spot, and *after all* . . .

She looked dreamily toward the moon.

She heard footsteps behind her. She looked back.

Oh Christ. Elon.

Coming on with a look of grim determination. He was brandishing a rake.

Lao-tse snapped around again quick and resumed growling at the stranger and hoped to hell Elon hadn't noticed any foolishness or dereliction of duty on her part.

66

*E*lon, no."

Romulus, on his knees, thought to try a chuckle, but it wouldn't come and it wouldn't have stopped Elon anyway. The rake came up over Elon's head, and he swung it down wildly. Romulus leapt back and the thing just missed him. Slammed into the dirt.

Elon tried to pull it out again but it was tangled in a root, and Romulus stepped on it and cried:

"Elon! No!"

Elon yanked at it. He was a small man but strong, and his yank knocked Romulus off balance, and he fell backward onto his butt.

"Elon! I'm on *your* side! For Christ's sake!"

Again Elon brought the rake back behind his head and brandished it, the tines quivering. He stepped forward and Lao-tse advanced with him, snarling.

Romulus, his hands splayed out on the ground behind him, tried to scuttle away from them. Scuttled backward like a crab. They kept coming.

"Listen, for Christ's sake! I'm just trying to get some answers, OK?"

Didn't seem OK at all.

"Elon, *I just want to know who killed Scotty Gates."*

It took a while. The name had to work its way through the impossible plumbing of Elon's brain, and meanwhile he kept coming on, the rake handle shivering in his clutch—and then he paused.

And said, in his high hoarse voice, "Scotty?"

"Do you know? Do you know who killed him?"

"Killed?"

"Right. He's dead. Jesus Christ, they didn't even tell you? Scotty's dead."

"No."

"Yes. Dead."

"Scotty's here. In the coach house. Scotty's in the coach house."

"Not anymore. He's gone."

"No! Scotty's always here! Always!"

"Did you like Scotty, Elon? Was he your friend? What did they do to him? Did they hurt him?"

The rake quivered again. The very suggestion of hurting Scotty seemed to rile him.

"At the parties, Elon. Did they hurt him at the parties?"

Elon shook his head. "I don't go to no parties."

"Whisper, OK? And tell the dog to cool it. *Bad dog,* Lao-tse. *Sit. Bad dog.* You got to tell him. Tell him to *sit."*

Suddenly Elon burst out in a giggle. "Loo-zoo's a *girl.*"

"Whisper. Tell her to sit."

Elon giggled again. "You said *him.*"

"I thought she was a drag queen. Tell her to fucking *sit.*"

Elon shrugged. And whispered, "Sit, Loo-zoo."

Lao-tse didn't. Whispers carried no weight with her. Perhaps nothing Elon said carried weight with her. But at least she did cut out the snarling.

Romulus said, "What did David do to Scotty at the parties, Elon? Can you remember? Did he have sex with him?"

"Sex?"

"Fucking? Jamming? Jesus. I don't know, what do you call it? Naked stuff?"

"Naked?"

"Did Scotty ever do naked stuff—"

"Scotty's always naked."

"Right. 'Cause he was modeling. But did David ever *hurt* Scotty when he was naked?"

"David is *gen*-tul."

"Damn it! You must have seen something! You must—"

The breeze brought a sound from the coach house. The storm door opening. Shutting. He glanced back. The lights were ablaze, and a dark figure hurried from the house and got into a car. Not the scarlet death car, but one parked next to it.

Romulus whispered, "Or maybe you didn't see anything. As you say, you don't go to parties much. Hey, I better be going. Keep Loo-zoo with you, OK?"

He walked backward. He heard the car door shut. The engine started up, headlights.

Romulus waved good-bye to Elon and Lao-tse. Then he turned and strode purposefully in the direction of the moon and the river.

Elon called after him. "Hurt? Hurt with a needle?"

Romulus looked back.

"What?"

Said Elon, "Needles hurt."

The headlights swept over the field as the car turned onto the long drive.

"Yes they do, Elon, but I have to run."

"Wait!"

Elon suddenly tore off toward his little house, Lao-tse with him.

He'd said to wait. But the headlights were headed this way and for Romulus to hang around till they had him pinned seemed ill-advised. So he took off. Sprinted hell-for-leather down the wide magnificent moony field, and when the headlights started to pick up his shadow he dove into the grass, and huddled there.

He heard the car pass on the drive behind him. Glanced over his shoulder and saw the lights wrap around the farmhouse and then he saw the glow on the far side. He watched, and though the breeze took the sounds away from him, he could follow the car's lights all the way to the main road, where they turned toward Gideon Manor.

So the hunter was still hunting. But had lost the scent.

Romulus got up and hobbled on down the field. When he came to another rock wall crossing through the blowing grass, he stopped, and sat on the wall, and rested.

Under the running moonlight, as far as the eye could see, Z-rays were telling their lies. Their sweet-talking lies. The shimmering Hudson River, the immaculate wind, the vast reaches of sky. Lord, they were glorious lies, and he stayed much longer than he had planned, just looking.

Then he heard panting beside him—right beside him—and he slid his eyes over, and there was Lao-tse, perched on the wall.

He scratched that spot on her back.

And then a voice at his ear: "Needles hurt."

Romulus turned, and Elon was holding something out to him. He looked down. Hypodermic syringe.

Said Elon, "I found it. He hided it, but I found it."

"Who hid it? David?"

"Needles hurt."

The syringe was caked with mud and broken at the tip. And there was another stain inside it. Kind of a brown in this moonlight—maybe some other color by daylight.

Romulus demanded, "*Who* did it hurt? Did it hurt Scotty? Did he say it hurt him?"

Elon nodded solemnly.

"What did Scotty say, Elon?"

Elon opened his mouth and started to shriek.

"No. Elon, *no*. Shhh! I get the picture."

Elon shut up. He was crying. He said, "Told me it *didn't* hurt, but it hurt."

"Who said it didn't hurt? Scotty?"

"Told me, Don't say, Elon. Don't say."

"You can say. It's all right."

"Needles hurt!"

"What was in this needle, Elon?"

Romulus grabbed for the thing. Elon snatched it out of reach. "Mine."

"I just want to borrow it."

"Mine! Needles hurt!"

"Give it to me, Elon."

"You hurt Scotty! Now Scotty's gone! Loo-zoo, come!"

The two of them ran off up the hill. Romulus watched them go. Strange and a little impolite, the way they kept coming and going so abruptly, but don't take it personally.

He drew a breath and started hoofing.

He hoofed it down to where the field became woods. Then the woods opened onto another field, then more woods. Down, down, and the moon set and he was dead tired and stumbling. He came to the edge of a railroad cut, a sharp drop to the tracks, and it took him half an hour to find his way down. Bits of coke got into his shoes, and when at last he got to the bottom he had to sit on the tracks and take off the shoes and pour sand and smoke from them.

He was next to the river now and he could hear the ice groaning but there was nothing moving except the wind, which was turning chillier and chillier. He wished to hell he had something more substantial on than this silly show coat.

He got up and followed the ties until the ties blurred. He wrapped his arms around himself as he walked, and marched on, and the wind whipped up a froth of dawn light and a few gulls.

The river changed color.

He heard a train coming from the north. He hid behind some boulders. It was a freight coming, a slow moan of boxcars, and lives there a soul in this country who has never dreamed of someday, in the right, necessary circumstances, hopping aboard a freight train?

This particular freight train was headed south, headed toward home, and would circumstances ever get any more necessary than they were now? They never would, thought Romulus, and he leapt aboard.

Z-RAYS

67

When at last, a little after noon, he made it home, trudged up the hill to his cave, he felt that he had been away for a long time. That nothing would be the same, that the cave would be stripped bare. By now they would surely have stolen everything he had.

In fact no one had valued his TV, nor his mattress, nor his answering machine, nor his clothes, nor even his blankets.

But still, just as he had suspected, nothing was the same. The huge beech tree seemed unfamiliar. Its skin struck him as less glossy than he recalled. The cave herself greeted him indifferently. Had she always been this cramped and shallow?

Cave wasn't the least bit happy to see him.

Well she doesn't know what I've been through.

Anyway, what's *with* you, Romulus, it's not as though she's yours, body and soul. This cave has made her bed for Algonquin Indians and drunken Dutchmen and whole families of poor Irish and what the hell sort of claim do you have on her?

She was simply stone, cave-seep, and forty million generations of moss, and she still remembered her mother the Ice Age, and she was not likely to be impressed by Romulus Ledbetter's comings and goings.

She did not fraternize with the tenants.

68

Taped to his answering machine, Romulus found a note.
CALL ME. ASAP. CORK.

Got a lot of nerve coming right in here, poking around my things. Did he have a warrant for this intrusion? Romulus crunched the note into a ball and tossed it into the wastebasket.

Then he jabbed the Message button on the answering machine.

A series of clicks, a *boop,* and a voice:

"Mr. Ledbetter, this is Special Agent Jake Claw of the FBI. Understand you've got an assassin hunting for you? Could be a violation of your civil rights—we'd be *tickled* to help you out. If you'll just report to our office in the Chrysler Building at fifteen hundred hours, why, we'll put you right into witness protection, a castle upstate, lovely place called Matteawan, we want to—"

The machine swallowed the rest of the message. *Boop.* Machine was a piece of trash. Ought to return it to the Dumpster he'd fished it from.

Then came a series of *boops.* Then Leppenraub, midmessage:

"—and needles *hurt,* or so I'm told. Come back, amigo, all is forgiven, come to my sister's arms—"

More *boops* and clicks and Romulus pulled a blanket over him and started to drift.

But then he heard shuffling footsteps and a shopping cart's squeaky wheels and he didn't have to pull the blanket down again to know who it was. It was Cyclops, the one-eyed old dying white woman from Alabama.

"I'm asleep, Cyclops."

"Not no more. You going . . . come with me. Caveman. You just got to see this."

"What? What's this that I've got to see?"

"Not telling." She coughed. "Surprise. Come see."

"I'll see it tomorrow."

"Tomorrow it'll be gone." Which sounded like *Tahmarrah hit'll be gaw-un.*

"What'll be gone, Cyclops?"

"Nothing."

"Well. Can't nothing wait? I think nothing can wait."

"OK, it's a bird."

"What kind of bird?"

"*I* don't know, Caveman. That's why. Came to you. Big red head."

"Cardinal?"

She shook her head. "Blue wings."

"Blue. You sure not black? Like a woodpecker?"

"Bright. Blue. White crosses on the wings."

He pulled the blanket off his head. "*No* such bird."

"But I saw it. And it's . . . it's hurt. They isn't no more. Like it. Last of its kind."

"Cyclops, I've got to sleep. You don't know how tired I am. I've had about twenty minutes of sleep in the last two days. I'm so tired I'm hallucinating. I'm hallucinating you coming to tell me about a mystical bird."

"Mystical. That's right, son."

"An accidental, right? Blown off course from another galaxy?"

"Sleep's just going to have to wait, son."

69

He walked beside her. He pulled her cart for her, but still she walked very slowly and drew long rheumy breaths.

Cyclops had been a gym teacher in Alabama. This was a long long time ago. Now she had so many wrinkles that from her bad side, from the side with the empty eye socket, her skin looked as though she'd molted—as though she'd taken her skull out, gone back to Alabama with it, and just left the skin bag up here to amuse passers-by.

Said Romulus, "Where is this bird?"

"Just. Li'l piece."

They walked up a hill and down another.

They passed three black kids who were hanging out by a bench. The kids whistled at Cyclops.

"Mmm-*mm.*"

"What . . . a . . . fox."

"Hey Mama."

When Cyclops looked over, one kid did a pantomime of jacking off.

"Show us your tits, Mama."

"Oh shit! I *see* her tits! See 'em? Down by her *feet,* man!"

Romulus gave them as nasty a look as he could dredge up, considering his eyes wouldn't open.

He said, "Shut the fuck up."

One of the kids said back, "Get a job."

The kid did his jack-off thing for Romulus. Then all the kids catcalled and grotesqued till Romulus and Cyclops were over the next hill.

Said Cyclops, "I'm sorry, Caveman. Walking so slow."

"It's OK."

"Hate this body."

"What?" Romulus shrugged. "It's an age, Cyclops."

They kept walking.

Said Romulus, "What you need is a home. You had a home, you wouldn't feel so bad."

A moist boiling of her breath, which was as near as she could come to a laugh. "Don't want a cave," she said. "Spiders. No. Want a big *old* house. In Mobile."

They walked all the way down to the low fields by the Harlem River. There was a swampy area and Romulus stepped off the path and reached down amid roots and uncovered a little hood of striped leaves. He opened it carefully. A blossom. He called to Cyclops:

"First flower of the year."

"What is it?"

"Skunk cabbage. Come by in a few weeks, I'll make a skunk cabbage soup."

"How does. That taste?"

He shrugged. "Pretty bad."

He came back to the path and walked beside her. He said, "Well, it's skunk cabbage, how would you expect it to taste?"

They passed the playground. They came to the river's edge. Cyclops stopped.

"Far enough."

He looked at her. "Well?"

Her one eye rolled away from his gaze. She said, "Well what?"

"The bird?"

"Oh. It was right here."

"It's not here now?"

"No."

"You said *blue* wings? *Bright* blue . . . ?"

"Oh. Maybe not. Maybe . . . maybe the wings were black. I think the whole bird. All black. Now I think. I think it might have been a crow."

Which came out sounding like *Ah thaynk hit miy-uht ah bin a cur-row.*

70

He left her on a bench by the water.

Then he hiked all the way up back to his cave. When he was nearly there, he heard voices and whispers and then silence, and a thought came into his weary head.

Setup.

Oh shit. Fucking fucking witch. *Witch.* If he got out of this she was losing her other eye. Let her and her fleas find their way down to hell by the light of her master's Y-rays.

Then he saw the balloon tied to a limb of the beech tree.

Then he considered the date.

71

The birthday cake had one candle. He blasted it. They all applauded. He looked close at the cake and asked:

"Hey, what is that? Is that . . . is that *birdseed?*"

Lulu took out the candle and handed the cake to him.

She said, "Birdseed in honey. When I bake a real cake, you won't take it. This you'll take, 'cause you can feed it to your damn birds."

Big laugh.

Romulus nodded. He didn't smile, but he *did* amiably lift his eyebrows, and he accepted the cake.

"Daddy, what's with the suit? And you've got a haircut, and you've shaved—what's going on?"

"Dressing for success, Lulu."

"You know, you're not so bad-looking, Daddy."

Then his brother Lycurgus's kid—Romulus forgot his nephew's name but he was the one with all the hair shaved off except a big star on top—he switched on his juice box and of course it was Mahler's Fifth. Because once when Romulus had been about fourteen, he'd said he liked Mahler, and now every year they played it at these birthday shivarees.

Trying to remind him that he was the sort of African-American that appreciated Mahler, and such a man oughtn't to be living in a cave, living on skunk cabbage soup.

He ought to be living like his brothers.

Like his big brother Lycurgus, for example, who was an administrator at Beth Israel Hospital, and who had brought his wife and two kids, the one with the star on his head and the other, the daughter, who was attending Brown University and had won the Theodore Roethke Award for a poem she'd written about Uncle Romulus.

> Sad uncle, the stars play their cadenzas,
> but in the dark cave
> of your exile you cannot see them! Society

has stolen the coat off your back, and your name
from our lips . . .

Something like that.

Or like his big brother Marcus, who was a producer of television commercials, and who wore a polka-dot scarf to work instead of a necktie. Marcus and his wife had brought the picnic basket. Fried chicken and ham-and-horseradish sandwiches, and potato salad and beet salad. Romulus didn't eat, but he could smell the beet salad, and he knew Sheila had fixed it. He knew that sometime later this week Sheila would get around to asking Lulu if Romulus had tried it. Lulu would say no, and Sheila would say, "Well, let the fool starve if that's what he wants to do."

Or like his big brother Augustus, who could not attend because of pressing business in Washington, but who had sent Romulus a nice card.

Or like his big brother Samuel who had four fine kids, who were all future rocket scientists and who ran around screaming, and who decided the park was the Arabian desert and the cave was a berm they had to blow up.

And while they were blowing up everything in sight, the grown-ups milled around outside the cave eating chicken and making talk.

Mostly they talked about Mom and Pop. They didn't try to talk too much to Romulus, because they knew better. They knew that sooner or later the talk would trigger his fury, and he'd harangue them all home, as he did every year, and they wanted to hold this off for a while.

But his daughter, Lulu, had brought her new boyfriend, and he talked to Romulus. He told Romulus he was a lawyer for an investment firm, and he had a place on the south shore, and his hobby was kites. Hadn't Lulu warned the kid? Romulus got the feeling she had, but the young man was the sort who felt he could finesse most anything. He'd dealt with sweethearts' daddies of all stripes, and he was dead sure he could handle the stripes of Romulus Ledbetter.

So he prattled on about his kites, and about his regard for Lulu, and Lulu's regard for her father. And Mahler's Fifth was blaring away in the background, which made his talk sound pretty dramatic. Like two lovers' blood-red kites dueling in a cobalt sky, and whatever this might signify.

Romulus called to the kid with the star on his head.

"Nephew. Come here."

The nephew approached Uncle Caveman—this guy from his nightmares—quite boldly.

Said Romulus, "Do you have any other tapes?"

"Yeah."

But big brother Lycurgus, in the middle of a chat with big brother Marcus, heard his son's "Yeah" and spoke sharply: *"Benjamin."*

"I mean, *Yes, sir.*"

"Well," said Romulus, "what tapes do you have?"

"Rappers and shit."

Lycurgus heard that, too. *"Benjamin."*

Benjamin amended, "I mean stuff. You wouldn't want to hear them."

"Play anything but Mahler's Fifth."

"Dad says this is your kind of music."

"Your dad knows as much about my kind of music as he knows about your kind of music."

A little catch of silence. Then they all made talk again. Some rapper started rapping. Romulus deemed it no worse than "Gentle on My Mind."

He turned back to the boyfriend and said, "Now what were you saying? Kites? Big redheaded kites with bright blue wings? What was the name of your firm again?"

"Wilcox and Lassiter."

"And what was that a subsidiary of?"

"Excuse me?"

"Subsidiary. Who *owns* Wilcox and Lassiter?"

"No."

That was big brother Lycurgus. The silence came crashing down again. Even the berm bombers shut up.

Said Romulus, "What did you say, Lycurgus?"

"I said, *No.* It's not a subsidiary of *anything.* It's not owned by Stuyvesant. Leave the boy alone."

"The boy is courting my daughter. I have a right to know who he's working for."

"My niece has a right to make her own decisions. Which she

does pretty damn well, considering the example you set for her. So drop the Stuyvesant crap, because nobody wants to hear it."

Lycurgus's wife touched her husband's arm.

"Baby," she said, "we're on our first piece of chicken. Not yet, all right?"

Lycurgus ignored her. "If you want help, Romulus, we'll get you help. But you've got to want it. We're not going to try to force it on you anymore. You've got to do something for your damn *self.*"

Lulu took her piece of chicken, which she hadn't yet bit into, and put it back in the bucket. Muttering, "OK, here we go. Go ahead, Daddy, let it rip."

Big brother Samuel's wife put the lid back on the beet salad. She said, "Come on, kids."

"Is it time for Uncle Romulus, Mom? Is he going to give the speech?"

"Just come on. Jeremy, where's your hat?"

But Romulus didn't launch. Apparently the Moth-Seraphs were all dozing.

He sat. On a stone by the beech tree. He shut his eyes. He felt Lulu come close to him.

"Daddy? Daddy, are you all right?"

He opened his eyes just to look at her face. All his kin were staring at him.

She said softly, "Daddy, you're supposed to lecture us about Stuyvesant and Y-rays and selling our divinities and all."

"I'm sorry, Lu. Have I spoiled the party? I'm just very tired. I haven't had much sleep."

"But you still believe it? The Y-rays and all, you haven't stopped believing—"

"I'm not worried about Y-rays anymore."

"Really?"

Romulus shook his head. "I'm too busy worrying about *Z-rays.*"

Somebody's wife murmured, "Oh Lord."

"But no speeches. Not now, anyway. No, you know . . . you know . . . would you all mind if I just lay down for a while? I mean, go ahead and eat, this is your home, too, and you're welcome to stay here as long as . . . you like . . . but if it's OK I'll just lie down. . . ."

"Come here, Daddy."

Lulu led him to the mattress in the cave and shooed away the

181

nephews who were sprawled out on it. Romulus lay down and she shook out one of his blankets and put it over him.

He heard the squeaking of wheels and then the voice of Cyclops. She was coughing, and saying, "Well. I got up that hill. Soon as I could. Have I missed? All the fun?"

Romulus looked up at Lulu, into her eyes. Those ragged irises, and the scaffolding of bone above the cheek. Incomparable. Except of course you could always compare her to her mother. She leaned over and gave him a kiss on his forehead. Then she sniffed the air.

"Hey Daddy?"

"Yes."

She said, "Have you . . . have you been with a woman?"

"Do not tell your mother, right?"

"Oh Dad, this is a little weird for me. This is—you're not supposed to—I mean . . ."

"Do not tell your mother."

"Do you think she'd mind?"

"Probably not. Still."

Lulu came close to his ear and whispered, "Not that one-eyed woman?"

"Cyclops? No."

A great many kin-faces had gathered around.

"Rom, you just go on to sleep for a while."

"You're fine, you're just tired."

Said Romulus, "Folks, I went to a party last night and I stayed out too late."

"That's right. Have a nap."

Romulus said, "But you're still all Stuyvesant's slaves and lackeys, and if you'd open up your damn divinities a little, you'd know it."

"Uh-huh. Catch some winks, brother."

He shut his eyes. Plenty of worried murmurs. He was holding Lulu's hand and he listened to those murmurs, and then they faded away. He wondered why they'd stopped, and he wanted to take a look. But it took him a while to get his eyes open, and by the time he did, all his brothers were gone and it was cooler and the sun had dropped close to the river.

But he still felt Lulu's hand in his. He looked over, and she was right there, stretched out on the mattress beside him. She was wide awake.

"Baby?"

"You feel better Daddy?"

"Yes ma'am."

"Are you hungry?"

"Yes."

"There's still some fried chicken and beet salad."

He looked away.

"Come on Daddy. I'm just going to throw it out. In fact maybe I did throw it out. I threw it in that can by the path but then I dug it out again. So that makes it kosher, doesn't it? I won't tell anybody."

Romulus was very hungry. He said to her, "OK, the fried chicken. Not the beet salad."

"Maybe Mom had nothing to do with the beet salad. Aunt Jane might have made it."

"No, not the beet salad."

"The potato salad, is that OK?"

"Yeah."

He ate. Three pieces of chicken and a pint of potato salad and he drank half a liter of ginger ale. Then he asked her:

"Lu, did you bring your car?"

She nodded.

"Did you have trouble parking it?"

She shook her head. "It's Sunday."

"Would you take me for a drive?"

"Are you serious? Daddy, you never go in cars. You haven't been in a car since—"

"Since last night. Come on, take me for a drive."

Down Payson Street to Dyckman Street to the Harlem
River Drive. The High Bridge. Golden light of sunset, which was
trying to work its sleight-of-hand on the Harlem River. But to no
avail. It was still the most disconsolate river in the world.

They passed Coogan's Bluff, up on the right. Great skirts of
Manhattan schist, in purple shadow.

"See there, Lulu, back there's the polo grounds. Where the Giants used to play. Was a woman owned the land in those days—old
widow Coogan. Your great-grandfather worked for her. Run her
messages for her. Have you heard this? Once a month he ran downtown to pick up her rent check from the Giants. Everybody thought
it was something that she trusted a *Ne*-gro with that. Old bitch. Paid
him shit wages. One of them rent checks could have carried his
wages the rest of his life. That was my father's father. They say he
was raised on a little farm across the river somewhere."

Somewhere over in the Bronx, where it was all hell-gray ghetto
now.

"Jesus, I'm getting as bad as your grandmother, Lulu. This is
what *she* used to do. Run on all the time about all the folks that have
passed on. Your great-*grand*father, Romulus. Your great-*great*-grand-
father. Your second cousin's great-aunt Hattie. Like they were some
kind of *weight* you just had to carry around. Or you were no good.
My Lord. And please pass the weight on down to your children."

He looked over at Lulu to see if she had anything to say, but
she didn't.

He said, "Been living in a *cave* to get out from under that
weight. Now listen to me. My . . . Lord."

After a while she said, "Where did you go yesterday, Daddy?"

"What? Nowhere. Little drive. Little pre-birthday party. Why
didn't my brother Augustus come today?"

"I guess he had business in Washington."

"I guess he thought it wasn't worth it anymore, right? Just not worth it trying to make sense of his baby brother."

"That's not true."

"No?"

She came out with it then. "I think he's sick, Daddy."

"What kind of sick?"

"They think he might have stomach cancer."

"Oh. No. Augustus? No."

"They don't know yet. He's going for more tests."

"Why didn't anybody tell me?"

"They all think you've got your own problems."

They rode in silence.

"Oh Jesus."

Under the Willis Avenue Bridge.

"My brother is dying? Augie is dying?"

"Daddy, they don't *know* that."

Under the Triborough Bridge, and onto the FDR Drive.

Then they saw the footbridge over to Ward's Island, and Romulus said, "You remember that little park on the other side over there?"

"When I was little, yeah. When we were living in the East River Project."

"Right over there. There was a sandbox. You think it's still there, Lu?"

"I don't know but I think so."

"I used to make these big castles for you."

"Yeah, and you said that Ward's Island was once a pirate island and they'd left buried treasure. And I used to dig in the sandbox for the treasure."

"Aha! Yes, I remember that."

"Once I found a balloon."

"You *thought* you found a balloon. It was a condom."

"No!"

"Yes. You cried when I wouldn't blow it up for you."

"You did blow it up for me."

"I bought a balloon on the way back and I blew that up. I wasn't blowing up any used condom."

"Where am I taking you, Daddy? Am I taking you to Cole Street?"

"I just want to drive by."

185

"You can come in, you know. Mom won't mind."

"She won't mind, 'cause she'll have a chance to cure my brains with a fry pan."

Over the Queensboro Bridge. In the rearview mirror he saw the sunset, which was giving up now, just letting itself go the color of rotten egg yolk.

"Daddy, if you don't want to tell me where you were last night—that's OK. None of my business. But don't go there again, all right? Promise me that? That you won't start wandering?"

"Good to get out of the city once in a while."

"Around here, they know you. They might not understand you somewhere else."

He said, "You know, once when I was a kid, my uncle died and Mama took me with her to North Carolina for the funeral. Did I ever tell you about this? That was my mother's brother, George—your great-uncle. I guess he was about the age that Augustus is now. Not nearly old enough to die, you know? Mama decided to go see him. Left all my brothers with Grandma Ledbetter, but me she took with her, because—I don't know why. Maybe because I wasn't old enough to be in school. I guess that was it. Anyway we went down on the bus, and I had Mama all to myself, which I liked. Except she never stopped worrying about my brothers. My Lord I remember that ride. We left New York and it was winter and we rode all night and when I woke up it was spring.

"But I don't remember the funeral.

"Maybe I didn't go to it. What I remember is being on the porch of somebody's house out in the tobacco fields. Like a share-cropper's shack? You know? And there were already fireflies, that early in the year, I remember that. And there was somebody had a guitar and somebody had a harmonica, and I think that's the first time I ever heard anything like the blues.

"My uncle's cousins. I never saw them again.

"And I remember on the way down, one other thing, I remember in the bus, Mama was going on about my brothers and then she said, 'What are you making those little bird chirps for, son?' And I didn't even *know* I was making them, till she told me. These little squeaks, about every five minutes I'd make one of these little squeaks in the back of my throat, and I *had* to make them because they were back there, and they just had to get out. And then when I woke up later and it was spring I wasn't making them anymore, but that's the first time I remember doing anything like that. I mean the kind of craziness that someone might notice."

Queens Boulevard to Woodhaven. Woodhaven to Pitkin. Darkness coming on, neon getting a hold. Left on Cole. Third house on the left. The ratty brick facing. The sills had been painted pink. New fence around the postage-stamp yard, where the grass was in fair trim and the forsythia ready to bloom. She had ceramic ducks. She had got herself a flag. Sheila, she was trying to do it up right, this "just another neighbor" deal.

"You want to come in, Daddy?"

"Just wanted to see it."

"*Rude* if I take you all the way here and you won't come in."

"Another time."

"But it's *your* house."

"No thanks," he said.

Then after looking at it awhile, he said, "Never was. *My* house. By the time we got this place I was pretty much an invalid—just hanging around watching the goddamn TV. Don't you remember? This place, this was your mama's doing. Except I *was* the one planted that forsythia there. And there were one or two times I paid the mortgage. You know what I remember? I remember coming home from a gig in Astoria, Greek place, middle of the night. Made good money there—took a cab home—that was all right. Then I felt like maybe this was going to be my home. But that's all. Rest of the time, I was out in . . . oh, space."

He looked up at the house again. He said, "Jesus."

Sheila had come to the window. She must have known the sound of Lulu's car. She was looking right at him. He couldn't see her very well. Mostly he saw the outline of her, silhouetted by the lamp behind her. He had known she'd put on weight. He hadn't imagined that the weight would be pulling down her shoulders that way.

He turned away from her and looked dead ahead at the street.

"Daddy, is Mama looking at you?"

"Yes, she is."

74

They were quiet on the way back until at last he asked her, "Will you give me a birthday present?"

"For you? Not for the birds? Of course I will. What do you want, Daddy?"

"You know what I'd truly love?"

"What?"

"What I've got my heart set on?"

"What?"

"What you could get me and then it would be like a true birthday for your old man?"

"What? Tell me."

"The autopsy report on Andrew Scott Gates."

First she gave him a six-block serving of black silence along Dyckman Street. Then she told him to go to hell.

Then she told him she'd like to just shake him, just *shake* all the paranoia and scheming out of him.

Then she started to cry.

75

Detective Jack Cork was out on the front steps of the church. Sitting to one side, contemplating his knees. Romulus spared him no more than a glance. He climbed the steps and headed resolutely for the front door.

The plan was to meet in the confessional. This was their custom, after all. Had the man no respect for tradition? What was the point of meeting in a church if you had no feeling for tradition?

"*Hey!*"

Cork's tone was harsh.

"Out here this time, OK? There's people in there."

Romulus asked, "What are they doing?"

"Jesus, *I* don't know. Looks like some kind of religious ceremony. Bizarre, huh? Hey, I'll call in the feds, we'll bust their freaking asses. First I gotta talk to you. Come here, would you? Have a seat."

Romulus shook his head. "It's not safe out here."

"Come. Here."

Romulus went and sat beside him on the steps. Cork was looking gone to seed. Wearing an oil-stained parka and one of his shirt buttons was missing and he had a day's growth of beard on his sunken-cake face.

Romulus supposed that together they looked like a couple of winos enjoying their evening libation.

Said Jack Cork, "All I want to know is, you going to cut out the shit or what? That's all I want to know."

"Who called you?"

"Deputy sheriff of Gideon Manor."

"Herman."

"You got it. Says you were trespassing, creating a disturbance, pulling some kind of crazy scam, which he described to me and which I did get a laugh out of—that concert pianist bit, you know? But he says he told you to get out of town and you didn't, and now there's a kind of . . . like a *movement,* it's not quite the size of a lynch mob yet but it's getting there, and it wants to see you institutionalized before you do further harm. *Deeply* fucking institutionalized."

"Somebody tried to kill me."

"You *too?* Jesus, this guy's gotta be *stopped.* And I bet the police aren't doing squat. Well, maybe you should stay away from his parties for a while."

"They tried to run me down. Then they shot at me."

"Oh yeah? Leppenraub?"

"I didn't see his face."

"No of course not. Real dark, huh?"

"He was wearing bandages over his face."

"Oh sure, of course. *The Mummy's Curse,* that was a good movie. Any witnesses?"

"Of course not."

"Of course not. But we just *know* it was Leppenraub, don't we?"

Romulus brooded. "Well . . . no. No, I'm not sure. I mean . . . my wife doesn't think Leppenraub's a killer."

"Your *wife?* You mean your ex-wife? Your daughter says she won't talk to you."

"Right. That's true. Sort of. But still I know what she thinks."

"Yeah, so do I. She thinks you're crazy. So does everybody else on the fucking planet. But since when did that ever make any difference to you? What's the matter with you, guy? You losing your nerve now?"

Said Romulus, "Listen to me, Lieutenant. I think I know how it was done. How Scotty Gates was killed. Lethal injection. That's why there were no wounds. There's this feeble-minded guy up at Leppenraub's, he showed me the needle."

"He showed it to you. Well goddamn good for you, Caveman, now we're talking *evidence.*"

"Also I saw traces of whatever the agent was."

"Agent?"

"You know. The poison."

"Oh like agent of *death,* I get it. Agent. That's like a forensic shop talk term huh? This is all over my head, Caveman."

"Brown stuff. There was a stain of it, still in the needle. Brown, flaky."

"Brown?"

Said Romulus, "You know what I think it is?"

Cork shrugged. "I know what *I* think it is. I think it's *shit.* Probably *your* shit. That'd be a highly lethal agent. It's killing *me,* I know that. Look, Caveman, this has been amusing but now I'm getting tired of it. This is my day off. I'm not supposed to do anything today. I'm supposed to be puttering about, planting my antique roses. But I'm not doing that, am I? No, I'm sitting here trying to talk you out of a trip to the nuthouse. Which is a total fucking waste of time, 'cause that's where you're hell-bent on going. Now, why do you think I'm wasting my time? 'Cause I like you? Why do you think?"

Romulus thought. Soon he came up with it.

"Because a fellow officer asked you to go easy on me?"

"There we have it."

Romulus frowned. "But I just saw Lulu. She didn't tell me. She didn't tell me you'd talked to her."

"I guess she decided it wouldn't do any fucking good. Of course Papa's not going to listen to his little baby girl, is he? But *I'm* telling you. You got her very worried. She's says to me, 'Detective Cork, do you have to take my father in?' It's sad. 'Cause she's not going to ask me *not* to—you know? But just the way she puts it, she makes it a real tearjerker. 'He's harmless,' she says. I told her, 'I know that. I already checked him out.' She says, 'He gets these obsessions, but he gets over them. But you put him in a mental hospital, he'll just shrivel up and die.' Is that touching, or what?"

Romulus stared down at the steps.

Cork said, "Wait, I didn't say it right. What she said was, 'He'll *fold* up and die.' And the way she said it, you know? With those big eyes of hers? Hey, I get the feeling she really loves you. True love, oh boy, it gets to me every time. I told her, 'Look, I'm not sending him to the zoo if I don't have to. But your daddy keeps screwing around with this witch-hunt of his, hey, what am I supposed to do?' She says, 'He'll stop.' I say, 'I doubt it. He's got these clues now. He's probably got about fifteen thousand clues. He's probably got 'em on three-by-five index cards. He's probably figured out that Leppenraub's middle name is an anagram for Cornelius What-the-fuck.' "

Romulus looked up. "For Stuyvesant? Is that true?"

"Oh Jesus," Cork said—then he shrugged. "Oh what the hell. *Real* cops do it—get all wound up in the fucking clues—why shouldn't you? I told your daughter, I said, 'Look, I do it. I take some stupid garden-variety spouse killing, and these clues start dancing around in my head and I can't stop 'em, I gotta work it out that the victim was done in by that scarred man I saw at the funeral. Then the husband confesses, and it breaks my heart. Ah, the clues! The clues'll make a sane man crazy. God knows what they'd do for somebody who was crazy to begin with.' "

"You said all this to my daughter?"

"Nah. But I'm saying it to you. You got clues jumping in your head? Get a doctor to pry 'em out. Do it quick, or you're a goner."

"A dead duck?"

"Caveman, *nobody's* trying to kill you, for Christ's sake. Oh, this is fun, wasting my breath like this. Don't you hear *any* of what I'm saying?"

"You're saying clues are worthless."

"You want to know something? You want to know the only kind of clue that's ever worth jack shit? It's the one that's not there. Something's missing, something's wrong with this picture. Sometimes that'll give you a jolt. But all the clues that waltz in front of your eyes? I'm telling you, they're going to waltz you straight to the bughouse. Jesus. If you weren't such a deadbeat already, I'd tell you to get some rest, take a vacation."

Romulus mulled this over. "Somewhere warm?"

"Yeah."

"Warm and restful? Some place that brings back memories of my childhood?"

Cork squinted at him. "Yeah—maybe. Why?"

"Oh, I don't know," said Romulus. "But maybe you're onto something there."

76

That night he stopped by Bob and Betty's. The Zouave doorman recognized him right away, and called up to Bob.

"The garbage collection is here."

"What?" they heard Bob say.

"The homeless guy."

"*Not* homeless," Romulus muttered.

Said Bob, "Send him up."

When he got upstairs, Bob fixed him a lime rickey. Betty was clearly dismayed to see him lapsed into his old duds, his old ways, but Bob took it all in stride. Bob seemed to understand that there were often messy knots in the loops of failure and recovery.

"Brought your clothes back," said Romulus. "In that bag. I'm afraid they got a little torn up though."

"Oh Romulus," said Betty. "They're yours, you're supposed to keep them."

"The underwear isn't in there. I must have misplaced the underwear."

Bob laughed a sly laugh.

Said Betty, "But tell us, tell us, how did the gig go?"

"I thought it went great. I did very well, and I learned a lot. Problem is, I got a little carried away afterward, a little too much celebration, got in a few scrapes, you know?"

"Sure," said Bob.

"Got to learn to control that old demon temper."

"That's the ticket," said Bob.

"I'm thinking, if I want to get myself a nice little condo like this someday, I'm going to have to learn to play the part."

"Keep at it," said Bob. He handed Romulus his drink.

"I did get a lead on another gig. Down in North Carolina."

"Romulus!" said Betty. "That's great!"

They drank a toast to North Carolina.

Then Betty showed him the telescope. She had it set up before the big picture window.

She said, "Bob never uses it. But I've been looking at Stuyvesant's tower. Haven't seen any Y-rays coming out of it, though. You want to take a peek, Romulus?"

"No, I'd rather . . ."

"All right."

Romulus told her, "Anyway, Stuyvesant isn't using Y-rays just now. Last week, though, that would have been a perfect time for a show."

"Oh."

And for the Z-rays, Romulus didn't need a telescope. Z-rays filled the whole sky in the big window. They dallied and sported above Manhattan, and shimmered as Romulus imagined the Northern Lights must shimmer. They put him in a storytelling mood.

At Betty's wide-eyed urging, he told her all about Stuyvesant. She gave him another shave, and while she did he told her about Lem Mulkhoo, Stuyvesant's genius-lackey, who was always at Stuyvesant's side, and who was so old now he had outlived his grandchildren.

But one day he might yet find a way to turn against his master, and this was the great hope for humanity.

Betty said she certainly hoped so.

He had two lime rickeys, which left him feeling drunk and happy. Then Betty brought out a light spring sportcoat and some slacks, for his trip to North Carolina.

The Z-rays romped, and Romulus gave Betty a kiss and Bob a firm "I believe in myself" handshake, and went on his way.

77

It could have been an RV-and-tent campground in West Yellowstone at the season's height. Campfires blazing, circles of lawn chairs pulled up around the fires. A chilly evening, but convivial. Everywhere folks were chewing the fat. One camper stood and stretched, and cracked a joke to his circle of friends, and while the circle cackled merrily, the camper went back to his tent tarp and fetched a big bottle of beer from the open cooler. He brought it back to the circle. Everyone reached out his plastic cup and the camper shared out the bottle.

The camper's name was Chore.

It was a night at the brink of spring in a vacant lot, corner of Avenue C and Seventh Street.

After the beer was served they passed around some herb. It had been donated by an angel who lived in the Christadora, the big co-op that overlooked Tompkins Square Park. The chunk of herb looked like a dried moth, finely veined. It crumbled in Penny's fingers as she wedged a chunk of it into the pipe.

She licked the dust off her fingers. She lighted the pipe. It burned voluptuously, with a sparkle. She gave the pipe to Chore, who was now tending the fire barrel.

"This is passable herb," said Chore.

"Passable" meant that it opened like a beach umbrella inside of his brainpan, and he could bask in the shade of it and watch the waves and the distant dolphins and the girls in maillots.

He sent the pipe over to Mourning Matthew.

Matthew was this nervous white guy who was in mourning for his lover who'd frozen to death. About halfway into his hit his face started to pucker: he was fighting back the tears. Manuel, who had the lawn recliner, leaned over and snapped his fingers in front of Matthew's eyes.

"*Pass* it, man. You want to mourn, that's fine, but pass the pipe to the living."

Penny giggled. She said, "Hey, Matthew. Want me to make you a veil?"

Chore clucked at her. "That's not a kind thing to say, Penny."

"Oh fuck you. He's gotta get over it, Chore."

Chore was a black man with a polished, strong-boned, faceted face. Firelight shone on the facets. From the pile of wood, he picked up a big piece of wooden floor joist, and he fit it into the fire barrel. He clucked again at Penny, and said:

"Not kind, Penny. Give the man time."

"Chore, you sound like a chipmunk, you know that? Your voice. Hey Manuel."

"What?"

"Want me to braid your hair?"

"Sure."

"For your trial."

"Sure."

"When is your trial?"

"This *is* passable. My trial?"

"Yeah, when is it?"

"Sometime. I forget."

"You better pay attention."

"Yeah. Penny, *you* better pay attention. The earth is going to crash into the sun."

"When?"

"Pretty soon. You better start worrying. You better start worrying about anything that might happen, ever anytime, anywhere. You better worry worry worry, fucking worry worry."

"Yeah? So when's your trial, Manuel?"

"I don't know, what's today?"

"Monday."

"Oh. Then I think it's tomorrow."

Chore was looking at Matthew, who looked unwell. "Matthew, you all right?"

Matthew was staring at something. He held his mouth slack.

Said Chore, "What's the matter, Matthew? You look like you be seeing a ghost."

Penny laughed. "Hoo shit. He thinks he sees the ghost of that frozen guy."

Said Chore, "Penny."

"*What*, Chore? You *are* a chore, you know that?"

Chore balled up a newspaper and threw it in the fire. "Don't call him 'that frozen guy.' That's just not kind."

Then he looked up, and noticed what Matthew was staring at.

They all noticed.

A ghost. Two ghosts.

Two ghosts who walked up into the sphere of firelight. One of them was big, and the other medium height. They wore old baggy clothes, and baseball caps. They had no faces. Their heads were wrapped round and round with gauzy white bandage, and it made them look like ghosts.

The lesser ghost carried a .357, which he held close to the pocket of his windbreaker. The greater ghost carried what looked like a chair leg.

The greater ghost spoke to Chore.

"Sit down, OK?"

Said Chore, "Fuck. Who the fuck are you?"

"Sit down."

His voice was heavy, slurry. Chore had the idea he was trying to mask his voice. Chore squinted, leaned in, peered at the bandages.

"Who the fuck?"

The greater ghost glanced over at the lesser ghost, as though seeking direction. The lesser ghost nodded. The big ghost snapped the chair leg at Chore's head. Sounded to Chore like the crack of a bat. What, are they playing baseball on the beach? Chore heard the roar of the crowd, but he couldn't see anything—the sun was in his eyes.

The greater ghost looked around at the circle.

"Anybody else?"

Nobody said a word. They all looked to Chore where he lay crumpled up by the fire barrel.

Now the lesser ghost jerked his head toward Matthew.

The greater ghost spoke in that slow heavy voice. He said, "OK Matthew."

Matthew moved. He spun out of his lawn chair, tried to run. But he was a weak and mourning sad-eyed weasel, and the big ghost took two steps and swung the chair leg and caught him where his neck met his skull. Matthew went down to his knees.

The ghost turned to the circle. "Is there anybody here didn't like that?"

Nobody said a word.

"Where's the videotape, Matthew?"

Matthew tried to rise. The ghost kicked him in the side, his boot coming up into the bottom of Matthew's thorax, and they all heard a rib giving way. A moist splintering.

"Now, Matthew. Where's the fucking tape?"

Matthew tried to speak and his breath heaved out of him. He clutched his side. He whispered: "I don't have . . . no . . . tape."

The ghost grabbed Matthew's wrist. Yanked it hard and spun him around and started to bend Matthew's arm in a way it wouldn't bend.

"Did you give it to the Caveman, Matthew? Does the Caveman have it? Answer me."

Matthew started to scream.

"Shut up."

The ghost rammed the chair leg into Matthew's sternum, and Matthew buckled up and the sound went out of his cry.

"If any of you got any problem with this, tell me now."

There were no objections.

"Where's the Caveman, asshole? Where's his cave? Central Park? *Where*, Matthew?"

"I don't . . . I don't know any—"

The ghost grabbed Matthew by the hair. He smashed the butt end of his club into Matthew's mouth and they heard the breaking of teeth and Matthew's groan. The ghost let him go and Matthew's face swooped down low to the grass, came up again. He looked to the circle, to the stony faces, and blood leaked out of his mouth and his eyes beseeched them. . . .

But nobody said a word until the ghost said quietly, "All right, let's go."

He dragged Matthew to his feet. He looked to the circle and the smaller ghost, the silent one, held the gun on them.

Said the big ghost, "How you folks doing? You having a good time?"

Nobody spoke.

The big ghost dragged Matthew closer to the circle. Raised the chair leg. Stood over Manuel.

"I SAID ARE YOU HAVING A GOOD TIME?"

"Yeah."

"Why? Lot of excitement?"

"Uh-uh. Same old."

The silent ghost put the barrel of the pistol against Penny's ear. He jerked his chin almost imperceptibly, and the big ghost spoke for him, asking her:

"What about your friend Matthew here? What *happened* to him anyway?"

Penny looked over at Matthew. At the blood oozing out of his mouth. Then she looked away.

"I don't know, I ain't seen him. Shit, I ain't seen Matthew in quite a while."

The no-face of the silent ghost moved slowly—he was check-ing out the faces in the circle. When he was satisfied that they all truly understood the value and honor of discretion, he gave the big ghost a nod.

The big ghost grabbed Matthew by his collar and dragged him out of the firelight.

"Let's go, Matthew. Let's go visit your buddy the Caveman."

The silent ghost followed them, walking backward, his gun still on the circle. Then he turned, and quickly the ghosts half dragged and half walked Matthew to their sporty scarlet sedan parked by the fence, and shoved him in.

$\mathbf{A}$t the same hour, the passengers on the number 7 subway train coming in from Queens were staring at their newspapers or staring across the aisle at one another or staring at their thumbs. Or reading the frieze of wonderful ads. Hemorrhoids. Cockroaches. Anal warts. Lonely nights. Smoking's ravages. AIDS. All the ads promised relief from these things, but where was the relief from these ads?

The train took them all under the river.

The door opened, and clashing and roaring came into the car till the door closed again. Some of the passengers looked up.

They saw a big black man wearing a moth-eaten coat and a saucepan for a hat. He had scratches all over his face. When he spoke, he did so in a composed voice that slowly drew everyone's attention from their newspapers or bitter musings, a voice that brought all their eyes up, pair by pair, to meet his own. He said:

"Well, I don't know if it's the time of my life or just the season but I've never felt this way before. Lazy, you know, sort of contented but at the same time restless and longing for something—are you feeling this?

"Also *nostalgic* as hell.

"Lately I've been dreaming of North Carolina, where my family's from. I've been remembering the fireflies in the sweetgums at the edge of the tobacco fields. I mean, the fireflies just load up those trees, you would not *believe*. Also I remember a hot day walking down to this little grocery store with my mother. And porches in the early evening. And the kind of music that is made on those porches, down in that country. Or that's how it was when I was a boy, though I suppose that by now North Carolina is just one long curtain of McDonald's and Popeye's Chickens. But they *can't* have vacuumed those fireflies out of the sweetgums—not *yet,* I don't think."

The subway arrived at Grand Central Station. The doors opened. A few got on, a few got off. The doors slid shut.

"I've never done much begging. In summer I live off food that I raise and gather in the park. In winter I scout the garbage cans. I'm not against begging, it's a profession at least as honorable as, say, bankruptcy law, but when it gets to be a habit then I think it gets to be at least as ugly as bankruptcy law. You know what I'm saying?

"Anyway, I *am* begging now. I'm asking you to help me with bus fare to North Carolina. I want to go south, and I want to go tonight. I'd like to go and see the fireflies in the scrub back of Mc-Donald's, and more than that, there's a man down there, a man who fled these parts, and I want to see what I can learn from him, and maybe what he tells me will teach me how to have the contentment without the restlessness.

"Fat chance, right?

"But anyway, you folks, if you take any foolish pity on such foolish desperation, you think you might help me out?"

He carried a Folger's coffee can up and down the car. Many gave, and some who looked into his eyes as they dug into their pockets were later surprised at how generous they'd been. A few even gave him five-dollar bills. The beggar did not say "Thank you" to them, but he nodded and smiled.

Someone tried to give him a ten spot, but the beggar studied it and said, "Uh-uh. No sir. This thing has been steeped in Z-rays."

He gave it back. The guy looked offended. The train stopped at Fifth Avenue, moved on. The guy tried to stuff the bill in the beggar's pocket but the beggar swerved his hips away. The guy looked at the other passengers, searching for sympathy. He got none. The other passengers understood somehow that if you took tainted money, you were just asking for trouble.

The train arrived at Times Square, end of the line, and the beggar got out and started trudging up the stairs. One of the passengers, as he hurried past him, heard him muttering to himself, "Well, that's enough, right? Isn't that enough, for Christ's sake? Can't I go home now?"

In less than half an hour Romulus was back at the cave and stretched out on the mattress, and he had wrapped a blanket around himself and turned on the TV. A Monday Night Football game—the new spring league. He wedged a candle into a chink of stone above him, and lit it, and then pulled the Folger's coffee can from his coat pocket and emptied the money onto the mattress. He started to count it, while he munched old pizza crusts from a plastic bag, while he kept one eye on the game.

Not a bad haul. The transit cops had chased him out of the subways only twice. Some of his pitches had fallen flat but some had soared.

He'd brought home six fives, forty-two ones, and such a weight of loose change as had distressed the seams of his pocket.

On TV, the football game was being played in the Roman Colosseum, which had been moved to the marsh flats of New Jersey and refurbished for the event. The teams were the New York/New Jersey Knights versus a legion of the Praetorian Guard from the time of the Emperor Caracalla.

If he weren't so tired, Romulus thought, he'd leave now. Right now. He'd catch a late bus so that when morning came he'd already be in Virginia and he could be reborn into sudden spring. Just the sort of jolt . . . well. You never knew. With the right sort of jolt you might get the whole of your divinity fired up again.

But he was too sleepy to start packing now.

And despite the chill, though winter was coming back to get its last licks, his coats and his blanket were keeping him quite warm. And there was a fine football game on the tube, and he was counting away at his money, humming and counting as contentedly as any counting-house fool.

Home, the game, plenty of money, and pizza crusts to munch on. What could be sweeter?

He'd take off tomorrow.

The ghosts parked the car at a pier. There was a river, and a warehouse with peeling walls. The ghosts got out and stood by the hood of the car and consulted quietly. They left Matthew waiting inside the car.

Matthew clutched his bloody towel close to him as if it were a comforter, and he tried to think about something.

His pain came in waves and he thought if he could find something to think about, maybe he could hold off the next wave. But he couldn't think of anything to think about except Scotty, and that was equal to or worse than the pain.

Outside, the silent ghost was saying something to the big one, and pointing at Matthew.

Then the pain welled up, and it wiped out the ghosts, and also the river and the warehouse, and Matthew passed out until the greater ghost slapped him awake again.

Now the ghosts were on either side of him in the backseat. The great ghost took the bloody towel and found a corner of it that wasn't drenched in gore. He put his arm around Matthew's shoulder. He drew Matthew's head close to him and held it in the crook of his elbow and spit on the towel and wiped Matthew's face with it. Like Matthew's mother used to do.

He said, "So you don't know nothing about no videotape?"

"No . . ."

"And you got nothing to tell us about the Caveman?"

"Don't . . . I don't . . . You stay away from the Caveman. His daughter . . . his daughter's a cop."

"Ooh. I bet she just loves the fucking deadbeat."

"She . . . they're close. She wouldn't let nothing happen to him."

"Oh yeah? So what's *her* name?"

"Nothing."

"Nothing? That's a dumb name. Where's this nothing live?"

"I don't. I . . . just don't . . ."

"Hey, that's OK, Matthew. But my colleague here, he wants to see the Caveman real bad. Wants some action, wants some fun. What's to fucking do here, while we wait for you, Matthew? We're bored. What are we going to do for kicks?"

The ghost had scrubbed Matthew's cheek to his satisfaction, and now he brought his face down low. Matthew looked up and the ghost's no-face was just an inch above his. He could smell the garlic on the ghost's breath, leaching through the gauzy bandage.

"Maybe," the ghost said, "he could draw a picture. Maybe my friend could draw a picture on your *face.* Is that OK?"

"On my—"

"Like a tattoo, Matthew. Right here. On your cheek where everybody can see it."

Matthew tried to squirm away but the arm held him securely against the ghost's breast.

Then he felt the fingers of the silent ghost. Felt them stroking his cheek. Long, gentle exploring strokes, like the strokes of a lover. The silent ghost opened a penknife. He put the blade against Matthew's cheek, and Matthew felt its coolness.

Said the greater ghost, "My colleague is an *artist,* Matthew. He'll do you a nice tattoo, for free. A tree, a big spreading tree, all over one side of your face—you like that? He don't have good tools, that's the problem. But then, he won't charge you nothing."

Matthew tried to cry out. The greater ghost made a wad of the towel and shoved it into his mouth.

"What was that? Was that a *yes,* Matthew? All right, we'll say it's a *yes, please carve a beautiful tree on my face.* Or, you could tell us where the videotape is."

Matthew tried to shake his head. His head wouldn't move.

"Or we could make it even simpler for you, Matthew. Just show us where the Caveman lives. That's all. It's so easy. You want me to take the towel out now? You got something to say?"

The greater ghost drew the towel out of Matthew's mouth. A pair of teeth came with it. The ghost opened his window and shook the teeth out onto the lot.

"OK Matthew?"

Matthew didn't speak.

"Oh shit. He's still fucking around. Better get started." He put the towel back in Matthew's mouth.

The silent ghost came close and raised the knife.

Matthew strained to look straight down. To the point near his chin where the knife was starting to work.

Said the big ghost, "One good thing, Matthew, is now nobody'll ever have to see your ugly face no more. They'll just see this big scar that looks like a tree, and they'll say, hey that fucker is a work of art."

Brisk crosshatching of tiny cuts, climbing up his cheek. Another wave of pain welled up and he tried to ride it but it washed over him, he was shrieking into the towel and tumbling end over end in the belly of that pain and then the towel came out again and he heard himself saying, "Inwood . . ."

"What was that?"

"Inwood Park, I'll show you. Cave. His cave's in Inwood . . . I'll show you. I'll show you. His daughter's name is Lulu. Here . . . here . . . her address."

He handed over the little piece of paper Romulus had given him.

81

In the waning moments of the game on TV, the New York/New Jersey Knights, trailing by three, launched a desperation pass. The Knights quarterback released the ball an instant before the Praetorian Guard reached him. Shields and swords aglitter, they cut him to pieces. The Knights responded with bursts from their semi-automatics. The ball soared into the night sky. Behind the ball could be seen the New York City skyline, most prominently Stuyvesant's tower in its mist of glowing green cloud.

Then the ball came down and was caught with full balletic flourishes by one of the Knights, who carried it into the end zone and kept on running.

He ran down terrace steps, through a crumbling ivy-covered arch into a garden, and up to a pool. He took off his helmet. It was

Bob, and Betty was a sylph in a translucent gown who lounged with her comely calves in the water. The trees were ancient oaks and mimosas. The color of the leaves was electric green. Betty embraced her hero, and offered him a wineskin, and when he had taken his fill, she put a tiny onion in his mouth, and he kissed her. During the kiss he passed the onion back into her mouth, and she giggled. The announcer told us that this broadcast was the sole property of the World League of American Football, and any rebroadcast for any purpose was strictly prohibited. Superimposed on the screen were the words

Tonight's game was brought to you by . . .
Z-rays
What could be sweeter?

Was it all fraudulent, then? Was the sweetness and rare contentment that he had been feeling, was it all a grand fraud? He killed the screen.

He listened to a plane overhead.

Then he was listening to something else.

Footsteps?

82

 T he great ghost had his arm around Matthew, and he helped him along the meandering path, over the roots and rocks, as one might support a drunken friend. The silent ghost followed along behind.

Matthew stopped.

The big ghost tried to pull him along. Matthew shook his head violently. He raised his hand, and flapped it.

The great ghost looked, looked through the trees, and saw in the moonlight a ridge of rock. A dark smear in the ridge. He whispered, "That's the cave, Matthew?"

Matthew pressed his face into the breast of the ghost.

The ghost laid Matthew down gently, where he was.

"Good boy. Stay. Don't say a fucking word. Don't make a fucking sound."

He motioned to the other ghost.

They moved soundlessly through the trees. Up the slope. They spread out a little as they approached the cave.

They saw the mattress. The blanketed heap on it. They heard sleep-breathing. The lesser ghost waited by the broad trunk of the beech tree, and the great ghost went up swiftly.

He stood over the sleeping figure and switched on his flashlight.

"Caveman."

The head of a one-eyed old woman emerged from the blankets.

"Not here. Who are you? You just missed him. He's on vacation. Down south. Will you please get that light? Out of my face? What now, are you cops? I got a right. To be here. I'm subletting while he's away. You just missed him. He just ten minutes ago up and went. He was. *Antsy.*"

PLAY

83

L ent, North Carolina, had one motel, a mile out of town on the Lumberton Road. Shady Rest, they called it. The shade was a few brutally pruned pines. The lawn had been mown within an inch of its life. Not a restful-seeming place at all.

In the office, the furnishings were fit for a prison. Fit for that dungeon Matteawan, Romulus thought. Everything was pin neat. There was a little display of rebel flags for sale. A bigger Stars and Bars hung behind the desk, next to a portrait of Pat Robertson. By the window, there was a green-gold parakeet in a cage, but it didn't dare open its mouth.

The white woman who came out from her parlor had all her hair pulled back sharply from her face and tied in a bun back there, and it looked as though she'd pulled her skin back and tied that up, too. She didn't answer when he asked her about vacancies. Her eyes were narrow to begin with—she narrowed them some more, and asked:

"Where's your car?"

"Ma'am, I came by bus."

"Came for what?"

"Excuse me?"

"What is it you want here?"

"I came to visit an old friend of mine."

"You got crumbs all over your shirt."

"Excuse me? Oh yes. Heh-heh. The bus, eating on the . . . haven't washed up yet."

"Who's your friend?"

"Clive Leif."

"I don't know him."

"Ah."

She said, "Maybe you got the wrong town."

"This is Lent?"

"*This* isn't Lent. This is outside of Lent."

"Right."

"Maybe your friend lives in Lumberton."

"Maybe you're right. I thought I heard him say Lent. Maybe he said Lumberton and I heard it wrong."

She turned to head back to her parlor.

"Ma'am?"

She spoke over her shoulder. "No sir."

"Ma'am?"

"You don't have no bags. You don't have no car."

She shut the door.

Romulus shouted, "So where the hell do I stay, *ass-face?* This is the only fucking motel in town, *where do I stay?*"

Through the door, she called, "Lavonia's. By the Jiminy Mart. Go stay there."

Before he left, he slid out the tray at the bottom of the parakeet's cage, and removed the newspapers and threw them in the wastebasket. Then he took the big Confederate flag down from the wall, folded it neatly—he respected this woman's need for neatness—and he put it in the tray and slid the tray back into the cage.

Then he went to look for Lavonia's.

84

At the Jiminy Mart they told him how to get there. But he still couldn't find it, so he stopped at an old wooden shotgun house and asked the black woman who came to the door if she knew where Lavonia's Motel was.

"Right here. Want a room?"

"Yes ma'am."

"Eight dollars."

"Yes ma'am. You Lavonia?"

"Uh-huh."

"But this isn't a motel."

"You want a room, I got two rooms, nobody in neither of 'em, you want one of 'em? Come on."

He followed her through her long hot living room. Kids' toys, *Enquirers*, sofa cushions scattered about. The VCR was on, but frozen. Freeze frame of some fancy kitchen in suburbia. Young white hunk with the nostrils of a racehorse was caught in midsnarl at some blond witchlet.

Romulus asked, "What you watching there?"

"My *story*. You can use the kitchen if you want. You want, I'll show you how to light the stove."

"What story?"

"Huh? 'Young and the Restless.' I'm catching up. I tape it when I'm working. Tell me when you want a shower, and I won't use the water."

"Is it a good story? Is it about restlessness?"

"Huh?"

She looked back at him. She was a scarecrow. So was the woman at Shady Rest, so was the pump jockey at Jiminy's. Whole town was famine-stricken. *Lent,* he thought, right.

His room was in the back, past the kids' room. A bed, too short, and a card table. And an old yellowing poster of Jesus as giant, knock-knocking on the UN building in New York.

"Kids make too much noise, you tell me, OK?"

"OK."

"How long you staying?"

"Long as it takes me to find who I'm looking for."

"Who you looking for?"

"Man named Clive Leif. You know him? White kid? Early twenties, I guess?"

"No. *Uh*-uh."

"He went to New York to work in the theater. But he didn't make it and he came back."

"Well, maybe Miz Peasley knows him. Her boy Joey went to New York."

"Yeah? What happened to him?"

"Oh, he did some acting, he made it *big,* uh-huh. He was even on my story. Once. He played a bartender. I don't know after that."

"Was he good-looking?"

"I guess. *Some* would say."

"You got that scene on tape by any chance?"

"Nope. That was more'n a year ago. Why you ask?"

"Beats me. Getting so I'll ask anything. I guess I'm getting to be a true pain in the ass. Where's this Miz Peasley live?"

85

M iz Peasley lived in the kind of neighborhood that Sherman's boys would have drooled over, if they'd happened to have swung their havoc a little to the north. The very cream of Doric mausoleums, of gables and pergolas and boxwood gardens and dovecotes and some fragrance heavy and maddening on the evening air.

Romulus peered through all the blossoming and saw some of the slave shacks, still standing, out in back of the big houses. Some looked as though they were still occupied. Well, why not? There were still plenty of slaves to occupy them.

He opened the gate at Miz Peasley's and went up the cracked flagstone walk.

He wove through spills of wild rosebush.

High up, under a scalloped attic eave, an eyebrow window looked down upon him.

It was that sort of house. Tall, turreted. Partaking of the town's general anorexia. A big brass knocker. He knocked.

A curtain fluttered in the bay window.

He knocked again.

Shifted over and peeked through the rose-colored sidelight into the hall. A bony woman appeared. She made a shooing gesture and shouted through the door.

"I've already bought plenty!"

"Ma'am?"

"Say I've already bought it and I didn't like it!"

"I'm not selling anything!"

"I've got Jesus in my heart! I pray all day long! Suit you? Go away!"

"Miz Peasley! I want to talk to your son! I'm looking for Joey!"

She opened the door. "Joey doesn't live here. He hasn't lived here for years. Go away."

"You know where he is?"

"What do you want with him?"

"I'm from New York, ma'am. I'm investigating a murder. Did your son use the professional name Clive Leif?"

"You a cop?"

"No ma'am. This is private. I think your son was acquainted with the murdered man. I think he might have some evidence I'd like to look at. I'd like to talk to him."

"Well you can't. I tell you, he doesn't live here."

"Where *does* he live?"

"Wouldn't know."

"Have you talked to him lately?"

"He doesn't want to have a thing to do with that life. You understand? He's finished with all that."

"I do understand. I know what they did to him."

"You wouldn't have any idea."

"Yes, I would. I do. Because they did the same thing to Scotty Gates, ma'am. The one who was killed."

"You don't know the way my son used to be."

"But I know how he is now. He's scared, right? He's quiet. He's got nothing to say. He doesn't want to talk about it. He doesn't want to do *anything,* right?"

She was silent. She squinted at him. "How do you know that?"

"Because I know what happened to him."

"What? What happened to him?" Panic in her voice. "What did they do to my son?"

"He saw something."

"What did he see?"

"He saw somebody getting hurt. Just to give somebody else a little thrill. And he couldn't do anything about it. So maybe, maybe he just sort of *went along* with things."

"My son would never—"

"I'm not saying he did. I'm just saying he saw—"

"What did my son see?" Miz Peasley demanded.

She looked to have been through rough times, worry times. There was something old-woman and grasping in the way her eyes would dart and then seize hold of whatever they lit on. Even if it was only the brass knocker or the mother-of-pearl button on Romulus's shirt—those eyes grabbed like an old woman's eyes. But her hair was still blond and full, and her brow was still handsome. She was probably, Romulus realized, younger than he was.

Her eyes grabbed at his.

"What? Tell me, for God's sake, just tell me! You said a murder, did he see—"

"No. He didn't see the murder. The murder was just a week ago. He saw torture, I guess. What *exactly* he saw—I don't know. That's why I want to talk to him."

"I don't know where he is."

"Ma'am, he probably doesn't even know there *was* a murder. If he knew, I think maybe he'd want to help me. If you'd just help me find him—"

"But I don't know how to find him. I'm telling you the truth. He came home in October, but just for a while. For a while he moved back into the cottage—"

"What cottage?"

"Just behind the house here. It's his own little place. I keep it clean for him. It's always ready for him. Always fresh flowers. And when he came back I thought he'd stay. I prayed he would. Because he seemed so . . . he was in pieces, he came back in pieces. If I could have . . . if I could only have figured out how to make him stay, I could have healed him."

"But he wouldn't stay?"

"He said they could find him here. He said he had to go and he couldn't tell me where he was going because if I knew, they could make me tell them. So he left, and I don't see him at all anymore. Except once when he came home for a visit because he just couldn't stand that life. And he cried in my arms for a day and then he was gone again and I don't know if I'll ever see him again. . . ."

She took a breath. She let it out.

"He's a temp now. He types. Some city somewhere in the South. He won't tell me which one but it doesn't matter, they're all the same. You know those horrible New South cities where they build the trashiest glass boxes imaginable and the theater's worse than watching TV but who cares, because Joey doesn't go out anyway. He just goes to work and comes home and watches TV and goes to bed. That's what he does. He calls me sometimes and tells me about the TV he watches. About the old movies he watches. He was going to be a great stage director. A movie director. A famous *artist*. That's what happened to my boy."

"You wanted that?"

"Wanted what?"

"You wanted him to be famous?"

"Oh, that's none of your business."

"OK."

Her eyes grabbed idly at the things on the porch. Then she said, "Actually, no—*I* never did. I never cared. His father cared."

"OK."

"None of your business though."

"No ma'am."

"And that man was not God's gift to the stage, whatever Joey might think."

"You mean Joey's father?"

"The only real acting he ever did was when he talked me into marrying him. Enough. Enough of this. Next time Joey calls I'll tell him you were looking for him."

"Thank you."

215

"Who shall I say came by?"

"The Caveman."

"The Caveman? That's your name?"

"That's what people call me. I live in a cave, ma'am. In Inwood Park. Can you remember that? It's in New York. Inwood Park, the Caveman. If he wants to, he'll find me."

"All right. I'll remember. The man who lives in a cave, I certainly won't forget that."

"Things may change, ma'am. Things may get better. I used to read a lot of history. All of a sudden, you know, the cruel lord gets overthrown, they hang his body from the tower he used to rule from. Then everybody comes out of hiding."

"Are you crazy?"

"Some have said so. But still—things may get better."

He turned and walked down that path, steering around the rambling roses.

86

Lavonia asked him did he want to eat supper with them? For three dollars he had lamb chops and coleslaw and rice and turnip greens. She fixed the turnip greens because he had asked her for something southern. Her kids, Millie and Frazer, took a few bites of the greens and left the rest on their plates. As soon as they were done they went to watch TV. Presently he and Lavonia joined them. They watched a rerun of something called "Laverne and Shirley." The kids sat on the floor, and Lavonia sat in an armchair with the stuffing busting out of it, and Romulus sat in an old white-lacquered captain's chair. All four of them stared. Ads came and went, the kids' attention did not falter for an instant. They seemed to have no more notion of what they were watching than Romulus did. They just gazed on, resolutely. Meanwhile Romulus shut his eyes and saw the face of Miz Peasley. Her anguish.

Now he had that to carry around with him, along with the images of Matthew's anguish.

At some lull in the blare, he heard a bird outside enunciating perfectly the words *Chuck Will's widow.*

At another lull he asked Lavonia, "Suppose you had to get away from here, you had to hide, go live in some city so big and so dull that nobody would know your name and nobody would care—"

She didn't let him finish. She kept her eyes on the set. She said simply: "Charlotte."

When the show was over, Millie, who was nine years old, turned to him.

"Do you watch TV a lot, mister?"

"Pretty much."

"What show do you like *best?"*

"That one seemed pretty good. Really they're all pretty good. They're all just the same, aren't they?"

Millie reminded him faintly of Lulu, so he tried not to look at her.

Frazer, who was eleven, said with stony conviction, "If I was from New York, I'd kill all the drug pushers."

"There are a lot of them."

"I know. I'd have to have commandos to help me. We'd have to kill for *five days."*

87

Romulus could not sleep in the tiny bed. In the utter silence, with fireflies flashing out the window, his eyes stayed open all night. However, in the morning the kids made a terrific racket, and that helped him to relax—he napped for an hour or two. Then he got up and went out. He walked to Miz Peasley's.

She didn't answer his knock. She was at work, of course. But he gave her a minute, just to be sure, and then he went around back.

Found the cottage where Joey had stayed.

Found it padlocked. He walked all around it. There were four small windows, but all were secure, and soon he was back at the door again, frowning at that padlock.

Romulus thought that perhaps a man raised in the ghetto ought to know how to pick a lock. Not he.

He went back to the big house. Tried the back door. Also locked. He walked around and found slanting cellar doors. He pulled at one of the old wooden wings—it resisted him. He pulled harder. Suddenly it sprang up. He grinned and shrugged and went down the steps into cool darkness.

The cellar had a lovely cave-smell, and a soft flow of sunlight from the doors, which he had left spread wide.

When his eyes adjusted, he saw the steps that led up into the house, and he climbed them. He came to the door at the top, groped in the dark for the doorknob and found it. It turned when he asked it to.

He was in the kitchen.

Such a tall kitchen. To find the ceiling you looked way up like you would in a church. The refrigerator was a museum piece. His great-uncle the dentist had owned one like that.

The key he was looking for was hanging on a string by the back door. He went out, returned to the cottage. The key opened the padlock.

The old door creaked open and he stepped into Joey's place. Simply furnished. The flowers in the vase on the checkered table-cloth were as fresh as Miz Peasley had boasted. There was also a shelf with every ribbon or medal or flattering gewgaw that little Joey had ever brought home. Romulus saw in this decor the hand, the grabby eye, of Miz Peasley. He didn't know Joey, of course, but it seemed unlikely that, on his own, the kid would have saved such trifles. No, the decor was his mother's and she'd done a handsome job. It was truly a wonder what you could do with slave quarters when you fixed the roof and put in plumbing and AC and cut the occupancy from fourteen souls to one.

Romulus searched through every drawer he could find. He checked behind the cabinet. He checked the closet.

Then he stepped into the tiny bedroom. Not much to see— just a bed and a hook rug under it.

He thought a moment. Then he lifted the bed and slid the rug out, and saw the loose floorboard. When he saw that, he felt his pulse go up a notch. He set the bed down. He got down on his

belly and slid under it a ways, and prized the board up with his fingertips.

A stink came up.

He slid forward a little farther and looked in. Not much light
but he didn't need much light—it was a shallow space. In the space
was a mousetrap.

In the trap was a mouse who had made its mistake some time
ago but still looked astonished.

Romulus stared at the thing. He understood that he had come
a long way and gone to a great length of trouble for nothing. However, this was more or less what life was about, wasn't it? He tidied
the room and went outside and locked up and stood a moment in
the shade of what he thought might well be a pecan tree. He had
never seen a pecan tree but he knew they had leaves like this, fan
leaves like a walnut had. And there were black husks, like shell cas-
ings, all over the grass. From last year's crop.

Then he noticed a line in the grass.

Near his feet. A faint break, maybe a foot and a half long, and
as he studied it, he noticed another break, at right angles to the first.
In a few moments his eyes had picked out the whole square. Where
someone had dug, and then carefully replaced the turf over the hole
he'd made, and in another month of this warm spring the place
would have been invisible.

Romulus knelt and got his fingers under that piece of turf and
lifted, and the whole thing came up, like a piece of carpet. He
moved it aside and scrabbled at the earth. He dug up a locked metal
box.

He found some loose bricks and put them in the hole where
the box had been. Rearranged the carpet of turf. Went back into the
big house and put the key on its nail, and retraced his steps down to
the cellar and up and out.

He carried the box back to Lavonia's.

Nobody there. Lavonia was at work. The kids were in school.
He spent twenty minutes picking at the lock on the box with an as-
sortment of kitchen knives and forks. Then he looked for a hammer.
It took him longer to find a hammer at Lavonia's than it had taken
him to find the locked box at Joey's. When he finally found one

under the kitchen sink it didn't help him any. He took monster whacks but they only dented the box.

This was not elegant detective work.

He heard a saw going across the street and went over there where three men were building a garage. He borrowed a sledgehammer.

That did the trick.

The lid flew open. Inside the box was a small cardboard box with a videotape inside.

He returned the sledgehammer. The men's T-shirts had cusps of sweat under the arms, bibs of sweat under the collars. If he could have given up his own work, and taken up theirs, he would have. If he could have been useful to them swinging that sledgehammer, if he didn't have that videotape waiting for him over there in Lavonia's . . .

He thanked them and went back and fixed himself some coffee.

He was going to watch the videotape while he drank the coffee, and then perhaps the indulgence of the one thing—fresh coffee!—in a kitchen!—sunny morning!—would assuage the ugliness of the other thing. But soon the coffee was all gone, and he still hadn't touched the videotape.

Then he got a bit brisk with himself—he pushed the cup away and brought the videotape into the living room, and turned on the TV.

He studied the VCR controls for a long time before selecting one. Using his dim memory of the Bible for his instruction manual, he decided that Power was surely the prime mover, the essential beginning of things. He pushed. The machine sprang to attention. He fed it the tape, which it devoured.

Now what? Why, we're all the frolicking children of Eden, what else should we do but Play?

It was a movie about pain.

Not about damage. The tape depicted some damage, but damage wasn't its theme. The damage seemed somehow incidental to the pain.

Scotty Gates was manacled to a white wall. His back was to us. His face was in profile. While we watched, something happened to him. He winced, screamed. Then it happened again. But you couldn't see what it was. The frame was cut off just above his waist, the damage was off screen.

All you saw was the look on Scotty Gates's face. A glaze of old tears. A single bead of blood where he had bit his lip.

Then his voice. With the dead-echo of a confining chamber.

"Please. Why . . . are . . . you . . ."

Next, Leppenraub's voice. Faint, far from the mike: "I love you."

The thing was done to Scotty again. His head lurched upward, his carotid artery pulsed, his mouth opened and he cried out again.

"Please. Please. Please. Please."

Leppenraub: "Look at me."

Romulus had the feeling that whatever was being done to Scotty, Leppenraub wasn't doing it.

He was having it done *for* him.

For David Leppenraub, Sheila. For his pleasure. You didn't believe me. You thought he was too gentle, or too afraid. Nobody believed me, but I knew. I know what Stuyvesant can do to people. I've known all along, but none of you believed me. Now what do you say? Now the shit is before us, Sheila, it's in plain view, *now* what do you say?

On the video, the thing was done to Scotty again.

Scotty: "I don't . . . *why?* Please tell me why, what's the *point*, what's the . . . what's the purpose? Do you think this is art? This is—"

Leppenraub: "Look at me. I want you to look at me with your wonderful eyes."

Cut to Scotty slumped in another white corner, staring up at the camera. His limbs were splayed, limp. No manacles now. There was no more need for manacles.

Scotty asked: "Is there . . . something . . . I can do? To stop . . ."

He was shuddering. His voice trembled. He brought his arms up to fold them across his chest and something flashed toward him. Snakelike, rubbery, and a sharp slap was heard on the sound track and Scotty's hands fell to his sides.

"Please. Isn't there something you want?"

Leppenraub: "What sins have you committed?"

Shuddering. Spasms. "I can't . . . I can't . . . no more."

Again he raised his arms, to wrap them around himself.

Again the blurred snake, Scotty too weary to flinch. He groaned.

Leppenraub: "You're too soft."

"You're brilliant. You're *brilliant.* All right? But I can't . . . it's not . . ."

The lash.

Leppenraub: "How annoying."

"Brill . . . brilliant . . . art . . ."

He tried to curl up fetally.

The lash stopped him. The lash liked him to stay open, undefended.

Leppenraub: "You're a glutton."

Leppenraub's voice seemed bored and remote. Seemed he was making this movie only because he and his friends had nothing better to do that day.

Fuck a kid up for life, it's fun, sure, it's something to while away a rainy day, but that's about as far as it goes. Really, it's scarcely worth the effort.

It was just *play* for Leppenraub. It was a break from making his gentle art.

90

R omulus heard the screen door shut behind him. He wheeled in his chair.

Millie was there. She was looking at the screen.

"What you watching?"

He rose. He tried to shield her with his body. She tried to see around him.

"Millie, it doesn't matter. Aren't you home early?"

"Half day. I have to wait and Miz Grey will pick me up. Is that a good show?"

"Wait outside for Miz Grey, OK, Millie?"

"That man don't have no clothes on. Is that man hurt?"

"Millie, here's fifty cents. Is there some kind of candy that you like?"

"Yes."

Behind him, Scotty groaned.

"Go buy it. At the little store. Don't cross any big streets, right? When you come back wait outside."

"OK."

"Is that a promise, you'll wait outside?"

"Yes."

91

F ull-length shot of Scotty facing the camera. Again the manacles. A hypodermic syringe dangled from his arm.

There was nothing left of him.

His lower lip was so weirdly slack you could see his gums. There were deep furrows between his eyes, but the eyes themselves had no expression, or they had drawn all expression deep within themselves. They had carried their lights inside and shut the doors.

Now it was more than pain, it was an *exhaustion* of pain.

Scotty spoke. It was hard to hear him. He said, "How . . . long?"

Leppenraub: "What? What's the matter?"

"Let me . . ."

"There's no way out."

"Fuck you. You . . . fucking bastard."

"Don't cry, little peasant."

No blood. No crimson or bruise-purple. All white, shades of white. Stuyvesant's favorite color.

Said Scotty, "Why don't you let me die?"

Leppenraub, mocking him: "Oh, if only this were over *quickly!*"

In the background, faintly, laughter could be heard. His audience.

Said Scotty, "Why not . . . mercy? Why not? This hurts. Let me sleep. Let me . . . why not . . . show some mercy?"

"What sins have you committed?"

Romulus heard the screen door slam again. He said, "Millie, I told you to wait outside!"

But it wasn't Millie.

It was a young white man, blond, strong, spare. He glanced at the screen, and then into Romulus's eyes. He went to the VCR and he hit Eject and took the tape out.

He turned to Romulus.

He said, "You don't want to watch this. I promise you, you don't. This will give you nightmares."

92

His eyes were bloodshot. He looked like he was familiar with nightmares.

"Joey?"

"Yeah, that's a name all right. It's not my name, not now."

"So what do I call you? Clive Leif?"

"Not that either. That sounds like some phony theater name, and I'm no longer involved with that life. You don't have to call me anything, mister. You won't know me long enough for this to be a problem."

Romulus asked him, "How'd you know I was here?"

"My mother called me."

"She said she doesn't have your number."

"Well, that was smart of her to say. Tomorrow I'll get my number changed, so next time she says it, it'll be true."

Romulus asked him, "But how'd you find me *here?* I didn't tell your mother where I was staying."

"Yeah, but from the way she described you, I had an idea Shady Rest hadn't given you the presidential suite."

"How did she describe me?"

"She said you were black."

"Oh."

"Also kind of scruffy-looking, but black would have been enough for Shady Rest. Safe bet you'd wound up here."

"Right."

"If you're planning on staying awhile, there's a nice cave down by Amos Creek."

"I'll keep it in mind."

"Is that for real?"

"Is what for real?"

"Mama says you live in a cave?"

"I do. I wouldn't say it's *for real,* but it's where I live."

"You're not a detective?"

"Not so I get a paycheck."

"But you found this tape in a hurry."

"Luck."

"*Tough* luck. I mean it, I'm telling you, for the next few years you'll be wanting to sleep with the light on."

"So why didn't you destroy it?"

"I don't know. I guess I thought one day it might come in handy. Somehow."

"It'd come in handy right now. You could let the world know what kind of man David Leppenraub is."

"Oh, yeah? Why should I do that? What's the world's interest in this?"

"He killed Scotty Gates."

Joey dropped his gaze. His voice changed. "Yeah. So Mama told me."

He shook his head. Back and forth, to get a thought out of it.

He asked Romulus, "Did the police find the copy of this that I made for Scotty?"

"No. I guess that's what Leppenraub killed him for. Leppenraub must have it."

Joey sat on Lavonia's battered couch.

He said, "So I killed him. After everything else I did, I had to do that, too."

"*You* didn't kill him."

"Sure I did, I gave him the damn tape. That was so stupid. So *stupid*. I should have known he'd try to use it. He was so naive. He was the dumbest hick you ever saw. I thought I knew hicks growing up around here. But he was incredible. He thought he could threaten a man like Leppenraub. *Stupid! Jesus.* After everything else I did to him, I had to do this, too."

"What else did you do to him, Joey?"

93

B ut then Millie called from the door.

"Can I come in now?"

Romulus didn't turn, but he called back to her: "What d'you get, Millie?"

"M&M's."

"Will you save me a few?"

"Yes."

"Where's that lady that's supposed to take care of you?"

"She's not here yet. What color you want? Green?"

"Green's OK. Could you wait out there for her?"

Reluctantly: "Yes."

He heard her dragging down the steps.

94

When her steps had faded, Joey asked him:

"Who are you? I mean, you're not a cop, you're not a detective, so what are you looking for? You want to send Leppenraub to jail?"

"That's a start."

"You got any evidence besides this?"

"Not in truth."

"Well then, you lose. Look, I've spent a lot of time thinking about this. A lot of nights. The tape isn't enough—this won't hold up. David's got a pack of million-dollar lawyers, you know they'd tear this tape to shreds. They'd say it was just a show. They'd say it was all makeup and special effects. So forget it. Unless you're just looking to make a few bucks. You could sell this to the *Weekly World News* maybe. SHUTTERBUG IN SADIST SEX SCANDAL. Is that what you want? A few bucks?"

"No."

"Then what *are* you looking for?"

"I'd like to know the truth."

"Why?"

"Because those lies they're telling . . . they dishonor Scotty Gates."

"*Dishonor?* Huh. I haven't heard that word in quite a while. You know, my mother thinks you're crazy."

"Yeah."

"That's true?"

"It's true I have done crazy things."

"You sure sound crazy. *Dishonor.*"

They sat in silence. A car stopped outside. It was Miz Grey, the woman come to pick up Millie. Millie ran in, dropped three green M&M's into Romulus's hand, gave him a hug, and ran out again. The car drove off.

Joey shook his head, slowly. "All right. You want to know why

I held on to this? If I tell you, will you go away and leave me alone?"

Romulus just looked at him. Joey seemed to take his look for an assent. He said, "OK. It had nothing to do with Leppenraub. It was for *me*. It was to remind me. So if I started to forget I could watch it and then I'd remember again. Not what Leppenraub did. What *I* did.

"Because I took those pictures.

"Nobody forced me. Nobody held a gun to my head. I did it because it meant that David Leppenraub trusted me, that he wanted me in his little circle. You understand? That's all I wanted. I . . . I didn't just love that man, I *revered* him. I thought he was the greatest artist of the human psyche who ever lived. I thought he had us all figured out. That he knew what it is that attracts people to suffering. Why people seem to *reach out* to it, you know, like suffering's some kind of holy mercy—David understood that, and to me that meant he understood everything. And *I* was one of his right-hand men. Fucking Joey Peasley from Lent, North Carolina. You wouldn't believe how proud that made me. He was like my father. He was like my Christ. I was his disciple.

"And so was Scotty.

"I mean Scotty always seemed . . . kind of *excited* by what we were doing. That wasn't the first weekend we hurt him. But he never scrammed. You get this? He could have just taken off, but he didn't, he stuck around. No matter what we did to him, he stayed. So I thought that meant it was OK, somehow. Though sometimes we came damn close to killing him. I say we, because I've got to say we, because I was part of it, I can't let myself forget that, ever. *Ever.* But I wasn't the one who actually hurt him. I just worked the camera. I wasn't honored enough to be the one hurting him. David's *special* boys did that. They did anything he wanted. They did everything they could think of, so long as it didn't leave a mark.

"See, David didn't want Scotty marked. Oh, every now and then a little scratch or bruise couldn't be helped, and internal injury—that was no problem. But he didn't want any permanent scars that would show.

"David just had a thing for Scotty. For hours, I mean endlessly, he could look at that kid. When he was tired of torturing him, he'd take him in his arms to comfort him, and he'd just keep looking at him and calling him 'my little piece of heaven.'

"Maybe also, though, the reason David didn't want to leave scars was he was afraid he'd push it too far someday and Scotty would rat out, and David didn't want any incriminating evidence. You know?

"But I didn't think Scotty would ever rat out. Oh, he'd whine a lot, he'd cry and he'd beg David to leave him alone, to let somebody else be the Pain-Challenger. That's what we called him—like these were some kind of sacred rites, and civilization was rotting because it had turned its back on the sacrament of pain, and here on this farm we were keeping the spark alive.

"And Scotty, he'd curse and cry and say we were killing him. But he never beat it out of there.

"I was working in Leppenraub's little theater up there, I guess you know that? For the summer. Assistant director. I'd be in rehearsal and one of the boys would stop by, and say David needed my expertise, and I'd come running back to the farm and they'd have the kid on the pool table, and David's boys had worked up some new torture. They were 'challenging the godhead,' that's what they called it. They used to read books on torture. I mean it—they used to read reports from Amnesty International—that's where they got some of their ideas.

"We were sick beyond your worst nightmare, mister.

"Every one of us. We were sick, we were out of our skulls, and I was back behind the camera and I don't think I could have done those things to him myself but how do I *know* that? I was never asked. I just stayed there behind the viewfinder and watched, and I think that makes me sicker than any of them. I thought these things that David Leppenraub was teaching me would make me the greatest director that ever lived. 'Cause I was looking into the very soul of human desire, and . . . horror, and suffering and—you know? And, see, David had friends who were Hollywood producers, and one day I just knew he was going to say to me, 'Your apprenticeship is finished,' and snap his fingers and I'd have a fucking job like that. OK?

"I just had to be patient. Be helpful. Believe in the fucking challenge.

"But then one day I had to go over to the farm to help Scotty climb a tree. 'Cause Scotty couldn't do it by himself—he was too weak. And I was watching the way he was moving and I realized, He's all busted up in there, he's moving like an old man. And I had to practically carry him up that tree. David didn't give a shit. He was fiddling with the camera, figuring out the f-stop.

"So here I am, I'm carrying this kid like a monkey on my back, and I get him way up there and tie him to a limb like he's crucified. And I wipe the sweat off his face with a towel. And climb down out of the frame, and I'm looking down at David. David keeps fiddling with his lenses. Finally he gives this disgusted look and he calls up, 'Scotty, what's the matter with you?' 'Nothing,' says Scotty, 'why?' And David says, 'You look like you're about fifty years old. You look sick. You're not taking care of yourself.' Scotty says, 'I'm all right, David.' And David says, 'If you won't take care of yourself, I'm sure not taking care of you.' And then he says to me, 'Get him down. I can't use him.'

"So I help him out of the tree, and I'll be goddamned if I know how I did it, 'cause he's a mess, he's bawling all over me and he's made of rubber, and the only thing that kept him alive is he was so scared he just clutched on to me like a tick all the way down.

"And then David says to me, 'Clive, would you go up? You know, you look an awful lot like Scotty. Would you be willing to go up?'

"And so just like that I was David Leppenraub's new angel. His little piece of heaven.

"I flew up that tree. And David himself climbed up to tie me on. We had the shot in less than an hour. And I came down and Scotty was still sitting there, up against this stone wall. I helped him stand up. Then we walked back. I had to carry a lot of these bird cages, these props, I don't know what they were for. And Scotty walked beside me, and David was still back at the tree, taking another shot.

"And something happened to me then. I don't know what it was. Or maybe it happened when I was hanging on that tree. But I knew that I was done with this. I didn't want to be David's angel. I didn't even want to be a director. I just wanted to get out of there.

"And I asked Scotty, I said, 'Scotty, why don't you run away?'

He didn't say anything. He just kept walking. Sort of hobbling. And I said it again. 'Why don't you fucking run away?' And then he said, 'Where am I going to run *to?*'

"See, he didn't know shit about the world. He thought he didn't have any world but what David Leppenraub told him was his world. And anywhere he went, he knew, David's boys would find him.

"And I guess he was right about that. They did find him. Maybe they wouldn't have if I hadn't given him that videotape. But I did. And you know, one of these days they're going to find me, too. That's their new challenge, and they're clever boys. And when they find me they're sure as shit going to kill me."

95

They sat, Romulus in the exploded armchair and Joey in the white-lacquered captain's chair, and they stared at the empty TV screen.

Joey said, "So is that enough for you?"

"Yeah, I guess. Except . . ."

But Romulus scarcely had a voice. He cleared his throat. He said, "The needle. What about that?"

"Huh?"

"What was in the needle, Joey? The needle hanging from his arm."

"I don't know. Some shit. Some shit to make it even scarier for Scotty. But cooking up the shit, that wasn't my department."

"Whose was it?"

"The boys—one of the boys."

"Which one? Vlad? Was Vlad one of the boys?"

Joey almost smiled.

"Vlad. So you've met Vlad. Good man, isn't he? Level-headed. Easygoing. Huh? A real pearl of a man."

"Was Vlad one of the boys?"

Still Joey wouldn't answer. The very name seemed to spook

him. "I'd rather not talk about Vlad, all right? In fact, I think I've talked way too much already."

"But I need your help, Joey. I need the tape."

"Why? So they can kill *you,* too?"

"Maybe they won't kill anybody if we can put the bastards in jail."

Joey shrugged. "Yeah, sure—but we can't. Not with just this tape."

"But you're an eyewitness! If *you'll* testify—"

"Yeah. If I'd just be willing to testify at my own execution . . ."

Joey rose. He tucked the tape back into its cardboard container.

"Look, I got to go. I got a long drive ahead of me, and then I got to get back to work. I got a life to grind out here. Did Mama tell you what I did? I type. All day long. I couldn't tell you what I type. I just enter what they put in front of me. I was sick of it the first day. I bet in another twenty, thirty years, it'll *really* get to me. So I kind of hope they find me soon, you know? Listen, will you do me a favor? Will you never tell another soul what you saw here? Or you can tell them *what,* but just don't ever tell them *where* you saw this. I'm worried, you know? Not about me—about my mama."

He headed for the door. Romulus went with him. Trying to think of something to say, some argument, but nothing came to mind. On the steps Joey stopped to look at him. To study him. The young man's eyes, those arctic blue eyes, were as grabby as his mother's—but they held on to things a lot longer.

Then he offered:

"Hey look, if you ever find some other evidence, I mean proof, you know, something *solid,* something that could really put the fuckers away—then I would do it. Then I'd give you the tape."

Romulus shrugged. "You mean, if I don't need it, I can have it? If it doesn't matter?"

"Oh, it'll matter. On its own, the tape won't swing a jury. But it'll give them nightmares—it'll put them in the mood. Still, you got to have something else to back it up. Otherwise, what's the point? What's the sense in getting us all killed?"

"How would I find you?"

"Call Mama."

"She won't have your number."

"I'll check in with her now and then. Just tell her the man who lives in a cave is looking for me, and I'll find you. And now if you'll excuse me, I got this fucking life to grind out."

96

Romulus left eight dollars in quarters on his bed. Added twelve quarters for breakfast. He had already paid for last night's supper. He left a note.

> Thank you Lavonia Millie and Frazer. I enjoyed your company. I enjoyed watching "Laverne and Shirley." Frazer, when I get back to NYC I'll tell the drug pushers you're coming, they better clear out. On second thought, let it be a surprise.
>
> See you,
> Romulus Ledbetter

He took the bus to Lumberton but then he didn't have enough money left for the fare to New York. So he bought a ticket for as far as he could afford, which turned out to be Wilmington, Delaware.

At Wilmington—it was the middle of the night—he got off, then got back on when the driver went into the station for coffee.

Romulus went all the way back to the bus's cramped bathroom, and shut the door.

He sat on the john, and as the bus pulled out he put his head in his hands and tried to conceive of how one might replicate, with an orchestral instrument, the song of the chuck-will's-widow. But the engine noise filled his head and made him sleepy, and as soon as he started to drift the chuck-will's-widow flew off and the nightmare of the tape presented itself.

He had to keep shaking that nightmare off him.

Then somebody rapped on the door. Well, he'd known that was coming.

He only hoped the bus wasn't full, so he could let whoever needed to come in, while he slipped into a vacant seat way in the back where the driver wouldn't notice.

But when he opened the door it was Sheila, and he sat down again. She wedged herself into the bathroom and shut the door behind her.

"Shit or get off the pot, Romulus."

She didn't fit very well. He was on the toilet, and she was crammed up against the sink, and their knees touched.

"I'm trying to nab a little shut-eye here, Sheila."

"In here? This place smells disgusting. Don't they ever clean these places? Or are you *living* here now? Is this your new home, is that why it smells so—"

"I'm tired, Sheila. Not tonight."

"You're always tired. Every time I see you, you're whining about how tired you are. Poor boy. What's the matter, you *working too hard?*"

She laughed.

Said Romulus, "I'm not whining, it's a good tired. I'm whipping the sucker. You thought he was innocent, didn't you? He's not the killer type, you said. He doesn't have it in him. Did you see the show? Did you see?"

"I saw."

"*What* did you see, Sheila?"

"I saw a lot of fishiness."

"Oh, bullshit. You just can't admit when you're wrong. That's why I couldn't stay with you."

"*You* couldn't stay with *me?*"

"All I need is one more break, baby. One little nudge of proof, and Leppenraub's in the monkey cage. You know, I think I may be finding myself with this work. I'm happier than I've been in a long—"

"All you are is way crazier. Lulu tells me now you're getting nostalgic. Talking about the *bloodlines,* she says, and all the good old days. Your brother could be *dying,* and Lulu says you've got this little smile—"

"I'm sorry about my brother. That news hurts me. But listen— that pain, and all these pains, they're teaching me something."

"Yeah? What are they teaching you, boy?"

"Don't you think you can learn from suffering?"

"Hoo yes. I do. I learn a shitload. Learn that I *don't want* to suffer no more. Where'd you get that shit anyway? Learning from suffering?"

"But it's true, isn't it?"

"Crazier and crazier. Romulus. You think you're on your way up? You're going down so fast we going to have to pay a well digger to go find you. What's with you? Your man Stuyvesant using some new kind of ray on your brain?"

"What?"

"Well you always say that's where your problems—"

"What do you know? What do you know about a new ray?"

"Shit or get off the pot, Romulus, don't be so selfish. Others have to use these facilities, too."

She went out. She shut the door. In a moment she knocked again, and Romulus opened it quickly and demanded:

"What do you know about Z-rays?"

Some white woman. Looked like the sister of the owner of the Shady Rest—though this one had let herself go. Her hair was slack and there were pouches under her lonesome eyes. Romulus bowed to her.

"Excuse me, ma'am. It was moving a little *slow* tonight, you know what I mean?"

He pushed past her. He felt her shiver. But she steeled herself and went on in and shut the door, and Romulus cast around quick for a seat to duck into.

There were no seats available. Everybody was asleep and singles were sprawled into neighboring seats. Romulus took an armrest next to a snoring sailor, and hunched down low out of range of the driver's rearview mirror. He listened to the crashing sea wind of the sailor's breathing.

He saw that they were on the Jersey Turnpike.

A minute later the white woman pushed past him on her way up to the front, and Romulus went back to his hiding place. Shut the door. Sat.

And he was just drifting off again when he heard some kind of hubbub.

He heard the sailor crying out, "What the fu—"

He heard something on the PA, indistinctly.

Then, quite distinctly, the sailor cried out in disbelief, "A bomb in the bathroom?"

And others: "A *bomb* in the *bathroom!*"

Then the bus hit some rough going and Romulus was pitched forward. Then he realized they'd stopped. He cracked the door.

Hubbub and havoc in the aisle.

Romulus looked quickly all about him. The white woman had not looked like any wild-eyed anarchist, but you never knew with these lonely white women.

Everyone scrambled out. The whole busload of them, spilling onto the turnpike shoulder. The driver waited nobly at his post until they had all stepped off. Then he got out himself.

Then Romulus came out.

The white woman said to the driver, "That's him."

"That's who?"

"The bum."

"*Bum?* What bum?"

"The one I told you about. The bum in the bathroom."

"You didn't say *bomb?*"

"I said *bum.*"

Another passenger said, "I heard you say *bomb.*"

"I never said *bomb.* I said there's a *bum* in the bathroom."

This went on, but Romulus had passed out of earshot. He walked down the highway, and thirty pairs of eyes followed him, and he kept walking. He walked seven miles through a cold wind to the Walt Whitman Service Area. Wondering all the while, *What is the nature of Z-rays?*

97

So far here's what he knew, or had divined, or believed he had divined, about Z-rays:

1. Z-rays are green. They had been a viridescent green when

they had issued from Stuyvesant's tower, and a kind of greenish burr or buzzing on the black grass in Leppenraub's moony field.

2. They're the color of fireflies, of contentment.

3. They're potent and dangerous. Perhaps they're even dangerous to the user (Stuyvesant), for he never used them before. He introduced them now only because he's worried, profoundly worried, about the course of the investigation.

4. Therefore the investigation must be hitting close to home. Romulus must be on the verge of some understanding that could prove damaging, even fatal, to the schemes and fortunes of Cornelius Gould Stuyvesant.

5. Dream on.

6. You're getting off the track here. You were trying to think about Z-rays, their unique properties. But all these *whoosh-whooshes* of cars, vans, tankers, and semis are making it tough to concentrate, to keep things in order.

7. All right, Z-rays. They're subtle and mean. They're not the generation of reality, like Y-rays. No, no. They're the *infiltration of illusion*.

8. In other words, even your dreams aren't safe.

9. And maybe the Z-rays are getting to you. Sweet-talking you, throwing you subtly off course.

10. Y-rays make you suffer. But Z-rays throw an arm over your shoulder and tell you, "Sure, suffering's tough, I know that, I'm on your side. But suffering has its place, doesn't it? We learn through suffering. All great art and understanding is born of suffering."

11. Z-rays whisper, "Cast a cold eye on suffering and you'll be rewarded by the good life—you know what I mean, amigo?"

12. Z-rays whisper, "You know, you're doing quite well these days, amigo. You're getting healthier. Sanity is just around the corner, don't you think? And by the way, don't you think it's about time to forget about that silly Stuyvesant character—to leave him alone?"

13. Z-rays whisper, "Considering the joys of fireflies and martinis and extravagant sex and great expansive lawns, aren't you tired of being such a pain in the ass?"

14. Z-rays whisper, "You could drop your childish paranoia right this second, right here on this highway, and welcome home to

sanity and sweetness—WELCOME HOME, AMIGO. How about it?"

15. *Whoosh. Whoosh. Whoosh.*

98

He caught a ride with a trucker back to the city.

NO-FACES

99

M essages awaited him at the cave.

Half a sheet of yellow legal paper had been speared on a stick:

> Hope you had a nice vacation. Hope you never
> come back. But if you do, call me right away.

> Cork

Furthermore, the little red light was winking on the answering machine. His friend Special Agent Jake Claw of the FBI.

"Mr. Ledbetter, we'd be interested in your conclusions regarding a certain greenish, kindly emanation from the Tower of the Perfectly Real and Good. How much do you know, fellow citizen? Have a nice day. Spring has sprung."

But in fact spring had unsprung. Romulus was freezing. Two of his coats had been purloined while he'd been gone. Only the worst-for-wear remained. He put that on, and wrapped a blanket around himself.

Finally he perused the cave drawings.

They had been sketched on a flat mossless slab of rock above the mattress. A stick figure with a black, oval head. A stick dog, showing its fangs at the stick man.

A piano, a moon, a pentangle, and a telephone number.

Beside the drawings, hanging from a knob of rock, was a brown grocery bag with a card pinned to it. No name on the card, just a red heart painted with fingernail polish. He opened the package. He found the pair of silken boxer shorts that Bob and Betty had given him and that he had last seen when Moira pulled them off him.

He walked down to Payson Street and called Cork, but Cork wasn't around.

Then he called, collect, the telephone number that Moira had left beside her drawings.

She accepted charges and he asked her, "How'd you find my cave?"

"I went to Inwood Park and I just kept asking. I was disappointed you weren't there. I wanted to see you."

"You'd have seen a dirty bum."

"I know."

"I stink. I wear a pot for a hat."

"A what? A pot? Why?"

"Keeps my head warm. I wouldn't have wanted to see you."

She held that one a moment. "OK."

"But thank you. I mean thanks for the drawings."

"Scrape my number off the rock before I get perverts calling, all right, Rom?"

"Who visited us?"

"What?"

"That night. Who came looking for me?"

"Oh. That was Vlad. I didn't let him upstairs, though. You didn't have to run."

"Moira, I saw a movie yesterday."

"Was it good? No good movies ever come up here."

"It was a movie your brother made."

"Oh. You better not tell me about it."

"I have to."

"No you don't. And I don't have to listen."

"Your brother's a fiend."

"No he's not."

She was weeping.

Romulus said, "You know he's a fiend. You were there when he tried to kill me."

"That was Vlad. I'm sure it was Vlad who tried to run you over. Vlad would have done something like that—if he thought it would please David. David swears he had nothing to do with it."

"And Scotty? What does David say about—"

"He didn't kill him. He didn't kill him."

"You *know*—"

"I don't care what I know. He's my brother. I love him. Stop it. He's a tough man, and sometimes he can be cold, and he's sick, but he's *not*—"

"Yes he is. And I'm going to find some way to prove it. Jesus, Moira. You can step out of the fucker's shadow now. He's a murderer, he—"

"Stop it. He didn't kill Scotty. I love him, he's my brother! He's scared, that doesn't make him a murderer. Please don't hurt him, Rom!"

He listened to her cry.

She said his name again. "Rom."

"What?"

"If I . . . if . . . Could we see each other again but not talk about . . . my brother? You wouldn't ask me about my brother?"

"I would. I'd ask you *everything* about your brother."

"Rom."

"I'd just keep asking and asking."

There was nothing from her end for a minute, then she whispered, "Please don't hurt him, Rom. He's going to die."

"Yeah. He's going to die in prison."

Then he flinched because he knew the dial tone was coming, and it did.

100

H e collected himself, then tried Cork again. This time he got him.

Romulus suggested, "Saint Veronica's? This afternoon?"

"No."

"You busy? Tomorrow then?"

"Cut the church shit. Cut all of your shit. All your fairy tales, stuff 'em. Where've you been?"

"I took a most intriguing journey—"

"Tell me where, Caveman."

"North Carolina."

"How'd you get there?"

"Bus."

"When did you leave?"

"Monday night. Just before midnight. Why?"

"No, that's what *I* want to know. Why?"

"Because you recommended I take a vacation."

"Odd time of night to start a vacation."

"I wanted to wake up in the South."

"What did you do Monday night before you left?"

"I was in the cave, watching the Knights game. Before that I rode the subways, raising a little scratch for the trip. *Why?*"

"See anything unusual that night?"

"I saw a million unusual things. I was on the New York City subways. Why?"

"How long you been back?"

"An hour."

"You heard any news about your friend Matthew Donofrio?"

Suddenly Romulus realized he was on the phone with a cop, and the phone went cold in his hand. What a cop knows about the people we know, we never want to hear.

"Matthew? What about Matthew?"

"Well. He's alive."

"What happened?"

"That's what so many of us are wondering. They found him out by the Henry Hudson Parkway, on the slope under the Cloisters. Just a heap, they found. Let me see. His jaw's busted, his hip's busted, his left tibia I understand looks like what we used to do to Turkish taffy bars on winter days, what else? His right wrist don't work. They carved something on his cheek, but you can't see what it is. They ruptured his spleen. They banged up his head. The left side of his face hasn't quite woke up yet but they say it will."

"What *happened* to him?"

"Who can say?"

"What does *he* say?"

"He says he was drunk and he walked into a tree. What do *you* say, Caveman?"

"I guess he's scared to talk."

"Or else they're just nasty fucking trees you got in your neck of the woods. You send your trees to guard school?"

Romulus didn't say anything.

Said Cork, "Hey, I'm sorry—sorry I was a wise-ass there. He was—you're pretty close to him, huh?"

"Where is he?"

"Bellevue."

"Bellevue? But that's way the hell down—"

"That's where they take deadbeats."

"I'll call you back."

"Wait a minute, Caveman. Just wait one goddamn—"

101

If you're in training for hell, thought Romulus, do your warm-ups in Bellevue.

The man standing before the desk had blood all over his shirt, which had been a beautiful satin thing with tassels. The nurse kept telling him over and over that he was at the wrong desk, that he needed to go to the emergency room. He didn't understand. An orderly told him in Spanish. The man said something back, but not in

Spanish, or English, or any other tongue that Romulus was familiar with. He tried to unbutton his shirt. The nurse said forcefully, no. The man then recited, in English, in a voice equally as forceful as the nurse's, the Pledge of Allegiance to the United States of America. Seemed to be the only English he knew. Also seemed to think that was *enough*.

As though all you had to do was flash a little loyalty, show them your puppy-dog devotion to your old pal America, and they'd take out the bullet. As though it were just that simple.

But he looked to be no more deluded than a dozen other suppliants in that waiting room.

Romulus marched past them all. Strode purposefully right through the double doors into the bowels of Bellevue, and no one stopped him, and he was instantly lost.

No one that he met in his wanderings had heard of Matthew Donofrio. Romulus kept shuffling along, kept asking. He shuffled through miles of corridors, serpentine and sulfurous. He received glimpses—slender, lightning peeks—of astounding horrors, before doors were shut in his face. He shuffled in circles, in barbed diagonals, in spirals. He went up and down stairs, up and down like a hospital graph. He made a handful of friends, and hosts—howling legions—of enemies.

For hours he journeyed. Then at the end of a long withering tunnel he came upon a fat little South Pacific idol, a pagan totem with a woman's face and a nurse's uniform. The totem asked him what he was doing out of bed.

"They told me Matthew Donofrio might be up on floor five."

"This isn't the fifth floor."

"No?"

"But really," she said, "you're not a patient? You've really come to visit Matthew Donofrio? Well, for Pete's sake. It's about time he had a visitor."

Then she took him to see Matthew.

His jaw was bandaged and his brow, and the rest of him was under a sheet, so Romulus could see only a bit of his swollen purple skin. He did see the eyes, which had no expression. Romulus turned back to the nurse.

"Is he in a coma?"

The nurse was gone, though. Matthew answered for her. "No. He's not in a coma."

A tiny voice. His mouth hardly moved. He said, "Did you bring me any morphine, Rom?"

"No, I don't have any."

"Nobody does. People I trust here, you know, people I never did no harm to, they lie like pushers. They keep all the morphine for themselves."

There was something on the next bed. Or it was part of the bed, a bed-tumor—except that it breathed. Romulus tried not to look at it.

"How long you been in here, Matthew?"

"I got no fucking idea. What month is it?"

"March."

"Yeah but what year?"

"Who did this to you, Matthew?"

Matthew murmured, "Guess what, I'm cured. I don't cry no more."

"Who did this to you?"

"Guys with no faces."

"No faces?"

"Just like the fucker you're always talking about."

"Stuyvesant."

"I always thought you were full of shit, Rom. Now I know better. You're right. Leppenraub and your fucker Stuyvesant, they're in this together."

"How many were there?"

"Two."

"Did you hear their voices? Leppenraub, did you hear—"

"I don't know. I know one of them never said nothing."

"But the other one? What did he say?"

"He didn't say much either. They wanted to know where you lived."

"Why?"

"They wanted the videotape. Did you see the videotape, Rom?"

"Yes."

Matthew winced, but he didn't cry. "It's all about Scotty?"

"Yes."

"I showed them, Rom—I showed them where your cave was. The guy used a knife on me. He was going to draw a picture of a tree on my face with a knife. He didn't though. I guess because I showed them where your cave was. I don't remember showing them. I mean . . . I *do* remember, but I wish to fuck I didn't. I wish to fuck you had some morphine."

"I don't have any. Who drew the picture?"

"He didn't, because I told them where you lived."

"But which one? Which one was the tree artist? The one that talked or the other one?"

"The silent one. Rom?"

"What."

"What did they do to Scotty in the videotape?"

"Scotty's dead. You can't do anything for him. You should try to forget about him."

"OK."

"You'll forget about him?"

"Sure. Rom?"

"What?"

"What did they do to him?"

"They hurt him. That's enough to say."

"Why does Leppenraub do that to people?"

"I don't know. I'll find out. Matthew, why didn't you tell my daughter about these guys?"

"Your daughter?"

"Yeah. I gave you her number."

"I lost it, Rom."

"So why didn't you tell the cops?"

"They wouldn't have believed me. They'd have said I was crazy."

"You should tell them."

"Or else they *would* believe me. Just for a minute, you know, Rom? You know how sometimes you believe people just for a minute before you realize they're fucking with your head? So they'd believe me like that till they called Leppenraub, and he'd set 'em straight, show 'em how I was just fucking with their heads. Then he'd come here to this room late at night like I keep waiting for and he'd carve the rest of that tree in my face and then he'd kill me. And they'd have lots of hospital forms, and all those forms would all say I just checked out. Checked out against doctors' orders. The way street people do, you know? No forwarding address."

Romulus had nothing to say, but to say nothing meant listening to that breathing in the bed next to Matthew's. So he said:

"Matthew, you've *got* to—"

"I'm not scared of him killing me, Rom, I want him to do that. He killed me already when he killed Scotty, so great, let him finish it off. But first, see, he'll want to finish that tree. Don't let him finish that tree, Rom."

"I can't do shit unless you help me. You've got to talk to the cops. Or let me talk to them—"

"No. If you tell the cops he'll finish that tree. You know he will. *Promise me* you won't tell the cops."

"Maybe they'd help."

"The *cops?*"

Put it that way, how could Romulus argue?

He stood for a long time looking down at his friend.

"All right," he finally said. "I won't tell them, Matthew."

"Can you get me any morphine?"

"I can't."

"Just a little something off the street?"

"Do you have any kin, Matthew? Anybody you want me to—"

"They've been notified. Nobody's come by yet, but I'm sure they'll all be piling in here any minute."

More silence. After too much of it, Romulus glanced over at the next bed.

Said Matthew, "He's all right, Rom. He just forgets to breathe sometimes. He'll remember in a minute."

102

Jack Cork came out of the Thirty-fourth Precinct house, hurried down the stairs, turned left, walked up to the corner of Broadway and West 185th.

He stood at that corner for about ten seconds, whistling through his teeth. He thought about how cold it was getting again, and how he hated springs that played these come-on games with you. Then he checked his watch, muttered, "To hell with it," and started back for the station.

The Caveman stepped out of a doorway. Beckoned Cork with a crooked finger and retreated into the shadows.

Cork stood his ground. He called:

"Come out of there. Right now, asshole! Christ's sake. I'm freezing to death."

The Caveman did not comply. They glared at each other.

Said Cork, "All right, fuck you."

He started back toward the station.

The Caveman emerged.

Cork shook his head and pursed his lips. "Not amusing. Cops and robbers, you think I find that *fun?* To the station, *now.*"

Said the Caveman, "I won't go to the station."

"You think somebody'll see us talking in there? You'd rather be out on the corner?"

"The station is linked to the tower."

Cork growled. Cast his eyes around. His eyes lighted on Cecil's Bar. Shamrocks in the windows. Shamrock time, rolling around again. Cork used to get a nice feeling when they brought out the shamrocks. Now he felt the headache and the cement stomach even before he started drinking.

He muttered, "Take that pot off your head, and come on."

He led Romulus across the street.

Saying as he went, "Cops and robbers, cloak and dagger, hound and hare, I don't need any of this shit. I am a hundred percent fed up to the gills with your shit, Caveman."

He swung the door to Cecil's, violently. He walked in and didn't give a damn whether or not the Caveman followed. But he could smell him, right behind him.

The place was day-lonely, thank God. Cecil gave him a nod. "What'll you have, Jack?"

"Alka-Seltzer."

"I'm sorry, Jack, I've none."

"Some kind of fizzy water then. You know? Anything fizzy."

He walked to the end of the bar and past it. Made for the farthest, darkest booth.

Behind him, he heard Cecil asking the Caveman, "And for you now?"

Without looking around, Jack Cork warned, "If you don't have any money, Caveman, don't order. NYPD is not treating."

Then he sat. Heard the Caveman ask for a cranberry juice. *Cranberry juice.*

Cork noticed that the pinball machine across from the booth was called Cloak-and-Dagger.

The Caveman took the seat opposite him.

Said Cork. "OK, what have you got?"

"Proof."

"Proof of *what?*"

"Of Leppenraub's guilt in the murder of Andrew Scott Gates. Any doubts I may have entertained have vanished. There's a videotape—"

"Oh Jesus, will you *cut this crazy shit?* All I want to know is, what tree did Matthew Donofrio walk into?"

"He walked into Leppenraub."

"That's what he told you?"

The Caveman shrugged. "I can't reveal what Matthew told me. He asked me not to. But it's obvious, anyway. Clearly Leppenraub had Matthew beat up to intimidate him, so he wouldn't talk about the tape."

"Oh yeah? That's obvious? You mean that's where all the *clues* point?"

Cecil arrived with the drinks. Cork threw down a couple of bucks. The Caveman fished around in his coat pocket and brought up a heap of dimes and nickels and pennies and put them on the table and started to count them, by twos.

Said Cork, "For Christ's sake."

He slapped another bill on the table.

He said, "Leave us alone for a minute—OK, Cecil?"

"Sure, Jack."

When Cecil was gone Cork galloped his fingers a moment against the tabletop. Then he nodded and said, "You know, now that you mention it, I guess all the clues do add up. I guess they all point to one man."

Said the Caveman, eagerly, "Leppenraub had to silence Matthew, or—"

"They all point to *you.*"

Now that shut him up good.

"See, Caveman, you're the only one who's got a motive for trashing all these deadbeats."

Watch him tremble. "A motive?"

Cork leaned forward and hissed, "You're *psycho.* And the only place for psychos like you is that place upstate. What is it? Matteawan?"

He let that one linger.

Black guys, they don't turn pale. They just go *gray.* Pleasant to see this joker running through the gray scale. A real satisfaction to see the muscles in his neck twitching wildly.

Said the Caveman, "I was classified once, long ago, by a pair of fools, as *schizophrenic.* It is not the case. I lead a complex life. I live well. I am *not*—"

"Why are you so nervous, Caveman?"

"What would my motive—"

"Your motive is you don't need a motive. You're nuts. That's the beauty of it."

"But what proof—"

"Ha! Look at you—you're a mess. You're turning into jelly there. How long do you think it'll take me to get a full confession? Half an hour?"

"Don't be silly."

"No sweat. Look at you. I could get you to confess to whacking McKinley."

"But why would I—"

"Who cares? For some psycho reason you decided Scotty Gates was the fucking Antichrist. So you *did* him."

"Talk sense."

"I'd rather talk psycho. And the *clues,* Caveman, think of all the juicy clues. For example—*you* were the one who found the body— yes? And it's goddamn very suspicious, how you took off on your little vacation just about the time your buddy Matthew walked into

252

that tree. Oh, it's suspicious as hell, all these homeless guys coming up to your neighborhood to get clobbered. Huh? Goddamn flood of clues, am I right? So what do you say, Cavey? You want me to write all this up so you can sign it?"

He took a sip of his fizzy water, then looked down at it distastefully.

Said the Caveman, "Are you arresting me, Detective?"

Cork gave him a dull stare. "Arresting you? Why would I do that?"

"You just said I killed Scotty Gates."

"I didn't say you killed Gates. I said that's what your *fucking clues* say. Didn't I tell you I pay no attention to clues?"

Suddenly the Caveman remembered his cranberry juice. He drank it all down thirstily. He drew a deep breath. Slowly the color came back into his face. He smiled back at Cork and said suavely, "Well, but how can you be sure I *didn't* kill Scotty?"

"Oh fuck you. A minute ago you were wetting your pants, you were so scared. Now it's Holmes and Watson again. How do I know? Cause I know. *Nobody* killed Scotty Gates. He froze to death."

"So then who beat up Matthew?"

Cork shrugged.

"That's a good question. Local punks? Yeah, but I doubt they'd drive him around. Gay bashers?"

Cork squinted thoughtfully into the middle distance. Waggled his fingers.

"Naw. It's fishy. You know what? I think it *was* you."

He rose. Threw a dollar on the table for tip.

Said the Caveman, "Wait a minute. I've got to talk to you about—"

"About the videotape? Let me guess. It's a beaut, its better than *3-D Zombie Strumpets*—but you don't quite have it in your possession."

He grinned and said, "Did I take the words right out of your mouth there?"

Then he leaned in till his chewed-up Irish nose was an inch from Romulus's nose.

"It was you, wasn't it, *Psychoman?*"

103

The vacant lot on Avenue C and Seventh was cold tonight. Also chilly. Romulus ambled up to the barrel fires, he smiled warmly, he greeted friends with big hellos, but what he got in reply were nods, grunts, and a petering out of conversation till he moved on.

He saw shadows in Chore's tent, and he stuck his nose in. They had a grease fire going in a coffee can. Burning blubber, like Eskimos. Hot as the dickens in here—but still chilly. Penny lay in her sleeping bag, reading the poems of Adrienne Rich. She never raised her eyes. The others nodded, grunted.

Conversation went to zero.

Romulus wondered aloud, "Anybody got any spare space for me, for a night or two?"

Nobody did.

"Just a little place to stretch out?"

Somebody muttered, "Why don't you dig a cave."

Chore said, "I got a blanket if you want to borrow a blanket."

Romulus thanked him but shook his head.

Presently he moved on.

He sat on a stoop across from the lot, and watched the spikes go by. Coming out of a spike bar on the corner, headed to their spikes' nests south of Houston Street.

Chore came and sat beside him. And said quietly, "Where you been, man? I thought you was dead."

"Why'd you think that?"

"You ain't come around in a while."

"I like it up in my cave. Anyway, I was here just a few weeks ago."

"Oh. Yeah."

"So why'd you think I was dead?"

"If you like it up in your cave, why don't you stay there?"

"Crime wave up there."

They watched the spikes go by.

Said Romulus, "You getting around to laying something on me, Chore?"

"Uh-huh."

"What is it?"

"Just . . . I think you'd be happier finding some other place to hang. That's all."

"You afraid I'm bringing trouble?"

"I don't know nobody *likes* trouble."

"That's true." Romulus shrugged. He said, "OK."

He stood.

"But if I go, will you tell me one thing? Man to man? Nobody's ears but these?"

"Sure," said Chore. "Fact, I'll tell you *two* things, Caveman. 'Cause that's how many there were, two of them, two bizarre fucking bozos, wearing masks. Looking for you. They did a number on my head. I don't want to *ever* see them again."

"Did you tell them? Where to find me?"

"They didn't ask *me*. They asked Matthew."

"Would you have told them?"

"Never in a million years. Of course I'd have fucking told them. Much as I know. Your cave's in Inwood Park somewhere, isn't it?"

"You think Penny would have told them?"

"Never in a million years."

"Manuel?"

"Never in a million years."

"Anyone would have told them, right?"

"Right."

"I mean," said Romulus, "it's not like I'm the hardest man in the city to find. It's not like I've got rottweilers and bodyguards, and I sleep in a different bunker every night, is it?"

"Uh-uh."

"If they wanted to find out where I was, they just had to ask. They didn't have to do what they did to Matthew. My Lord. *Fuck* this son of a bitch."

104

He could not go back to the cave. He knew if he did, Stuyvesant's No-faces would find him and kill him. So he went that night to stay in the men's shelter on Ward's Island.

They took his name and he waited in line about an hour and they issued him a towel. Then he waited in another line for another hour and he took a shower.

Later there were NYU students who came around and asked people if they'd model for sketches. A kid asked Romulus if he'd model and he said OK and he sat on a bench for ten minutes till his patience ran out. He went and wrote on the kid's sketch, on the brow of his own image:

RL
One Who Fathoms the True Nature of Z-rays

Then it was lights out, and he put his shoes under the legs of his cot so nobody would steal them. He put the silk underwear, which he had not worn since Moira had returned it, under his pillow.

He stayed awake and listened to all the moans, maunderings, and typhoon outbursts in the sea of beds around him.

He knew that in truth he did not fathom jack shit about the nature of Z-rays.

All he knew about Z-rays was that he hadn't felt their presence in a long time. And that he missed them.

He was strung out on Z-rays. In their absence, he was quickly breaking down. He was losing the threads. There were so many threads, and they were hopelessly tangled up and knotted, and he was tired, and there was *no evidence of murder,* just phantoms. All the phantom witnesses who wouldn't come forward, the phantom videotape that couldn't be exposed to the light of day. There was no daylight anywhere.

No more shimmering green lawns for you, asshole. No more sweeping vistas and sudden breakthroughs.

Just this chamber of horrors. The smell of flesh roasting in the shelter furnace. But then, this is more like it, isn't it? This is more your style.

You've been seduced, misled, fucked with, and discarded, and your home's been thieved away. Hope you had a good time. Now run along and get back to your miserable life.

Oh, and before you go, here's a little nightmare to remember your glory days by:

He dreamed all night of the suffering of Scotty Gates.

105

In the morning he walked down to the little playground where he used to take Lulu, where she'd dug in the sandbox for pirate treasure. He sat on a bench and slept some more, dreamed some more torture. When he woke he could see Stuyvesant's tower, just across the river, glittering in the light. A yellow bolt of Y-rays shot out. Old-fashioned Y-rays, aimed somewhere on Long Island. Romulus was sitting here in plain sight but Stuyvesant wasn't concerned with him.

Romulus Nobody, former Caveman, failed composer, failed prophet, failed detective, burned-out old Z-ray junkie, why waste any energy on him?

Stuyvesant had bigger fish to fry.

Then Romulus crossed the pedestrian bridge over the East River, back into Manhattan. He walked to Central Park, found a bench and again tried to sleep. A cop on horseback came by and told him to move on. The cop had silver spurs and the spurs were tipped with blood.

Homeless. Nowhere to go. Everybody always said he was homeless, well they were right, weren't they?

HOMELESS! HOMELESS! BURNED-OUT SCARED-OUT FOOL OF A HOMELESS Z-RAY JUNKIE!

He called Lulu at her precinct house. He tried to seem cheer-ful.

"Hey baby."

"Daddy where have you been?"

"I found a man who's got the proof, Lulu. A videotape—is that amazing or what?"

"I went by the cave, Daddy, but you weren't there."

"They're trying to kill me. They beat up Matthew and now two of the No-faces are after me."

"Daddy . . ."

"Please, Lulu. I know how it sounds, coming from me. But please believe me. Please. Can't you believe your old man?"

"Daddy, do you need any help?"

"I need you to believe me. I need you to believe it's not that I'm a coward. It's just—it's too much for just one man. Too much. They got all the guns. They got all the rays. All I've got is the truth. What good is the truth if nobody believes it?"

"I believe some of the things you're saying."

"Like what?"

"I believe you're trying to say you need help."

"Right. I need help with the case. Do you believe that Leppen-raub killed Scotty Gates?"

"No. I don't believe that one thing, Daddy. But I love you."

"Did you get the autopsy report for me?"

"No."

"That was supposed to be my birthday present!"

"Daddy."

"If they did any kind of decent autopsy the torture would *have* to show up."

"That's true, Daddy. And if they'd found evidence of torture I'd know about it."

"Not if Stuyvesant didn't want you to."

"Daddy I gotta go."

"Why?"

" 'Cause I gotta go. I got work—"

"Work for who? Huh, Lulu?—who do you work for? Give your boss a message from me, OK? Tell Stuyvesant he was wise to discontinue the Z-rays—they didn't do squat. They didn't fucking seduce me, did they, 'cause I'm still here. Call me chicken but how come I'm still here? I'm still on the case, right? Tell him I'm going to see his boy Leppenraub *fry*. Tell him—"

"Bye Daddy. I love you!"

She hung up.

Then there was a terrible rasping noise. It was the Seraphs of Divinity and Vengeance, rasping their dried-up old wings against the dried-up old walls of his brain.

"Love?" he said into the phone. "You cannot discuss love if you don't discuss honor in the same breath. A civilization that dishonors its citizens, that herds them into concentration camps at night and makes them roam the streets like dogs in the day, right?—that kills and maims and calls it Art, that encourages its daughters to spit upon their fathers—oh, such a regime cannot speak of love, can fucking *not speak of love!* LOVE WILL DEFEAT SUCH A REGIME! *GODDAMN YOU ALL TO FUCKING HELL!"*

The rest of the day was not eventful.

In fact, it was gone, and he had no idea what had happened to it.

It was night, and the NYU students were fanning out in the shelter, and again he had his portrait done. But Romulus's hand shook too much to send another message to Stuyvesant. And anyway why bother to write a message to Stuyvesant when Stuyvesant could read his mind. Read this, Stuyvesant: *Love will defeat you. Love will defeat you.* He put his shoes under the legs of the bed. He was wide awake as he dreamed. His nightmares of suffering were so vivid they spilled out of his skull and the whole shelter dreamed them, all at once.

106

Ⅰn the morning he went to the New York Public Library and studied back issues of *The Wall Street Journal, Scientific American,* and the *New York State Law Journal.* He took copious notes. He deduced that Genentech Inc. and Union Carbide had worked in concert on the development of Z-rays, which were produced by lacing human bone marrow through a superconductor.

Accidents had occurred. Bhopal, for example.

A few years ago Stuyvesant had traveled to Utah to test Z-rays for the first time.

Anomalies during the firing produced the illusion of cold fusion in a lab *on the other side of the state.*

High school students *in New Jersey* had skipped the prom and made suicide pacts instead.

Where are we going with this, Romulus?

The pot fell off his head and bounced on the library table.

Damn you. DAMN YOU ALL TO FUCKING HELL!

He was shuffling down Sixth Avenue when he saw a crowd gathered in front of a TV store. There was a bank of TVs, and on each TV the same scene was showing. A criminal was being drawn and quartered.

"Yes," several of the onlookers said reverently.

Said Romulus, "What's this garbage?"

"It's not garbage, it's a challenge to our notions of the preordained psyche."

"Just watch."

"Watch."

"Just watch."

"Caustic."

"His cries give voice to our alienation."

"They prod the frontiers of our animal essence."

"But they're in dispraise, in dispraise of disempowerment, so it's OK."

"And a little thrilling."

Screams came through the plate glass. Romulus went into the store and told the salesman:

"Turn it off!"

"Excuse me?"

"TURN IT OFF! TURN IT OFF! TURN IT OFF!"

"Sir, maybe you better leave."

"If you don't turn it off right now, misery will boil up in waves and drown us."

"Yeah, but you better go."

"Where can I go?"

"I don't know that."

107

Up at Bob and Betty's, where he went to return the silk underwear, there were two other Bob and Betty–type couples. "It's a Bob and Betty festival!" said Romulus, and they all laughed.

Bob—the original Bob—offered him a drink, and Romulus took it, and proposed a toast.

"To the Eternal and Everlasting Cycles of Failure and Resuscitation," said Romulus.

Bob said, "Hear! Hear!"

The other Bobs and Bettys murmured their approval, and everyone took a sip.

Romulus toasted again. "To the fact that the Cycle Seems to be Stuck, and the Bobs and Bettys are Always on Top."

They all chuckled at this, and murmured their approval.

Said Romulus, "Let's drink to the cycle being Just for Show, that it's got No Moving Parts, and that Those on Top Stay on Top—Bob knows it, and Betty knows it—and for those poor losers down below, hey, let's drink to them, too, mucking around on their Hungry Bellies with the Thorns and Dogs Snapping at them. Because they're always going to be shit slogging, right? *Right?* I'll drink to that. I mean we can lend them some nice threads and clean them up and invite them up for a cocktail but they never will *get* it, will they? They'll always be animals!"

He threw open the sliding door, and went out on the balcony. It was cold out, and the lights of the city were crystal clear and twinkling. He went to the balcony's edge, and looked way, way down at the dark courtyard.

He cried: "They got their noses in the fucking ooze, poor suckers, and they'll believe *every lie you tell them.* Throw down a *clue* once in a while, watch 'em scurry around like rats trying to figure it out. *Right,* Bobs and Bettys? Piss on 'em, they'll think it's manna from fucking heaven!"

He unzipped, pulled out his equipment which shriveled from the cold, and it took a mammoth act of concentration but he got it working. He splashed the iron balusters, and then he found his aim and the stream opened up as it fell, scattered into thousands of golden droplets.

He shouted into the abyss, "Drink it up, folks! It's *stardust!*"

Then a wind kicked up and blew the stream back at him, and he got some of it on his pants. He humiliated himself in front of all the Bobs and Bettys and in full view of Stuyvesant, who watched the performance of the beaten man with glee.

He zipped, and went back in, and one of the Bettys was on the phone. He told her, "Don't trouble yourself. You don't need the police up here. You're safe up here. *Nothing* can touch you."

The original Bob held the door open for him and he left.

108

H e didn't go back to the shelter. He slept that night on the subway trains. And the next night, and the next. A friend saw him there, and said, *"Romulus,"* and he didn't know what the guy was talking about. He said to the guy, "Don't say it if you haven't got proof."

109

H e called Moira again.

"Is Elon there?"

"Elon? Who's this? Rom?"

"I want to talk to Elon."

"Elon doesn't talk on the phone, Rom. Are you OK?"

"Just . . . Elon."

"What do you want to say to him?"

"I want to try. I just want to try. What else am I supposed to do?"

"I'll tell him that, if you want."

"I want to talk to Elon! What is he—is he your brother's prisoner? Like they say? Does Leppenraub open his fucking mail? What does he do, does he put him in chains and shove stuff up his asshole? Why won't you let him talk to me?"

Nothing that he said was what he planned to say, though he'd been planning for days. It was pointless to plan.

Next he planned to call Lulu, but the moment she answered the phone he put his fist on the buttons and played all the notes at once.

110

Nor did he *plan* to go back to the cave.

But one day he was sitting on a water hookup on Madison and thought if he only had his notebooks, he might find it, find it, find the clue. Find it, he thought, and in another hour he was climbing up the slope to the cave.

The beech tree ashimmer. Tiny green slips of leaves. Cyclops sat on the mattress.

"Hello Romulus."

"Any messages?"

"Two men came by. Had no faces. Night you left."

"I heard about that. I mean in the last few days."

"No."

There was a squirrel hole in the trunk of the beech. He got down on his knees and reached up into that hole and felt around. Two chickadees were at play just above him. Old friends of his.

Said Cyclops, "How was the trip?"

"It was fine. But now I'm dying. I'll die soon, Cyclops, we'll go out together. You're from the South, right?"

"Uh-huh."

"Help me with something that puzzles me. I was in the library, checking an atlas, and I noticed an odd thing. It seems that within a twenty-five-mile radius of Tifton, Georgia, are the following villages: Omega. Eldorado. Enigma. Sunsweet. Glory. Mystic. Do you know why?"

"I never been to Georgia but once."

"I hear Stuyvesant has a factory built of stain glass somewhere around there, where he manufactures brain chemicals."

"What you got there, Romulus?"

Out of the squirrel hole he had pulled a plastic bag, and he was shaking off the shit and cobwebs. Then he opened it, and inside were the notebooks for his biography of Cornelius Gould Stuyvesant.

He meant to leave right away, but it was a nice day and he could *think* in the cave, with his back up against a certain ergonomically contoured slope of rock. So he stayed and pored over the notebooks there.

Cyclops got up and went away and he didn't notice her leaving.

It may have been that day, or it may have been on his return visit the following day, when he looked up and saw Miz Peasley was standing there. Joey's mother. Come all the way up from Lent, North Carolina, to see him.

111

M a'am."

"They took Joey."

"Who did?"

"They said you sent them."

"Who said that?"

"I don't know. They wore white bandages over their faces. They said you sent them. They said they were soldiers of justice. They said they had a message from you that they had to give Joey. They stayed with me for a day, and when Joey called me, they answered the phone and spoke to him. Then he came. He talked to them a long time, in his cottage. Then he told me he was going away with them. He was scared. He said he had to go away with them. He said if I went to the police he'd be killed. He said good-bye to me. Then he drove away with them."

She stood there. Gray coat, gray scarf. He put down his note-book. He wished he could think of something to say to her, but his thoughts had no spring to them. He could only think that every-thing about her was gray, except the strands of lovely blond hair that got loose and blew in front of her face, and these she quickly caught and tucked back under her scarf.

Her son was surely dead, but Romulus supposed that no one would ever bother to let her know that.

He asked her, "When did this happen?"

"Three days ago. I didn't know what to do. I remembered you said you lived in a cave in Inwood Park in New York. It's insane for me to come here, I know this. But what else was I supposed to do? I don't know what I'm doing. I don't know what I'm supposed to do. So I came. Do you know who they were?"

"Yes."

"Did you send them?"

"Of course not."

"Oh. For just a second I had hoped . . ."

"I don't see grounds for hope, ma'am."

She asked him, "Who are they?"

"One of them's named Leppenraub. The other, I'm not sure. They work for a man named Stuyvesant."

"Why did they take Joey?"

"They're enforcers. They enforce Stuyvesant's Law of the Per-fectly Real."

"What can I do?"

"Tell the police."

"Wouldn't they kill Joey if they found out—"

"Yes. But they'll kill him anyway."

"Have they already killed him?"

"There. That's something you can hope for. You can hope they've already killed him. In fact, let me assure you that they have. And let me take you to see a friend of mine, a policeman."

She thought about it. "No. Joey told me not to."

"He was just trying to protect you."

"You said—that day you came looking for Joey—you said things would get better."

"I said they might. I was wrong. As a prophet, I suck, ma'am.

How can things get better? We've got every kind of ray cutting us up. There's twenty thousand TV rays right now telling your brain every kind of lie in the world. And Y-rays and Z-rays and who knows what else and we can't see any of them but they're cutting our divinity to confetti. Right now I think I'd kill my daughter for another dose of Z-rays."

She said, "Oh shut up. I want you to help me. Help me! This is more of this craziness! Has *everyone* lost his mind? Please God, what is this?"

"Everyone has lost his mind. I used to think I still had mine, but nope, mine's gone, too. Go away, Miz Peasley. Go home."

"For God's sake! Can't you do *anything?*"

She was gone for an hour or maybe all afternoon before he put down his notebooks again, and answered her:

"Yeah, I can do this for you. I can get them to kill me, too."

112

Again he called Moira.

"I'm sorry I flew off the handle at you."

"Oh. Well." She spoke slowly. She picked her way carefully. "Rom, I don't think I should talk to you anymore. OK?"

"That's fine. We'll just sign off, right?"

"I'm sorry."

"Hey I understand. We'll meet in another life. But before you walk out on me, my darling, could you do me one tiny favor? Tiny tiny?"

"I don't know, Rom. I'll try."

"It's easy. I want you to give your brother a message."

"*Please,* Rom."

"Just tell him the psycho Caveman's been bothering you again. Tell him I called up and you've got to get your number changed 'cause I was ranting and raving. And tell him that this is what I raved: tell him I said *I made a copy of the videotape.* Right? Where I was staying in North Carolina, I made a copy of Scotty Gates's videotape. Joey took the original, but I've got the copy. If he wants it, I've got it. Will you tell him that?"

"Rom!"

"I'll never ask anything again. Just tell him what the madman ranted and raved."

113

Then he went back to the library and wrote down everything he knew about the death of Andrew Scott Gates in one of his notebooks. Then he wrote a letter to his daughter, Lulu. He went to the post office and mailed it. He went back to the cave and hid his notebooks in the beech tree. He tidied up. Cyclops came by, and he told her if she showed her hideous face here again, he'd have her arrested. He watched her limp away. He sat on his mattress. He threw pastry crumbs to the chickadees. He had not eaten in two days. He stared at the tiny pale leaves of the beech. He waited.

When they came to call, they'd find him at home.

114

The letter was waiting for Lulu when she got home from her shift. It was on the kitchen table. Mama sat with a cup of coffee, didn't say anything. She must have seen it, must have known it was Daddy's handwriting, and you could tell Daddy was in a bad way just by his handwriting on the envelope. But Mama didn't say anything. She was quiet. She asked Lulu about her day, but she didn't listen to the answer.

Lulu took the letter into the bedroom.

Darling daughter,
    By the time you read this I'll already be murdered. There

won't be any body, they'll say I'm missing persons, but no, I'll be dead.

Go see Matthew Donofrio. Tell him you know all about the no-face men, and tell him that for the sake of your father's divinity, he must come forward.

Then go talk to Elon, the retarded man who lives with Leppenraub. Tell him you want to see the needle. Take the needle to the lab, and find out what was in it.

Go to Mrs. Peasley in Lent, North Carolina, and tell her the Caveman is dead and for the sake of his honor and divinity to tell you the truth. Tell her that her son is dead, that this the Caveman swears on his own grave, and so there's nothing any more to be afraid of.

Then take all this truth you've gathered and with it drive Leppenraub through the gates of hell. I'll meet him there, just inside, and deal with him.

Leave Stuyvesant alone. You're not strong enough to take on Stuyvesant directly. Not by yourself. Not yet. But keep looking for the prophet who will deliver us. As I go now, I tell you that prophet is coming.

At this very moment, Lulu (at the moment I write this, I mean) in some other chord of time, I live not in a cave but in a treehouse, a treehouse built in a beech tree of great proportions, and it's by the sea, and you and I are down on the sand making a castle and your mother is wading through the shallows gathering enough sand dollars to make us all filthy rich.

I love you.
Daddy

The New York Public Library, Inwood Branch Sometime near the Vernal Equinox

"Oh Daddy," she said.

It took Mama two hours to bring herself to ask. They were watching the news and a headache ad came on, and finally Mama said:

"So what damn-fool nonsense is your father writing you?"

"Mama. He's pretty sick."

"He's always been sick. Sick before I knew him, if I'd had the eyes to see."

Lulu said, "Mama, I think . . . I mean I think we're going to . . ."

"What do you want to say, girl?"

Lulu sighed. "There's nothing I want to say."

"Well what are you *trying* to say?"

"That I'm going to have him committed."

A bad thing happened to Mama's lips. She gave them a fierce tug downward, then let them slide slowly back into place while she watched the rest of the ads. She glared at Peter Jennings for a while. Then she went into her room and shut the door.

115

But at the cave, that very evening, Romulus was still waiting.

Days had gone by, and they still hadn't shown.

Tonight, he thought. Tonight would be a good night for them. Right, Seraphs?

The Moth-Seraphs, those that were still alive, seethed.

Romulus watched it get dark.

He watched the moon come up.

The neighborhood mockingbird chose that night to perform one of its bitter, beautiful routines. Sitting up at the tiptop of the beech and slamming everybody it knew. Mockers had drifted into New York recently, but they were at home here. Even cabdrivers couldn't surpass their knack for nastiness. They had the *gift*.

Romulus leaned back against the stone and drank in this bird's music.

He was trying to remember the names of all his great-uncles and aunts. That had been his strange occupation the last few days, dredging up the names of his kin. And all the random shreds of their history that his mother had passed down to him. He had no idea why he was doing this. But it served to pass the time.

Along about one in the morning, he went for a walk. He hated leaving the cave—he might miss his visitors!—but his limbs were restless and there was a trio of crocuses on the slope behind the cave and he wanted to check on them. He walked around the top of the ridge and came down to the little grove of ironwood, and the crocuses were under there, waxed with moonlight, perfect.

Also the ironwood leaves, which he appraised with his fingers, were coming along. Though they were still so small they scarcely registered to his touch.

He heard footsteps. He looked down the slope. The two No-faces were coming up the hill.

He shrank back into the shadow of the ironwoods, and they passed within a yard of him and didn't see him. It was such an easy game, it was all he could do to keep from giggling.

But once they'd gone past, there was no point in playing any longer.

"Gentlemen," he called. "Would you be heading by any chance to the Caveman's place? I'll walk with you, if you don't mind. I'd be grateful for the company. It's a dark night, and I have fears that evil might be afoot."

The larger No-face produced a pistol. Pulled it from the pocket of his loose dark windbreaker, and aimed it at Romulus.

Said Romulus, "So you yourselves are highwaymen? Just my luck. I might have known."

"The videotape, Caveman."

"Ah. So you'd like to make a purchase?"

The greater No-face looked to the lesser. The lesser nodded. The greater said, "How much?"

"Well, I'm inclined to be fair, since the tape's of no value to *me* at all. Shall we say a million dollars?"

No response.

"Plus *that*, of course."

Romulus pointed upward. The greater No-face followed the angle of his finger and found the moon.

Then he came very close to Romulus.

"We don't have no time to fuck around. Where's the tape?"

"I don't negotiate with underlings. Tell your friend to speak up, I'll talk to him."

The lesser No-face made some kind of impatient gesture, and the greater No-face cracked the side of Romulus's head with the pistol, just under the rim of his pot hat. The hat went flying.

The moonlight turned to oil, swirled and sloshed.

"You'll do what we fucking *tell* you to. Now where's the fucking tape?"

Romulus was on his knees. He put his hand down, and the moonlight stopped rocking, and he rose. "I will not tell you. You better kill me now. It's a good time, a good place. In a minute, you might lose the opportunity. A word to the wise—this park is well patrolled. Do it now."

The big No-face brought his face close to Romulus. Romulus stared, but all he saw were the tiers of gauze.

Said No-face, "You're going to tell us. You understand?"

"No. Explain it to me. Are you going to torture me? Fine, let's get to work. I'll consider it a challenge."

Said No-face, "What, do you think we're crude? We're not going to torture *you*. We're going to torture your daughter."

Romulus stopped breathing. Terror took hold of him from behind and squeezed all the air out of his chest.

No-face was saying, "Little Lulu. 135 Cole Street, Ozone Park, Queens. We're on our way there right now. You want to come? You want to watch?"

Romulus's hands lashed out and he grabbed the smaller fucker, the silent one, the boss, by the throat. It was a small throat and it would have taken Romulus only six seconds to kill him. But he didn't have that long. Somebody started knocking on the door, knock-knocking insistently, and that pounding was so annoying it distracted Romulus from his murdering. He turned to see who it was.

It was the moon. He was gazing up at the moon, and his head was in flames, and through smoke he saw those white faces, except they were dark now, against the light sky. They were standing over him.

"You don't *have* to come, Caveman. If you want, we'll take you someplace and tie you up, and we'll go by ourselves to see your daughter. But you really ought to come. We're going to party with that girl all night long."

271

Think.

Forget the flames, the howling in your skull, the smell of your own blood, the feel of it as it trickles into your ear.

Climb above all this, and think.

What's important here is that you can't afford to die. Not yet. You can't let them kill you before you've warned her. You've got to warn Lulu.

"What?" said the greater No-face.

"I said, I've got to make a call."

"You're not calling nobody."

"No, I've got to. I've . . . the tape is . . . with a friend. I told him if anything happens to me to give it to the cops."

"Give us your friend's name."

"Yeah, I could do that."

"Then do it."

"But you'd have to kill him, and his wife, and the guard in his apartment house, and maybe his children—"

"We don't have to kill anyone. We'll handle it real smooth. Who?"

"And it'd get messy. Too fucking messy for you guys. And for me. I can't do it."

"Then we play with Lulu."

"Do what you have to. But I asked him as a favor. I'm going to let you kill his whole family? Little part of the favor I didn't tell him about?"

"Fuck you."

"No, fuck *you.*"

The No-face was frustrated. He gave Romulus a kick. Romulus took the pain, folded and refolded it, and put it away.

He got his breath back, and he tried to sound reasonable when he said, "Look, what's . . . what's the problem? You let me call him, I'll tell him to make the drop. We've got a drop all worked out. He'll do it any time I ask. I'll tell him to make the drop, all we've got to do is go pick it up."

The big No-face kicked him again.

But then the smaller, the silent one, put a hand on his colleague's arm.

For a moment the figures swam out of Romulus's vision. Then

he felt himself being hauled to his feet. The greater No-face was lift-
ing him up by his lapels. Saying, "Listen to me, fucker. If you're trying to fuck with us . . ."

Said Romulus, "What would be the point? I cross you, you kill
me, and you get Lulu. So what would I get out of crossing you? For
God's sake, let me just get over this. I was being stupid, all right? I
was playing some stupid game, trying to make a few dollars, and
now I see that was dumb. I'm persuaded, all right? Let me make the
call."

116

Not a soul on Payson Street. He stood at the little three-
sided telephone coop, and pressed his ear hard against the receiver so
the No-faces wouldn't hear, and started to dial.

But the big one was watching his fingers. Romulus hung up.

"Stand back," he said. "Don't watch."

"Don't tell me what to do."

Romulus insisted. "I'm not getting my friend involved. If you
involve him, the deal's off."

The No-face stepped back again. Romulus cupped one hand
over the numbers and dialed again.

Don't answer, Sheila. Let Lulu pick it up.

A groggy, pissed-off voice. "Hello."

Of course it was Sheila.

"Hey. This is Romulus."

"Oh you crazy goddamn son of a bitch. What the hell are you
doing—you know what time it is? What are you calling for? Not
one soul on earth's got any patience for you. Not one soul on earth
feels sorry for you."

"Darling, I've got to speak to the Cap'n."

"The who? The *Cap'n*? Who the hell is the Cap'n? Jesus
Christ, Romulus. Jesus Christ."

Then she just breathed.

He said, "I know it's late, but I've got to talk to him. I'm
sorry."

Sheila. It's our little girl, they're going to kill her. If you don't help me, they'll do this thing.

Please. Please. Please. Please. Please.

The breathing stopped.

Then again he heard Sheila's irritated voice, but this time it was far off, another room of the house.

Then he heard a click and an echo—the extension had been picked up.

"Daddy?"

Women when they're sleepy sound like five-year-old girls, like little girls that you used to bring home from the neighbor's in your arms, and you could have sworn they were dead to the world, but when you set them down in the bed, at the last minute they reach up to give you a dry good-night kiss.

Romulus said, "Hey there, Cap'n. Need a favor. The owner of that little videotape—he wants it back bad."

The gun barrel showed up in the corner of his eye. The No-face murmured to him, "No explanations. Just tell him to make the drop."

Had she heard that? *Listen, Lulu. Listen to this.*

He said, "So, Cap'n, if you'd kindly just bury that treasure for me."

"Daddy, what are you talking about?"

"Yeah, well I know it's kind of late in the night for this *pirate* thing, but it's important to these guys that you do it now. Bury that treasure where we decided. Then clear out."

"Bury the treasure? Daddy, did I hear someone with you—"

"You sure did, Cap'n. You heard right. I'm sorry, but it's got to be now. You've got to do it, and then get your ass out of there. Right?"

The voice behind him: "Hang up."

Romulus turned.

"What?"

"I said hang up the phone."

"Daddy, who *is* that?"

"Thanks, Cap'n. I won't ask you anything else ever again. Ever. That's a promise. You know, I'm kind of crazy but I do keep my promises."

117

The car was not the old death car. Leppenraub was too smart to use the same old death car. The car was a big tacky American boat.

Romulus rode in the back with the big No-face. The boss drove.

He had Ravel's *Bolero* on the tape deck.

There was no other car in sight. The FDR Drive was bright, lit up like a movie, and the tacky car was the star, and Ravel was the theme music.

Romulus said—and it was the only thing he said on that drive:

"Hey Leppenraub. Ravel sucks. Would you turn it down? It's my dying wish."

The silent No-face ignored him.

So he was forced to do his thinking to the tempo of Ravel's simpering.

Ah, but so what? He didn't have any thoughts anyway.

Just a slender wild hope.

That by some miracle he had gotten through to Lulu—that she understood he was talking about the little playground on Ward's Island, the sandbox where he'd played pirate with her when she was a little girl. And that despite his thousands and thousands of earlier wolf cries maybe she had heeded this one, and she might be waiting for him at that playground and he'd see her from the pedestrian bridge, from far off, and he could shout, warn her. And of course they'd kill him but she'd have time to get away.

Was that crazy or what?

But it was the best show in town.

And for now all he could do was keep playing it over and over inside his head. So he wouldn't have to watch the other show. (*Lulu decides her father has really lost it this time, and she shrugs and goes back to sleep. A few hours later, she hears a knock on the door.*)

118

There wasn't another soul on the pedestrian bridge.

He was crossing it with the big No-face. The silent one had silently elected to hang back with the car.

It used to be that homeless men would loiter here, on this bridge. Till one Hallowe'en when a posse of punks from the East River Projects had come through on a wilding spree. One victim they'd bludgeoned to death. Some others they'd played slash 'em, forget 'em. There was this poor guy on the bridge, they'd told him to jump in the water. Jump in the water or we'll slit your throat. Six of one, half dozen of the other. The man demurred. Slash 'em, forget 'em.

So now people kept off this bridge at night, and Romulus and the No-face were all alone here.

Below, the dark, heavy muscles of the river. Overhead, a string of bridge lights and a blotter sky. The moon was gone.

Romulus looked across to the shore at the end of the bridge. On the right, the little playground.

But Lulu wasn't there.

That was that.

Leaving only one way open. He'd have to scare this guy into killing him—not knocking him out or otherwise subduing him but a clean *kill*—and well, once the Caveman was dead, there'd be no point in molesting the Caveman's daughter, right?

Wasn't that right? He had never been good at this kind of reasoning but it seemed orderly enough.

He just had to rush the bastard, lunge so suddenly that the guy would panic and blow him away. And up here on this bridge, with the guy walking just a few paces behind him, this was as good a place as any.

But he couldn't do it. The lunge didn't seem to be in him. Where were the Moth-Seraphs? All he needed was a little burst of anger. Where the hell are you, Seraphs, when for once I can use you?

"Move it, fuckhead."

He kept walking.

They came to the end of the bridge. The ramp led left, then right, then they went down some steps and they were at the water's edge. An old pin-oak tree, and under its spreading limbs, the simple playground.

No-face cast his eyes about anxiously.

"This is it?"

"This is it."

"So where's your fucking treasure?"

Romulus nodded at the sandbox.

Said No-face, "Get it."

Romulus stepped to the edge of the sand.

Now?

Just turn around and jump. He's *got* to panic, he's got to make this my grave. That's all I have to do. I can do it now. Screw the Seraphs. Just turn around—

There was an *X* marked in the sand.

Someone had scratched it out with a shoe tip. *X* marks the spot.

He knelt before it, and dug, and found a plastic shopping bag.

No-face took it from him. It was tied with a bread-bag tie. No-face untwisted the tie with his teeth. He kept one hand in his pocket, holding his gun. He tipped the bag. A videocassette fell into the sand.

Said No-face, "What's *this* shit?"

"What does it say?"

But Romulus could see perfectly well what the box said. In bright letters it said *The Adventures of Cap'n Crunch*.

"You trying to fuck with us?"

Then Lulu stepped out from behind the pin-oak tree. Romulus, still kneeling in the sand, was looking right at her, but No-face had his back to her. She came and stood ten paces behind No-face and leveled her pistol at him.

"Freeze! Police! Put your hands over your head!"

No-face glanced back at her. He let the bag go, and it fluttered into the sand. He said:

"I got a gun pointed at your daddy's brains, bitch. So be careful you don't spook me."

Then, slowly and steadily, he drew the gun out of his pocket. He held it two feet from Romulus's skull. He turned to face Lulu. He said:

"Don't either of you *fucking move*! Now drop your gun, bitch."

Romulus said, "Kill him, Lulu."

"Want to see his brains, bitch? I said *drop your fucking gun!*"

Lulu held her stance, but her hands trembled and her eyes were full of terror.

Romulus said, "Lulu. Don't drop the gun. Kill him. If you drop the gun, he'll kill both of us."

No-face said, "No fucking way! I know you're a cop—think I'm going to kill a fucking *cop*? I got nothing to do with this fucking shit! I was doing this for pocket money! I just want to get the fuck out of here! Drop your gun and I'll run like hell."

"Don't listen to him, Lulu!"

But she *was* listening. She was wavering. Her eyes flicked to the ground, came back up. She was letting his lies work into her.

"Oh Jesus. Lulu, *kill* him! Let him shoot me! I'm a dead man anyway. Lulu, do *what I say!* I'm your father, do what I say!"

"He's your father, bitch—you want to kill *your own father?* Drop the gun."

Then Romulus saw the strength go out of her arms. She was slowly lowering her pistol.

And in an instant she would toss it down and then there would be no more discussion, just dying.

But still, Romulus thought, there was that one way open to him.

All he had to do was reach. Reach up quick, Romulus, flash your arm out and take hold of the pistol barrel and hold on tight, and remember to keep on holding even after the eruption of pain and absolute light and absolute dark, just don't let go and if you're lucky before you lose everything you'll get to hear the sound of Lulu filling the fucker with bullets—and it'll be a wonderful gift-music, and you can compose a split-second March of the Great-

Uncles to wrap around it, fiddles and flügelhorns, but you have to do it *now.* Now.

If you've ever been worth anything.

Now, while her arm is still dropping, before she tosses her pistol down.

If you've ever deserved anyone's love or honor.

If you've held on to an ounce of your divinity, you'll unfreeze yourself, wink at that pistol's little black eye, reach, and take hold of death.

And then he felt the Seraphs swarm. All at once they rose up from their multitudinous nests, legion upon legion of them, beating their ragged wings and darkening the whole vault of his consciousness with their fury, and Stuyvesant in his tower across the river felt them and sent down a green-gold-red-black blast of utter destruction, but there were too many of them, they had too much momentum, they kept coming. They hurled themselves against the selfish light of Romulus's fear, and they put that light out. And then there was nothing but smoke and soot and the beating of their wings, and the fear of death was utterly extinguished, and he did what he had to do.

His arm flashed out.

119

At that instant No-face must have had his eyes on Lulu's surrender, because Romulus's reaching took him by surprise. He saw it in the corner of his eye, and quickly turned his no-face to Romulus, and pulled the trigger—but too late. Romulus's hand slapped against the barrel and knocked the gun's aim off. Romulus heard the blast, and heard the bullet whistle past his ear. Then he heard another shot—this one from Lulu's gun.

No-face yanked his pistol barrel free of Romulus's grasp, and swung it toward Lulu, but her gun went off again.

Then No-face lost his grip.

His pistol flew away from his hand and hit the pavement of the playground and skittered to the base of the swing set. No-face reached after it. He looked like a desperately thirsty man reaching for a skinful of water. He fell to his knees and his head dipped to the sand, kowtowing.

Romulus rose and came toward his daughter. She was still in stance. She was furiously in stance, and terrified, and barking orders to a dying man.

Romulus looked down at No-face. No-face was trying to lift his head. There was a hole in his neck and blood poured out onto his jacket, and he put his hand over the wound. The blood spouted through his fingers. His faceless head moved, he seemed to be looking all around him as though searching for something he'd lost.

He turned his no-face up to the pedestrian bridge and he murmured, "You fucker. You fucker."

And Romulus looked up, too, and he saw what the dying man was seeing.

The other No-face.

The silent one—up on the bridge with his pistol drawn and aimed.

Romulus cried to Lulu:

"The bridge!"

He leapt at her, smothered her body in his own, and they went down together, and even as they fell he heard the shot. They hit the soft playground pavement and his hand was under her and his huge chest was on top of her head. More shots. His eyes were shut. He was bellowing, bellowing to black out the noise of the shots raining down on them. One two three four five six.

Then there were shots right at his ear. He opened his eyes. Lulu was shooting back. She was peering out from beneath her father's shoulder blade and firing cooly toward the man on the bridge.

The shots stopped. There was no sound left in the dark but Romulus's own bellowing. Lulu squirmed out from under him, and shouted above his roaring:

"Daddy! It's all right! He's gone! It's all right!"

He shut up and looked at her. Then at the empty bridge. A far-off echo of running footsteps. He looked back at Lulu, who had risen and was kneeling by the No-face in the sandbox.

Romulus looked over across the river at Stuyvesant's tower. It was dark now, pitch black. There was a smear of last moon in the clouds.

"Lulu. I'm confused. Help me out with this. I don't understand. Why are we still alive?"

She didn't say anything. She was bent over the body of the No-face.

Romulus said, "I don't understand. Did he *miss* us?"

She told him quietly, "He wasn't aiming at us, Daddy."

Then Romulus saw the No-face lying on his side and half of the man's head was gone, and he was bleeding from half a dozen wounds.

Said Lulu, "He was finishing off his partner here."

She looked all around her. "Is that all of them, Daddy?"

He nodded.

He lay there and stared up at Stuyvesant's tower.

"But why didn't he kill *us,* Lulu? He could have, easy. Why not? You're alive, I'm alive. How did this happen?"

She knelt beside the No-face, breathing deeply, still looking all around her. "You complaining, Daddy?"

"No, but I would like to know. How in the world does it happen that we're still alive?"

He lay on his back and thought about it.

And then suddenly a tumbler fell into place, and he did know.

THE
VAMOOSED
VALENTINE

120

E ver seen this face before?"

Romulus looked through the snapshots. There wasn't much face to see. One whole and staring eye, one whole cheekbone, the cleft of the chin—the rest wasn't face at all.

"I'm not sure. It could be—I mean, he looks some like a man I saw a couple weeks ago. Guy who hustles drugs down on First and Ninth."

"Bingo," said Jack Cork.

They were sitting in one of the little windowless interrogation chambers in the precinct house.

Cork asked, "But you didn't know him?"

"Uh-uh. His partner, Eel, that's Matthew's pusher—him I talked to. I just got a glimpse of this one, from across the street."

"Right. We're looking for Eel. *This* one they called Shaker. Real name was Robert Jackson. Bright guy, you know? Or anyway semibright. Graduate of PS 140. Spent a year in Queens College— yes he did, would have been a brain surgeon, too, but first they canned him for peddling shit on campus. Six arrests, two convictions, four months in the hole. Going nowhere. Not what you would call a big cheese in the drug world. Neither mover nor shaker, just another asshole in the parade. Running a little garbage, here and there, waiting to get burned out or dead.

"You know, Caveman, when I was a kid I had this friend that used to catch flies right off the wall. He'd pull their heinies out and put a little twirl of toilet paper in the wound, and those flies would buzz around with that banner flapping away behind them, you get this?—and they'd just spiral down"—Cork made a spiral in the air— "down . . . down . . . till they ran out of gas. Real tragic, but nobody felt particularly sorry for them. Now I've forgotten why I told you that story. Oh, yeah. Robert Jackson. Guys like Robert Jackson remind me of my friend's flies."

Romulus asked, "Have you found his connection with Leppenraub yet?"

"I'm sorry, do my stories bore you? No. Nothing so far. But we got people asking. We're checking out everything you gave us. Talking to all of Leppenraub's known boyfriends. Got the police in North Carolina to search Mrs. Peasley's place. Nothing. And nothing she's telling us is of much use, either. FBI's checking to see if anybody's turned up missing in Charlotte."

"FBI?"

"You got it. The mightiest law enforcement agency in the mightiest republic in the history of the world, at your service. No story of yours too crack-brain that we won't check it out. You're a man of great power, my friend."

"I'm not powerful."

"No? Well, all I know is, you could turn my life into a nightmare in a hurry."

"*I* could?"

Cork scowled, lowered his voice. "You may have noticed, on your way in, a pack of vermin out on the sidewalk? Critters that look sort of like jackals and sort of like sewer-ooze? If you wanted to, Caveman, you could go down there and give them the whole story. They'll take your picture, they'll stick mikes in your face, they'll put you on the six o'clock news. They'll give you headlines big as cathedrals. They'll make your cave into a national monument. And they'll make me look like the evilest great Satan who ever lived because I never listened to your sage advice. Do you want to do that, you want to talk to the press?"

"Do I have a choice?"

"Sure, your choice is you can do me a favor and keep quiet for a while."

Cork checked Romulus's expression. Romulus gave him nothing, waited patiently. And Cork went on:

"See, what the press knows now is this: They know who died, they know he was wearing some kind of mask, they know he abducted a homeless man and this man got a call through to his daughter, who's a cop, and the cop found them and there was a shootout. Everything else is *pending investigation*. They're going nuts. You go out there and take a look at them. They're biting people. This is juicy stuff and we're giving them *pending investigation*. And the name *Leppenraub* hasn't come up yet. Once Leppenraub gets into this, it'll be like opening night for *Gone With the Wind*. That's why I want to keep him out of it. Till I've talked to all his boyfriends, till I find out what Robert Jackson was doing the last few weeks."

"Right."

"Right? You'll keep quiet? It's that easy?"

"Right. You want a favor. You want me to seal my lips? Be happy to."

"Wow. Thank you."

"Naturally I expect a little something in return."

"Hey fuckhead, you don't shake down cops. Supposed to be the other way around."

"I'm not asking much."

"Uh-huh."

"All I want is the autopsy report on Andrew Scott Gates."

"Oh Caveman. Caveman, Caveman. You drive a hard, mean bargain, you son of a bitch."

Cork opened a drawer, pulled out a little gift-wrapped package, and tossed it on the table. The card read "Belated Happy Birthday, Daddy."

"Your daughter asked me to give this to you. Officially I don't know what's in there. Privately I expect it'll bore you to tears. Whatever it is, get rid of it after you've read it, OK?"

"OK. Thanks."

Said Cork, "Anything else I can do for you?"

"Yes, one little thing."

"At your beck and call, crack-brain."

"I need a ride."

"Sure. Where to?"

"Gideon Manor."

"Caveman. Listen to me. You've done good work. You deserve the thanks of all Gotham—but now it's time to turn this over to the pros. Let us break this mother open. You know what I mean?"

"Right," said Romulus. "I know what you mean. You mean you still don't think Leppenraub is behind this."

They confronted each other.

Romulus said: "Bingo?"

Finally Cork shrugged. "Look. I'm not telling you he's *not* guilty. Like I say, we're checking it out. But OK, you want to know what I think? I think you and Matthew Donofrio, you were always shooting your mouth off about this videotape. This precious videotape. So a guy like Robert Jackson, he's always got his eye on the main chance, and he and his buddy Eel hear the rumors, and decide if they could get hold of that tape, they could turn it into cash. A lot of cash. So they go to work. Neither of them are what you'd call subtle. Naturally they screw up. What do you think?"

"Sounds reasonable."

Said Cork, "Well, *I* like it, you know, 'cause it doesn't involve a lot of fucking clues."

"Also it doesn't involve accusing the most famous photographer in the world of murder."

"There's that. There is that. It's a low-hairiness solution, yeah, that has its appeal."

He grinned.

Said Romulus, "And your theory is, all you have to do now is find the partner, find this Eel guy, and get him to confess?"

"Caveman, you are astonishing. I mean your sanity is fucking astonishing. What's happened to you?"

"Shock therapy. You'll take me up to Gideon Manor? Tomorrow morning?"

"Oh, please. Who do you want to talk to, anyway?"

"*I* don't want to talk to anybody. I want *you* to. I want you to have a chat with David Leppenraub's sister."

121

Cork arranged for Romulus to spend the night up at the little shelter run by the Franciscans on Broadway and 112th.

It was a high-rent, man-on-the-move-up shelter. Everyone was a *guest,* everyone slept in his own cubicle. Every cubicle had a crucifix above the bed. Light poured in through the transom. Romulus sat up in bed and read the ME's report.

As Cork had warned him, it was not delicious reading. The ME was a squeamish man, and he'd tried to bury the truth under an avalanche of jargon. Scotty he diminished to "the decedent." The boy was no longer beautiful, he was only a "well-developed white male whose appearance is consistent with the reported age of 20." The ME noted the blizzard of "ice crystals in the blood," the skin condition "suggestive of hypothermia"—but he did not dwell on these troubling details. He tried to emphasize the positive. He found to his delight that "the periorbital spaces are free of extravasated blood or edema." Furthermore he was pleased to announce that the "sclerae are anicteric, with bulbar and palpebral conjuctivae that are free of petechiae."

He went over Scotty with a fine-tooth comb and noted his smallpox vaccination, a birthmark on his shoulder, a few needle tracks in his left arm, some lacerations and abrasions that were minutely described, but no other significant marks. *No evidence of trauma.* Nothing to fret about. Oh, if it weren't for those pesky ice crystals, *decedent* could have gotten up and downed a double cheeseburger.

Those ice crystals. The cold of that night.

On such a fine spring evening as this, Romulus could no longer remember the feel of that cold. He dredged up a dim image of sitting in the cave under a mountain of blankets. Shivering like an old washing machine. He had that image. But the way it had *felt?*—this had flown.

And he thought that if we could only remember, conjure, imagine the feel of suffering, surely we would stop inflicting it.

It seemed a good, pious thought for such a place as this.

He desperately missed his cave.

He picked up the ME's report and read it again.

Nothing had changed. The sclerae were still anicteric. Decedent had that birthmark on his shoulder. No other significant marks. No evidence of trauma.

That was all.

And what Romulus was looking for—that was still missing. Now where in the world, he wondered, could it have gotten to?

The valentine. That heart-shaped brand that Matthew had said he saw on Scotty's butt. OK, maybe to the ME just a tattoo. But still, how in hell could you report the birthmark, the smallpox vaccination, this little flaw and that little zit, and leave out a glaring red, heart-shaped tattoo on decedent's buttocks?

Unless you had some powerful reason for leaving it out . . .

122

$\mathbf{H}$e woke up once in the middle of the night when the man in the cubicle next to him had a coughing fit. He woke, and the realization that he was still alive—that he hadn't been killed in that sandbox—came to him as a shock. It flooded him, it terrified him, his heart skipped a beat, it was so strange and huge he thought he was having a heart attack.

He calmed himself by reciting the names of all his great-uncles and great-aunts.

123

$\mathbf{I}$n the morning he awoke refreshed and full of fire. Cork picked him up and they cruised northward. Cork started out grumpy, whining about missed appointments, but they stopped for breakfast at a diner in Yonkers and after that he was in a better mood.

They talked. They discovered that they had been born in the same year. Two months apart, two miles apart. They griped about the flight of time. They griped about cold things that girls had said to them in high school. They found that they were both youngest children. Romulus said he thought it was because he was a youngest child that he had never felt himself anything but a kid, that the image returned by mirrors always looked incomprehensibly aged to him, et cetera.

Cork said, "I know exactly what you mean, my friend."

Cork said that at the ceremony when he was promoted to lieutenant, his mother, right in front of everybody, had knelt and retied his shoelaces for him because she thought they were too loose, he might trip over them.

They agreed that George Steinbrenner, not content with plucking, oiling, and spit-roasting the Yankees, was also secretly in control of other sports franchises, among them the New York Mets and the New York Knicks, the New York Giants, and the South Korean Olympic boxing team.

They pulled off the Taconic Parkway at Peekskill Hollow Road, for gas. Romulus borrowed Cork's credit card and called Information, got the number for the only Reynolds in Gideon Manor. He called the number and asked the woman who answered if he could speak to Darcy. He waited.

"Hello?"

"Cassandra?"

"Yeah, who's this?"

"The guy from Walter's bar. The black guy who played piano."

"Romulus! Hey man. What's up?"

"Not too much," he told her.

"Easy living?"

"That's about it. What I'm doing, I'm trying to put a puzzle together. Thought maybe you could help."

"I love puzzles. I'm in kind of a hurry right now, but—"

"Hot date?"

"Lukewarm."

"Another lapse in judgment?"

She giggled.

Said Romulus, "Well listen, what I want to know, it's real quick—"

"OK."

"Scotty Gates was your boyfriend."

"Mm."

"When you knew him, now here's my question—did he have a heart-shaped tattoo on his butt?"

She laughed. "A what?"

"A heart-shaped tattoo."

She laughed some more. *"Scotty?"*

"I take it he didn't."

"No, but it's really weird you ask me that."

"Why?"

Another spasm of laughter. She couldn't stop laughing.

124

By the time Cork came ambling out of the little country grocery, happily and dreamily peeling down the wrapper of a Mars bar, Romulus was back in the car waiting for him. They got back on the Parkway, and Cork munched at his candy and told Romulus about the antique roses he was trying to grow in his little backyard. Romulus discoursed on the difficulties of cultivating squash along city highway embankments.

With a few words, Cassandra had given him the missing piece. The heart of the puzzle. So that now in all the chaos of landscape rushing by—the blossoming apples, the nook-and-cranny drumlins—Romulus saw nothing but coherence, golden-crowned coherence.

He said, "This used to be the Leatherman's country. Up around here."

A hundred years ago, he told Cork, there was a man who wore an astounding suit made from bits of leather sewn together, and who lived in caves up here north of the city. Walking from cave to cave, living by begging. Never speaking a word to anyone—begging by gestures. His circuit of caves was a hundred miles around and he traveled that circuit on a schedule so rigorous that farmers along the route knew exactly when to look for him, and they always had a little something for him.

"He lived that way for forty years," said Romulus.

A few miles farther along, he said, "Maybe it's about time for me to get out of New York. Retire, you know what I mean? Come on up here to the country and live the good life. Right?"

Cork went back to bitching about the Yankees.

In the horse-farm country of Dutchess County, Romulus asked him: "You ever do any surveillance, Jack?"

"Sure. Some."

"Tailing people?"

"Some."

"You good at it?"

"Not really. You know how boring it is, waiting around for somebody all night? It's unbelievably boring. You wait five hours, then close your eyes ten seconds and they're gone. That's happened to me."

"But except for the boredom, you're good at it?"

"Oh, I guess. Why are you asking this?"

"Just thinking that whatever skills you've got in this regard, you're going to be needing them today."

125

At Gideon Manor they stopped at the Country Market convenience store and Romulus used the phone. He called Moira. He told her he was sorry for all the things he'd said and wondered if he could meet her. She hemmed and hawed.

He wheedled and cajoled.

Finally, with a sigh, she gave in.

He said, "The Country Market, you know that? Twenty minutes?"

Then he hung up and called the main house, and got Vlad. He

reminded Vlad of who he was. He told Vlad he was in town and could he see him for just a minute?

Said Vlad, "Why? I got nothing to do with you."

"Just for a minute."

"What you want to say to me, hah? You say it now."

"Not over the phone. What's the matter, Vlad? You a wimp? You scared of me? Scared of my soul? Scared of the soul of the American black man?"

Vlad muttered, "Where?"

"There's a bank across from the Country Market, you know that? In about twenty-five minutes?"

126

Then he got back into the car and they drove toward the farm and Romulus told Cork:

"In a little while David Leppenraub's sister is going to drive away from the farm and you're going to follow her."

"No, I'm not."

"Yes, you are. Because she's heading for a rendezvous and it's going to be very intriguing what happens during that rendezvous."

"Who's she going to rendezvous with?"

"That's why you need to follow her. To find that out."

"You're not telling me the whole story."

"That's true."

"You gotta be crazy, you think I'm—"

"You do this for me, we can go home right after, I promise, and I'll never ask you anything again, and I'll be just as good as gold with the TV reporters."

"No."

It took another fat dose of wheedling and cajoling, and still Romulus wasn't sure Cork would go along with his plan.

Even after they'd driven past the entrance to the Leppenraub farm and gone on for a quarter of a mile, and turned the car around and come back and pulled over, way up the slope from the entrance, still Cork hadn't said he would do this thing. Still he was murmuring, "Uh-uh, no. This is nuts. This is just going to get me in trouble."

And when Moira's car emerged and turned toward the town, and Romulus opened his door and got out, Cork just stared at him.

He said, "Wait a minute. You're not coming with me?"

Said Romulus, "I've got to stay here and see if anybody follows her. Come pick me up in forty-five minutes. Just stay with her, watch what she does, who she meets."

"This is nuts."

"Come get me in forty-five minutes. I'll be right here. Go—before she gets away."

"What's the sense of this, Caveman?"

"I'll never ask anything of you again. And I promise you that this will be an exploit of great discovery."

"Eat shit. Shut the door."

Romulus did. Cork drove off.

A few minutes later Vlad's car showed at the end of the drive, pulled out onto the road, went toward town.

And Romulus walked briskly down the hill. He turned in at the drive. Birdsong, haze, the orchard in blizzard-bloom. If he got nothing more from the trip than this stroll, it was plenty. At the farmhouse Lao-tse came running out to take his head off. He knelt and smiled. She recognized him. She slithered up for her back scratching. Then he climbed up the steps onto the porch, and found the door open. He went into the parlor and sat down before the piano and started playing.

He played Ravel's *Le Tombeau de Couperin* and blended in a medley of the Carpenters' greatest hits. He pushed the pedals down to full throttle and the whole house shook.

Then suddenly he quit. Held his fire. The piano throbbed, the throbbing faded. Romulus said without turning:

"Put the gun down, the gun's no use to you."

He waited for the house to return to silence. When it was absolutely still except for a few far birds and Leppenraub's breathing, Romulus said, "All these guns, they're no use at all, are they? But it's all right. I know what you want, David Leppenraub, and I can arrange for you to get it."

127

Half an hour later he was on his way home. Cork was driving much too fast for these twisty roads. He seemed put out.

"So?" Romulus asked him.

"So, what?"

"So what did you see?"

Cork spoke quietly, but his voice had a razor edge of fury in it. He said:

"You want to know what I saw? I saw the best-looking broad in history standing by her car in the parking lot of a little store. I saw her fold her arms and check her watch and pout. The pout was something, I must admit. Then this guy who looked like a gigolo except he was too short, this guy got out of a car across the street. He saw her but she didn't see him. We all waited awhile. Then the telephone rang behind the woman and she answered it. When she hung up she looked like she was really pissed. She noticed the gigolo and she crossed the street and she had a few words with him. I wasn't as bored as I usually am on a stakeout because watching this woman cross the street was a wet dream. But anyway, then she just stormed back into her car and drove off and the gigolo followed, and I followed, and she led us back to the farm."

"Hmm. What a story. Very intriguing. You've got a real eye for details."

"Oh, I saw a *lot of clues,* Caveman."

"What do you make of them?"

"What do I make of them? I make a dead fucking Caveman tossed out of a moving car at seventy miles an hour in Nowheresville, New York. *That's what I fucking make of them.*"

Romulus leaned over and checked the speedometer. "Better watch out around here, the cops are vicious—"

"All that rigmarole just so you could have a private chitchat with Leppenraub? Was that it, Caveman?"

"Well, you wouldn't have let me talk to him alone. Neither would Moira. Neither would Vlad."

"I hope you had fun. 'Cause when we get back and he's got a warrant out on you for harassment, I'm driving you personally to Matteawan."

"He won't do that."

"No? Why not? Christ, you didn't kill him, did you?"

"We had a civilized talk. I invited him to a meeting."

"Another fucking rendezvous?" He bore down on the gas pedal.

Romulus was not comfortable at this speed. To get Cork to slow down, he told him the interesting piece of news he had learned from the ME's report and from Cassandra.

It worked. Cork not only slowed, he hit the brakes hard and pulled wildly off the road into a bumpy church parking lot, and Romulus hit his head on the roof. Cork put the car in park, turned to Romulus and said:

"*What?* What the—? Oh, Jesus. Jesus Christ. Jesus Q. Christ, Caveman, *tell me you're making this up.*"

128

In Matthew's hospital room, the dying thing in the next bed was gone. The bed was empty.

Romulus said, "Matthew, are you ready to get out of here?"

Matthew didn't meet his eyes.

Romulus said, "Where's your neighbor, Matthew?"

"Huh? Oh that guy. I don't know. He forgot to breathe, I guess. I think breathing just slipped his mind, so they took him away. Pretty stupid, huh?"

"Same thing'll happen to you if you don't get your ass out of here."

"Yeah, you're right."

"So you ready to go?"

"Sure."

"Let's go then."

"Oh I don't think I can, Rom."

"They won't release you?"

"Doctor said he wouldn't make me go. Not yet."

"Well, I'm making you. I need you."

"Rom. I'm OK here. Let me stay here."

"Matthew, what do you want most in the world?"

"A swimming pool in East Hampton full of morphine."

"Think about it, Matthew. If you could have anything . . ."

"Don't, Rom."

"Anything."

"You know what I want. I want Scotty."

"You can't have Scotty. What else?"

"*Nothing* else! I don't want nothing else!"

He threw the bedclothes off. He sat up, faced away from Romulus. Naked, emaciated. "Except I'd like to get the fucker that got Scotty."

"Well, that you can have. OK, Matthew? You can meet the fucker at last, and we'll put the fucker away. That can be arranged. In fact, it already has been arranged. Tomorrow at noon. Get dressed, right?"

129

A collect call from Romulus Ledbetter. Charges accepted.

"Rom."

"How are you, Augie? I hear you've been sick."

"Well. Just taking a few tests."

The old wariness, arrogance, in his brother Augustus's voice. But also a new thickness.

Romulus said, "I'm sorry."

"Early for that. You talked to Sheila lately?"

"No I haven't."

Said Augustus, "Well I did. She sent me some cookies last week. Beautiful woman. She and I had a long talk. She says you're up to your usual stunts. She said you pulled some carnival act that almost got Lulu killed. She's in a holy fury, Romulus. I don't know why you can't keep her feelings in mind a little."

"Augie, we haven't lived together for seventeen years. I haven't spoken to her for six. What are you talking about, keep her feelings—"

"She says it's high time for you to get a little treatment."

"I got the *treatment* from her already. From all of you, last me a lifetime, your treatment."

"Oh, goddamn it, did you call me collect so you could get my damn blood pressure up?"

"What about *my* blood pressure? Right? Every time I talk to my brothers, boom-*boom,* going off in my head, what about . . . No."

He stopped and took a breath. He said, "No I didn't call you to . . . No. I just wanted to say I'm thinking about you."

"Well. Thanks Rom."

"Take it easy, Augie."

"I'm trying."

"Love to everybody."

"Love to you."

130

He went to the New York Central Library and sat down with Chekhov's *The Cherry Orchard.* The play that Moira had told him they'd done a reading of, up at the farm last summer.

He wondered if he'd be able to guess which part Leppenraub had chosen for himself.

Oh but it was easy. He came to the landowner Lopahin's first speech, and right off he caught something of the Leppenraub tone:

I remember when I was a boy of fifteen, my poor father . . . punched me in the face and made my nose bleed. Lubov An- dreyevna . . . she was still young and so slim . . . led me to the washbasin in the nursery. "Don't cry, little peasant," she said, "it'll heal in time for your wedding." . . . It's true I'm rich. I've got a lot of money. . . . But when you look at it closely, I'm a peasant through and through. . . .

Romulus enjoyed the entire play. Especially Lopahin's speeches. Lopahin's speeches, they were exactly what he'd been looking for.

I don't get to the theater much, Romulus thought. I should try to go more often.

131

When he got back to the shelter, one of the priests was playing Brahms on the piano downstairs, and even up in his room Romulus could hear it.

He said fuck it, and left, and went and spent the night in the cave.

He listened to the howls of the city all night. Great descant of sirens. Lightning storm of Y-rays, but they weren't touching him, and the Z-rays were transparent to him. On the TV, on C-SPAN, Stuyvesant's Undersecretary of The Perfectly Real and Good warned of conspiracy, treason, and a gnawing away at the roots, but his voice sounded shrill, it echoed in an empty studio.

"Tomorrow," Romulus said to the figure on the screen. "Noon tomorrow, tune in. You won't like it, though."

The Undersecretary paused for a moment, and lowered his eyes, then continued.

132

The next day, a little before noon, Matthew Donofrio sat on the last bench of the subway platform at Times Square. The red line, the old IRT, numbers 1, 2, 3, and 9. Matthew's head was shaved and he wore a cap with the visor pulled low and he sprawled on the bench facing the downtown express track. He was all the way down near the end of the platform. Nobody around—the midday commotion didn't get this far. Down here it was just him and a drunk passed out and slumping against a post.

Matthew waited.

He was scared to death.

He shifted position. He waited. He glanced at the clock by the bright Salem ad: three minutes till noon.

At last he heard steps, and he slid his eyes to his left, and though he'd only seen David Leppenraub's picture once, he knew him right away.

Leppenraub was carrying a black attaché case. He was coming on in a slow, infirm shuffle.

Matthew lowered his head, glared down at the cement.

Leppenraub took a seat on the bench back of Matthew. Facing the other way, facing the local track. Matthew felt him there, felt his sickly aura, heard him breathing right behind him and just a little to the side. But he didn't turn around to look at him directly.

Instead Matthew looked to a control room at the end of the platform. Three dark slabs of window. A tiny red light inside, no bigger than a wolf's eye. Maybe Matthew also saw, in the gloom, the suggestion of a shadow.

The shadow would be Rom. Rom had said he'd be in there, watching.

And he had told Matthew not to budge until the little red light in there went out, and a little green light came on.

So Matthew kept waiting.

Leppenraub gave off a faint reek of antiseptic, and though it was the same smell Matthew had been breathing for a week, coming from Leppenraub it made him sick. Just being this close to the bastard made him sick. Matthew wanted to do the thing now. He was ready. He knew what he was going to say. *You killed my love. You killed Scotty Gates. You killed. You killed, fucker, and now you're going to be killed.* And he would look in Leppenraub's eyes, and *know*, and Leppenraub would know that he knew.

But then what?

That part he didn't know. Rom would have to take it from there.

He glanced at the dark control room. Still the steady red light. Oh Jesus, what was Rom waiting for? Rom, let me do this before I chicken out. Before the sense of this guy makes me so sick I can't face him, before I have to run. Please, Rom—before I start thinking about Scotty.

But it was already too late for that. Scotty was moving through his thoughts, Scotty was caught in his throat and stinging his eyes. And Matthew was crying again.

And he knew that when he confronted Leppenraub, the man wouldn't fear him. Leppenraub would laugh him to scorn. Matthew glanced over to the control room, but still the red light was burning. That tiny blob of red shimmering through his tears. What the hell was the matter with Rom? Shit, maybe the light was broken. Maybe, Matthew thought, maybe he should just do it anyway, do it now. No, damn, a train was coming in, on the local track. He'd have to wait some more.

The train squealed and rattled its bones behind him. Matthew heard the doors open. He heard the passengers getting out.

Over the PA the train's conductor was saying, "Stand clear of the closing doors." Over and over. "Please stand clear of the closing doors." Matthew could hear, behind him, the doors start to close and then kick open again. Somebody was holding them open. And Matthew flicked his eyes and caught a quick glance at the first car, where somebody was just standing there, holding the doors open and checking out this platform.

Matthew lowered his eyes.

And then he heard the doors slide shut, and the train pulled out.

He looked toward the glass room.

The little light was green.

But it was too late. Matthew was weeping. His throat was wrenched closed with sorrow, and fear, and sweat was seeping from every pore of him and he had to get out of here. I can't help you now, Rom. I've lost my nerve, I don't have the guts to face Leppenraub. What does it matter anyway? What matters is that Scotty's dead, and nothing's going to bring him back.

Then he heard a voice behind him. Someone talking to Leppenraub.

"I got what you want. You got what I want?"

For a moment, a fever-instant, Matthew thought he knew the

voice. Then he realized he was only going crazy, he had caught Romulus's craziness and he had to run, he had to get out of here.

But then he heard the voice again.

"Answer me, Leppenraub. You got what I want?"

It couldn't be, but it was. It was *his* voice. Matthew pushed himself up, and turned. Faced the man who was standing before Leppenraub.

The man was looking into Leppenraub's attaché case. Then he raised his eyes, and saw Matthew.

They stared at one another.

The two lovers.

Matthew and Scotty.

133

*B*ut *you're dead! They said you were dead!"*

Scotty's ghost cast him as cold a look as the living Scotty ever had, and there was also sudden terror in his eyes. He took a step back.

Matthew came around the bench. Came toward him, saying, "Scotty? *Scotty!* Don't you know me?"

Leppenraub spoke softly. "Sir, I'm afraid you're mistaken. This man's name is Joey Peasley."

Then Scotty turned his cold gaze on Leppenraub. "What the hell is this? You setting me up, fuckhead? What the fuck is Matthew doing here?"

Said Leppenraub, "I swear to you, I've never seen him before in my life."

Scotty snarled, "Then what's he doing here? What, this is some kind of coincidence, he shows up here? It's just fucking *coincidence?"*

"Scotty," said Matthew. He reached and touched his fingers to his lover's cheek. Nothing more than that, a gentle caress, but Scotty flinched back from it.

"Get your hands off me, you stupid cunt. Scotty's *dead,* haven't you got that through your fucking head yet?"

But Matthew wasn't listening. He tried to embrace him, crying, *"Scotty!* Oh for God's sake, Scotty—"

"Get the fuck off me!"

Scotty gave Matthew a violent shove. Dropped the attaché case. Money, wads of hundred-dollar bills, slid out, scattered on the platform.

Just as another local train came down the tracks.

Matthew pointed to the scar on his face and cried, "Did *you* do this to me, Scotty? Did *you* carve this? It was *you,* wasn't it?"

Scotty ignored him. He was gathering up the money. He was scared and his gaze flickered all around him.

Matthew came toward him again. "But it doesn't matter, Scotty. I love you, I still love you!"

"I'm *dead!* I'm *dead,* you dumb cunt! Stay the fuck away from me!"

"Scotty, we gotta run, we gotta get away. They're here, Scotty, they want to catch you, come on, *run* with me—"

Scotty looked at him. Then at Leppenraub. "Is this a setup, Leppenraub?"

He pulled a pistol from under his jacket.

He looked everywhere. He looked at the drunk on the ground. He looked at the train coming and at the other passengers way down the platform. He tried to look in the glass room, but that was still dark except for its green light. He pointed his pistol at Leppenraub and said:

"If this is a setup, I swear your little home movie will play in every bar in the country! You perverse asshole, you want the whole world to know?"

Matthew cried out, "Scotty, I *love* you!"

"Shut *up,* faggot!"

Scotty glanced again at the approaching train. He tucked the gun into his jacket pocket.

The train stopped, and the doors opened. In the first car there were half a dozen passengers, and Scotty quickly slid in among them. Matthew tried to step aboard, too, but the drunk got up from the floor and came up behind him and caught him in a bear hug.

Matthew screamed, "Scotty! It doesn't matter! You're alive! You're *alive!"*

The doors closed. The train went nowhere. Matthew looked at the other cars and they were all empty. Then he looked back to the first car and he saw the half-dozen passengers pull out guns and take aim at Scotty. They flashed badges and they shouted and one of them moved up swiftly behind Scotty and clamped handcuffs on him.

Matthew cried, "It's OK! Scotty, I love you! Don't worry, I still love you!"

But Scotty didn't see him. He was staring out the subway windows at Leppenraub and raging: *"This'll ruin you, you shit! You sick shit!"*

He tried to spit in Leppenraub's direction but the spit caught on his lip and dribbled down his chin. And with handcuffs on he couldn't wipe it off.

And then David Leppenraub got up and walked away down the platform, went the way he had come.

134

B y the time Romulus stepped out of the little control room there was no one left on the platform but Matthew. The cops had hustled Joey Peasley away. It was just Matthew and when he saw Romulus he went for him. Hitting at him wildly, and Romulus grabbed his arms and held them and Matthew shouted:

"You lied to me! Rom! YOU LIED! You didn't tell me you were setting up Scotty! *YOU LIED!* YOU FUCKER! YOU FUCKER!"

Then he sagged, went down to his knees, and Romulus let him go and Matthew was just a well of tears.

Romulus knelt beside him. He said, "Matthew, that wasn't Scotty. You never knew Scotty Gates. That was the guy who killed him. You remember he never wanted you to look at the pictures Leppenraub took? Because he was afraid if you looked long enough, you'd figure out it wasn't him in those pictures."

"I don't . . . I don't understand, Rom. I don't . . ."

"Remember when you told me that Scotty had this heart tattoo on his ass? That Leppenraub's boys had put it there? But then I never heard about it again. Wasn't in any of the pictures Leppenraub took. And it wasn't in the videotape either. I kept wondering, whatever happened to the heart? Where the hell had that valentine vamoosed to? Finally I guessed, but I checked the autopsy report just to be sure. No mention of it. And then I called Scotty's girlfriend, Cassandra. And I asked her about the heart, and she thought it was a weird question to ask, but she did remember the thing. But not on Scotty. She'd seen it on Clive Leif, the actor. She'd slept with him, too. And Clive Leif's real name is Joey Peasley, and that's the man you just saw. That's the man you loved, Matthew. That's the man who killed Scotty Gates. And he told you so many lies that you'll never get them all untangled—so don't even try. You've got to tell yourself you just had the worst nightmare anybody's ever had and you've got to keep waking up from it, Matthew. Keep trying to wake up, you hear me, Matthew? There's nothing else you can do."

THE
NEWBORNS

135

Detective Jack Cork sat in the confessional at St. Veronica's and bowed his head, and was a true penitent.

"Forgive me, Father, for I have really made an ass of myself."

Caveman's voice:

"You should have listened to me from the start."

"That's true, Father. Although if I *had* listened to you from the start, I'd have clapped David Leppenraub in irons, wouldn't I?"

The Caveman conceded, "I was thrown off the track for a while. Stuyvesant's deceit—"

"Oh, yeah. And I would've had to raid the Chrysler Building with a fucking SWAT team—"

"Never do that! Never try to assault Stuyvesant head on! He'll crush you. He's more powerful than you can imagine."

"I bet he is."

"Yes. Well. For your penance, say twenty Hail Marys every time you take a drink."

"Please, Father."

"OK, one. Say one Hail Mary every time you take a drink."

"Deal."

"And tell me how much Joey Peasley spilled."

"I think just about the whole cup of soup. You want it?"

"Yes."

"Every drop?"

"Please."

"Ah, every drop means all his pitiful boyhood in North Carolina—you know, all the sick stuff about how his saintly sick fuck of a father believed in him, but his mama never did—the kind of nasty dog shit that bores me to death. But along about last summer, things get interesting. That I'll give you. But speaking of drops . . . did I ever tell you how confessions always make me thirsty, Father?"

"No, you didn't."

"Well, they do. So I was wondering if, please God, we might adjourn us outta here? Down the street?"

"Cecil's Bar? Are you saying that?"

"Please God, Father."

136

At Cecil's, Cork drank Scotch and Romulus had a vodka and cranberry juice, which every now and then Cork stopped to shake his head at. While he related the troubled history of Joey Peasley.

"See, by last summer, the kid's great directing career in New York was a big fizzle. But he did manage to get work in that summer stock company run by the Leppenraub Foundation. Joey figured now here were the connections he'd been looking for all his life—and he started hustling.

"One night last August Leppenraub had the whole theater company over to his farmhouse for a reading of this old play called *The Cherry Orchard*. Leppenraub's favorite, and he himself took the part of this Russian merchant, Lopahin. Didn't think I knew my Chekhov, did you, Caveman? Truth to tell, two days ago I didn't know Chekhov from Mr. Spock. But anyway, Joey was quite an accomplished techie, and he ran the video camera for this little event.

Jesus, you're really *drinking* that stuff. Don't you think it's going to make you sick?"

Romulus shook his head. "Any kind of drinking's going to make me sick. I don't hold alcohol well. But I'm obliged to celebrate, right?"

"Right. It's your civic duty. Ready for another?"

"Let me buy this one?"

"How can you? You're a fucking bum. You don't have any money."

"Right. I forgot."

"Another one, Cecil!"

Cecil brought the drinks, and Cork put away three-quarters of his Scotch in one swallow. He held that swallow in his left cheek for a moment, let it nestle there—then slipped it quietly down his gullet. He looked down at Romulus's vodka and cranberry juice and shook his head. He said:

"So. After that, Joey turned himself into Leppenraub's unpaid assistant. Did everything—lugged the cameras, mixed the chemicals in the darkroom, fetched the coffee. Hell, he even modeled for him. There was one time when our boy Scotty was too chicken to climb a tree for this weird picture Leppenraub wanted. So Joey, he looked a lot like Scotty, and he went up in his place. And I guess Joey thought he was getting to be Leppenraub's protégé or something. 'Cause when he comes down out of that tree and puts his pants on, he's got these stars in his eyes, and he tells Leppenraub, 'You know, maybe we ought to try a little collaboration, you and me. What do you say?' And Leppenraub—he was in a real nasty mood that day—he says, 'But we *are* collaborating, Joey. I'm making art. You're looking gorgeous.'

"Now this hurts Joey very deeply. He quits Leppenraub in a huff and goes back to New York and starts getting sicker and sicker in his head. Feeling more and more humiliated by Leppenraub's disrespect. Joey's daddy had always told him he had a wild, glorious, radiant mind. Who the fuck was this asshole to call him a pretty boy?

"And in early October when Joey heard Leppenraub had gone into the hospital—well, he decided to make another visit to the farm.

"There was nobody there except Scotty and that retarded guy

311

Elon. Vlad was in Europe. The sister was staying in a hotel next to Leppenraub's hospital. So the field was clear for Joey. He visits, he stays, he goes to work on Scotty Gates. And makes his fucking art. The same kind of stuff that Leppenraub did—only Joey's making *videos,* see, the true medium of the times, you follow me? I mean Joey's stuff is really *alive.* Like he does a scene of Scotty's ass with blood all over it, and ants crawling in the blood. Crap like that. Or for example we see Scotty fucking something—humping away, you get me?—and we zoom in and what is it he's diddling? A dead bird. Something they scraped off the highway. I mean really. I mean what we're talking about is *an explicit assault on American violence.* You like that? I should have been a critic, huh? I'm telling you, these videos, they were really . . . bold—huh? And, and *vital* and . . . all that shit."

Romulus said, "If you're a critic, you can't say things like 'all that shit.' "

"You can't? Why not?"

Romulus said, "I don't know. Truthfully, I have no idea."

"Yeah, well, all right, I'm still a cop then. Boo hoo. But any-way, Joey Peasley, you couldn't tell *him* he was no critic. He thought he had it all scoped out—what really great art was. It was these sicko videos he was making with Scotty Gates.

"Only problem was, Scotty Gates had no aesthetic taste, no imagination whatsoever, and he never quit whining. He said he didn't *want* to fuck dead birds. Joey had to smack him around a little. And still Scotty was such a brat. Once he even lashed out at Joey—he said, 'You call this art? You're just a maniac.'

"Which pissed Joey off no end. But also sort of inspired him. He came up with a great idea for his next video. It would be called *Chill.* It would make Scotty very sorry for ever saying anything nasty about Joey's artistic gifts.

"He took Scotty up to the coach house and put him in that big walk-in freezer and he locked him in.

"After a while he opened the door. He brought lights in, and the video camera, and he taped a torture show.

"And yet still Scotty didn't seem repentant enough. He was weak, but he was still whining. So Joey let him freeze some more.

Then he went back in and shot another torture episode, and finally Scotty came to understand and appreciate Joey's gifts.

"Joey felt much better. But he locked Scotty in again anyway.

"Because he realized that now he'd gone too far to turn back. He'd gotten carried away. The way sometimes geniuses will. There was no letting the kid loose *now*.

"He'd have to kill him.

"Joey sat outside the freezer, and let his imagination run wild, and then he came up with this scheme—a way to punish Scotty and Leppenraub at the same time.

"But the way he had it worked out, one very important detail was that Scotty have the HIV virus.

"OK, no problem.

"He took a trip down to the city and paid five bucks to a homeless guy with AIDS for a pint of his blood. He came back up and injected that blood into Scotty.

"But while Joey was injecting Scotty, the retarded guy walked in on them. That guy Elon—and he started bawling. And Joey had to do a real song and dance to persuade him that this was all for Scotty's own good, and Elon was being a *bad boy*, and leave us alone, *we're playing*, three's a crowd, you know?

"As soon as Elon was gone, Joey locked the freezer up tight and left Scotty in there to die while Joey drove down to North Carolina. To visit his mama, what a good boy. And that's where he edited the videotape.

"On the sound track, he spliced in snippets from that reading of *The Cherry Orchard*, from Leppenraub doing the part of Lopahin. *'Don't cry, little peasant.' 'You're too soft.' 'I'm fed up with you.'* So anyone seeing the tape would think that Leppenraub had been right there watching Scotty getting tortured, getting his jollies.

"Joey made one copy of the tape and buried the original. Then he came back up to New York and put on his amazing show. He became the man he'd killed. Are we ready for another round?"

"Huh? I guess so," said Romulus.

"Except the problem is, if I have another round, I'm not going to be able to drive home. Wait! Wait! I just remembered—my wife's staying at her sister's tonight. How about a change of venue?"

Cork got up.

Romulus said, "Your place? You sure?"

"I don't have any cranberry juice though. We'll have to pick some up. Come on. I'll show you my roses."

137

Cork paid the tab and they drove to his place in the North Bronx.

Along the way he said, "Hey listen, Caveman, something I been meaning to ask you. When I talked to Moira Leppenraub today, she was . . . she was very solicitous as to your well-being. You know what I mean? She said I had to remember to tell you to call her. Just as soon as you can. I mean I think you made quite a favorable impression on this woman. You didn't, by any chance, you didn't *get it on* with her, did you?"

"Let's watch the road, Jack. You're weaving."

"Yeah, well I swear to you if you say yes I'm going to weave right onto the fucking sidewalk."

"Then I won't say yes."

"No, answer me. You want me to accept that such a stinking bum as you could ever get so lucky? Not a chance. The very idea is disgusting. Tell me the truth."

"I want my lawyer present."

"You son of a bitch."

138

They stopped at a deli for cranberry juice and frozen pizza. While they were waiting to pay, Romulus looked at the front page of the paper and there was a picture of a cave on it. Since when were caves news, Romulus wondered. Then it dawned on him that it was *his* cave. He read the headline:

CITY
CAVEMAN
FOILS
MURDERER

So it was as big and splashy as Cork had said it would be, and that was a disturbing development. Also sort of amusing.

When they got to Cork's place, Cork put the pizzas in the oven and took Romulus out back to look at his antique roses. They weren't in bloom yet but even the buds were nice to look at under the yard light. Then they went back in and Cork fixed the drinks, and they sat at the kitchen table and ate their pizzas and drank.

Said Cork, "Where were we?"

" 'He became the man he'd killed.' "

"Yeah. Yeah, right. Joey moved in with the downtown lowlife. And he pretended to be Scotty Gates. He created Scotty Gates eye-witnesses all over the place. He went to gay bars and played the wounded yokel, he hammed it up all over the streets. Critics who'd said he couldn't create theater—they should see this show! Oh, the way he got the rumors working, got the word percolating through the art world. 'Hey, did you know that the model for Leppenraub's tree pictures is now this homeless junkie with AIDS? Did you know that Leppenraub fucked him and ruined him and then discarded him?'

"And he found the most gullible and vulnerable and forlorn soul in the city—Matthew Donofrio—and made him the number one witness to Scotty's suffering.

"Then when he figured the time was ripe, he snuck back to the farm and fetched the body, and brought it down and left it in your park, Caveman. Matthew had told him all about you, and he wanted you to find the corpse. He knew all about your harangues. He guessed that Matthew would talk to you, and you'd go all over preaching the word against Leppenraub—spread those rumors.

"Meanwhile he took his videotape up to the farm, and told

Leppenraub Scotty had given it to him. Leppenraub said it was a fraud, a travesty. Joey said Oh sure, surely Scotty had gone off the deep end there, hadn't he? But still Joey would appreciate a little reward for not showing the thing to anyone else.

"And Leppenraub asked him, 'How much is a little reward?'"

"And Joey said, 'Say a hundred grand?'"

"And Leppenraub was sick, and worn out, and the only thing he cared about was his place in the history of art. So he paid.

"After all, the truth about Leppenraub is that he's kind of a timid, *gentle* guy."

Romulus murmured, "Not gentle."

"What?"

"Not a murderer, but not gentle. Kind of nasty, in fact."

"Well maybe you didn't know him at his best. You know what I mean? I had the impression he was sort of a prick myself but now think about it. I mean, he's got that disease. He's got that death sentence hanging over him. That's got to be tough."

"That is tough," Romulus concurred.

"You know he's got nothing but kind words for *you.*"

"He threw me out of his goddamn party."

"You were drunk."

"No. I'm drunk now. Then I was just pitching a fit. His sister's a better artist."

"You were really getting it on with that broad?"

Said Romulus, "I do not understand squat. A week ago I understood everything. Then I solved this mystery, and now I'm completely confused. I'm supposed to like David Leppenraub? But he's still a nasty son of a bitch, isn't he? He wanted me dead. Right?"

"Forget about it," said Cork. "My advice is, no matter what the problem is, my advice is, *forget about it.*"

"A gentle guy? Truly? I do not have a single clue as to what the world is up to."

"Didn't I tell you about clues? Forget about 'em."

"Right."

"Another?"

"Oh all right," said Romulus. "Thank you."

Jack Cork poured them new drinks. Romulus suspected that

the drinks were getting progressively stiffer, but he had no way of knowing—his tongue was numb.

Cork got comfortable again.

"So Leppenraub came up with the money, and gave it to Joey on a Saturday morning. That afternoon he held a party—and *you* showed up, Caveman. Rattled him pretty bad, what you said to him. He called Joey several times at his motel—begged him to do something about you. And Joey told him to send you home on the bus.

"Joey decided you'd taken your shit way too far, and he had to get rid of you.

"Though just in case you spotted him and got away, well, he fixed himself up in a way to completely discredit any story you might tell. He wrapped bandages around his head and made himself look like your worst paranoid nightmare. It was perfect. Who would listen to you after you went into your Stuyvesant routine?

"Then he drove into the village of Gideon Manor and waited for your bus. He saw you get on, he saw you get off. He tried to do you, but as it happened, you *did* get away.

"So he decided he was going to need a little help. He got hold of this guy Robert Jackson—a guy he knew as Shaker—somebody he'd met during his lowlife stint. He and Shaker went to the tent corner on C and Seventh and snatched Matthew. Shaker did all the talking, of course—Matthew would have recognized Joey's voice in a heartbeat.

"Matthew led them to your cave, but you'd slipped him again. The one-eyed woman said you'd gone south for a vacation.

"So Joey just beat Matthew within an inch of his life. Chiselwork worthy of a da Vinci, you know? And then he called it a night.

"And it wasn't till the next day it occurred to him—what if 'going south for a vacation' meant that somehow you'd tracked him down to North Carolina? Joey called his mother, and sure enough you *were* down there. So he drove like a bat out of hell, and got to his hometown just in time to catch you watching the videotape you'd dug up from his mother's yard.

"Then he put on his performance for you. He was eloquent, he says. He thinks in a just world they'd give him the Academy

Award or something. Don't *look* at me like that, Caveman, those are *his* words. All right?

"Anyway, after he was done with you, he figured now he wouldn't have to bother with killing you. You'd swallowed his story hook, line, and sinker, and he could rest easy.

"He could retire.

"Though as a curtain call, as a little stinger at the end, he made himself disappear—I mean his Joey Peasley self. He staged his own abduction in front of his mother's eyes, with the help of his buddy Shaker. He completely destroyed her, and it was the happiest day of his life.

"Oh, he thought he was the fucking Cézanne of terror.

"And that's when he made up his mind a hundred grand wasn't even in the ballpark of what he could get out of Leppenraub.

"He called the guy and told him another donation was in order.

"Another . . . five million, say?

"And when Leppenraub got his breath back he said he'd have to think about it. Also he told Joey that the Caveman had sent him a message. The Caveman said he'd made a copy of the videotape.

"OK—that was it. Joey was just fed up with you. He called Shaker again and they found you in your cave where you were waiting for him.

"And once again Joey underestimated you. He made that colossal blunder—he let you call your daughter. And then when he looked down from that bridge and saw Shaker get shot, he had to finish him off, so the guy wouldn't talk. If he could have killed *you* he would have, but he'd have hit your daughter, too, and he knew that once a cop gets killed . . .

"So he just went back to his hotel room and laid low for a while. Then he called Leppenraub one more time and said, 'When are you going to pay me, fucker?' And Leppenraub did just what you'd told him to, Caveman. He said he had the money, and talked Joey into meeting him at the subway platform.

"Where I got to play a sleeping drunk, which was a marvelous performance for which I'm due an Academy Award.

"And where we nailed him. Thanks to my friend the crackpot caveman. And that's the whole story. Any questions?"

Romulus thought awhile, then shrugged. "No. I mean, I'm sure there are, but I'm too drunk to think of any. You got a bathroom?"

"Back there. All the way down, take a leff."

Cork was pretty high himself.

139

Romulus wove his way back to the bathroom. When he passed the glass door leading out to the rose garden he thought he saw Sheila sitting out there. He didn't stop. He went into the bathroom and found the switch and the fluorescent light flapped on and nearly blinded him. He stood unsteadily before the toilet and then worried he might make a mess, so he sat to pee.

When he passed by the glass door again he saw Sheila was still out there. He slid open the door as quietly as he could and stepped out and whispered to her, "What are you doing here?"

Sheila said, "You always had a lot wrong with you, boy, but at least one thing, you weren't a lush. Now look at you. You're going to wind up a wino on the—"

"I hate wine."

"You're drunk as a skunk though."

"I'm celebrating."

"What you got to celebrate?"

"I accomplished something."

"You sure did. You nearly got your daughter killed, and yourself in the bargain, and you rearranged the lives of a couple of white folks that you have no business with at all—"

"I put a nick in Stuyvesant's armor."

She silently clapped.

Said Romulus, "And I put a murderer behind bars."

"Ha! I did about half your thinking for you."

"But you're in my head."

"I don't care where I am, I don't want you taking all the credit. You'll get on your high horse."

"Sheila, why are you always trying to belittle me?"

"Lower your voice. Because you're always doing *little* things. You're not doing your music, and everything else is little."

"I'm in no condition for—"

"Rom."

"What?"

"I'm *sorry* if I seemed to belittle you. I didn't mean to. It was . . . *something*, what you did."

"Thank you."

"But still, you're getting too old for this life—that's for sure. You're going to get arthritis living in that cave."

He said good night to her, went back in and slid the door shut.

Cork put him up in one of the kids' rooms. His head was spinning, and it was hard to fall asleep. Then he did fall asleep, but some time in the night he woke up and he was deadly sick. He staggered into the bathroom and knelt before the bowl and puked. The water in the toilet started out a deep, dizzying blue, but he filled it with the corpses of dead Seraphs, and it turned a reddish brown. There were thousands of them, floating in their own faint blood, pouring out of him, all the casualties. He retched, and his fingers were cold as ice where they clutched the porcelain, and his groans echoed in the bowl. He retched until there was nothing more to retch, and then he dry-heaved. He gazed down into that sea of carnage. The bits of broken wings, the thousands of tiny blind eyes, the delicate bodies scorched by Y-rays, corroded by Z-rays. What this victory had cost. And then he lifted his head and leaned back, and Cork was holding him. Romulus put his head against the tile wall, turned his cheek to it. The cool tiles. Cork flushed the toilet, and the water swirled the Seraphs away.

140

In the morning Jack Cork's wife woke Romulus and fixed him breakfast.

He took a shower, then he called Moira Leppenraub. Then he rode with Cork back into Manhattan. They were too hung over to talk. They said about six words to each other. Cork left him off at the edge of the park.

He climbed the slope. His head was still throbbing, but he was essentially healthy. He climbed nearly to the top and angled around, down and then up, approaching the cave warily.

Stopped when he saw the crowd.

Cyclops was standing before his cave, holding forth. There were four or five TV cameras trained on her, and reporters barking questions, and a simmering mass of spectators. There were twenty kids up in the beech tree. Romulus watched for a while, and then he heard a voice behind him.

"Daddy."

She wore a shawl and dark glasses. She took off the glasses, and she looked tired. She said, "I've been waiting for you. I wanted to warn you."

Romulus turned back to look at the crowd and he shook his head.

She said, "I guess you know there's reporters up there who would give their right arms for an interview with you?"

"Yeah. How about you, Lulu—how are you taking all this?"

"Oh, the attention was fun. For about twenty minutes. It's weird, how quickly it got old."

"Lu, have you seen Matthew?"

"We're putting him in the rehab clinic, just like you asked. And it's Leppenraub's treat. But I couldn't find one with a swimming pool full of morphine."

"Then he probably won't stay."

"Daddy, where are *you* going to go?"

"Haven't figured that out yet. Might spend the summer in the country. I have an invitation from David Leppenraub. My former enemy. The world goes around."

"I was thinking . . . you . . . Daddy, why don't you come home for a while? I think Mama wouldn't mind having you around. Just for a while, I mean—"

"Did she say that?"

"She didn't *say* that but I know her, Daddy."

He considered the offer.

He tried to speak but he couldn't. He cleared his throat and tried again. "You know what, Lulu, I don't think so."

They looked at each other and he said, "Maybe some other time. Thank you just the same, though."

141

A night full of katydids, a hot night, damp stars, and on the TV, on C-SPAN, the Undersecretary of the Perfectly Real and Good was testifying:

"What has gone wrong? Nothing has gone wrong. What have we lost? We've gained. Really. We've gained cunning. Why do we seem to hesitate? We're only resting. Come on, everyone deserves a rest. We haven't stumbled, you only imagine we've stumbled. You always let your imagination run away with you. Really, *really*, we are on the verge of great exultation. So why don't you join us? Why don't you *cease* with all these defeatist questions? Why don't you rein in your foolish imagination, and join us before it's too late for you?"

Then the Undersecretary laughed a sad, bitter laugh and tucked his lower lip under his teeth thoughtfully.

Romulus threw a shoe at the screen, and it went dark. Elon threw another shoe. Romulus said, "What do you think of *that,* Elon?"

Elon didn't answer. He seldom answered, but he liked to hang out here in Romulus's cave, in the cave Moira and Vlad and David had made for him, in the pear orchard at the edge of the Leppen-raub farm. Elon liked to watch the shows with Romulus. He brought the bags of Doritos and the jugs of cranberry juice. When he was tired he'd fall asleep on the mattress. And on a clear night like this one, Romulus would drag the mattress with Elon asleep on it out from under the eave of the cave and stretch out beside him. Lao-tse would come over and curl up by his head, and Romulus would reach back and scratch her where she liked to be scratched. He'd gaze through the pear boughs at the stars and say to himself the names of his wife and daughter, and of his older brothers, and the names of his mother and father and of his uncles and aunts and all the cousins he could remember, and of his great-uncles and great-aunts, and so on, the circle growing wider and wider until he came to the circle of the stars themselves. Then he would carefully arrange the names into the form of a temple around the nest of the Seraphs, so that the newborns might sleep peacefully, guarded by the music of all these names, undisturbed by any alien ray or poisonous influence.

It was a lot of work but clearly necessary.

Some work you could squirm out of, but it was a lost cause to try to shirk this. You either got that name-music under way or the newborns would keep you awake all night. You wanted sleep? You gathered the names. You got the temple set up for the night, the lamps glowing, everything secure, everyone snoozing, even the katy-dids, even the owl—and then in that rhythm of absolute stillness and patience you could permit yourself to roll over onto your side and grab some shut-eye yourself. You did your work, and when it was done and not a moment before, you could let yourself tumble away.